BEYOND DEATH.
INTO THE LIGHT.
ANOTHER BATTLE AWAITS.

"No!" she screamed, and felt the same force emanate from her that had kept the Shadow Monster away from the little girl before. The Shadow Monster recoiled as if physically struck. Its eyes widened with surprise, its mouth clamped shut, and a howl of anguish rose from the smaller mouths that were in constant eruption all over its surface.

It occurred to Deedee that the Shadow Monster couldn't touch her, couldn't eat her, unless she gave in to it and let it. She tried to take it a step further and will the thing away from her, but her power did not extend that far; the thing remained, enveloping her in darkness that began a few feet from her body in every direction.

She was trapped.

HIGH PRAISE FOR
THE AUTHOR OF *TUNNELVISION* AND *DEATHWALKER*
R. PATRICK GATES
"A TRUE MASTER OF FRIGHT!"*

"If you haven't gotten around to R. Patrick Gates, it's time. . . . Give Gates the remote control and you won't be tempted to change the channel."
—*Fangoria*

"A NEW MASTER OF PULSE-POUNDING TERROR! READ HIM AT YOUR OWN RISK!"
—Joseph A. Citro, best-selling author of *Dark Twilight* and *The Unseen*

"R. Patrick Gates is a fresh new talent. He does what many in the horror field find impossible: something different."
—Ray Garton, author of *Live Girls* and *Crucifax*

"R. PATRICK GATES WILL KEEP YOU ON THE EDGE OF YOUR SEAT."
—*Rave Reviews**

"R. Patrick Gates is a writer to be reckoned with. [He] spits in the face of contention and goes straight for the throat."
—Mike Baker, *Afraid Magazine*

"AN EXPERT IN TERROR!"
—Gary Brandner, bestselling author of *The Howling*

Previous books by R. Patrick Gates:

Deathwalker
Tunnelvision
Grimm Memorials
Fear

R. PATRICK GATES

Jumpers

A DELL BOOK

Published by
Dell Publishing
a division of
Bantam Doubleday Dell Publishing Group, Inc.
1540 Broadway
New York, New York 10036

If you purchased this book without a cover you should be aware that this book is stolen property. It was reported as "unsold and destroyed" to the publisher and neither the author nor the publisher has received any payment for this "stripped book."

Copyright © 1997 by R. Patrick Gates

All rights reserved. No part of this book may be reproduced or transmitted in any form or by any means, electronic or mechanical, including photocopying, recording, or by any information storage and retrieval system, without the written permission of the Publisher, except where permitted by law.

The trademark Dell® is registered in the U.S. Patent and Trademark Office.

ISBN: 0-440-21471-8

Printed in the United States of America

Published simultaneously in Canada

May 1997

10 9 8 7 6 5 4 3 2 1

In loving memory of my mother, Rose

ONE

ANNA AND THE BAD GUYS

1

Christmas Morning.

Is there any other day of the year that is more exquisite, more magical, more anticipated?

Anna Wheaton didn't think so. Next to Halloween, Christmas was Anna's favorite day of the year. She liked it even more than her birthday.

At age nine (going on ten, as she always said), Anna still believed in things magical like the tooth fairy and the Easter Bunny, but she especially believed in Santa Claus. Where her peers' beliefs in such things had grown thin with skepticism or had disappeared altogether, Anna held on strongly to hers. Deep down she knew, logically, that there could be no such thing as a tooth fairy, an Easter Bunny, or a Santa Claus, but she insisted on believing in them anyway. The way she saw it, life would be pretty boring without *some* magic in it. And, oh! there was so much *wonderful* magic in Christmas morning.

But Christmas Eve was absolute torture.

Her parents made her and her sisters, Haley and Jayne, go to bed so early on Christmas Eve, but they were always too excited to sleep. Anna would lie awake in bed, staring at the shadows thrown on the ceiling by the Little Mermaid night-light that Jayne, the youngest at five years old, insisted be left on every night to ward off the *boogerman* (as she called him). She and Anna and Haley (who was seven going on eight, as *she* liked to say) would talk in subdued voices about what Santa was going to bring them. They would pause often at the slightest sound in the house, straining their ears to hear the pitter-patter of tiny hooves on the roof or the jolly *ho ho ho* of Saint Nick himself.

Jayne was never able to stay awake for long, and Haley would eventually follow her younger sister into slumberland, leaving Anna to lie awake in the darkness counting the endless seconds until dawn.

If asked, Anna would swear she never slept a wink on Christmas Eve. In truth, she would begin to doze around one in the morning, but would never sleep for longer than twenty minutes at a stretch. Her eyes would pop open, and she'd sit up in bed to look out the window, searching the dark sky for the slightest sign of dawn. Seeing none, she would lie back, listen to Haley and Jayne's deep-sleep breathing, and try to imagine Santa in his sleigh winging through the winter night toward her house. First, she imagined him soaring over Mount Wachusett, reindeers' heads high, hooves beating the air. The sleigh would wobble, then dip and swoop down into the Nashoba valley. She imagined Santa stopping at all the ramshackle farms in the town of Winchendon, on the other side of Bean's Hill, then sailing around to deliver presents in Groton, Shirley, Lunenburg, and Crocker, getting closer to Towns End with every house visited.

She could see him in her mind's eye, slicing through the air, crossing over the Squannacook River and passing over Towns End, where she lived. She could see the sleigh stopping at the big mansions on Ridge Road, just below Turkey Hill, and moving on to the farms surrounding the wetlands of Towns End Harbor, the small village adjacent to Towns End. Closer Santa would come, over Pheasant Lane Middle School, over Towns End High School, stopping at the modest houses and cottages along the way. Finally, the sleigh would head for the poor section of Towns End (saving the best for last, Anna always told herself), and she imagined it stopping at the little houses—nothing more than shacks, really—that lined Hickory Street. Her heart rate would speed up, her breathing come quicker as she thought of Santa stopping at her friend Elli Winston's house on the corner of Hickory and Chase streets, then hopping over to Dave and Cory Teags's (her *sometime* friends) house.

Just one more house to go until Santa was at her house! Anna would strain to hear Santa's sleigh touch down on the roof of Old Man Roberts's house across the street. Roberts was a mean guy, but Anna knew that even mean people got something from Santa because, like God, Santa loved everyone, good and bad.

At last Santa's sleigh would settle onto the roof of the dilapidated ranch house that Anna and her family called home. It had been a nice place when they first moved in, and Anna's father's construction company was making bundles of money during the building boom of the 1980s. But soon after Anna was born, things had gone steadily downhill. Business had fallen off until her father, Joe Wheaton, was forced to lay off all his workers and sell his heavy construction equipment piece by piece to pay the mortgage. Last year, he'd had to get rid of the three ponies he had bought for his daughters—every Christmas Anna prayed for Santa to bring her pony, Pepper, back to her. When the ponies were gone and the construction business still hadn't picked up, Joe Wheaton was forced to take a job pumping gas at the Exxon station in Towns End

Harbor and sell off parcels of the forty acres of land that were part of his property.

Barely able to contain herself, letting her fantasy work her into a frenzy, Anna would get out of bed and rush to the window. She would search the sky and listen for Santa's approach and for the sound of hooves on the rooftop.

And there it was! The jingle of sleigh bells! The tiny thump of reindeer hooves on the slate roof! The faint, jolly laughter of old Saint Nick himself!

He's here!

She woke from the dream, Santa's laughter fading into the stillness of the night.

"I didn't fall asleep," Anna whispered to the dark. "That really was Santa. He's been here!"

Excited, she got out of bed and went to the window. The first gray tendrils of dawn were stretching across the sky over Bean's Hill.

"It's time!" Anna breathed. Putting her flannel robe on over the large T-shirt (her dad's) that she wore for a nightgown, she woke Haley and Jayne.

Now came the hardest part, waking her parents. Hurrying her sisters out of bed and into their robes and slippers, Anna led them into the hallway.

"Mom? Dad? Are you awake?" she called through their open doorway down the hall, on the other side of the bathroom.

"What's wrong? Are you sick?" Her mother's voice, full of concern, came out of the darkness.

Jayne giggled nervously behind Anna.

"No, Mom. It's Christmas morning. Can we open our presents now?"

There was a deep groan in the darkness—her father waking up. "Jesus Christ, Anna. It's not even five A.M.," he growled.

"It's all right," her mother soothed him. "I'll get up with them. You sleep."

That brought another groan from Joe Wheaton. "No. Forget it. I'll get up too. Might as well. Won't be able to sleep with them squealing and fighting over their presents."

"Yeah, right," Bev Wheaton said sarcastically. "It couldn't be that you're as excited as they are and wouldn't miss them opening their presents for anything, could it?"

Joe Wheaton chuckled, and Anna and her sisters giggled.

"Wait here," Joe said to his children as he came out of the bedroom, dressed only in a T-shirt and boxer shorts.

Anna, Haley, and Jayne danced in anticipation in the dark hallway while their father went into the living room to turn on the Christmas tree lights. Anna's mother came out of the bedroom wearing her silk robe, the one that Anna loved the touch and smell of. It felt like warm ice to her and always smelled good, like her mom.

"Excited, girls?" she asked. Anna nodded her head rapidly, her eyes shining.

"Me too," answered Haley.

"Me three," Jayne piped up, making her mother laugh.

"What's taking so long?" Anna asked, barely able to contain herself. The colored lights of the Christmas tree came on at that moment, sending their green, red, and blue auras into the hall to light the excited faces of the children.

"Boy! Has Santa ever been busy!" Joe Wheaton called from the living room.

The girls giggled excitedly.

"I don't know if there's enough room in here for you girls with all these toys!" Joe called again. "We may have to throw some out."

"No!" Haley and Jayne screamed in unison.

"Dad-ee!" Anna said with loud exasperation.

Mother laughed. "Come on, Joe, stop torturing them."

"Okay. I guess you can come in now."

Anna, Haley, and Jayne ran down the hallway and into the living room. Their father stood by the tree, his smiling face bathed in its colored lights.

Jayne immediately pounced on the presents under the tree, ripping the paper off a large box without regard or concern as to whether it was hers or not.

"Whoa!" Bev Wheaton said, pulling her youngest daughter back. "That doesn't have your name on it. Your sister will give out the gifts. Anna, you pass them out."

"Get the camera, Bev," Joe told his wife. Anna started going through the packages, reading off the names on the gift tags and handing them to her sisters. Though there were as many presents as in years past, they were neither as large nor as expensive. The girls didn't notice—all they cared about was the quantity, not the quality, of the gifts, and they were delighted with the load of presents they each received. But it bothered Joe. He and Bev had done the best they could, but they each felt shame that the toys were not up to the level of gifts they had showered on their children on previous Christmases.

Bev came back with the Polaroid and snapped pictures of the girls opening their gifts while Joe got a plastic trash bag and started picking up the growing mound of discarded wrapping paper. It took nearly an hour for the girls to open all their gifts. When they were finished, they sat comparing what they had got, each more interested in what her siblings had received than in her own gifts.

Joe and Bev had made a point of getting each of the girls at least one expensive gift that they had asked for. Haley got the Creepy Crawler oven kit she had wanted, and Jayne got a new Barbie doll.

Anna noticed this, but she didn't see anything special for herself. Of course, the thing she always asked for was to have her pony, Pepper, back, and of course, she didn't expect him to be gift-wrapped under the tree.

She went to the kitchen window and looked out at the barn. Nothing unusual. The corral next to the barn, where Pepper had been kept, was empty. Disappointed, Anna turned away from the window.

"There's one more thing for you, Anna," her father said, going to the hall closet. "Close your eyes."

Anna did as she was told, a thrill of excitement coursing through her. Though she knew it could not be Pepper in the closet, it might be the second thing she had been asking for since the first heavy snowfall back in November.

"Just a minute," Joe said. Anna could hear her father removing something large and awkward from the closet.

"Wow!" she heard Jayne exclaim.

"Oh, Anna! You lucky dog!" Haley joined in. She couldn't wait to open her eyes. It *had* to be what she'd wanted almost as much as Pepper. She crossed her fingers, hoping silently it would be.

"Open your eyes now."

A new sled!

"Yes!" Anna cried, tears of joy filling her eyes. "I knew it."

The day was sunny and sparkling cold, with a fresh cover of snow over everything. After playing with their toys for a couple of hours and breakfasting on their mom's delicious homemade cinnamon rolls and hot chocolate, Anna and her sisters were ready to play outside and try out her new sled.

Bundled up in snowsuits against the cold, they trudged out of the yard and up Chase Street single file. Anna pulled her sled behind her, turning frequently to admire it. She didn't' know it, but the sled was quite old, practically an antique. Her father has bought it at a yard sale in Lunenburg on his way home from the gas station one evening. It had been beat-up and worn, with the middle wooden plank missing from the seat and the runners corroded with rust. He'd kept it hidden in his workshop at the back of the barn and spent hours renovating it until it appeared to be brand new. The wood was repainted a bright red, and the runners sanded free of rust and painted a brassy gold. On the new wooden middle plank, he had stenciled Anna's name in gold lettering.

Behind her, Haley and Jayne pulled their plastic saucers along, also admiring Anna's new sled, not without a good deal of envy. At the end of Chase Street they met Cory and Dave Teags. Cory was the same age as Anna, and Dave was a year younger than Haley.

"Where you guys going?" Dave asked. Cory ignored them. He secretly had a crush on Anna but would never be caught dead showing it.

"We're going sliding at Hillman's Farm," Haley answered.

"What a bunch of wimps," Cory said disdainfully. "That's a baby hill."

"Really?" Anna said coldly. "And where are you going, to the sandlot?"

Haley and Jayne giggled at that. The sandlot was a large and deep sand pit in the woods behind the

Teagses' house. In the summer it was a fun place to play. You could slide down the sides and clamber back to the top no problem. But in the winter, when the sand froze, it became treacherous. The slide down was more exhilarating, but as Cory had found out when he fell into it last winter, it was impossible to climb back out. The Towns End volunteer fire department had to come and rescue him with a rope ladder, so he could climb up.

"Not!" Cory said angrily. "We're going to Cemetery Hill. Why don't you come with us? 'Less you're too scared."

That stopped their giggling. Haley and Jayne looked at each other, then at Anna. Cemetery Hill was closer than Hillman's Farm, but they were forbidden by their parents to sled there.

The name of the cemetery was really Restive Pines. The place known as Cemetery Hill by generations of townspeople going back to the 1700s was the largest hill in Restive Pines and faced Route 13, which ran through Towns End before crossing the state border into Greenfield, New Hampshire. The hill was really two hills—a high steep one, and a smaller sloping one adjacent to the first on the left. At the bottom of the hills, separating them from Route 13, was a six-foot granite wall.

The wall was the reason Anna's parents, and many other parents in town, forbade their children from sledding there. Back in 1978, a few days after the momentous blizzard of '78, the snow had been piled up to the very top of the wall. Billy Jameson, a twelve-year-old, had ridden his sled down the hill and right over the top of the wall, crashing onto Route 13, where he was hit by a truck and instantly killed.

"We're not scared. My mom and dad won't let us slide there," Anna retorted.

"Oh yeah, right," Cory sneered.

"Yeah, right," Dave mimicked.

"If I remember correctly, *your* parents won't let *you* slide there either," Anna said.

"Nuh-uh," Cory answered.

"Yah-huh."

"No way! They said we couldn't slide there only if the snow was up to the top of the wall, like it was when that stupid kid got squished by the truck."

Anna didn't know what to answer to that.

"You're just a bunch of wimpy girls," Cory taunted.

"Are not!" Haley shouted.

"Yah-huh!"

"No-suh, you, you, camel puke!" Jayne blurted out, causing Anna and Haley to burst out laughing. Dave joined them until his older brother shot him a dirty look.

"If the snow ain't up to the top of the wall, then Cemetery Hill ain't dangerous. Everyone knows that. You guys are just scared cuz it's not a *baby hill.*" Believing he had had the last word, Cory turned away and started around the corner to Route 13.

"Come on, Dave," he called back to his little brother, who obediently followed.

"Come on," Anna said to her sisters, and started after Cory and Dave.

"What're you doing?" Haley asked, fear in her voice.

"We're going to Cemetery Hill."

"But what about what Mom and Dad said?"

"I don't care. I'll be damned if I'll let Cory Teags, or any boy, call me a wimp."

"Oh!" Jayne said with shock. "Anna, you said a bad word like Daddy."

"So? Why don't you run right home and tell Mom, you little tattletale?"

Jayne's eyes filled with tears at the rebuff.

"I'm sorry, Jaynie," Anna said quickly. "Come on. One thing that spaz said is true: The snow isn't up to the top of the wall at Cemetery Hill. Mom and Dad won't get mad, cuz it's perfectly safe. Besides, I want to try out my new sled on a really big hill and see how fast it will go."

Haley and Jayne looked unsure.

"Okay. If Mom and Dad find out and we get in trouble, I'll take the blame. I'll say I made you come with me." That satisfied her sisters, and the trio set off through the snow, following the deep footprints and sled tracks left by Cory and Dave.

Cemetery Hill was teeming with sledders and skiers of all ages. Anna, Haley, and Jayne arrived right behind Cory and Dave. Anna ignored them when the older boy expressed surprise at the Wheaton girls' courage.

Anna's new sled was the center of attention among the younger kids. Several of her and Haley's classmates were there, and they crowded around to ooh and aah over it. Anna ate it up. This was almost as good as getting a pony—better in some ways, since many of the children in town who lived on farms had ponies or horses. But *no one* had a sled like hers.

"Haley, you and Jayne slide on the small hill," Anna directed her younger sister, pointing to where the little kids were sledding. The small hill was a gentle slope, not more than thirty-five yards from top to bottom.

"I don't want to go on the baby hill. I want to go on the big hill with you," Jayne complained.

"Yeah, Anna. We want to go down the big hill with you. There's enough room on the sled for the three of us," Haley added.

Anna didn't like the idea. The sled was hers, and she wanted to be the first to christen it, but Haley and Jayne looked so hopeful, she couldn't say no. The youngest girls left their saucers at the bottom of the hill, out of the way of the other sledders, and followed Anna up the side path, through old headstones and pine trees, to the summit of Cemetery Hill. Once there, Anna had definite second thoughts on whether going down it was such a good idea for herself, never mind taking Haley and Jayne down with her.

The hill looked so much bigger and steeper from the top. She could see clear across town to the white steeple of St. Boniface's. Looking down the slope made her slightly dizzy, it was so steep, running for a hundred yards at least before ending at the stone wall. To the right of the wall was a snowbank piled high. Anna watched as kids sledded, whooping down the hill, and veered away from the wall, into the snowbank to stop themselves.

"That's the way you got to do it," Cory Teags said, pulling his sled up next to Anna's. "You got to turn at the bottom and use the snowbank to stop, or you'll get flattened against the wall."

"I can see that," Anna replied coldly. She watched as Cory and Dave sat on their sleds, pushed off, and flew down the hill, turning at the bottom, easily avoiding collision with the wall.

"Let's go, Anna," Jayne said excitedly. "That looks fun."

"Why don't you guys let me go down one time alone first?" Anna said hesitantly. "You know, to test it out. Then you can go with me on the second turn." Jayne didn't like that idea and pouted, but Haley didn't mind. She seemed intimidated by the steepness of the hill and agreed.

Anna sat on her sled, clutching the steering rope

in both hands, then thought better of that position. She lay on the sled, on her stomach, and gripped the steering handles, figuring she'd have more control that way.

"Be careful, Anna," Haley said. Jayne was still pouting, sitting on a tree stump a few feet away.

"No sweat," Anna replied bravely, though she didn't feel brave. "Here goes."

Raising herself on one knee, she used her other foot to push off. The sled started over the top slowly, the runners sticking in the wet snow. When she lay down again, putting all her weight on it, the sled went over the edge and began to pick up speed.

Anna knew the hill was steep, but she was unprepared for the speed with which the sled went down it. From the top, the slope had looked smooth, but riding down it, she discovered it was full of dips and bumps, causing her to flop and bounce wildly. Snow flew in her face, and she almost fell off twice. She screamed with fear and laughed with excitement at the same time. This was definitely better than the little hill at Hillman's Farm. She hated to admit it, but she was glad Cory had goaded her into coming here.

The sled went over a particularly large bump and left the ground, sailing for several feet before landing. Anna held on and whooped as the sled returned to earth, sending up a spray of sparkling snow around her. She couldn't believe how fast she was going. It was amazing! This was the fastest ride she'd ever had, even faster than the big roller coaster at Whalom Amusement Park.

She was nearing the bottom, the gray stone wall looming larger. Afraid that if she turned too quickly at this speed she'd tip over she tried to turn the sled gradually.

It wouldn't respond.

She yanked on the right steering handle, but it was stuck. She pulled harder. Nothing. She looked up a second before she and the sled smashed head-first into the wall. She had just enough time to let out a short piercing scream.

2

"Hey, Rod, what's with the gun? I thought you said this was a safe job. Easy in, easy out, no one gets hurt."

Rod Baylor looked at Gary Jergins in disdain. At six feet, ten inches, and 320 pounds, Gary was big and powerful of body, but small and weak of intellect.

"Don't sweat it. It ain't loaded. The gun's just for show, so's no one will get hurt. Believe me, this job will be a piece of cake. So stop worrying about it, and go and start the van—it's almost time to go."

Satisfied with Rod's explanation, Gary did as he was told. When he had left the room, Tom Wayne and his brother, Fred, looked quizzically at Rod.

"Why'd you tell Dumbo that?" Tom asked. "I know you loaded that Uzi. I saw you do it not twenty minutes ago, when Pea-brain was in the john."

"That's right, I saw you too," Fred agreed.

Rod smirked at his two henchmen. The Wayne brothers were two of the meanest, toughest psychopaths he'd ever known, but in the brains department, he ranked them only slightly above Gary Jergins. Tom Wayne had a mile-long rap sheet and was wanted in Canada most recently for raping a budding young fashion model and then performing radical plastic surgery on her beautiful face with a razor blade. Fred Wayne had served time for armed robbery and rape and had a penchant for little girls, and sometimes little boys.

"You guys know nothing about management strategy," Rod said. "You got to treat Gary like a mushroom."

"A mushroom?" Tom asked, confused.

"I don't get it," Fred added. "How's that?"

"You got to keep him in the dark and feed him lots of bullshit."

Tom laughed heartily, but Fred only smirked a little, evidence that he still didn't get it.

"All right. Let's go over the plan one more time," Rod said.

It was actually very simple, but Rod didn't trust any of his cohorts to be able to keep things straight. He reviewed the plan from start to finish. The target was Middlesex Regional Hospital, which bordered the towns of Lunenburg and Towns End. As he went over how Jim Bush, a security guard at the hospital, would let them in, lead them to the hospital pharmacy, and open it up for them, he marveled at the originality of the plan. A hospital pharmacy was the last place the law would expect to be robbed—and on Christmas Day, no less. And if they were careful, no one would discover the theft for a whole day, giving them plenty of time to transport the drugs to Carlo in Providence. Carlo, a player in the Rhode Island mob, had promised to pay twenty-five grand for a truckload of prescription drugs, the likes of barbiturates, amphetamines, and tranquilizers. Twenty-five grand was peanuts to split among four people, but Gary would take whatever Rod gave him and be happy with it, and the Wayne boys would get their fair share when the job was over.

Rod smiled at the thought. He finished the rundown of the plan and sent the Wayne boys out to the van. Checking his Uzi one last time, he followed them.

The plan was running smoothly. The only thing Rod didn't like was that the entrance to the hospital that Jim Bush had let them in was right next to the hospital emergency room. But since it was Christmas Day, he figured there would be very little action there. The chances of running into any cops would be slim. But even if that slim chance proved true, Rod was ready with his Uzi.

They parked the van outside the door—the ER lot was empty and quiet. Jim Bush was waiting inside the unlocked door with a wheeled shipping cart, as they had planned. Rod and his men were dressed in gray overalls, looking like plumbers or workmen of some kind—a precaution in case they ran into anyone inside who might question who they were. Rod Baylor didn't mind killing if someone got in the way—in fact, he rather liked it—but he wasn't stupid. If he could talk his way out of a tight spot, he'd do it. If not he'd gladly shoot his way out.

Jim Bush was nervous and sweating profusely, evidenced by the large sweat stains under his arms. The plan was to bind and gag Jim and leave him in the pharmacy storeroom before they left.

They made it to the pharmacy without incident. The hospital was quiet, except for two PA announcements requesting a doctor on call to report to the intensive care unit and for housekeeping to go to the maternity ward.

Jim Bush's hands were shaking so badly, he twice dropped his key ring before fitting the master key into the pharmacy door and opening it.

"The storeroom is over there. Barbiturates are along the back wall. Tranquilizers to the right. Amphetamines to the left."

"What about narcotics—morphine, codeine, pharmaceutical coke, and stuff like that?" Rod asked. He figured if he got enough morphine and cocaine, he'd be able to demand another ten grand from Carlo. Hell, why not twenty grand more?

"Morphine's kept in those locked cabinets over there. I don't have a key for them, but you can bust the locks easily," Jim Bush explained, pointing to the back wall of the main room of the pharmacy. "But before you do anything, you got to tie me up quick in case someone comes along."

"Sure, Jim," Rod said with a smile. He had a coil of nylon rope and a roll of heavy duct tape in his deep coverall pockets. He took Jim Bush into the storeroom and tied his hands and legs securely, while the Wayne brothers and Gary began carrying out boxes full of drugs and stacking them on the cart outside the pharmacy.

Rod put two wide pieces of duct tape over Jim's mouth and pushed him into a closet at the back of the storeroom. He waited until Gary and the Wayne brothers had left with the shipping cart filled with boxes before pulling up his pant leg and taking his knife out of his boot, where he always kept it. Jim Bush's eyes widened at the sight of it, and he began to make frantic noises in his throat.

"Sorry, Jim," Rod apologized softly, "but I just can't trust you, man. You're so nervous and scared now, you'll blab everything to the cops as soon as they lean on you a little. Nothing personal." With a quick thrust of his arm, Rod plunged the knife into Jim's heaving chest and twisted it, watching him die.

3

Bev Wheaton hung up the phone as her husband came out of the bedroom. "That was your sister. She wants us to pick up a can of coffee at the Cumberland Farms."

"Are they open today?" Joe asked.

"Yeah. They had a sign in the window, said they would be open from noon to four."

"What time are we supposed to be at Kara's for dinner?"

"She said two, but you know her. We probably won't eat until four or five."

"You want to get the coffee on the way over?" Joe asked.

Bev looked at the kitchen clock. It was twelve-fifteen. "No, it's in the opposite direction from Kara's. I'll go now."

"I'll come with you," Joe said, pulling on his tan work boots. "You can drop me at Hillman's Farm. I want to see how Anna's making out with her new sled."

At Hillman's Farm, as Joe was getting out of the car, a friend of Anna's told him she'd seen Anna, Haley, and Jayne heading in the direction of Cemetery Hill. Joe was furious as he got back in the car, but Bev calmed him.

"The snow's not near as deep as it was the year the Jameson boy got killed, Joe. Take it easy."

"I don't care," Joe retorted. "They were expressly

forbidden from going there. They deliberately disobeyed."

He fumed, muttering under his breath, until they neared Cemetery Hill and saw the crowd of sledders gathered around something on the ground near the wall at the base of the hill.

"Anna!" Joe breathed, seeing Haley and Jayne looking pale and frightened and sobbing wildly.

4

Sparks.

A flash of white.

Darkness.

Fast darkness.

A rushing darkness.

A mad escalator ride through a darkness so deep, it made black look like a light color.

Anna felt sick, her stomach doing flipflops and somersaults. It felt like it was being pulled out of her body, right up through her throat.

The darkness turned to gray.

She had the strange sensation of being deep under water, of lying on the bottom of a lake and looking up at the gray-silver surface far above. She held her breath and tried to reach it. The water was thick, like syrup, making her rise in slow motion. Her lungs felt ready to burst.

Closer to the surface she came. Her lungs were burning. Just a little bit more, just a little bit more. Reaching. Almost there. Just a little more, just a—

—with a gasp she burst through the surface and was immediately frightened by a circle of faces looming over her, growing larger. She raised her arms to ward them off—

—and passed right through them.

"I'm dead! I'm dead!" a far-off, eerie voice wailed. It sounded strangely familiar. A vast expanse of blue sky freckled with clouds spread out above her, and she rose toward it. She was floating, flying, and it felt wonderful. She wanted nothing more than to keep going until she could touch the wisps of clouds far overhead.

"I'm dead! I'm dead!"

But the moaning voice wouldn't let her. Reluctantly she turned back toward the voice, rolling in the air until she was facing the earth again.

What a strange sensation!

There was a crowd of kids standing in a circle around someone lying in the snow near the wall. Haley and Jayne were there looking down at the person and crying.

Why?

Anna waved her arms like a swimmer and moved closer. The moaning voice was coming from the person on the ground. It was a girl. Anna saw blood covering the girl's face and wondered who it could be. The answer came a moment later as she recognized the girl's coat, snow pants, and boots and the shattered remains of a new sled strewn around her.

That's me! Anna thought. A mixture of fear and wonderment filled her.

What am I doing down there?

"I'm dead! I'm dead!" her body below cried out, as if in answer to her question.

The fear in Anna grew. *Oh, no! Am I dead? Am I really dead?*

The fear reached the point of panic.

But I can't be dead if I'm still thinking, she realized. *Then what am I doing floating around up here while my body's down there?*

Before she could figure out the answer to that question, she was buffeted by a strong gust of wind that sent her rolling and spinning. Strangely, she was the only thing that seemed to be affected by the wind. The branches of the trees around Cemetery

Hill remained unmoving. The wind was followed by a rushing, sucking sound, as though a giant can of vacuum-packed coffee had just been pierced.

A wondrous, dazzling light that was both right in front of her, yet far away, blinded her, blotting out everything else. It encompassed her, caressed her, and made her feel warm. She reached out to it, trying to touch it, but she felt it begin to recede from her. At the edges of her vision, a darkness crept in, forcing the beautiful light to contract and withdraw. There were things in the darkness—Anna could sense them—horrible laughing drooling things. All the things from every kid's worst nightmares lived in that darkness, and they wanted her. She could feel their eyes looking at her, could hear them smacking their rotting lips and grunting with anticipation as they forced the light farther away. It was just a circle now, like the light at the end of a very long tunnel. Anna tried to swim to it, but the darkness was moving closer, surrounding her, and it was thick and gluey. Strange slimy and furry things brushed against her in the darkness, making her recoil in disgust.

"Anna."

The voice came out of the light. She looked and was filled with joy at the sight of her friend Mary. But how could it be Mary? Anna wondered. Mary had died two years ago from leukemia.

"Anna, you have to go back," Mary said.

"No!" Anna cried, her voice coming out of her mind instead of her mouth. *"I want to come with you."*

"No," Mary said. *"It's not your time. You have to go back. Go back now, or the darkness will eat you."*

Mary's voice grew faint over the last few words she spoke, and the circle of light shrank rapidly. The hungry darkness rushed in.

"No!" Anna screamed.

"Anna! My God! Anna!" a voice from below cried.

"Daddy," Anna sobbed. She began falling at a rapid rate. Hands with tentacled fingers reached out of the darkness to her, trying to pull her back, but she slipped from their grasp and sped toward the earth.

"Anna! Speak to me!"

"Daddy?" Anna mumbled, opening her eyes. Her father was kneeling over her, his eyes shiny with tears.

"It's okay, baby. You're going to be okay," he said, his voice thick with emotion.

"Daddy? Am I dead?"

"No, honey, no. Sssh. Don't say that," her father said quickly, his voice cracking and the tears spilling from his eyes. He put his arms under her, lifting her, and Anna slipped back into the deep dark lake of unconsciousness.

5

Officer Dan O'Dea wasn't happy having duty on Christmas Day, but that's what happened when you were the youngest rookie cop on the town police force—even if the force only consisted of three officers and two dispatchers, one full time, one part time.

Even if he wasn't the rookie of the force, he figured he would have gotten stuck with duty today anyway since he was the only one without a family, still single, and no living relatives in the area.

Considering that, he knew he probably would have volunteered for holiday duty anyway. He guessed what rankled him was not having a choice. That, and the fact that the other two officers, Bob Joy and Chief Harper, had taken perverse pleasure in teasing him about being a rook and having to pay his dues.

Dan was cruising Route 13, on his way to Luv'n Donuts for his morning cup of java and a jelly cruller, a daily ritual with him. He was looking forward to—no, actually, dreading—a long boring day, a long boring *twelve-hour* day. Then he'd be on call for the rest of the night. The only good thing about it was that he'd get the next two days off.

He rounded the bend near Hillman's Farm, and a

half mile down the road he saw a silver Subaru station wagon stopped smack in the middle of the road, near Cemetery Hill, its driver and passenger doors wide open.

"What the hell?" Dan wondered aloud. He flicked on the flashing roof lights and pulled up behind the Subaru. There was a crowd of kids and a few adults gathered on the other side of the wall at the bottom of the hill.

Dan got out of the cruiser as a tall, well-built man, wearing a leather bomber jacket and cradling a little girl in his arms, climbed awkwardly over the wall, followed by a pretty blond-haired woman, her face streaked with tears.

"Help us!" the woman cried, seeing Dan before the man did. The man looked up as he jumped gingerly off the wall to the road, trying not to jostle the girl in his arms. Dan recognized him as Joe Wheaton, who worked at the Exxon station at the edge of town.

"What happened?" Dan asked, running to the woman and helping her off the wall.

"She hit the wall on her sled. Her head's bleeding," the man said over his shoulder, carrying the girl to his car.

"I'll take her," the woman said, running over and getting in on the passenger side so that her husband could put the child on her lap.

"You taking her to Middlesex Hospital?" Dan asked, running to his cruiser.

"Yeah," the man yelled, getting behind the wheel of the Subaru.

"I'll take care of Haley and Jayne," a woman, a neighbor, called from the other side of the wall. Joe Wheaton nodded his thanks and started the car.

"Follow me," Dan shouted, and got in his cruiser. He flipped on the siren and pulled around the Subaru, slowing only to be sure the wagon was following him before putting the pedal to the floor.

6

"What's that?" Gary Jergins asked, coming back to the pharmacy storeroom for the last carton of prescription drugs. He pointed to a pool of blood seeping out from under the closed closet door.

"Don't worry about it," Rod told Gary. "Get the last box, and let's get the hell out of here."

"Why'd you off Bush?" Fred Wayne asked Rod after Gary had left with the box.

"He was a liability, Freddy boy," Rod said, not adding what he was thinking: And so are you.

Fred looked nervous.

"Don't worry about it, Freddy. This gives us more time to get away. Believe me, he would have spilled his guts the minute we left and told the cops everything. Now he's spilling his guts, but he'll never say a word about us." Rod laughed at his own joke, but Fred looked like he didn't think it was all that funny.

"Let's go," Rod said, pushing Fred out of the pharmacy.

Gary was loading the last box into the van, and Tom was behind the wheel, starting the engine. Rod told Gary to get in the side and started to close the door.

"Uh-oh," Gary said. Rod didn't know what he was talking about at first. Then he heard it. Sirens. Getting closer. Coming up the hospital hill, and fast.

"Let's get out of here," Gary said, his eyes wide with fear.

"Don't sweat it, Dumbo," Rod said calmly. He reached into the van, took out his Uzi, clicked off the safety, and turned toward the sound of the siren.

"What're you gonna do?" Fred asked, his voice excited.

"You think this piece of shit van can outrun a cruiser? We're gonna ambush 'em and give us some time to get outta here. Get over there so we can catch them in a cross fire."

"All right," Fred exclaimed, his eyes gleaming. "Let's waste some fucking pork!" He ran over near the ER entrance and pulled his .44 Magnum out of his coveralls, cocked it, and assumed a police-style, crouched firing stance and waited.

The siren was very loud now. Under it, Rod and Fred could hear the roar of engines climbing the hill. Any second they expected to see flashing blue lights crest the top of the hill less than thirty yards away.

There.

The cruiser nearly left the road as it came over the top of the hill, reaching level ground. Seeing only one police cruiser disappointed Rod. He'd expected more and was looking forward to a major shoot-out. No matter. Even a chance to waste one pig was a chance he wouldn't pass up. A small silver station wagon crested the hill a few seconds behind the cruiser, and Rod's spirits rose. Maybe there are plainclothed cops in the wagon, he thought, or off-duty cops responding to the call on Christmas Day. It was probably the latter, he figured. All the towns around Middlesex Regional Hospital employed very few policemen, and only one, Towns End, had at least one cop on duty twenty-four hours a day.

The cruiser roared toward him, but Rod calmly waited until it was less than twenty feet away. He raised the Uzi, smiled at the look of shock on the face of the cop behind the wheel, and opened fire.

7

Dan O'Dea knew the girl was badly hurt—and with a head injury, no less, the worst kind. Her eyes had been showing the whites only, and her face was pale. He'd seen head injuries on children before, usually the result of a car accident, and knew how serious they could be.

What a terrible thing to happen on Christmas Day, he thought, racing his cruiser up the hill road to Middlesex Regional Hospital. He checked the rearview mirror. Joe Wheaton was keeping right up with him. Dan could see Mrs. Wheaton in the passenger seat, cuddling her daughter to her breast and rocking her gently.

The cruiser crested the hill. Dan was glad to see that the emergency room parking lot was empty, except for a van parked off to the side, at a door away from the emergency entrance. He didn't think twice about the van, so glad was he that the ER wasn't busy and its personnel would be able to devote all their energies to the Wheaton girl—until he noticed a man in coveralls coming around the back of the van. At the same moment, out of the corner of his eye to the left, he saw another man, also dressed in coveralls, standing, legs apart, against the ER wall. The stance of the man on the left was familiar. Dan O'Dea realized, a moment too late, that the man was in the standard police weapons-firing position. There was a popping sound, and the right side of the cruiser's windshield cracked and starred. The man by the van was bringing up a weapon with both hands. Dan saw that it was an Uzi. He slammed on the brakes and swerved. The last thing he saw was the rapid succession of flashes as the Uzi opened fire.

8

Joe Wheaton never saw the two gunmen, never had an inkling that they were there. What he did see was Officer O'Dea's cruiser suddenly swerve out of control and slam into the left sidewall of the hospital emergency room. The next thing he knew, there was a rapid popping sound, and the windshield was crashing in on him. He slammed on the brakes, reaching for his wife, but half her head was gone. A second later, most of Joe Wheaton's head went the way of his wife's.

9

Like shooting cats in a crate, Rod Baylor thought, laughing wildly as he sprayed the cruiser and the following Subaru with bullets. He thrilled at the sight and sound of lead striking metal and smashing glass. Adrenaline surged in him, making him cackle with excited glee as the cop car spun out of control and slammed head-on into Fred Wayne and the wall of the ER opposite him, pinning Fred to the wall. Even the screams of Fred being crushed to death by the cruiser did nothing to diminish Rod's enjoyment of the moment. If anything, Fred's death pumped him up even more.

He turned his attention, and the Uzi, on the Subaru wagon. Relishing the glass and blood flying, he fired into it until it crashed into the ambulance dock to the right of the ER entrance. For good measure, he pumped a few more rounds into it.

Whooping loudly, he opened the back of the van, pushed a frightened Gary Jergins out of the way, and climbed in.

"Let's get the fuck out of here!"

10

Far away there was the sound of glass smashing. Anna opened her eyes and looked up at her mother. One second she was smiling down at Anna, happy to see her daughter awake; the next second her face was gone in a cloud of red.

"Mama!" Anna tried to scream, but there was another crashing sound, and she was flung from her mother's lap onto the floor, striking her head hard again in the process. As blackness closed over her, she felt a great weight crashing in upon her, crushing her.

Suddenly she was outside the car, hovering in the air, looking at the smoking remains of the smashed station wagon wedged under the concrete dock used for unloading ambulance patients. A few feet away a police car was crushed up against the building, a man pinned between it and the wall.

With the speed of a camera shutter clicking, she was back inside the car, back inside her body. She felt an immense weight on her again, which caused intense pain. She couldn't move. She opened her eyes but could see nothing. Something wet dripped onto her face, trickled down her cheek and into her mouth. She tasted blood. The image of her mother's face disintegrating into a bloody mist flashed before her eyes, and she knew it was not her own blood she was tasting.

She started to scream—

—and found herself outside the car again, floating in the air. There were doctors and nurses running out of the ER doors. Several ran to the police car, where the man crushed against the wall had stopped screaming and was just making a low gurgling noise, his head slumped against the crumpled metal of the cruiser's roof. The other medical people ran to her parents' Subaru.

"I think there's three people inside," a nurse shouted. "Two adults and a child. The adults look like goners, but the kid might still be alive. She's on the floor, trapped under the dashboard, front seat, passenger side. We'll need the Jaws of Life to get her out." A doctor instructed another nurse to go inside and call the fire department.

Anna tried to descend to look in the car, but she had no control over her weightlessness. The nurse's words about the adults being goners frightened her. At first she didn't realize the nurse was talking about her parents. She felt so disconnected from everything, as though she were watching a movie on television.

"That's my mom and dad," she tried to say to the nurse, but her voice was faint and seemed not to come out of her mouth at all but from far away.

Anna grew frantic with fear. What was happening to her? What had happened to her parents? The last thing she remembered was sliding down Cemetery Hill on her new sled. She'd been going fast, too fast. She remembered trying to turn the sled to avoid the wall and the steering handles had jammed.

I hit the wall, she realized. *And I was talking to Mary—Mary who died two years ago!*

The memory of the beautiful light Mary had appeared in returned and made Anna feel a little better, but with it also came the memory of the encroaching darkness and the horrible things she had sensed within it.

I'm dying, she thought with an overwhelming sense of sadness. She began to cry. The wind picked up, buffeting her, yet she felt no chill from it.

"Don't cry," a voice said to her, but it was a man's voice, not Mary's. The wind turned her, and she saw a man rising through the roof of the smashed police car.

"Don't cry," he said again, turning to her. His body was encased in a sphere of bright yellow light. He appeared to be naked within the sphere, but that didn't matter to Anna; it seemed perfectly normal.

"I want my mommy. I want my daddy," Anna cried. The man floated to her and embraced her. Before he could say anything else, the air was rent with the loud suction sound Anna had heard before, when her dead friend Mary had appeared to her.

In the next instant, Anna was blinded by the beautiful all-encompassing light. The man let go of her and began moving toward it. Anna wanted to follow him but could not control her movements. Where the man was moving effortlessly into the light—actually being drawn to it like metal to a magnet—Anna could only flounder about in the air.

Suddenly there was a crackling noise. Rays of the light began to poke through the man—tiny ones at first, but getting larger. The man seemed to diminish in size, as though being pulled into a long tunnel. He began to disintegrate into the light, and though the process looked as if it should have been a painful one, Anna could see by his face as he turned to look at her, just before disappearing, that he was full of joy.

And then he was gone. The light began to recede.

"No!" Anna screamed.

She became aware of another man and realized it was the one who had been crushed between the police car and the hospital wall. Through the haze of the diminishing light, she saw that he too was rising out of his body. He looked frightened and confused until he saw the light, and then his expression changed to wonderment. He reached for the light, but the light withdrew from him quickly, seemingly repulsed by his presence, and disappeared. In its place, the foul darkness rushed in. There was a numbing flash of weird light that Anna could only describe as black lightning, and suddenly the real world around her was gone. The darkness boiled and swirled around the man, slowly taking form, coalescing into a huge creature, the likes of which Anna had never seen.

The thing was a mass of darkness and shadows that seemed to go on forever. Far above it, Anna could see what looked like thousands and thousands of black balloons hovering over it, connected to it with bloodred neon strings. The thing had a massive head. Its mouth was a yawning cavern lined with cruel-looking teeth. Its eyes were yellow with red pupils that glowed horribly. As hideous as the head was, the body of the thing was worse. It was a myriad of shifting shadows that became tentacles, with hands sprouting from the ends of them. And there were tiny horrid faces with beady eyes all over the body—the eyes were human, pitiful human eyes, all looking at her. These faces with screaming, tortured expressions, mouths opened in pain, surfaced and submerged constantly around the tiny eyes, but the eyes remained, some staring at her with fear, some with pain, most with hatred.

The man screamed, but the sound was lost in a terrible roaring sound of rushing air. His body, which was encased in a dark purple sphere, began to distort and stretch. The huge mouth of the black creature widened, and Anna realized the sucking sound of rushing air was coming from it. The creature was sucking the man into its mouth.

His eyes were bulging now, his body and face becoming distended as the cavernous black mouth pulled hm in. He fought it, but to no avail. His aura turned black and began to dissipate, like smoke, inhaled into the creature. His body began to break up and shred. Large pieces of him tore free and flew into the creature's mouth. The man's eyes turned to Anna, pleading with her for help. There was nothing she could do but watch in terror as his entire form disappeared into the black hole of the creature's mouth. It was only then that she heard his scream, resounding faintly and far away, but still horrible enough to give her chills and bring tears to her eyes.

Slowly, the creature's massive head turned toward Anna. The knob of rubbery black flesh that passed for the creature's nose was sniffing for her. She saw with a sense of revulsion that there were two tiny, beady eyes set in each nostril. The nose twitched, and its tiny eyes locked on her. The thing smiled with its cavernous mouth. All the many eyes of the thing turned on her now, and a red light began to seep from them in tendrils, groping for her, reaching for her.

She tried to back away, but she still had no control over the movements of her transparent body. The creature's mouth widened. The red tendrils came closer. The eyes of the thing narrowed cruelly. Just above the thing's nose, the blackness began to boil and a face appeared. It was the face of the man the thing had just consumed, his mouth open in a howl of pain and terror, the eyes wide with torture.

One of the bloody tendrils of dark light touched Anna's arm, and she felt a burning sensation throughout her body, but the red shaft of light recoiled from her at the same time.

The creature paused in its shape-shifting and appeared confused, hesitant. Suddenly it let out a bellow of rage that was a mixture of the tortured screams of the faces embedded in it and the sound of a train roaring past. Its many eyes blazed, the mouth widened, and it rushed at Anna.

She threw her arms up in front of her face and screamed—

—and opened her eyes to daylight pouring through a gaping hole in the side of her parents' car. Two firemen were working a machine with steel jaws that chewed through the metal of the car, opening it like a tin can.

Anna felt terribly cold and shivered. The shivering brought intense pain, and she moaned.

"Easy, darlin'," one of the firemen said to her. He caressed her hair lightly with his left hand. "We'll have you out of there in a minute." While they repositioned the cutting machine to tear away the last chunk of metal confining her, the fireman called to a doctor nearby, "Can you give her something? She's in a lot of pain."

The doctor, a young man with short black hair and thick glasses, came forward, leaned into the car, and gently put a needle into Anna's arm. The sound of the cutting machine renewing its assault on the car accompanied Anna into unconsciousness.

11

"Where's Fred? Where's Freddy? Where's my brother?" Tom Wayne, turning from behind the wheel, screamed at Rod Baylor, crouching in the back of the van.

"Shut the fuck up and drive. He didn't make it," Rod shouted back, panting with excitement.

"What'ya mean he didn't make it?" Tom cried, his voice on the edge of hysteria.

"Just what I said. He bought the farm. Kicked the bucket. Shit the bed. Fucking cops wasted him," Rod explained, his tone of voice amused.

"No!" Tom screamed, a half-strangled cry of pain and rage. "We're going back for him."

"He's dead, goddammit!" Rod shouted.

"Then I'm going back to kill the fucking pigs that wasted him. We're not leaving my brother back there, dead or not." Tom started to slow the van to turn around.

Rod grabbed the back of the driver's seat and jammed the muzzle of the Uzi under Tom's right ear.

"We're not going back," Rod said in a quiet, even voice. "You keep driving, or I'll blow your fucking head off."

"But my brother—"

"I don't give a sweet fuck about your brother. He's dead. The dumb bastard didn't know enough to get out of the way of the cop car when it went out of control, and he got flattened."

"No!" Tom choked. "You bastard! I'll get you for this, you fucker!" he screamed at Rod.

"Sure you will," Rod answered, a slow smile breaking over his face, his even tone of voice never changing. "Anytime you want to have a go at me, I'll be happy to oblige. But right now you're going to keep driving. We've got to ditch this van and lay low for a while."

Tom started to speak, tears streaming down his face, but Rod silenced him by pushing the muzzle of the Uzi harder into his neck. "Just quit your fucking bawling, Tommy boy, so I can think where we can get another vehicle."

Tommy did as he was told, grumbling tearfully. Rod pulled the gun out from under Tom's ear and sat back against the van wall, but he kept the Uzi aimed at him.

"You said no one was gonna get hurt," Gary Jergins blubbered from the back of the van. "You said there was blanks in your gun. You lied, Rod. You lied to me." He sat with his knees drawn up to his chest, hugging himself with his massive arms.

"Yeah, Gar, well, you know, sometimes, shit just happens. It was either us or them."

Gary shook his head and sobbed.

"Look, Dumbo. You want to go back to the slammer and be a bitch for all the spics and niggers?"

That stopped Gary's blubbering. Rod and Gary had been in Walpole State Prison together, where they had met. Gary had been gang-raped several times by two different gangs of blacks and Puerto Ricans. As big as he was, he was too gentle to fight back. It wasn't until Rod had taken him under his wing and into the protection of the white gang of cons that he belonged to that Gary had been left alone.

"No," Gary whimpered, shaking his head, his voice full of terror.

"Then shut the fuck up and be glad I wasted those cops. If I hadn't, you'd be on our way back to the can, and you wouldn't come out until you had an asshole the size of the Grand Canyon and you'd have to wear fucking diapers for the rest of your life. If you didn't die of AIDS first."

Gary paled at that, stifling his sobs against his legs and rocking himself slowly back and forth.

Rod made Tom stick to the back roads that run through the countryside of north-central Massachusetts and that intersect frequently with the New Hampshire border. They were heading in the opposite direction from where they were supposed to be going, but that couldn't be helped. Rod knew it would be suicide to head south in the van for the rendezvous with Carlo. He was certain there was an APB out on the van, and the longer they stayed with it, the stronger the chances became of their getting caught.

On a long, winding, desolate road called Turnpike Street, outside of a small town bordering the New Hampshire state line, Rod finally saw what he was looking for. It was late afternoon and the sun was going down, the sky becoming prematurely dark with the help of a layer of heavy gray storm clouds rolling in from the east. Parked on the side of the road, with its lights off, was a new model Toyota pickup truck.

Rod made Tom drive past while he moved up front into the passenger seat and checked out the truck. It looked like a couple of teenagers were parking, hiding their faces in each other's necks as the headlights washed over them. Rod waited until

Tom drove the van around a bend in the road, passing out of sight of the truck, before telling him to stop and turn around. With the headlights off, he directed Tom to pull in behind the truck. Before the van came to a full stop, Rod was out the door, running to the driver's side of the Toyota. He yanked open the door, grabbed the driver—a young kid with his pants down and his girlfriend's face buried in his crotch—by the arm, and jammed the Uzi into the girl's shocked, upturned face.

"If you know what's good for your little cocksucker there, you won't do anything stupid," he said, smiling at the kid.

Tom got out of the van and went around to the passenger door and pulled it open. He reached in and grabbed the girl by the hair and dragged her out of the truck. Her winter coat was off and her blouse was open, exposing pert little breasts that jiggled as he manhandled her. Tom grinned lecherously and grabbed her breasts roughly, making her squeal with pain.

"Hey, you like that, Tommy?" Rod asked, laughing. "This is more like it, huh?"

Tom grinned sadistically and bit the girl's left breast, making her scream. He slapped her silent, knocking her to the ground.

"Leave her alone, you asshole!" the boy shouted, trying to pull away from Rod's grip to go to his girlfriend's aid. Rod shoved the gun into the boy's testicles hard, making him gasp painfully.

"Shut up, lover boy, or I'll make a girl out of you," Rod told him. He pulled the boy from the truck and dragged him, pants down around his knees, to the rear of the vehicle, between the van and the truck.

Tom Wayne was on top of the girl in the snowbank at the side of the road, mangling her breasts with his teeth and tearing at her clothes while she moaned in pain. Rod kicked at Tom's legs.

"Get up. There'll be time enough for that shit when we get the goods transferred from the van to the truck."

Tom didn't respond but kept on at the girl. Rod kicked him hard in the ass. "Get up and get Dumbo and put the goods in the truck like I said."

Growling and cursing Rod under his breath, Tom got up, zipped and buckled his pants, and went to the rear of the van.

"Lay down next to the slut, lover boy," Rod instructed the boy, pushing him forward with the muzzle of the Uzi. The boy did as he was told, clutching at his pants and pulling them up before lying next to his girlfriend in the snow. She was curled into a fetal position, and she whimpered and trembled uncontrollably when the boy tried to put a consoling arm around her.

"Hurry up, you guys!" Rod shouted at Tom and Gary, who were coming around the van, each with a box of stolen drugs in their arms.

"What the fuck are you gonna do, just stand around and watch us?" Tom groused, hoisting his box into the truck bed.

"No. I'm keeping an eye on your fresh piece of ass here so they don't get away and bring the heat down on us. The quicker you guys get that shit unloaded, the sooner you'll be able to have some fun, Tommy boy."

Tom considered that for a moment, looking at the girl in the snow, and hurried back to the van. He carried two boxes each trip and urged Gary to do the same.

The stolen cargo was transferred in less than twenty minutes. Tom loaded the last box into the truck, closed and secured the tailgate, and looked lustfully at the girl. Her boyfriend tried to cover her with his arms, glaring balefully at Tom all the while, but she began crying and tried to pull away from him.

"Please don't let him hurt her anymore," the boy pleaded with Rod. "You can have the truck. Take it. Take me with you as a hostage if you want, but please let her go."

"Shut the fuck up," Rod said loudly. "You can have the truck," he said, mimicking the boy. "Like I need your fucking permission, asshole." He turned to Gary. "Get in the truck and start it. And turn on the heater, it's getting fucking cold out here. Wait here for us, we'll be right back."

Gary, looking nervously at the couple in the snowbank, hesitated a moment, then climbed into the cab of the truck and started it.

"That clearing we turned around in, back about thirty yards, looked like snowmobile tracks leading into it. We'll ditch the van there," Rod said to Tom. "You drive." He kicked the boy in the back. "Pick up the slut and get in the back of the van."

"Please don't kill us," the boy whimpered.

Rod kicked him hard in the side of the head. "Shut up and do as you're told."

The boy helped the girl to her feet. She tried to pull away and resist him, but he spoke soothingly to her, calming her, and led her to the open doors at the back of the van.

"Get in," Rod instructed, and climbed in after them, pulling the doors closed behind him. Tom was already in the driver's seat. He started the van, backing up and turning it around to head up the road to the spot Rod had indicated. He turned off the road into the clearing, the van traveling through the deep snow for nearly two hundred yards before it got bogged down and could go no further.

"All right. Get out," Rod told the boy. The boy grabbed the girl's hand and started toward the rear doors.

"Leave the girl," Tom said, climbing in the back and pulling the girl from the boy. The boy looked pleadingly at Rod.

"Do as he says. Come on." Rod grabbed the boy's shirt-sleeve and pulled him from the van. He fell face-first into the snow at Rod's feet.

"Please, mister, please don't do this," the boy pleaded, his voice muffled by the snow.

"Look, I ain't the fucking tooth fairy, and I don't grant wishes," Rod said. He stood over the boy, pointed the Uzi at the back of his head, and let loose one quick burst of fire. The boy's head was immediately pulverized, turning the snow red for a radius of several feet around him.

Rod turned back to the van. Tom hadn't even noticed that Rod had wasted the boy, so busily was he ripping the clothes from the girl, biting and grabbing at her, and pulling down his own pants. He was sitting on her chest, forcing himself into her mouth and grunting.

Rod stepped into the van and shoved the muzzle of the Uzi into the crack of Tom's ass. "I know you'd like to go this way," he said with a smirk before pulling the trigger. The bullets ripped through Tom's rectum and into the girl's head, killing her instantly. Tom fell off her and thrashed about, screaming and gagging and holding his shredded privates with both hands. Rod finished him with another quick burst from the Uzi that tore open his chest and sent chunks of flesh and a spray of blood throughout the interior of the van.

"Where's Tommy, Rod?" Gary asked as Rod got into the truck.

Rod looked at him and debated for a second whether to tell him the truth. He decided that his method of treating Gary like a mushroom was the best course.

"He's taking the boy and his girlfriend over the border into New Hampshire, to dump them in the boonies and give us a good head start. He'll catch up with us in the van and meet us at Carlo's," Rod lied.

Gary looked uncertain. Something didn't sound right about that, but his plodding mental process couldn't immediately finger it.

"Let's go," Rod told him. He took off his gloves and held his hands over the heating vents in the dash. "Go back the way we came, and head for the interstate—I think it was left at the end of this road. We should be able to make Providence in a couple of hours."

Gary put the truck in gear and started driving, but he kept thinking in his slow, ponderous way and casting doubtful, sidelong glances at Rod.

12

"Okay, let's move her from the stretcher to the table on three. One, two, three."

Anna felt herself being lifted and put down again. She lay unmoving, listening to the voices around her.

"All right. Let's get the blood cleaned off her face and head. Looks like a pretty severe head trauma. Type her, and get an IV started, and get her stabilized. Then I want full head and body X-rays and an EEG."

Anna had no idea what the voices were talking about, but she vaguely knew that she was their focus. She knew in a distant way, the way one might know that a moving speck in the sky far off is a bird, that she was hurt and hurt bad. She also knew, in a more immediate sense, that her parents were dead. The pain of that knowing was so intense that she felt as though she could die from it.

"She's going into convulsions!" she heard someone shout, and suddenly she was outside of her body again, floating above herself. There were a group of doctors and nurses working frantically over her body, which was jerking and flopping about like a fish on dry land.

Anna was mesmerized by the spectacle below her and tried to move closer. Like a swimmer, she moved her arms and kicked her legs, but she felt as though she were swimming against the current. She began to be frightened. It dawned on her that if she couldn't even get closer to her body, how could she ever hope to get back inside it? And if she couldn't get back inside her flesh, then that meant that she was . . . dead.

Like Mom, she thought. Tears welled up inside her, and she heard the sound of someone crying. At first she thought it was herself, the sound being distorted, as everything seemed to be on this other plane of existence. She soon realized the sound was coming from elsewhere. With a great effort, she turned away from the scene below. As she did so, everything around her changed, as though a shade had been drawn over the world, or a near-transparent veil. Everything around her became darker, as when a cloud passes over the sun. She had the strange sensation of seeing everything tripled for a moment before it all coalesced into a slightly less distorted image. It was like looking through a large storefront window; through the glass she could see the real world—the emergency room with the doctors and nurses scurrying about—but on the surface of the glass, she could see a reflection, the reflection of a whole new world where her spirit now existed.

The new world was darker than the old and was filled with perpetual twilight. Its dimensions were distorted to the point where it almost made Anna dizzy to look around. There was a dark gray and blue spongy material all around that resembled earth but couldn't rightly be called that. From the material, which stretched out around her and above her, too, in great rolling plains, sprouted strange funguslike plants that undulated in an invisible current, the way underwater plants will. The superimposition of this new world on the old was very disconcerting to Anna's senses. The gray-blue earthlike matter grew through, around, and over the walls, floors, and ceiling of the emergency room. To the right, it seemed to stretch for miles, right through the walls of the hospital and out into the air. To the left, it banked against the hospital walls and went upward, passing through the roof until it disappeared from sight in the twilight overhead. All around Anna there were great rents and holes in the spongy matter, giving it the appearance of moldy Swiss cheese. Some of the holes gave off a faint blue or reddish glow, and others gave off a dark glow that was as black as pitch. Every so often a thin tendril of darkness would seep from them, wriggling and curling into the air like a snake in pain, then flit away into nothingness.

Sound was distorted also at this new level of perception. The sounds of the real world—the voices of the doctors and nurses—were alternately loud then soft; near then far away. At times the real world sounded speeded up, like a tape recorder on fast forward; then it would slow to the point where every sound was deep and drawn out to the point of being incomprehensible.

But through it all, like a radio playing in the background, or a song that repeats itself over and over in your head, she could hear the crying and sobbing of someone in distress.

That sounds like Haley, Anna thought, but she knew that couldn't be so. She distinctly remembered seeing Haley standing over her at the bottom of Cemetery Hill, when she'd had her first out-of-body experience. It had to be some other child.

Anna looked around trying to pinpoint the source of the crying. She concentrated on finding the person in distress, and the more she did so the more the real world retreated, telescoping away from her until it was a bubble, a minute oval image floating in the twilight of this new world, like a scene viewed from the wrong end of a pair of binoculars.

Behind Anna, where the gray-blue spongy earth erupted into a tall pillar that seemed to stretch into eternity above her, she pinpointed the direction the sobbing was coming from. With the real world withdrawn to a balloon at the extreme periphery of her vision, she found it easier to move where she wanted to and to control her body movements—which scared her, telling her that she belonged more in this new other-existence than in the real world.

Stretching her arms in a breaststroke, Anna propelled herself forward toward the pillar.

I'm flying, she thought, a fantasy she had always entertained and that was the reason she was such an avid swimmer in the summer. But this wasn't really like swimming in water—it was more like being immersed in a thin gel that could be breathed. Though a small part of her found the air to be suffocating, a larger part felt completely at home and exhilarated in the weightlessness of this new existence.

"Mommy! Where are you?" the cry echoed through the thick air, and Anna was absolutely sure now that it came from behind the pillar. Large fan-like growths protruded from the spongy pillar and vibrated slightly in time to the sound of the voice, which made barely visible ripples in the thick atmosphere.

Anna did the breaststroke again and moved closer to the pillar. Out of the corner of her eye, she could see that the real world had receded to less than the size of a dime. From very far away she heard a tiny, tinny voice proclaim, "She's stabilized.

Heart and respiration normal, but she's lapsed into a coma. Let's get her to the ICU."

Though she knew that the voice was talking about her real, mortal body and its state in the real world, the words made no sense to her, and she didn't care. All she cared about was finding the child who was crying. She felt so lost and alone herself, she thought that if she could find the child, it would help herself somehow. She didn't know how that could be or why she felt that way—she just did, strongly and irrevocably.

She kicked her legs Australian-crawl style, breast-stroked again, and came within touching distance of the spongy pillar. She reached out and tentatively brushed her hand against it. It felt warm and wet to the touch, and there was a faint palpitation to it, as though a tiny heart was buried deep inside it, beating away as though it were alive.

Her first sensation at touching the pillar was one of shock, and she quickly withdrew her hand from it. Her fingers came away tingling not unpleasantly. She held them to her cheek, and a soothing, comforting feeling came over her. She was about to reach out and touch and caress the pillar again when the crying voice from behind the spongy protrusion broke through her thoughts and dispelled the feeling, leaving her only with concern for the owner of the lamenting voice.

Anna reached out with both hands and grabbed the pillar, aware of the life within it but more focused on using it as leverage with which to move herself. Like a hider behind a post, she felt along the pillar to peer at the other side. At first she saw nothing but deep blue darkness—nothing like the blackness of the horrible creature that had swallowed the man or the deep darkness that tendriled from some of the holes in the sponge-ground—that was broken only by the ripples of sound undulating upward and outward from the base of the pillar.

She pushed herself around and closer, lowering her position as she did. A shape came into focus, blurred, then crystallized. It was a child. A little boy. He held something cradled in his arms and rocked it to and fro gently as he sobbed.

His aura was a pale yellow. The thing he held in his arms had a slightly darker aura than his own. Anna looked down at herself and realized her own aura was a bright blue. She moved closer.

"Mommy! Please come and get us. Mommy! Please!" the child whimpered, his voice barely a whisper. He hugged the thing in his arms to his chest and sobbed deeply over it.

Anna pushed against the pillar and lowered herself to the base of it, settling next to the child. Her knees sank into the spongy surface, and she felt a tingle, like a mild electric shock, course through her transparent body at its touch.

"Hey, what's wrong?" she asked, though her voice came from her mind and not from her mouth, which moved completely out of sync with the words she was speaking. The child jumped and looked up in shock, then scrambled away from Anna while trying not to drop the thing in his arms.

"It's okay. I won't hurt you," Anna said as soothingly as possible. The boy stopped his sideways slide away from her and looked cautiously up at her, hugging the thing in his arms more tightly to his breast.

"Who . . . who are you?" the boy asked, his mouth open but his lips not working to form the words. Anna could feel, could hear, could almost see the words coming from the center of his forehead.

"I'm Anna," she replied, trying not to move her lips as she projected her thoughts, but she felt them moving anyway. *"What's your name?"* she asked shuffling her knees over the yielding sponge-ground to move closer to the boy.

"T-T-T-Tony," the boy stuttered mentally. The sound of the repeated T's reverberated into the distance.

"Tony what?" Anna projected the question. This was becoming easier, and she was able to keep her mouth closed this time.

"T-Tony Driscoll, and I live at 425 River Street in Leominster," the boy recited quickly, as if he'd practiced it under coaching by an adult many times. *"I can't see you too good,"* the boy went on. *"Are you a policeman? Can you take me to my mommy?"*

"No," Anna replied, floating closer. *"I'm not a policeman."* To her left, a rent opened in the surface of the spongy matter, and a blue light poured forth, mingling with her aura and allowing Tony to see her better.

"You . . . you're just a girl," Tony said with disappointment.

"Sorry," Anna replied, and had to chuckle at his reaction, *"but yes, I am."*

Tony hugged the thing in his arms closer. *"You're no help. You'll go into the light, or the bad black thing,"* he said with a shudder, *"just like everyone else. Nobody wants to help me. Nobody can help me. I want my mommy."* Tony began to cry again.

Anna pondered over what he'd just said. What others? *"Who did you see go into the light and the bad black thing?"* she asked, settling her floating body next to the boy.

"Lots of people," he answered. *"Everyone I seen has gone into the light or been eaten by the*

black thing. When it comes, I hide. I know it wants to eat me too, but it can't unless I let it. I don't know why." Tony sat silent, clutching his shadowy bundle.

"What's that you've got?" she asked, leaning over, her movements as graceful as a ballet dancer's in slow motion.

Tony drew his arms away, looking at Anna distrustfully. He considered her smiling face for a moment, then seemed to come to a decision and held his arms out for her to see.

"It's my baby brother, Billy," he said softly. He held up a tiny infant, its eyes open, its body moving feebly. It was emaciated, so thin, Anna could see the bones of its skull outlined in the transparent flesh.

Anna almost let out a gasp at the sight of the baby, but she managed to contain herself. *"What happened to you and your brother?"* she asked, reaching out with both hands, one to touch Tony's shoulder, the other to caress the baby's forehead.

Tony hesitated a moment, tears spilling from his eyes and falling on the chest of the starved infant in his arms. *"It was Mom,"* he said in a voice that was barely perceptible. *"She changed. She stuck sharp things in her arms, and then she'd get far away and didn't care about anything; not me, not Billy here,"* he said, nodding his head toward his brother, *"not nothing. She left our 'partment for a long time, for days I think, and me and Billy got real hungry. I tried to feed him as long as I could, but there wasn't much food, and I ran out of milk. I don't remember too much after that. I think I slept a lot, so did Billy, though he cried a lot too.*

"Then one night I woke up, and Mom was there. She was crying and holding one of the needle things she used to stick in her arms and go far away. I told

her I was hungry and Billy was too, and she told me to lie still and close my eyes, and she'd make the hunger go away. I did what she said, and she stuck one of the sharp things in my arm. It hurt, and I cried, and then I started to go far away in my head, just like Mommy did, and I ended up here. There was a bright light calling to me, but I was afraid to go inside it. I wanted my mommy. I want her now. I want my mommy!" The tears came hard from Tony's eyes, and his chest heaved with sobs. The baby in his arms joined his crying with a feeble wailing.

Anna felt like sobbing too. As soon as she'd touched Tony's aura, she'd been flooded with empathic feelings of his loss and understood in rapid, vivid flashes all that had happened to him. Anna put her arms around the two of them and rubbed Tony's shoulder, amazed that though their bodies both appeared to be transparent, there was still substance to them.

"How did your brother get here with you?" Anna asked softly.

"When I was hiding from the light, I saw Mommy and Billy being brought into the hospital down there." He pointed at the oval scene floating above them, which had grown a little larger in diameter. *"I saw my body in there too, and they were covering me up with a sheet over my head. I tried to go back inside my body, but I couldn't. Then I saw Mommy and Billy float out of their bodies, and I was so happy, cuz they were coming toward me. I hugged her, and we cried, and she said everything was going to be all right now, but it wasn't. She lied, cuz then the bad black thing came and swallowed her up. She tried to get away, but she couldn't. It just sucked her right in. It would have sucked me and Billy in too, but Mommy*

put Billy in my arms and told me to hide, so I did. I've been hiding ever since."

"How long have you been here?" Anna asked.

"I don't know," Tony replied. *"A long time."*

Anna thought for a moment. She remembered hearing her parents discussing a story in the newspaper about a young mother from Leominster who had given her two kids overdoses of drugs and then killed herself the same way. That had been over a month ago, just before Thanksgiving, if she remembered correctly.

"You have been here a long time," Anna said softly. Tony nodded sadly in agreement and hugged his little brother closer.

"Tony, you said you've seen a lot of people go into the bright light and the bad black thing. Who were they, Tony? Did you know any of them?"

"No," Tony answered slowly.

"Do you remember what any of them looked like?"

"There's been lots," Tony explained. *"Most come out of the hospital down there, and more of them get eaten by the black thing than go into the light. There was a nice lady and a man, though, that went into the light just a little while ago."*

Anna's heart quickened. *"What did they look like, Tony?"*

"The lady had long blond hair and pretty blue eyes. She was real pretty. And the man had blond hair too, and lots of muscles." Tony stopped and looked at Anna curiously. *"They kinda looked like you,"* he added.

Mom! Dad!

Anna started crying. They really were dead. *Dead.* What an awful, horrible word. It sat like a molten hot weight in her thoughts.

"That was your mom and dad, wasn't it?" Tony

said, a statement more than a question. He reached out and touched Anna's face through her aura.

Anna could only nod in reply.

"It's okay," Tony said, stroking her hair. *"The bad black thing didn't get them. They went into the bright light, and they were happy. The light is a good thing. I think it is, anyway. It feels good when I look at it, not like the black thing."* Tony's voice grew softer. *"When I see it, I want to take my brother and go down the tunnel to it. It's like it's calling us, but I'm afraid to go, cuz if I do and Mommy comes back looking for us, she won't know where we are, and—"*

"—Hold on, she's coming out of it."

Anna's eyes fluttered open, and she was dazzled by an intensely bright light. *Are you in there, Mom, Dad? Are you in there?*

A face loomed into view over her, blocking out the light, and she realized it wasn't the light at the end of the tunnel that she'd seen Mary in and that Tony said her parents had gone into. It was just a ceiling light, and she was back in her body in the emergency room.

I'm not dead, she thought, but the realization brought no joy. Mom and Dad were dead. Mom and Dad had gone down the long tunnel into the light, and she wanted more than anything to be with them.

"How are you, little lady? You gave us quite a scare," the head looming over her said. It was a young man with dark hair and dark eyes and teeth so white, they seemed to leap from his mouth. Anna tried to tell him that she wanted to die, wanted to be with her mother and father, but the words wouldn't come out. All she could do was moan.

"Don't try to talk. It's okay. You're going to be okay. I'm Dr. Donaldson. We're going to move you to a room now where we can take better care of you. You're going to be okay."

Anna tried to speak again and still couldn't. The effort brought a sharp pain, and she grimaced. She didn't want to be okay. She wanted to be with her mom and dad. She wanted to be dead.

13

"What do you mean he's not here?"

Rod Baylor stood with Gary behind him in the dark hallway of the dank tenement house and felt his bowels go cold.

"Like I told ya, man, he got busted. Feds pulled a raid last night at the docks, when he was takin' delivery on a shipment of guns. You shouldn't even be anywhere near here, man, if you're hot. If the feds ain't already watching this place, it's only a matter of time before they do. I'm on my way out now. Gonna lie low for a while. Orders from the Patruccis."

Rod was furious, but even more than that, he was scared. His first reaction to hearing that Carlo wasn't at the apartment where they were supposed to meet was anger and distrust—a sense that he was being set up or about to be ripped off. But looking at the heavyset, Neanderthal-browed Italian in the doorway, and listening to the nervousness in the thug's voice, Rod knew he was being told the truth.

Nothing's gone right with this operation from the start, he thought, and had the distinct feeling that things weren't through going wrong—not by a long shot. He tried to shake the feeling off.

"So what am I supposed to do now?" he asked the guinea, who'd said his name was Pauly. "I've got a truck full of prescription drugs that Carlo promised to pay me twenty-five K for. Since he worked for the Patrucci family, they must know it was coming. They must still want it."

Pauly laughed. It was a phlegmy, greasy sound in his throat. "No, man. They didn't know nothin' 'bout this. Carlo was doin' this on the sly. He was pissed at bein' cut outta the coke action by Don Patrucci, but it was his own fault—everyone knows he's got a coke jones real bad. Who's gonna trust him to handle delivery to the dealers when you know he's gonna cut the shit out of it and keep the best to put up his nose?"

"Oh! That's just fucking great! Just fucking *great*!" Rod slammed his fist against the wall. Gary whimpered softly.

"Hey! Chill out," Pauly said, his eyes narrowing and taking on a dark look Rod didn't much care for.

Rod chilled. "Sorry. Listen. You gotta help me move this stuff. I gotta unload it, get some cash, and get outta New England."

Pauly eyed Rod and Gary carefully and smiled tightly.

Watching Pauly's eyes, Rod had the distinct feeling that this greaser wasn't as stupid as he looked.

Pauly took his wallet out of his pocket and handed Rod a crumpled, grungy business card. "The Dew Drop Inn," it read in faded blue letters over an address.

"This place is used by the family. It's safe. It's up near Federal Hill. Go there and ask for room thirteen. They'll know you're there for protection. I'll see who I can sniff out for buyers and get in touch with you there."

A warning signal began to flash in Rod's mind. Don't trust this greaseball, it said. But what choice did he have? He was stuck.

"How long?" Rod asked, unable to keep the hint of a whine out of his voice and hating himself for it.

" 'S long as it takes," Pauly answered.

The motel was set back on a dusty parking lot, with a shopping mall down the road from it. Otherwise there were no other buildings in sight. The road was a short loop off one of the main streets. Rod figured if the place hadn't been owned and used for clandestine activities by the Patrucci family, it would have gone out of business a long time ago.

Gary pulled the pickup truck into the lot in front of the motel office and killed the engine. Rod got out, went in, and did as Pauly had instructed him. The clerk, an elderly balding man with a nose that looked like it had been used as a pincushion, didn't bat an eye when Rod asked for room 13.

"It's around back. Number on the door says twelve, but it's the one you want," the clerk explained.

As Rod took the key and walked out, he realized that not once had the clerk looked directly at him. Probably a smart practice, considering the clientele the motel had.

The room was dingy and poorly lit. There were two double beds next to each other, their headboards against the wall, a bad print of a foxhunt hanging over them. Opposite the beds was a cigarette-burned dresser with a cloudy oval mirror atop it. There was a badly frayed upholstered chair in the corner of the room near the bathroom door; its purple floral design was stained and faded. The carpet on the floor, also purple to match the bed coverings, was worn thin around the beds and on a path leading to the bathroom. On a small table near the window was an ancient black and white television set, with crooked rabbit ears sitting on top. The room smelled of stale sweat and smoke and gave Rod bad vibes from the moment he opened the door.

But it was more than just the room. The whole situation with Carlo getting busted and now having to deal with goomba Pauly had him paranoid. Carlo was a sleazeball, but he was basically a coward and wouldn't have dared cross Rod. After seeing Rod slit the throat of a hooker who'd tried to steal a hundred bucks from him, Carlo knew Rod was no one to fuck with. But guinea Pauly didn't know Rod, and he didn't look like he'd have second thoughts about fucking *anyone* over if the payoff was big enough. He might do it in a cowardly way, like with a knife in the back while you were taking a piss, but he'd have the balls to do it and make sure he got away with it.

I'm being set up, Rod thought, not for the first time that day. I'm on Pauly's turf, at his mercy. What's to keep him from coming in here, blowing me away, and then taking the goods for himself?

Rod decided he needed a plan for just such an event. Leaving Gary sleeping on one of the beds, Rod left the room and walked down the road to the shopping mall.

14

Pauly Garibaldi was excited, but you'd never know it to look at his face. He wore the same expression no matter what emotion he was experiencing. Only his eyes gave anything away as they became more furtive, darting about as Pauly went over the night's work ahead, considering all the possibilities for fucking up.

Not that he really thought there would be any fuck-ups—Rod Baylor looked and acted like a wuss; easy pickings. The other guy, Gary, Baylor's muscle, was big enough to be trouble, but Pauly wasn't too worried about him either. Pauly knew how to handle muscle. What Pauly had to worry about was his superiors in the Patrucci family finding out about this and coming down hard on him. He knew they'd find out eventually, but how hard they came down on him would depend on if he pulled it off cleanly or not, and whether he cut the family in for a piece of the action.

And that he would most certainly do. He was greedy, but he wasn't stupid. The family didn't mind its soldiers delving into a little entrepreneurial activity once in a while, as long as it got its share.

Pauly relaxed a little and settled back in the plush seat of the T-bird. He had three trusted guys with him—nonfamily members, but guys who owed him big time. He'd promised each to wipe out his debt if he helped him with this job, and each had readily agreed. Being completely ruthless men, none of them had any qualms about performing the task ahead.

Henry, a mixed-breed Hispanic Jew with a face pockmarked from a bad case of teenage acne, was driving. His black hair was long and tied back in a ponytail. At his left side, between the seat and the door, rested his sawed-off twelve-gauge shotgun. In the front passenger seat was Stretch, a tall bald-headed black man with gold hoops in both ears and bad teeth that caused a constant foul odor to emanate from his mouth. He, too, carried a sawed-off twelve-gauge. Next to Pauly in the backseat was Mike, half Puerto Rican, half Irish, with red hair cut short and dark crazy eyes. He carried a .38 special stuck in his belt.

Pauly carried his own favorite weapon, a .45, in a handmade Italian leather shoulder holster under his jacket. He patted the bulge the gun made and looked out the window. Another couple of miles, and they'd be at the motel. He had talked to Old Dingle, the guy who ran the motel for the family, on the phone right after Rod Baylor had checked in. Everything was set. Dingle would be out of the office, but he'd leave the key to room 13 just inside the office door, which he'd also leave unlocked.

Pauly planned to send his three goons into the room, guns blazing, while he stayed outside in case Baylor or his sidekick managed to get out. He doubted that would happen, but he liked to be cautious. He was ninety-nine percent sure his men would waste Baylor and the other guy before they even knew what hit them. Then it was just a matter of tidying up, disposing of the bodies in the landfill the family owned, and taking the goods Baylor had stolen. Pauly figured to come out at least fifteen grand richer, after the family took its cut.

Yeah, he thought, this is going to be a piece of cake.

15

Rod Baylor stood at the window of the room next to room 13, watching the parking lot. Around the corner, out of sight, was the van he had heisted from the shopping mall parking lot earlier in the day. It was loaded with the goods they'd stolen from the hospital. The truck they'd come in was parked right outside the motel room, a blanket thrown over several trash bags in the rear to make it look like it still held its cargo.

Rod had taken the trash bags from the bin at the side of the motel, after he'd paid the old guy who ran the place a visit. The old guy was tied up and gagged on the floor by the bed, with Gary watching over him. Rod wasn't taking any chances that the guy would tip greaseball Pauly off when he came to steal the truck and the drugs. And Rod *was* sure Pauly would come—gut sure.

He heard the car approaching before he saw it. Its headlights were out. The reflection of the moon off its polished surface was all he could see of it as it pulled up outside the room.

Rod tensed. Four guys got out of the car and moved to both sides of the door to room 13. They were all carrying guns.

"Shit," Rod swore under his breath. These guys meant to waste him and Gary! He'd expected them to just heist the truck and its cargo, but to waste him! That really pissed him off.

One of the men, it looked like Pauly, took a key from his pocket and inserted it into the lock on room 13. Rod heard the door bang open, and the night erupted with the sound of gunfire. The wall adjoining room 13 shook as it was riddled with bullets.

"That's it, you sonsabitches," Rod muttered. He brought up his Uzi and flung the door open. Greaseball Pauly was the first to go down, the short burst from the Uzi nearly cutting him in half at such short range. Rod stepped to the door of room 13 and wasted the two gunmen standing just inside. The bullets ripped up the back of one of the men and across the side of the other's head, tearing it open. The walk and door were slick with blood.

Rod flattened himself against the outside wall next to the door, unsure of where the other gunman was. He heard a metallic click and slide sound and immediately identified it as a pump-action shotgun. He leaned back into the doorway of the other room and motioned Gary to bring the old man to him. Grabbing the elderly clerk by the back of the shirt, he pushed the clerk into the doorway of room 13.

The clerk screamed, a muffled sound under the gag on his mouth, and was lifted off his feet by the force of the shotgun blast that caught him in the midsection. He flew backward, landing on the black T-bird the gunmen had come in, his guts splattering the hood and windshield around and behind him. Crouching, Rod jumped into the doorway and opened fire before the man inside could pump the shotgun for another blast. The first burst from the Uzi tore up nothing but carpet and one of the beds before Rod saw the guy crouching by the chair in the corner. Rod spun the Uzi, letting loose a second burst that shredded the chair and the man's right arm and shoulder. He screamed and fell back, dropping the shotgun onto the bullet-ripped carpet. The third blast from Rod's Uzi disintegrated the guy's head and sent him sprawling against the wall, his blood and brains painting the cheap wallpaper like a bad imitation of a Jackson Pollock painting.

Rod stood surveying his work, a grim smile on his face. Gary came out of the room behind him, slipped in the thick blood all over the walk, and fell hard on his ass. Rod burst into hysterical laughter that stopped as abruptly as it began when he heard sirens in the distance.

"Let's get the fuck out of here," he said to Gary. Helping his partner up, they headed for the stolen van around the corner.

16

Consciousness came and went. During the blackouts, Anna dreamed of her family, of happier days with her parents and sisters. She dreamed of days they spent at Hampton Beach, afternoons on the rides at Whalom Amusement Park, and simple picnics at Coggshall Park, listening to the merchant marine band playing oompah music (as her dad called it) on the bandstand that jutted out into the lake.

During the moments of wakefulness, she stared at a world that was a blurry fog and that came into focus only sporadically. She saw vague shapes that she guessed were doctors and nurses come and go and felt them inserting needles and tubes into her. Though what they did was uncomfortable and often painful, she didn't care.

One afternoon Haley, Jayne, and Aunt Kara came to visit her. She was aware of their presence, could hear them talking to her, but she couldn't bring herself to respond. She kept her eyes closed throughout their visit, even when Haley began crying and begging for her to wake up and say something. She heard the doctors come in and explain to her aunt that she was in a semicomatose state, whatever that meant, but they expected her to pull through. Anna hoped he was wrong.

The evening after the visit by what remained of

her family, she woke in darkness to hear a familiar voice calling her name. It was little Tony.

Anna sat up in bed and saw Tony crouching in the corner of the room, hugging his infant brother protectively to his chest. It wasn't until she floated off the bed, moving toward him, that she realized she was outside of her body again. She looked over her shoulder and saw her physical self still lying on the bed attached to tubes and needles. She heard an alarm going off as she floated to Tony, and she was aware of several nurses and a doctor rushing into the room to work on the body she'd left behind, but it was like being aware of something that was happening far away, something that didn't really concern her.

The closer she moved to Tony, the more the real world withdrew into its bubble.

"Anna!" the little boy called out to her, his face brightening, then turning sad. *"Why'd you leave us? You went away so quick. Me and Billy were scared."* She heard his voice in her head, though as before, his lips didn't move.

"I'm sorry, Tony," Anna replied, keeping her mouth and lips from moving. She was getting better at this. *"I don't know what happened. One minute I was with you, and the next I was back in the emergency room and the doctors were working on me."*

"I know what happened," Tony said sadly.

"What?"

"You're not dead, and me and Billy are."

Anna started crying. *"I don't want to be alive, Tony. I want to be dead too. I want to go into the light and be with my mom and dad. I don't want to be alive. I want to be dead!"*

Tony hugged his brother closer and bent his head over the infant.

Anna knelt next to the brothers and put her arm around them. *"You should go into the light too, Tony. You shouldn't be hanging around. The light is good—it leads to a better place. It leads to Heaven, I guess. I bet if we thought hard enough about it, we could bring the light here, and we could go into it together, all three of us."*

"But what about my mom?" Tony whined.

"Maybe she's already in the light. Maybe the dark thing didn't get her."

"But I saw it," Tony countered.

"Maybe you saw wrong. Maybe the light was behind the dark thing. She could be in Heaven right now waiting for you."

Tony looked hopeful. *"You really think so?"*

"I don't know," Anna said truthfully, *"but it's worth a try and better than hanging around here hiding from the dark thing."*

Tony said nothing, but Anna could tell he was almost convinced.

"Come on, let's try," she coaxed

"I guess so," he murmured in answer.

Anna held his hand. *"Think of the light the last time you saw it. Try to picture it. Concentrate hard."* Anna thought of her friend Mary, who had appeared in the light the first time, and called to her mentally.

The scene in the hospital room of the doctor and nurses working over her body had telescoped away until it was a tiny bubble floating far above her. The surreal landscape of pulsing pillars, weird growths, and burping holes seemed to float and ripple before her eyes. She became aware of millions of stars overhead, but they were untwinkling, set as if frozen in the bright neon purple sky.

The dark eerie colors of the landscape took on an iridescent hue. The weird ferns and pillars of ghostly vegetation became filled with flitting sparks of light. In the distance, in the middle of an especially large pillar, a spot of light brighter than all the others appeared and began to grow. Everything around it grew dim, the larger it became. It began sending out shafts of light around it until it formed a dazzling tunnel of light. Anna began to see shapes moving in the light of the tunnel.

"Momma! Daddy!" Anna called. A strong wind began swirling around her and Tony and Billy. The two brothers floated into the tunnel, which had become huge, encompassing everything. Anna tried to follow, but the wind held her back, anchoring her.

"No!" she screamed. *"I want to go too!"* Tony looked back at her once, a happy smile on his face but sadness in his eyes at having to leave her behind.

"It's not fair!" Anna cried, reaching for Tony. He waved, then turned into the light and was gone in a dazzling flash.

"No! No! No! It's not fair," Anna sobbed. The light began to recede, the tunnel retracting until there was nothing but a pinpoint of white left that blinked out of existence, leaving her alone and crying facedown on the rippling carpet of vegetation.

She lay there a long time, her face buried in her arms, sobbing. A thousand images and thoughts raced through her mind. All the recent events played themselves, rewound like a tape in a VCR, and played again. She remembered the excitement and anticipation of Christmas night; the joy of Christmas morning, when she got her new sled. She cringed at the memory of her wild ride down Cemetery Hill and the accident, hitting the wall with her sled. She felt again the sense of awe she'd first felt upon leaving her unconscious body as she remembered floating above it and her broken sled, then fear at the approach of the bad black thing. But the worse memory of all, playing in her mind in blaring staccato bursts of imagery, was waking in the car, in her mother's arms, and seeing her mom's smile disappear in an explosion of blood and flesh. Another image came to her—an image she hadn't remembered until just now—her father reaching out for her mother at the moment of her death, and his head seeming literally to come apart on his shoulders, ripped to pieces by . . . by what?

Bullets! the thought came to her.

She remembered the sound of firecrackers going off, but she realized now it wasn't firecrackers, it had been gunfire.

They were murdered!

The thought crystallized in Anna's mind, became a diamond-hard fact.

Mom and Dad were murdered!

Someone killed them!

But who?

She remembered floating above the smashed car in the hospital parking lot and seeing the man go into the light.

No, not him. The light was a good thing; the light was Heaven. Anyone who'd committed murder couldn't go into the light.

But there had been another man, the one crushed against the wall of the hospital by the police cruiser. The light had shunned him. Then the evil dark creature had come and eaten him.

He was the one. *He* was the murderer, and now he was dead, getting what he deserved by being swallowed up by that horrible creature of darkness.

Hell. He'd gone to Hell.

For a moment, Anna felt a sense of satisfaction at the thought, but then doubt crept in. *Had* that been the man who killed her parents?

She wasn't sure.

The scene in the hospital parking lot played in her mind again. The man who'd been consumed by the darkness had been way across the lot, crushed by the police car. Just before his spirit had left his body, Anna remembered seeing his gun—a pistol—still in his hand. She remembered the way her mother's face had disintegrated and her father's had just come apart. She recalled the sound of glass shattering and, most important of all, the sound of gunfire. It had sounded like a string of firecrackers going off in rapid succession. She knew next to nothing about guns, but she *did* know that a pistol firing wouldn't make a sound like that. She'd heard enough gunfire on TV and in movies to know that. What that had sounded like was *machine-gun fire*, which she'd also heard in various violent TV shows and movies.

There had to have been someone else with the bad man in the parking lot. Someone with a machine gun. And that someone was the person responsible for killing her parents.

He, or they, were still alive, still out there, living while her parents were dead. It was unfair.

It was *wrong*!

But what could she do about it?

I can find them! I can kill them! she thought furiously.

Yes! A rage built in her, reaffirming the thought. She could make her parents' killers pay for what they had done. She didn't know how, but she had to find a way. She *had* to do it.

Her sadness was gone now, replaced by a desire for revenge.

She noticed that she was beginning to feel very cold, a coldness that seemed to get inside her. She lifted her head and saw that the weird otherworldly landscape was gone. She was in the midst of a thick cold fog, and she was floating.

The fog broke suddenly, and Anna gasped. Far below her was the earth—hills and the lights of a town. The moon was full and bright to her left, and the sky around it was filled with stars. She looked behind her and saw that what she'd thought was fog was a cloud floating lazily away from her.

I'm flying! she thought, her rage and thoughts of revenge suddenly pushed aside and replaced by a feeling of indescribable exhilaration. Her heart was hammering in her chest, and she was panting, feeling a heady dizziness at being so high. She put her arms out like airplane wings and laughed at the sheer thrill of the experience. She discovered that by moving her arms, dipping them or raising them, she could make turns or fly higher or dive, the way a real airplane would.

She brought her arms in close to her side and plummeted toward earth. The speed of her descent frightened her, but as soon as she put her arms out again, she leveled out.

This is fun, she thought, laughing some more. She descended again until she was soaring just over the treetops. The landscape looked familiar, and as she crested the top of a hill, she realized the town in the valley below her was Towns End.

She could see Route 13 winding its way like a black river through the town. And there was the white steeple of St. Boniface's church, the gold cross atop it glistening in the moonlight. The snow covering the town looked so pure and white, like a satin quilt cushioning the land.

A pang of sadness overcame her when she saw her house at the end of Chase Street. She lowered her left arm and dipped through a thin cloud, descending on her home.

The house was dark. The moon reflected in the windows gave her an eerie feeling. She floated past the maple trees and the huge weeping willow in the front yard and sailed up to the large picture window looking into the living room. She peered inside and felt an overwhelming sadness at the house's emptiness. She touched her hand to the windowpane, and it passed right through the glass. She withdrew her hand quickly, shocked at what had happened. She tried to touch the glass again, and again her hand went right through it as if it weren't there.

Anna drifted to the left until she was at the front door. Cautiously, she reached out to touch the door and had the same experience as with the window. This time she did not withdraw her hand but put her other hand and both arms through the wood also. She noticed that unlike putting her hand through the glass, she encountered a little more resistance pushing through the wood door. It was like putting her hand through heavy wet snow.

Anna closed her eyes, took a deep breath, and pushed her head through the door. The rest of her body followed slowly, feeling as though it were being squeezed through a slim opening.

Anna looked around the living room. Everything was as it had been Christmas morning. She had no idea how much time had passed since then. The Christmas tree was still standing, the presents she and her sisters had opened were still lying on the floor where they had left them. The Christmas decorations were still on the mantle over the fireplace. The manger was there, the tiny statues of Mary and Joseph, the three wise men, and the little drummer boy. On either side of the manger were the candle figures of Santa, Rudolph, Frosty the Snowman, and a trio of Christmas carolers with their mouths open in perfect and perpetual O's.

Anna floated to the kitchen, which was separated from the living room by a four-foot-high paneled partition. There were two cups of coffee on the table in her mom's and dad's mugs, the ones that said "World's Greatest Mom" and "World's Greatest Dad" on them that Anna, Haley, and Jayne had bought for their parents on Mother's and Father's Day last year.

The surfaces of the liquids had a yellowish film on them, and her dad's coffee, which he always seemed to spill on the table, had dried to a varnish-like circle around the mug. At the sight of the coffee mugs, Anna began to cry. The heart-piercing grief she had felt when Tony and Billy had gone into the light without her returned. She felt completely and totally alone, alienated, desolate. She couldn't go into the light to be with her parents, and she couldn't return completely to her body to be whole again. With great sadness and a return of anger, she realized she'd never be whole again until she had tracked down her parents' murderers and made them pay.

The tears came harder and faster. In her young life, Anna had never known real heart-wrenching sorrow and despair, nor all-consuming rage, but she knew both now. The only sadness and anger she had experienced previously that came close was when she'd had to give up her pony, Pepper. But even that, as bad as it had been at the time, was mild compared to the pain and fury that filled her now. She would never have thought that emotions could be so strong as to cause physical pain, but now she knew better. She felt sick, sicker than she'd ever felt from any flu or cold or the various childhood illnesses she'd had. This was a sickness, a tearing pain, that permeated her entire being.

It was awful.

I have to find the murderers and make them pay, she thought, *and then I want to die.* She repeated the last thought over and over like a litany. She closed her eyes and curled into a fetal ball and drifted slowly to the floor, where her lighter-than-air body bounced softly once, then settled.

Anna. Anna. Anna.

The words were no more than a faint whisper, but they sent a chill through Anna. Before she even opened her eyes, she knew who had spoken. Though the words, the voices, sent a cold fear through her like she'd experienced whenever she'd watched a scary movie, she wasn't truly afraid.

Anna. Anna. Anna.

The words, voices, came again. It sounded like hundreds of people barely breathing the words, the cumulative effect being a whisper that was soft yet strong.

Anna opened her eyes and saw nothing. The kitchen, all her surroundings, were gone. She was surrounded by darkness, but not just any darkness. What surrounded her was the living darkness that was the antithesis of the light that had taken Tony and Billy. It swirled around her, blotting out everything else.

Anna. Anna. Anna.

She became aware that the darkness was full of faces, hideous faces, deformed faces; faces full of torture and pain, full of fear and anger and loathing for anything that was not part of the darkness too. The darkness was like a mass of quivering, rolling black jelly, the faces emerging and submerging constantly, their features pressing through the slimy surface, visible as outlines in black. Their eyes, the whites in stark contrast to the blackness around them, stared balefully out at her.

Far off in the distance, yet coming from the darkness, perhaps from its very heart, Anna could hear screams and moans intermingling with lewd, taunting laughter and a jumble of shouting voices speaking a variety of languages that all ran together until they were unintelligible.

Anna. Anna. Anna.

The whisper was louder this time, and the voices out of sync, creating an echo effect that went on for several seconds. The miasma of background screams, moans, laughter, and strange tongues grew louder, then subsided and grew louder again.

Anna . . . Anna . . . Anna . . . Anna . . .

A woman began singing in an operatic voice, hitting screeching high notes. Her song ended in a gurgling scream.

Anna . . . Anna . . . Anna . . . Anna . . .

"What?" Anna spoke softly, but despite the swirl of sounds emanating from the darkness, her voice sounded like a shout in her own ears.

The darkness grew quiet when she spoke. There was a stifled giggle that was quickly cut off in a strangled cry of pain.

"What do you want?" Anna asked the darkness.

There was a deep rumbling, bubbling sound from within the darkness, and the answer came back sounding like someone speaking underwater.

Nothing.

"Who are you?"

Again the voice bubbled up from the depths of the dark gelatinous mass.

No one.

Ear-piercing laughter followed the answer, and the darkness quivered with it. There were shouts and screams, and a horde of writhing black snakes emerged everywhere from the darkness, slithering and crawling over one another, their tiny red eyes malevolently fixed upon Anna.

"What do you want?" Anna asked. The darkness was frightening, but she was too weary with grief to be truly afraid, and her voice reflected it.

Nothing, came the gurgling answer.

Disgusted with its stupid answers, Anna gave up. She tried to rise but found she could not move; the darkness had drawn so close, pressing in on her aura so much, that she was hemmed in as though sitting in a tiny box. Voices from within the darkness began speaking rapidly, the words mingling and tumbling over one another:

Who are you? We want nothing. You are no one. We want nothing. Who are you? You are nothing. We want nothing. Who are you we are no one we want nothing . . .

Then a bellowing shout came that brought a shriek from Anna:

WE WANT YOU!

And the voices started again, hundreds, maybe thousands of them, whispering, the sentences intermingling to create a chant that was hypnotic in its effect.

Come with us Anna you are no one we are no one come be dead with us dead is nice dead is good in the dark yes in the dark with us dead is nothing dead is no one you are no one you are nothing we are nothing we are no one come with us in the dark and the dead the dark and the dead is nothing death is nothing you are no one come down in the dark with us where we can embrace you and hold you and lick you and make you nothing down here in the dark down here in the nothing and the no one down here come down here in the nothing with us . . .

Anna listened to the voices and felt them drawing her in, could see the darkness seeping closer the more she listened. She felt sleepy. She felt as though she could just curl up and fall asleep forever.

Yes sleep in the darkness sleep is good sleep is nothing . . .

She knew the darkness was evil, could sense it. She also knew that she should get away from it, but she was to the point of not caring. She was caught between life and death. Her parents were dead, her home was empty, the light didn't want her. Why shouldn't she go into the darkness?

Yes! Come with us we want you we want nothing you are nothing no one no one we want no one in the dark where you belong come down here with us with your mother and father . . .

Anna perked up at that. Mom? Dad? Were they in the darkness?

Yes! We're all here in the nothing we're all here in the dark come and see and be with your mommy and dadee . . .

Anna we're waiting for you to come to us.

The latter voice rose above the litany of the others and *sounded* like her dad's voice, but it was distorted just enough by the others that she couldn't be sure.

"Daddy? Is that you?"

Yes honey it's us come into the darkness with us and be nothing foreveeeeeeeer . . .

It was her mother's voice this time—Anna was

sure of it. Tony had told her that her parents had gone into the light when they had died, but she didn't know that for sure. They *could* be in the darkness, couldn't they?

Yes we could we are here in the dark in the no one in the nothing come in come in come in . . .

As final proof, the faces of her parents emerged from the slimy surface of the darkness. They smiled at her, and her father winked.

Anna reached for them and felt the darkness encircling her, caressing her with a hundred seeking fingers.

Come with us Anna, her mother and father said in unison.

"Yes," Anna sobbed, giving in to the darkness.

"No!"

The shout came from everywhere at once and with such force, it caused the darkness to stop enfolding Anna.

"Leave her alone! Get away from her!"

Anna felt her head clearing at the sound of the new voice, and she shuddered at the realization of what she had been about to do. The faces of her parents became hellishly distorted, bending and stretching. Screams of pain and frustration, like the howls of wounded animals, emitted from their mouths.

"Get out of here. Leave her alone. You can't have her."

The darkness, groaning and growling, screaming and gnashing, withdrew, shriveling into itself. The weird other world of flowing plants and towering iridescent pillars came into view as it receded. And there, sailing toward her, dispelling the darkness as she came, was a petite young woman with short raven-black hair and eyes the color of a winter's sky.

Anna floated into her arms, felt the woman embrace her, felt a confusing rush of feelings and images as their auras touched, and heard the woman whisper, *"You're okay now—"*

—and awoke back in her hospital room, back in her body.

two

Deedee and the Good Guys

1

Deedee Blaine was horny, and that meant she was afraid too. No blushing virgin or innocent youth, Deedee was 26 years old, with short black hair, large icy-blue eyes, and a pretty small-featured face. She was blessed with a body that was tight and tiny—and it required little effort on her part to keep it that way. The only thing she had ever thought to change was her breasts. They were small, almost prepubescent looking, and she had seriously considered having implants. But luckily, due to an aversion to hospitals in general and surgery in particular, she kept putting it off. Then when she learned about all the problems women with implants were having, Deedee was glad she hadn't done it. Besides, the men she had known had never complained about the size of her breasts—they had complained about other nonphysical things—and several had found her tiny tight mounds to be an extreme turn-on.

Deedee worked as a secretary in a doctor's office during the day, and as a waitress at the Rockland night club Thursday through Saturday nights. Being single, she made a decent living, enough to be comfortable, not that she needed much, especially in Missoula, Montana.

Missoula was a nice enough town, being where she grew up, but there wasn't a hell of a lot to do in town outside of going to the movies or going to

Rockland. Of course, if you were a nature buff, which she most definitely was not, and into mountain climbing and fishing and hiking, Missoula, surrounded by the Rockies, could be considered paradise. But for someone like Deedee, who yearned for more excitement and action in her life, it was a boring place. She wanted, almost needed, the energy and vitality of a big city, yet she was afraid to move to one, just as she was afraid of being horny, though not for the same reasons.

Deedee was afraid to move to the city not because she feared the dangers inherent in city life for a single girl. Just the opposite—she feared moving to the city because there was a part of her that yearned, at times even lusted, for the danger of life in the big city. She was truly afraid of that desire and sensed that if she ever did go to a big city, she would lose herself in it and plummet to depths (or maybe heights) she could not even imagine.

But Deedee *was* afraid of being horny because of the dangers inherent in sex. And it wasn't just a fear of AIDS, though that was enough to scare anyone away from any type of casual sex these days. No. Her fear went deeper—but so did her horniness, making the battle between the two, between lust and denial, monumental.

And lying here in bed thinking about it isn't helping matters, she thought. She pulled her hand from between her thighs, where it had been unconsciously goading her into lustful thoughts. Her fingers were wet and slightly sticky. She sat up, wiped her hand on the sheet, and stood. Across the bedroom was a full-length, floor-to-ceiling dressing mirror. As she did every morning upon getting out of bed, Deedee strolled to it, scrutinizing her body. She always slept naked, and the morning sun through the venetian blinds cast bars of light and shadow across her flesh. She studied her stomach, turning sideways to check her hips and buttocks, and bent to run her fingers up her legs from her ankles to her waist. Her nails left long red lines in her pale skin.

She had to admit it was a good body, especially considering what her own mother had looked like at twenty-six. She had been a dumpy fat housewife with the complexion of an acne-ridden teenager. Deedee had been blessed with her father's skin. There was not a blemish anywhere on her body, not even a beauty mark, and she had never had a zit on her face as a teenager. Everywhere she looked, her skin was creamy smooth.

She faced forward again and came to the last part of her morning examination—her breasts. She cupped them easily into her small hands but did not have to lift them at all. They were so small, they naturally inclined upward, the equally small nipples pointing up at a forty-five-degree angle.

"Perky," an ex-lover had called them. *Ex-lover! Ha!* One-night stand was more like it. Nearly all her ex-lovers had been little more than one-night stands. One night with her was enough to scare most men away. Only Jesse had hung in there—for a while, anyway.

At the thought of him, her fingers squeezed the nipples of her breasts, and she flicked the fingernails across them, making them hard and hot.

"Stop it, girl," she muttered through clenched teeth at herself. "You're making yourself crazy." Removing her hands from her breasts, she clenched the fists so hard, her long fingernails dug painfully into her palms. She went into the bathroom to shower for work.

Though the sun was bright, the morning air was cold, the kind of cold that stabs into the sinuses and hurts the lungs when it is breathed. Deedee breathed it deeply, punishing herself. She'd almost lost it while soaping herself in the shower. She'd become extremely aroused and had come too close to danger. She was angry at herself for having so little self-control and hoped the cold air would give her a headache to teach her a lesson, not to metnion the fact that she wished it would cool her loins too.

She walked to the street and followed the sidewalk around the corner from the two-story brick Victorian where she rented the second-floor apartment. She kept her beat-up Hyundai parked at her uncle Bill's gas station around the corner. It was especially convenient in the winter since there was a snow-removal parking ban on the Missoula city streets.

It was only a walk of six blocks—three down Mountain Avenue and another three over Main Street—to Dr. Pembroke's office. She often walked it, but this morning she was running late, thanks to her horniness. She got in the car, breathed on her hands to warm them, held her breath with hope, and turned the key. The engine rattled and groaned, tried to catch, and gave up. She tried again. The engine chugged and sputtered, started, then immediately stalled. She waited a few seconds before trying again. She held the key in start too long this time, trying to coax it to start, and heard it winding down as the battery lost power. Knowing it was futile, she tried again anyway and heard only dead clicking.

Cursing the car—and herself for not buying a new battery as her uncle had told her to—she got out and walked around to the front of the gas station. It wasn't open yet—no hope of a jump from her uncle. There was nothing else to be done; she started walking.

A block and a half down Mountain Avenue, she heard a beep and the sound of a car pulling to the curb alongside her.

"Hey! Kind of cold to be walking, isn't it?"

She turned to see Paul Beltzer, a bartender from the Rockland, leaning out the passenger-side window of his Jeep Cherokee. Clouds of steam came from his mouth as he spoke.

"Yeah," Deedee replied. "But my sorry excuse for a car died, and I have to get to work."

"Get in," Paul said, opening the door from inside for her.

Grateful to get out of the cold, Deedee obeyed. "Thanks. Boy! It is really cold out there today."

"Yeah. Big storm coming in tonight," Paul replied.

Deedee noticed him eyeing her legs as he drove. Her long coat had fallen open, and her white skirt was riding high on her thighs. Ashamedly, she felt a tingle of excitement under his gaze.

Normally, Deedee considered herself demure, an almost strait-laced type. She didn't flirt, she never was a tease, she'd never been one to sleep around a lot. At twenty-six, she could count the number of lovers she'd had on one hand—five exactly. One of those was just a one-night stands, one was a date rape, and the other three barely qualified as relationships. In her mind, only her time with Jesse qualified as a true love affair. Only with him had she been able to let herself go, acting flirty and sexy at times, but always and only toward him. He was the only man who had ever tried to understand her special problem and who hadn't been frightened away by it, at least not initially.

Since the breakup with Jesse two years ago, she'd noticed herself going through cycles, like the one she was in now, where she felt increasingly horny to the point where she did things that were out of character for her.

Like what she was doing now, for example.

Instead of pulling her skirt down or covering her legs with her coat, as she normally would have under a man's gaze, she opened her legs, causing her skirt to ride higher.

Paul licked his lips, glanced at the road, then back at her thighs. She'd never really noticed before, but Paul was kind of sexy. He had a good build, looking like he worked out regularly. Though he wasn't what she would call handsome, he had a rugged face that was really kind of a turn-on now that she got a good close look at it.

She opened her legs wider. The skirt rode up more, revealing a glimpse of her white lace bikini underwear.

Paul cleared his throat, his eyes dancing back and forth between the road and her legs. "So how long have you been working for this doctor?" he asked, speaking to her crotch instead of her face.

"Since I got out of college," Deedee answered. Slowly, she ran the fingertips of her right hand up inside of her right thigh, letting her hand come to rest against the edge of her panties. There was a quick, sharp intake of breath from Paul, and it appeared to be all he could do to tear his eyes away from her and glance at the road to avoid running into anything.

They were at the doctor's office on Main Street. Paul pulled the Cherokee to the curb and leaned across Deedee to open the door—and, she knew, to get a better look between her legs. She accommodated him, disgusting and yet exciting herself. She spread her legs more and actually slipped two fingers inside the edge of her panties. He stopped breathing then, his hand on the door handle, his eyes riveted to her crotch.

Deedee smiled and pulled her coat closed over her legs. Paul let his breath out and opened the door. As she got out, Paul leaned over to pull the door closed, and she noticed a large bulge in his pants. Mentally, she envisioned what his penis looked like. From the looks of the bulge, he was big. She felt herself getting wetter at the thought of it.

"See you tonight at the club?" Paul asked, his voice husky, before closing the door. "I'll be there a little early for inventory."

"Sure," Deedee answered, flashing him a sexy smile. He gave her legs one last going-over, licked his lips, and drove away.

Deedee immediately felt ashamed. "You acted like a slut," she chastised herself, muttering. What really bothered her was that she hadn't been able to help it. It was as though she'd been on autopilot; her horniness had just taken over, and she'd done things that were so out of character for her that she despised herself for it.

But no amount of self-loathing was going to soothe that hot itchy feeling between her legs.

The workday was one of the slowest Fridays she could remember. Four o'clock seemed to take days to arrive. When it finally did, she left the office quickly, declining an invitation to go out for a drink with Dr. Pembroke's nurse Julie.

She walked home at a brisk pace, as if she could outwalk the horniness that had driven her to distraction all day and leave it behind. Back in her apartment, she quickly changed into a sweatsuit, put an aerobics tape into the VCR, and for the next forty-five minutes tried to exercise the lust from her body.

And she thought she was successful. Dripping

sweat, ripe with the odor of perspiration, she lay on the floor, reveling in that wonderful feeling of healthy exhaustion that comes from any good exercise. The hungry itch was gone, or so she thought until she got into the shower and began lathering up with soap. Her hands, soaping her breasts, brought the feeling back immediately. The hot water, the slippery sensation of the soap on her skin, the touch of her own hands, and soon she was panting. Her right hand automatically moved to her crotch, where it slid the bar of soap back and forth over her clitoris. She experienced several small orgasms, but they only fueled her desire and left her frustrated. Masturbation had never been easy for her. She threw down the bar of soap and rinsed, then toweled herself dry, more horny than before.

She made a salad for supper, hoping food might quell her hormones, but she had little appetite. She dressed early for her waitressing job at Rockland and went down to her uncle's service station to get a new battery for her car.

She arrived at Rockland a half hour before her shift was due to begin, and the club to open. The place was quiet and dark, the only light coming from the storeroom behind the bar. Paul Beltzer was in there getting booze to stock the bar for the night. She stood in the doorway admiring his tight buns as he bent over cases of alcohol.

She licked her lips, her breathing becoming heavier, as a small and growing smaller part of her mind chided her for such animalistic behavior.

She unbuttoned her blouse halfway, realizing she'd forgotten to put on a bra and now glad she hadn't. Her breasts were small enough that she could get away with it, but she almost always wore one anyway. Except for tonight. Tonight she hadn't worn one and hadn't even realized it. She felt as if her body were conspiring against her.

She took the pen she used for taking orders from her pocket and dropped it. As Paul, who was on one knee now, turned at the sound, Deedee bent over to retrieve the pen, letting her blouse fall open. With it unbuttoned so low, it exposed her taut breasts fully to the bartender's hungry eyes.

She looked up at him as she straightened, and smiled. He stood, turning toward her at the same time, and she saw the hard bulge in the front of his pants. And that was all it took for her to lose it. All the lust and horniness that had been building in her for weeks reached its peak and boiled over, taking control of her mind and body. Later, she would realize it was akin to what a drug addict must experience when the urge for a fix is upon her. Her body was going to do what it wanted, no matter what her will might say. Not that she felt much willpower. There was still a small chiding voice inside, but after one feeble attempt to stop what was about to happen, it grew silent, and Deedee was left to the storm of her emotions.

She crossed the storage room floor in three steps, drawing close to Paul, and placed her left hand on the bulge at his crotch and squeezed. He let out a growling gasp, and both his hands came up to her breasts, cupping and squeezing them through her blouse. He rubbed his fingers over her nipples and caught them, pinching them gently.

She moaned, his tongue in her mouth, sucking on it, her hands undoing his belt, his zipper, freeing his penis, which was big and hot and throbbing in her hand. He pulled his mouth from hers and bent over, pushing her blouse all the way open with his hand, popping the last two buttons, and began sucking on her right breast. After a few seconds he switched to the left one.

Jolts of electric pleasure made her shiver and twitch. He nipped at her breasts, and she gasped, arching her back, squeezing his cock and thrusting her crotch against it. He licked his way up her neck, and then she was sliding down his shirtfront, her face pressed into the fabric, smelling the faint scent of laundry detergent, her breath coming back at her off the shirt—hot and sour—and then she was on her knees, his cock in her face, and she sighed. It was as big as she had hoped it would be—big and thick, with a heavy set of testicles to go with it. There was a pearly drop of liquid nestled in the slit of its head, and the sight of that excited her more than anything and sent waves of tingling hot shivers through her body. Juice flowed from between her legs, hot and creamy, and she moaned again.

She opened her mouth and slid his cock into it until she felt she would gag. But it was only halfway in, and she wanted it all, was suddenly ravenous for it all. She took a deep breath and pushed his cock deeper into her mouth, felt the head hit the back of her throat, pushed again, moaning as the thick head of his penis actually went down her throat, plugging it like a stopper in a drain. Her nose pressed against his belly, tickled by his coarse black pubic hairs, and her bottom lip rested against the sack of his testes.

"Oh, fuck!" Paul exclaimed as she deep-throated him. "Fuck! Yeah!" He grabbed her head with both hands and began moving his hips, sliding his cock in and out of her throat, fucking her face. She began to moan in rhythm to his thrusts, her tongue working furiously in her mouth, licking the underside of his penis as it slid between her lips.

The electrical feeling was growing stronger.

Every nerve end in her body seemed to be buzzing. The ones in her breasts and groin were damned-near dancing, the rest jiving hard to keep up. Her clitoris itched unbearably. She squeezed her thighs together, but it didn't help. There was only one thing that could.

She took Paul's cock from her mouth. He gasped, whimpering a little. He'd been close to coming, she knew.

"I want you in me," she breathed as she stood, undoing her pants at the same time. Paul didn't need to be told twice. He pushed his pants down, struggled to pull his wallet from the pocket of the downed trousers, and took out a rubber. Deedee was surprised, then grateful, then ashamed. She hadn't even been thinking of protection, she'd been so horny. And *that* was *really* scary.

Paul put the condom on and grabbed her pants, pulling them down, pulling her to him.

"No, not that way," Deedee said. "In case someone comes, I want to be able to pull them up quick." She turned and closed the storage room door. "I'll bend over, you get behind me."

Paul willingly complied. Deedee spread her legs and bent over, grabbing the doorknob with both hands. Paul pushed his pants down to his knees and shuffled up behind her, placing his hands on the small of her back.

"Hurry," Deedee nearly pleaded. Paul thrust at her and missed penetration. She reached between her legs and guided him into her. It slid in easily—the condom was obviously lubricated, though she was so wet, it didn't need to be. She inhaled sharply as she felt it filling her, deeper and deeper, until she thought it would ram into her gut. Then it was all the way in, and she could feel his body against her backside, his balls slapping against her clitoris with every thrust of his hips. She became very hot as waves of tingling electrifying pleasure spread out from her vagina to engulf her entire body. Each time he thrust into her and his testicles slapped against her clitoris, she felt an added jolt that made her gasp and twitch with ecstasy. She was panting, her vision blurred. Tiny sparks of white light began to dance before her eyes, and she became afraid.

It was starting again. She had hoped and silently prayed that this time would be different, that in the two years she had gone without sex, she had changed somehow. But now it was happening all over again just as it always had. Her breathing came quicker. The jolts of raw pleasure from her clitoris began to run together into one long current that set her hips and ass to gyrating.

Sparks of light began to explode in her vision. Her breasts were hot and itchy and wouldn't stop tingling. Like a fast-moving storm, the feeling spread over her whole body, carried by the electrical pleasure current emanating from her crotch.

Her breathing became a shriek. The popping lights grew larger. She felt an orgasm rising, rising, speeding toward fruition, grabbing at every nerve end in her body and pulling them all along for the ride. Higher and higher, faster and faster, until the universe exploded in a white-hot light inside her head. Her hips and buttocks jittered wildly. Her head snapped back with an audible click from the force of the orgasm. She screamed, was dimly aware of Paul moaning as he came, and then she collapsed, banging her head on the storage room door on her way to the floor.

Paul Beltzer wasn't quite finished coming when he felt Deedee falling away from him. He tried to catch her, more from a desire to keep his cock inside her than to keep her from injury. But her skin was so sweaty, his hand slid off her waist. He let out a short cry akin to pain as his penis popped free, still ejaculating into the condom but with less force.

Instinctively, he grabbed it, pulled the rubber off, and pumped his cock with his right hand to finish himself off, not caring for the moment that Deedee lay unconscious at his feet.

He finished coming, opened his eyes, and realized something was wrong. He had thought Deedee had just lost her balance, or had perhaps got a cramp in her leg, or had just finished her own orgasm and had become too sensitive. Now he saw that he was wrong on all counts. She was lying in a fetal position, unmoving, her head jammed against the door. She didn't appear to be breathing, but the thing that scared him the most was that her eyes were wide open, staring at the floor, unblinking.

"Oh, Jesus!" Paul cried and knelt next to Deedee. He gently shook her shoulder. "Deedee. Babe, wake up." His jostling did nothing more than cause her tongue to slide out of her mouth and hang slackly in the corner of her lips. He bent over and put his ear to her mouth.

Nothing. No breathing, no sound. Nothing.

"Oh, fuck! She's dead!" Paul said hoarsely and began to cry.

2

There was an explosion of sound and light around Deedee. A whistling, whining, almost singing noise, accompanied by a vast darkness, streaked through with burning incandescent beams of colored light. She felt as though she were falling, then rising, then tumbling, falling, and rising again. She was riding a roller coaster through a cavernous tunnel and doing it flat on her back. She was unable to see where the coaster was going, where it had been, or anything else around her except for those beams of light, which shot like lasers across her field of vision, making a sizzling noise as they did.

She began to turn and do a low somersault through space. There, far below her, the size of a postage stamp, was the storage room at the Rockland club. Paul Beltzer, ridiculously tiny, stood with his pants down around his ankles, jerking off over . . . *her half-naked body lying prone on the floor!*

Oh, no! Not again! Deedee thought with a sick churning feeling in her gut. The tumult of noise around her grew louder and faster, sounding like a tape of a choir played at high speed. The sound hurt her ears, but she was unable to lift her hands to cover them. A beam of red sizzling light whizzed by her face, and she could feel the heat of it singeing her hair. Another flashed out of the darkness to her left, went up, then bent in a way she had never seen light bend before and headed straight for her. She screamed a second before the light smashed into her eyes, and she came to a jarring stop.

All was darkness around her, a darkness that was impenetrable. She was on her hands and knees. The surface beneath her was soft and spongy.

"No! Please, no," she whimpered. She knew where she was; she'd been here before. She looked around in a panic, straining her eyes at the darkness, as if expecting something to be creeping up on her.

"I don't want to die," she whispered prayerfully. She was very afraid.

Her eyes slowly became accustomed to the darkness, and she began to make out shapes. A red bubble of light, shimmering ike a great corpuscle, floated by her. Within it she could see people. There was violence going on. A man held a gun, pointed it at a woman, fired.

As the red bubble floated away from Deedee, it was suddenly infused with a great white light. From out of the bubble rose the naked transparent body of the woman who had been shot. Immediately, an answering white light, a thousand times brighter than the first, came out of the darkness. It coalesced into a giant tunnel of radiant light. The woman was literally sucked into it, and then it was dark again. The red bubble continued on its way, its color shifting from red to dark purple to blue.

Deedee looked around at the millions of different-colored bubbles of reality that streamed past and around her. She tried not to look into any of them as they went by; it made her feel like a Peeping Tom.

A dark shadow passed over her, and she felt a chill along the back of her neck. *It's here!* she thought. She could feel Its presence. Another shadow passed over her, and this time she caught its source: in the distance, a black mass periodically sending out great beams of opposite light.

The Shadow Monster.

"Daddy, is that you?" A little girl's voice came to her.

A child? Deedee felt a chilling breeze blow through her transparent being. What was a child doing here? On all her previous visits to this strange other place, she'd never heard nor seen another human being who wasn't being consumed by either the white light or the Shadow Monster. At the thought of the latter, Deedee let out an involuntary whimper and shuddered. The last time she had been here, the Shadow Monster had attacked her and nearly devoured her. It was the fear of that creature that had kept Deedee sex-free for two years.

The creature whose voice (voices) she heard now—

We are here in the dark in the no one in the nothing come in come in come in—

—and the child's sobbing.

With a great effort, she began to move toward the sound. She was afraid, more afraid than she'd ever been. Though she was by no means brave, the one thing she could never stand was to hear a child in distress. And though her own fear might be so great as to make her heart burst with terror, the sound of a child crying was the one thing, the only thing, that could make her brave anything.

She floated over the weird spongy surface of the other world, between the fungus growth of pillars and the different-sized bubbles of reality swimming around her. She negotiated carefully around the latter and over the fluorescent holes regurgitating streams of color.

She began to move faster through no effort or will of her own. The landscape grew grayer, bleaker.

The eerie fluorescent colors had bled out of everything, and the colored spheres that were people's lives became rare, then disappeared altogether. Only her own remained, shrunk to the size of a golf ball and floating far above her. Everything was gray and shades of black. The holes spewed an oily black substance, some of which touched her as it floated by. It felt alive on her transparent body and seemed to wiggle and squirm, digging its way into her ethereal being until she had to rub her arms and claw at her legs to dispel the feeling.

She looked up, and there it was. A great roiling mass of shadow, interlaced with veins of bloody red that pulsated inside the thing. A horde of dark spheres hovered over and around the thing, each one connected to the shadows by a thin red vein. Eyes appeared, stared balefully at her approach, then sank away, to be replaced by more eyes and other facial features, not to mention snakes and insects, most of which she was certain had never crawled upon the face of the earth.

The child was a young girl. Deedee could barely make her out through the darkness that was seeping around her, trying to envelop her, to *eat* her. The child was sobbing, reaching out to the darkness as if to embrace it, as if she *wanted* it to devour her.

"No!" The shout came out of Deedee without her even realizing it. It came like an explosion from her head, the force of it making her reel. The girl jumped, drew back from the Shadow Monster. Howls of pain and screams of rage rose in a tumult from the hideous black form.

"Leave her alone! Get away from her," Deedee's inner voice shouted again, and she felt a thrill at the power of it. The blackness began to pull away from the girl and turn toward Deedee, its surface

swimming with volcanic change as faces and shapes erupted and sank with incredible speed.

"Get out of here! Leave her alone! You can't have her!" Deedee commanded. For the first time since meeting this horrifying creature years ago, she felt power over it.

The Shadow Monster withdrew, snarling and howling. All its horrid little eyes turned on Deedee. Its many mouths erupted with gnashing snarls and groans and garbled shrieks of pain. Recognition flashed in the eyes and faces appearing and disappearing on the surface of the thing. A huge long tongue lolled from one of the open mouths to reveal a tiny face at the end of it, its even tinier mouth screeching: *She's back! The bitch is back!*

Then the Shadow Monster was gone. Like time-lapsed photography of approaching storm clouds thrown into reverse, the creature buckled and collapsed in upon itself, getting smaller and more distant until there was nothing left of it. The weird landscape returned, as did the swarms of bubbles zooming past. Deedee reached for the girl and drew the child into her arms.

"You're okay now," Deedee whispered to the child. She bent to tip the girl's face up to hers, but as she reached for her, one of the bubbles passing by sucked the girl in, and she disappeared. Deedee was left embracing air and hearing the hideous laughter of the Shadow Monster taunting her from far off.

3

Deedee opened her eyes.

"Jesus Christ Almighty! I thought you were dead."

Paul Beltzer was bending over her, his face tear-streaked and worried. She looked beyond him and saw that she was lying on the couch in his small office at the other end of the dance club. She was dressed. He must have done that and carried her here.

Deedee tried to speak and couldn't. Her mouth worked, but the words wouldn't come out. Her throat felt tight, closed up. She tried clearing it and went into a prolonged coughing spasm. Paul helped her sit up and patted her on the back until she had it under control.

"I'm sorry," she managed to say, weakly.

"You really scared the shit out of me. I thought you were a goner. You stopped breathing. I couldn't get a pulse. You were fucking *dead*!"

"I'm sorry, really" was all that Deedee could answer.

Paul looked bewildered. He started several times to say something and stopped.

Deedee knew she had to tell him something. The poor guy deserved that, at least. But not the truth. She'd tried before to tell the truth about what happened to her when she had an orgasm, and no one but Jesse had ever believed her.

"It's not your fault," she said at last. "It's me,

it's . . . it's a condition I have. I get these seizures sometimes."

Paul looked doubtful. He got up from the couch, ran his hand through his thinning hair, and went to the desk, where he pulled a cigarette from a pack lying there and lit it.

"I've never seen a seizure like that before, and I used to work as an orderly at a hospital in Helena. I know what death looks like, and I'd swear in a court of law that you were dead."

He took a deep drag of his cigarette and pondered the lit end of it for a moment.

"I don't know what to tell you, Paul," Deedee said softly.

For a moment, he looked as if he were going to ask her to tell him the truth, then thought better of it.

"Look, I'm sorry about, you know, what happened in the storage room. I'm engaged to be married next year. If my fiancée ever found out about this, she'd call it off."

"It's not your fault," Deedee said quickly. "It was me. I wanted it to happen. Don't worry, no one but you and I will ever know about this." She got up unsteadily from the couch.

"I should go. I don't think it would be a good idea for me to continue working here after what's happened."

Paul looked as though he might argue but again thought better of it. "Yeah, maybe you're right," he said, and Deedee heard relief in his voice. "I'll send you two weeks' severance pay. Okay?"

"You don't have to do that," she answered, "but thanks. That would come in handy."

There was an awkward silence between them as she put on her coat and grabbed her purse. "Thank you, Paul," she said, and kissed his cheek before leaving the club quickly, never looking back.

She wept on the drive home. They were angry tears for the realization that nothing had changed for her as far as sex was concerned. She had sincerely hoped that it would be different after two years of abstinence, but it wasn't, and she found herself missing Jesse immensely. Jesse was the only one who had understood, even though her "condition" had finally driven him away too, no matter what he said.

Maybe I should see a doctor again, a specialist, she wondered. But what kind of specialist? She'd seen neurologists and gynecologists, and neither had been able to help her. And to have to go through the embarrassment again of telling her story to a stranger—not the whole story, of course. She always said she experienced blackouts and catatonic states after sex. She'd had all kinds of tests, and none of them showed any abnormality. There was no treatment for her condition, no cure.

Except for abstinence. That was the only treatment, the only cure.

She reached home, parked her car at her uncle's service station, and hurried up to her apartment. She undressed, ran a hot bath, and slipped into it, taking a glass of white wine into the tub with her.

She wanted to forget, forget everything that had happened with Paul, everything that had happened in that weird fucked-up world she'd been in. The wine and hot bath helped, but she couldn't stop thinking of the past, of how this had all started.

She had been fifteen, a sophomore in high school, when she lost her virginity to a boy she hardly knew. Nowadays, she supposed, what happened that night would be called date rape. The boy, Joey Singleton, was in her class and had asked her to a party at his cousin's house. The cousin's parents were out of town, and more than fifty kids from the high school showed up, bringing a variety of booze and drugs with them. She had got a little drunk and very high on grass and let Joey Singleton take her into one of the upstairs bedrooms. They made out, and Joey got aggressive, putting his hands under her sweater and undoing her pants. She told him no, but he wouldn't listen. He pulled her pants and underwear off.

She started crying, pleading with him to stop, but his lust made him deaf to her cries. He took off his shirt and pants and, pinning her shoulders, forced her legs open with his knees and entered her.

She had cried out in pain as he forced himself inside her. She screamed for help, but no one came to her aid. And after a few minutes, the pain subsided, replaced by a tingling sensation that was not unpleasant. The tingling grew into a warm electric current that swiftly reached a peak.

A very strange thing happened. She felt as if she were weightless, rising off the bed, actually rising right out of her body. But then Joey came (causing her great anxiety over the next month, wondering if she was pregnant) and pulled out, causing the sensation to come to an abrupt, almost painful end.

Joey had sat on the edge of the bed afterward, buckling his belt, and he had looked at her with a smile that made her feel dirty. "You really liked it, didn't you. I could tell." And then he laughed a soft, snickering, dirty laugh.

Deedee became furious. As Joey bent over to put on his sneakers, she reached over to the night table at the side of the bed, grabbed the porcelain lamp with the flowered shade that sat there, and smashed it over the back of his head. He let out a soft airy grunt of pain and tumbled headfirst off the bed, crumpling to the floor.

Deedee's fury quickly turned to fear. She could see blood trickling down the back of Joey's neck. Certain that she had killed him, she quickly dressed and ran from the house. She ran all the way home.

She spent the next two days in agony, expecting the police to show up at her parents' door any moment to arrest her for murder. Her mother and father, noticing something was wrong with their daughter, asked her repeatedly what was bothering her, but she was too afraid (and embarrassed about the sex part) to tell them.

She went on suffering in silence, alone. She berated herself constantly for having hit Joey with the lamp. Even though he had done what he'd done, that wasn't the reason she'd become so angry. The truth was, she hadn't felt fury until he'd said she liked it. Then she had become furious because it was true and she felt ashamed and guilty. But the worst part had been the way he'd said it, like she was something dirty, a *slut*.

She spent the weekend living in a horrible nightmare, and come Monday she was afraid to go to school. She tried feigning illness, but as always, her mother saw right through her charade and packed her off.

As she walked up the long stone steps at the front of school, Deedee saw Joey Singleton standing off to the side of the front doors with a gang of his friends.

He's alive! He's okay! He's—

Joey said something to his buddies, and they all looked at her and laughed, one of them whistling and another howling like a wolf.

—an asshole!

She had really wanted to kill him then, and if

she'd had a gun, she would have—him and all his stupid friends. She ran into school instead and spent the rest of her high school years hiding from Joey, and all boys in general, like the plague. And it wasn't easy. Joey made sure that word got around about her, and lots of boys came on to her and asked her out. She could always tell by the tone of voice and the look in their eyes that they'd been talking to Joey and expected to get an easy piece from her.

If, during those high school years, her parents had said they were going to move away from Missoula, Deedee would have been overjoyed. But they never did, and those were the worst years of her life. And during it all, she never forgot the weird sensation of starting to float free from her body that she'd had while Joey was raping her. Eventually she chalked it up to shock, and by the summer of her graduation, finally free from high school, she was able to forget about it a little.

After graduation, she enrolled at Missoula Community College, in the medical secretary program. She'd always been a good typist and was told by her high school guidance counselor that medical secretaries were among the highest paid.

At college, things changed. Few of her high school classmates attended the school, and the campus was so big, she rarely saw them. Near the end of her first semester, she started seeing a nice boy, Tod Bartholomew from Helena. Within a month, they were going steady. Tod began to constantly proclaim his love for her and pressure her to have sex with him. She liked Tod a lot, but she couldn't honestly say that she loved him. She allowed him to feel her up, and she even masturbated him when he got very excited, but she wouldn't allow it to go any further. Memories of that night with Joey invariably invaded her mind whenever Tod got amorous, but more often than not, they were curious thoughts, wondering if the same thing would happen again if she made love to Tod.

By the summer of her first year of college, Tod was asking Deedee to marry him. Over time, she had grown to love him, or at least to believe she did. On the night she said yes to his proposal, she went to bed with him, and the relationship was destroyed forever.

They had gone to his apartment, which he shared with another guy from the college. They had a dinner of pizza and beer, and at the end of it, Tod had gotten down on one knee in front of Deedee, taken her hand, and pleaded with her to marry him.

Her assent led to embraces and kisses, which led them to the couch. When he pushed her blouse up and undid her pants, she let him.

They did it that first (and only) time sitting up on the couch, with Deedee straddling Tod's lap. He was very gentle as he entered her, and after an initial slight pain, she loved the feeling of him inside her.

Taking both her breasts in his hands, he kneaded and suckled them as she rode him faster and faster. A deliciously hot wave of pleasure was building in her, starting in her loins and spreading outward like a flame on the surface of a pool of gasoline.

Her breathing came in short, gasping grunts. She could feel Tod building to a climax inside her, could feel his cock swelling to the point of orgasm. The burning wave of pleasure spread upward through her stomach, connecting with the excitingly hot tingling sensation in her breasts, then outward into her arms, hands, and fingers, down through her legs, to her feet and even to her toes. Sparks of light began to dance before her eyes, and she came with such force, she screamed and collapsed, falling like a rag doll backward off Tod and onto the carpet in front of the couch.

She had opened her eyes and was amazed to see her body below her on the floor, Tod bending over it. The sight was shocking, and in a panic she tried to reach out to her body. But she was rising away from it, rising to the ceiling, through it, through the roof and into the sky.

Only it wasn't the sky. There were no stars, no moon, no clouds. There was no earth below her. There was only an impenetrable darkness. She felt herself begin to move at an incredible rate of speed through the darkness, but she could not tell in which direction she was going. Beams of laserlike lights began to play across her vision and all around her, until one dazzlingly bright light hit her right between the eyes, and she felt herself being propelled down a long shimmering corridor. At the end of it, she landed hard on a surface that was spongelike and iridescent.

The Shadow Monster was upon her before she even had a chance to survey her surroundings. It came at her like a beast, with smoky tendrils shaping themselves into arms and tentacles as they reached for her. And the hideousness of the faces coalescing within that black mass, but especially the eyes, filled her with a terror she'd never experienced before, a terror no human was ever meant to endure.

The thing touched her with its slimy appendages, burning her with its touch and filling her mind with shadows. In that instant of touch, she understood that it knew every bad thing she'd ever done, every evil thought she'd ever had, and in some strange and horribly twisted way, it loved her for those things and wanted to possess her.

It spoke to her, its voice invading her mind, welcoming her, praising her, while its huge mouth gaped, ready to devour her.

With every ounce of willpower at her disposal, she had pulled away from the thing. She felt it fighting her, trying to hold on to her and pull her in. It almost succeeded, but with one final desperate mental effort, she pulled herself free and felt herself falling back into the laser-filled darkness—

—and awoke with Tod cradling her head in his lap.

4

Deedee took another sip of the wine and sank further into the hot water. "Tod," she murmured. "Poor Tod." She hadn't been able to blame him, of course, for finally leaving her. The sexual experience had been so frightening to her that she'd refused any further sexual contact with him. And when he pressed for an explanation and she'd told him what had happened, she'd seen the doubt and disbelief in his eyes, though he never voiced them.

Within a month, they went their separate ways, plans for marriage tossed aside. She didn't have sex again for over a year.

Sitting in the tub, the hot water making her drowsy, Deedee suddenly couldn't remember the name of the guy she had done it with after Tod. But she remembered the circumstances clearly, maybe because it was her first one-night stand.

She had been out with a couple of her girlfriends from college, Lisa and Sue, who were in the med sec program with Deedee. The three of them were slumming, hitting the many bars and clubs that, at that time, still thrived in and around Missoula.

By the time they reached the sixth club of the night, a place called the Wigwam, they were all quite drunk. And as often happens among women out on the town with a few drinks in them, their conversation turned raunchy.

They were having a good old time, checking out guys, estimating cock sizes by the bulge in a man's pants, and dissecting the many bimbos that were in the club looking to get picked up. Lisa was commenting on the fact that it must be kennel night at the bar because the place was full of dogs, when Deedee, feeling no pain by that point, claimed she would have no trouble at all, considering how ugly all the other women were, picking up any guy in the place. Her friends took her up on it and, picking out the best-looking guy in the club, challenged her to make good on her claim.

Weaving more than a little, Deedee stood and checked out the guy her friends had chosen. There was no doubt about it, they *had* chosen the best-looking guy in the bar. He was downright gorgeous—tall, long blond hair, well built, blue eyes, and the kind of square-jawed face that is common among male models.

Deedee undid a couple of buttons on her blouse, revealing a lot of skin and the curve of her small but firm breasts. She sauntered over to where he stood at the bar, trying her best not to stumble.

The next day she wouldn't be able to remember what she'd said to the guy, but she would remember that she practically threw herself at him, acting unashamedly slutty. Within fifteen minutes, they were making out at the bar, and within half an hour, his hands were in her blouse. Before the hour was out, they were in the backseat of his Bronco making the beast with two backs. Because of the amount of alcohol she'd imbibed, it took longer for Deedee to build to an orgasm, but come she did, and the only thing that was different from the last time was that she was able to get back into her body at the first touch of the Shadow Monster. She'd awakened to find herself lying in the bushes at the edge of the parking lot, the blond hunk and his Bronco gone.

Over the next several years, Deedee had had only two lovers, and each affair had ended after she had sex with them. And each time she did have sex and left her body, she found the Shadow Monster waiting for her. Only now it didn't rush at her, trying to engulf and devour her. It changed its tactics and tried to entice and tempt her instead. It sang to her—a song whose melody she would not be able to remember upon awakening—of deliciously dark sexual pleasures, where massive cocks penetrated her every orifice and her orgasms were endless. The last time she'd seen it, the Shadow Monster had formed itself into a large throbbing cock and entered her, sending her into the throes of the strongest orgasm she'd ever had and, ironically, right back into her body.

Then she met Jesse. She was, by this time, working for Dr. Pembroke, having graduated with honors, and had just moved into her apartment. Her parents had retired to Arizona, and the only family she had left in Missoula was her uncle.

Jesse came into the doctor's office for a physical for a new job. Deedee had immediately been attracted to him, and as he would tell her later, he had been equally attracted to her. He was tall, with light brown hair worn longish but not too long, and he had piercing olive green eyes. His face was slender, almost feminine in its prettiness, but his broad shoulders, big arms, and thin waist were all masculine.

While Deedee made out his receipt, they made small talk about the weather; it was winter, a generally interesting weather time in Missoula. After he left, Deedee was disappointed that he hadn't asked her out—and disappointed in herself for not being liberated enough to have asked him out. It wouldn't matter.

Three days later, as she left the office a little after four o'clock, Jesse was waiting outside, clad in a black leather jacket and jeans and sitting astride a chopped Harley. Even though she had her car, when he asked if she needed a ride home, she said yes and left her vehicle in the office parking lot. When he dropped her at her apartment, he asked if she'd like to go riding in the mountains on the weekend, and again she said yes.

That was the beginning of what was to become a three-year affair, Deedee's longest.

"Sweet Jesse," Deedee murmured to herself, and drained the last of the wine. The combination of drink and steamy bath was making her drowsy. She pulled the plug from the drain but remained in the water while it ran out.

She felt an urge to call Jesse, to tell him about what had happened tonight, about the little girl she'd seen being nearly devoured by the Shadow Monster. Jesse had been the only one who hadn't run away from her when she'd confided in him about what happened to her when she had an orgasm. He had listened, he had understood—or tried to, anyway. But he was engaged to another woman now. And though they had said they would remain friends, she hadn't spoken to him since the last time they'd been together. The last she heard, he was living with his fiancée in Helena.

A feeling of loneliness swept over her. The

emotion was surrounded by the thought of the poor child facing that intense evil all by herself.

Deedee got out of the tub and wrapped a towel around herself. She dried off and climbed into bed. She lay in the dark, wondering about the little girl. Was she real? Had the experience itself been real? That was a question that had been dogging her since the very first time she'd left her body.

Jesse had believed it was a recurring dream, at first. He hypothesized that she fainted when she had an orgasm, and her out-of-body experience while unconscious was a dream. She had thought of that before meeting Jesse, but hearing someone else propose it made it seem so much more real and logical. She clung to it, and for a long time while she was with Jesse, she was in denial, much as a cancer patient denies they have a disease. But deep down she knew the experience was real, and she finally proved it to herself, at least, when she was able to accurately describe what Jesse had done after she fainted, because she was watching him from above.

Despite the proof, Jesse still found it hard to believe she was having out-of-body experiences in which she crossed into some other dimension where the souls of the dead go. That had been the beginning of the end. Eventually he had come to believe her. He never said so, but Deedee could tell when he started to avoid having sex with her. Once convinced it was real, Deedee had gone into a phase of being intrigued by the phenomenon and had started to research it. She became so wrapped up in it, she didn't notice that Jesse was drifting away until it was too late.

Deedee snuggled deeper beneath the covers.

No, there was no doubt the experience was real, and that meant the little girl was real. But who was she? Was she dead? Dying? Deedee didn't know. The only thing she was sure of was that the little girl was in danger from the hideous Shadow Monster.

5

Anna awoke to the sound of birds singing. Sunlight streamed in the open window, and a warm breeze blew across the bed. She sat up suddenly, rubbed her eyes, and looked around. She was in her room, her own room, but she was alone. Haley and Jayne's beds were made and empty. Outside the window, she could see that the trees were heavy with green. The air was warm, the sky a sun-washed blue. The scent of flowers wafted to her on a gentle breeze. In the kitchen she heard pots and pans rattling.

"Anna! Come and get your breakfast. If we're going to get to the lake early, you'd better get a move on."

It was her mother!

Anna threw back the covers, tears streaming from her eyes, and tried to put on her bathrobe with hands that wouldn't stop trembling.

"Anna! That means right now!"

Her father!

Anna blubbered with tears and had to sit back on the bed to try and bring herself under control.

Her mom and dad were alive! Could it be true? Could it all have been some stupid, evil nightmare that she'd forget by the end of breakfast?

Joy swelling in her, she stood and was able to slip into her bathrobe, despite her trembling hands. She caught her reflection in the mirror on the dresser and started laughing at her tear-strewn face.

"What are you crying for, you dope?" she said to herself. "It was just a dream."

The kitchen was brimming with the scent of pancakes, fresh-brewed coffee, and bacon. Anna's father and sisters sat at the kitchen table, digging into stacks of pancakes smothered in maple syrup. Her mother was at the stove, pouring batter onto a sizzling hot griddle.

"Mornin', hon," her mom said. "Sit down, and I'll give you some pancakes."

Anna went to her and hugged her as she flipped pancakes with the spatula.

"I love you, Mom."

Her mother looked flustered and mildly amused. "What was that for?"

Anna just smiled and shrugged in answer and went to her father, hugging him and kissing his cheek. "I love you too, Daddy."

"Yeah, yeah. Now sit down and eat, or we won't beat the traffic to the lake," he replied gruffly but not without a smile and a wink for Anna.

"Don't even think about kissing and hugging me!" Haley exclaimed as Anna approached her. Everyone laughed, and milk ran from Jayne's nose, which made everyone laugh longer.

A shadow passed over the window, darkening the room, but Anna was the only one who seemed to notice. The others kept laughing, their laughter lasting much longer than it should have.

A chill passed down Anna's spine. Her family's laughter began to take on an eerie reverberating quality.

The room grew darker.

Something was wrong. Anna could feel it. Something was terribly wrong. The light in the room disappeared altogether, plunging the kitchen into complete darkness.

Anna let out a shriek. There was no sound from her family. She looked around but could not even make out their silhouettes, the darkness was so thick.

"Mom? Dad?" she called into the dark. No answer. She reached for the table but found only empty space. Something red flashed in the darkness for a moment, was gone, then reappeared. It was a pair of eyes, red glowing eyes, gazing malevolently upon her.

Anna! came the voice, softly and seductively out of the darkness.

"No," she whispered, and was answered with laughter. A red glow appeared at the windows. Glass exploded, pelting her with shards. The black thing was rushing in upon her. It was going to consume her. It had tricked her. Where was the pretty woman who had saved her?

A yawning bloody red maw stretched before her, the glowing eyes gleaming cheerfully above it. She smelled its foul breath and heard the screams of the lost souls within it as the mouth closed around her—

—and she awoke.

She opened her eyes and saw a white-tiled ceiling overhead. From the sounds around her—a beeping in time with her heart, and an airy sound in time with her breathing—she realized she was still in the hospital. She couldn't move her head—in fact, she couldn't move any part of her body. She was aware of a tube in her mouth and nose that was helping her breathe, and tubes were running from each arm, plus there was a very uncomfortable attachment at her privates.

What's going on? Anna wondered. One minute

I'm dead, floating around outside my body, the next I'm in the hospital. The thought occured to her that it had all been a dream; all her out-of-body visits to that weird other world were just a very bad dream brought on by the accident and the deaths of her parents.

But something told her no, it hadn't been a dream. It had been real enough. Tony and his little brother, her friend Mary in the heavenly light, the evil black thing full of damned souls, and the pretty woman who had saved her were all too real. The memory of them didn't fade or become fuzzy the way the details of a dream would.

Something very strange is happening to me, Anna thought. She was frightened and felt very much alone. She wished her mother and father were there to comfort her, but they would never be there for her again. That's why I have to make their killers pay, she thought, bringing the rage that was now always lying just beneath the surface into sharp focus. Somehow, she knew, she had to find them. Somehow she had to exact revenge. Somehow.

6

Deedee tried to resume the normal routine of her life and forget about what had happened with Paul Belzer and after, but the experience wouldn't let her go as easily as she would have liked. She went to work at Dr. Pembroke's office, shopped, cleaned her apartment, and watched TV, but thoughts of the little girl threatened by that evil creature were never far from her mind. She dreamed of the girl at night and awoke sweating and scared in the darkness, the dreams only half remembered but leaving her with a terrible sense of forboding.

Friends she had waitressed with at the club called wanting to know why she had quit, and she had lied, saying she didn't need the extra money and wanted the weekends to herself.

And she thought about Jesse a lot. She still wanted to call him and discuss this latest development with the little girl, but she couldn't. Though his parting words to her had been that if she ever needed him, to just call, that had been before he'd met someone he wanted to marry. Deedee was sure he'd meant it at the time, but she couldn't hold him to such a promise under the circumstances.

A week of sleep-disturbed nights went by, and it began to show on her face in the dark circles under her eyes and in a distracted attitude that caused her to make mistakes at work. By Friday night, she was overtired and overstressed, and her worries over the girl and how she was had grown to the point of obsession.

Deedee bought a bottle of wine on her way home from work Friday night and sat in front of the television drinking glass after glass in an attempt to numb her thoughts and get a complete night of sleep. By ten, she was drunk and dozing in the recliner. She roused herself when the eleven o'clock news came on and staggered to her bedroom, collapsing into the bed fully dressed. She was snoring loudly within seconds. The dream state followed soon after.

She dreamed she was at a club dancing with Jesse. They were holding each other close, dancing slow and sexy to every song, no matter what the tempo. Jesse was whispering in her ear, describing detailed sexual acts he wanted to perform on her. She was getting aroused, listening to Jesse tell how he would suck on her breasts and slowly lick his way down to her vagina, sucking and nipping at her clitoris. She began to rub against him as they danced, gyrating her hips, feeling her body begin to tingle with preorgasmic excitement.

"Let's get out of here," she whispered fervently to Jesse, but it was too late. An orgasm began to wrack her body. She closed her eyes, arched her back, let out a scream—and opened her eyes again to see her body slumped in Jesse's arms below her. She pushed herself down toward her body, but she saw that it wasn't her body anymore, it was the little girl below her. And Jesse wasn't Jesse anymore but the Shadow Monster, and it was devouring the screaming girl. The girl was beating her hands futilely against the thing. Deedee watched in horror as the creature's massive jaws clamped on the girl, shoveling her deeper inside itself with every bite, reminding Deedee of the great white shark in the movie *Jaws*. As the Shadow Monster took its last bite, engulfing the girl's head, she cried out to Deedee, "Help me!"

Deedee awoke in a cold sweat, her heart slamming inside her chest, wondering if that had been a nightmare brought on by the alcohol or if she'd really had another out-of-body experience. The idea that she could leave her body during her sleep frightened her tremendously. If that became a regular thing, she didn't know what she would do.

And what of the little girl? Deedee was certain she was in danger from the Shadow Monster. The dream had been so vivid, so real, that she couldn't be sure that it had been just a dream and nothing more. At best, it had been a premonition, and not a very happy one.

"I've got to do something," Deedee whispered to herself in the darkness of her bedroom. She thought a moment, then threw back the covers and got out of bed. Upon standing, her head began a dull pounding and her stomach did queasy flipflops.

That's what I get for drinking a whole bottle of cheap wine, she thought.

She went to the kitchen, poured herself a glass of water from the tap, and dropped two Alka-Seltzer into it, drinking it down before the tablets were completely dissolved. She placed the glass in the sink and began rummaging through the refrigerator, coming out with a half stick of Carrando pepperoni that was about eight inches long and three quarters of an inch thick.

"You'll do nicely," she said to the pepperoni, and took it back to her bedroom. A half hour later, she was very hot, sweaty, and horny as hell, but she could not bring herself to the point of orgasm with the stick of pepperoni. Her head was still pounding from the alcohol, and the Alka-Seltzer had done little to settle her stomach. That, and her urgency to get out of her body to see if the girl was all right, made her too tense to achieve an orgasm, and she knew it.

Frustrated, she tossed the pepperoni into the wastebaseket by her bed and lay back. Eventually she fell into a troubled, restless sleep.

Saturday was Deedee's day off, and she awoke tired from her restless night. She also awoke with a knot of anxiety and apprehension lodged in the center of her chest. Thoughts of the little girl refused to dissipate with the morning light.

She tried cleaning her apartment to get her mind off the girl and was fairly successful for the short time it took her to straighten up and vacuum the small place. Then she went grocery shopping, but that did little to distract her, since the market was full of mothers shopping with their children, nearly all of whom seemed to be little girls.

Back in her apartment by three, the conviction that the little girl was in extreme danger weighed heavily on her. Deedee was at her wit's end. By four, she could stand it no longer. She knew she had to leave her body, go to the other side, and find out if the girl was still there and, if so, help her. And Deedee knew there was only one way that was going to happen.

Putting on skintight leather pants with a low-cut blouse, she made up her face and went out. She thought briefly about going to see Paul Belzer but quickly decided that would be too awkward. Which also ruled out the Rockland Club. Though it was only four-thirty in the afternoon, the Rockland, and nearly every other bar in Missoula, was open for happy hour.

Bars did a good business on Saturdays during

happy hour, offering two-for-one drink specials and free munchies. Deedee decided to head for the nicest of the happy hour bars, the Mountain Lounge in the Holiday Inn at the northern edge of the city.

The melodic strains of Tommy Dorsey greeted her as she went in. The place was atmospherically dark, with fake lanterns on the wall flickering dimly and giving off neon candlelight. The room was done in a pirate ship motif, which made no sense to Deedee, considering the place was called the Mountain Lounge. The bar was horseshoe shaped and fashioned to look like the aft section of an old wooden ship. Fake portholes and tin cutlasses adorned the walls. The bartender and waitresses were dressed as buccaneers.

Deedee sat at the end of the bar nearest the entrance and surveyed the lounge, which was about half full. The crowd was decidedly older than Deedee, people in their late forties to mid-fifties. In the corner farthest from her, three silver-haired ladies sat at a table chatting, with colorful drinks sporting little umbrellas in front of them. An attractive middle-aged couple sat at the next table, holding hands and talking softly to each other, with furtive glances around the room and toward the entrance. Deedee guessed they were having an affair. The other tables in the lounge were filled with men in business suits wearing name tags on their lapels, obviously attending some sort of convention at the Holiday Inn.

The barmaid, a young blonde with big teeth that were not unflattering in her pretty smile, came over and took Deedee's order—tequila and a slice of lemon, hold the salt. As the tequila came, she was thinking she should have gone to one of the other bars that had happy hour.

Deedee picked up the tequila shooter and downed

it. She followed it by sucking on the lemon, wincing at the sourness of it. She waited for the effect to settle in before she left, but a good-looking guy from one of the convention tables came over and sat down next to her.

"Hi. Can I buy you another one of those?" he asked, placing his right elbow on the bar as he turned to her.

"Sure," Deedee replied. He looked to be in his forties, but he was very handsome, tall with dark hair and chiseled features. His convention name tag read "Hi! My name is Barry."

He joined her in a tequila shooter and gasped afterward while Deedee laughed at him.

"So, Barry. What's the convention for?" Deedee asked when he'd recovered from the breathlessness of the tequila.

"I'm here for a hospice convention—the International Hospice Institute and the Academy of Hospice Physicians."

"Oh, yeah," Deedee replied. "I heard about that. I work for a doctor, and I remember we got some info in the office mail about it."

"Oh?" Barry seemed interested. "Are you a nurse?"

"No. I'm a medical secretary."

"Oh."

An awkward silence followed. Deedee glanced at her watch. It was nearly six. She didn't realize she'd been in the bar for close to an hour. With every passing minute, the feeling grew stronger that the little girl was in trouble and needed her help. She had hoped to meet a man who was, quite frankly, a pig—one who would be hot and horny and ready to go. Instead she'd met a nice, intelligent (and probably married) man. Looking at him, Deedee doubted he would ever make the first move—he was too much the gentleman. Deedee decided that if she wanted to get out of her body and help the girl, she'd have to be the pig and act like a slut. And the thing that bothered her the most was that a big part of her (too big really) enjoyed acting slutty. She felt guilty about that, but her concern for the little girl on the other side overrode the guilt.

"Um, Barry," Deedee said softly, seductively, sliding closer to him at the bar, "why don't we get out of here and go back to my place." Deedee put her hand on his thigh and slid it up to his crotch.

Barry inhaled sharply, the breath whistling between his teeth. He glanced furtively around, as if he thought everyone in the bar—especially his colleagues—had seen Deedee rub his crotch.

Deedee squeezed his balls lightly, and he groaned.

"I, uh, uh—I have a room upstairs. We could go there," Barry stammered.

"I'd rather not," Deedee said quietly, continuing to massage the growing bulge in Barry's pants. "I know too many people who work here. Let's slip out the side door. My car is right outside, and I live only five minutes away."

Barry hesitated until Deedee again squeezed him. She accompanied it with a nibble and lick of his ear.

"Okay," he breathed.

Once inside her apartment, Deedee wasted no time on small talk. She led Barry to her bedroom, shedding her clothes as she went. By the time she reached the bed, she was naked. She began pulling Barry's clothes off. She got as far as removing his shirt before he pushed her down on the bed, got on top of her, and began sucking hard on her left nipple while kneading her right breast with his fingers. She reached down and undid his pants, freeing his penis. She wanted him inside her *right now*, but he wouldn't let her. He grabbed her hands and pinned them above her head and went back to work on her breasts with his mouth.

Deedee squirmed. "Fuck me. Please. I want you to fuck me," she pleaded.

"All in good time," Barry murmured to her breasts.

Great! Deedee thought. Nine out of ten guys would have been slam-bam-thank-you-ma'am; but she had to get *the one* sensitive schmuck who believed in foreplay and giving as much pleasure as he received. Normally his attention to foreplay would have been great for her, would have excited her immensely, but now the fact that he wouldn't stick it in her, so she could come and get to the other side to help the girl, annoyed her. His lips began to irritate her breasts and nipples instead of arousing them. When he began kissing his way down to her crotch, his lips and tongue tickled her, and she couldn't help but laugh and try to squirm away from him.

Barry was persistent. He buried his face between her legs, and she giggled louder until his tongue found her clitoris and the giggle turned into a moan of pleasure. Until his tongue reached that secret spot, Deedee hadn't realized just how horny she was. The touch of his tongue was electric and sent her immediately spinning into the void of orgasm—and out of her body.

She arrived on the other side the same way she had the time before, dizzy and feeling slightly disoriented from the ride. There was neither sign nor sound of the girl.

The Shadow Monster got her. At the mere thought of the thing, it began to materialize, as though pulled by the power of her mind. The rents in the surface of the other word began disgorging huge pliant bubbles of blackness that quivered, floating toward each other to coalesce into a mass of darkness whose blackness was unfathomable in its depth. The other bubbles of reality fled from it, and soon only Deedee and the Shadow Monster remained.

Deedee watched in growing terror as faces boiled to the surface of the thing, emerging from the blackness with eyes open and staring malevolently, only to submerge again and be replaced by other faces.

Tentacles and long-jointed spiderlike legs sprouted from the sides of the Shadow Monster as the last of the dark bubbles joined with it and it took its final shape. Two large eyes appeared in the center of the blackness and fixed their gaze on Deedee, and the thing scurried toward her.

Deedee shrieked and backed away.

You came back! Its voice slithered through her head, coming from everywhere and nowhere all at once, coming from inside Deedee's head as much as from anywhere else.

I've been waiting for you.

"Fuck you," Deedee said, her mental voice trembling.

Love to, the Shadow Monster replied.

Deedee stepped back and nearly lost her balance. She was still unused to the weightlessness of the other world. The Shadow Monster rushed closer, as if to pounce, but halted when she righted herself.

"Where's the girl?" Deedee asked, struggling to maintain her balance and keep the trembling fear out of her voice.

Which girl? I've had so many, a myriad of voices answered her from out of the thing. Some were deep, some shrill, some whispering, some shrieking. They hurt Deedee's head and made her dizzy.

"You know the girl I mean. The one I saw you with the last time I was here," she replied.

The Shadow Monster laughed, and the sound was nails on a blackboard to Deedee's ears.

I ate her! the Shadow Monster cried, its eyes rolling, nostrils flaring. Its mouth yawned open, and it belched a gray stinking cloud filled with tiny flying insects that buzzed around Deedee's head.

The Shadow Monster moved closer. Deedee backed awkwardly away.

"Liar!" she said.

Why don't you come on in and find out? There's lots of your friends, relatives, and especially ancestors in here with us. The creature was growing larger as it spoke. Its mass increased the way a storm cloud will expand just before letting loose explosions of thunder and lightning and torrents of rain.

Deedee moved away and found herself up against a massive pillar of vegetation that stretched for yards to either side of her. The Shadow Monster swelled and closed in on her, cutting off escape to the right or left. She looked up, hoping to float over the thing, but an array of hateful faces stared down at her, their mouths slavering hungrily.

The main face of the Shadow Monster reappeared. It came closer, and terror grew in Deedee. The eyes of the malevolent creature grew larger, and she could see more evil, tormented faces within the eyeballs, like rats scurrying over one another in a frantic attempt to get out of the enclosed place. Its mouth opened, revealing an abscessed tongue, running with sores. Its teeth were black but serrated and sharp like shark's teeth. Its breath was foul—a mixture of animal feces, dead flesh, and rotten eggs. Deedee gagged on it as the mouth widened and drew closer, ready to consume her.

"No!" she screamed, and felt the same force emanate from her that had kept the Shadow Monster away from the little girl before. The Shadow Monster recoiled as if physically struck. Its eyes widened with surprise, its mouth clamped shut, and a howl of anguish rose from the smaller mouths that were in constant eruption all over its surface.

It occurred to Deedee that the Shadow Monster couldn't touch her, couldn't eat her, unless she gave in to it and let it. She tried to take it a step further and will the thing away from her, but her power did not extend that far; the thing remained, enveloping her in darkness that began a few feet from her body in every direction.

She was trapped.

Deedee began to lose track of time. She looked for the bubble that was her real life but couldn't find it. She tried willing herself back to her body, but nothing happened. The Shadow Monster's flesh boiled and changed faces, eyes and body parts emerging and submerging constantly. Its foul breath washed over Deedee in regular waves. For a long time, the thing said nothing, was content to just sit there and stare at her with its huge frontal eyes and hundreds of other smaller ones that came and went.

Deedee began to recognize faces in the miasma that was the Shadow Monster. She found herself staring intently into it until she noticed that the more she stared, the closer the thing came, inching imperceptibly nearer every second. She forced herself to look away, lest the thing draw her in.

After a while, the Shadow Monster began a new tactic.

Deedee, it said.

She shivered to realize the thing knew her name.

Deedee, it repeated.

She tried to ignore it.

Deedee, it said again, and kept on repeating it every few seconds until she gave in and said, "*What?*"

You're stuck with it, the Shadow Monster replied.

"*What?*"

You're stuck with it.

The Shadow Monster smiled—a hideous expression—and winked at her.

Deedee, it said again a few moments later.

"*What?*" she responded automatically.

You're stuck with it. Deedee?

She looked away, refusing to answer.

Deedee?

Deedee?

Deedee?

Deedee?

Deedee?

On and on the Shadow Monster went, speaking in a monotone with the exact same questioning tone and inflection each time. It began to grate on her nerves, going from irritating to annoying, to the point of driving her insane if she had to hear the thing say her name one more time.

Deedee?

Deedee?

Deedee?

"*What!*" she screamed angrily at last, unable to stand it any longer.

The creature paused a moment, watching her, a smile playing at the corners of its cruel mouth, and said, *Stuck with it!*

Deedee shrieked in frustration.

The Shadow Monster laughed.

And moved closer.

Deedee? It began the sequence all over again.

Deedee?

Deedee?

Deedee?

Why is it doing this? Deedee wondered. The thing was driving her crazy, driving her to the point where she didn't care about her safety any longer—she just wanted to shut the thing up, just wanted to grab it and shake it—stuff something in its mouth and shut it up and—that was it! That's what the thing was doing! It was *trying* to drive her crazy. Trying to drive her to the point where she'd lose it and throw herself at the creature, and then it would be all over. The thing would gobble her up. It was unable to consume her as long as she resisted, but if she were to attack it, she would be gone in seconds.

"Fuck you," she said, and suddenly she was out of there. The sphere that was her life reappeared, suddenly descending swiftly, growing larger, until it recaptured her soul and returned it to her body.

She entered herself, gasping for air, just as Barry was finishing his oral sex performance on her. He was naked now, having removed the rest of his clothes while performing cunnilingus on her. He had been so intent on what he was doing that he hadn't even noticed the change in her when she'd left her body. He put on a condom he had taken from his wallet, flipped her over onto her stomach, and pulled her to him. She tried to cry out for him to stop, but she was too breathless from her journey to make a sound. Barry thrust his manhood inside her, forcing her open, and began pumping her with pistonlike ferocity. His testicles slapped against her clitoris as he invaded her, and she immediately began to orgasm again. Again she left her body.

* * *

Welcome back, the Shadow Monster said. *Just couldn't stay away, could you?*

Deedee let out a groan. She had been catapulted back to the same spot in the other world so quickly, she didn't remember the journey—it all happened with the rapidity of a blinking eye. She felt weak, exhausted. Her eyes were heavy, and she wished she could just drift off into sleep.

Can't do that.

She awoke with a start. The Shadow Monster was closer, its mouth looming before her.

Go back to sleep, it crooned. *Just drift off.*

It can hear everything I think, she realized. The dark cloud that was the creature answered with an insidious chuckle.

She struggled to keep her eyes open, to keep her mind alert, but she felt as though the Shadow Monster were already inside her, filling her brain with its oily darkness. Something brushed against her face and caressed her breasts. With great effort, she opened her eyes—was shocked to discover they weren't already open—and saw the Shadow Monster's tongue protruding from the thing's mouth. It was licking her breasts, tickling the left nipple with the tip of its tongue. Despite the revulsion she felt at being touched by the thing, she felt a tingle of arousal too.

Yes, crooned the creature. *You like that, don't you? Come inside with us, and we'll make you come forever.*

The words flowed over her with the physical sensation of stroking hands and fingers.

She felt its tongue, hot and oily, slithering inside her vagina. She tried willing the thing away from her, the way she had before, but she couldn't concentrate and focus enough. She felt herself losing to the Shadow Monster, felt it enveloping her, pulling her into its cold, horrid existence. And yet the feeling was immensely erotic, extremely arousing.

She was too weak, too aroused, to fight it anymore.

I'm dying, she thought.

"No, you're not," came an answer that was not the conglomerate voice of the Shadow Monster. She felt the thing recoil slightly at the sound of the new voice.

"You can fight it," the voice came again, *"just like you told me to."* Deedee realized it was the voice of the little girl. The creature pulled away more, and she found she could open her eyes. Through a dark mist of swirling eyes and faces, she saw the little girl floating toward her.

The Shadow Monster receded from around her and began moving toward the girl.

"No!" Deedee shouted, and the Shadow Monster hesitated. In that moment, the girl's life sphere descended, and she disappeared. The Shadow Monster turned back toward Deedee but came no closer. She could feel her strength returning, and as it did, the landscape around her, including the Shadow Monster, became transparent. Her life sphere came to her, grew huge in front of her. She could see the real world behind the fading image of the other world. She entered the sphere and began falling. She saw her apartment house below her and fell slowly through the roof, then through the ceiling of her bedroom. Her physical body was lying facedown on the bed. Barry was hurriedly dressing, tears streaking his pale face.

Gently she reentered her body, opened her eyes, and rolled over to face the frightened Barry.

"Don't worry, I'm not dead," Deedee said. Barry let out a shriek of fright and ran, half naked, clutching the rest of his clothes in his arms, out of her apartment.

Deedee couldn't help but laugh and was soon hysterical. The hysteria graduated to tears, and she lay on her bed crying until sleep dried her eyes and comforted her.

She awoke feeling tired. She rolled over, with going back to sleep the only thing on her mind, when the phone rang. Drowsily, she fumbled for the phone on the bedstand and answered it.

"Deedee? Where are you? It's eleven-thirty. Aren't you coming into the office today?"

It was Julie, the nurse at Dr. Pembroke's office.

"What?" Deedee asked, confused.

"What's wrong with you? Are you sick?" Julie asked.

"Is it Monday morning already?" Deedee asked.

"Are you kidding?"

"I'm sorry," Deedee said quickly. Where the hell had the weekend gone? "Yes, yes, I'm sick. Have been all weekend. You woke me up. I should be okay by tomorrow."

Deedee returned the receiver to its cradle and collapsed onto the pillow.

Where the *hell* had the weekend gone? She'd been asleep since when? Saturday afternoon? The last thing she remembered was a shocked and frightened (and funny-looking, being half naked) Barry hurriedly leaving her apartment.

She giggled a little at that, but the giggle quickly faded when she remembered her encounter with the Shadow Monster. She shuddered at the thought of that thing being inside her, raping her. She felt sick at the thought of how close she had come to letting that thing consume her.

But the girl had saved her. Deedee tried to

picture the girl in her mind, to recall the details of her face, but sleep was rapidly overtaking her again. She succumbed to it, stretching and yawning luxuriously, welcoming the somnolent bliss.

Frantic dreams.

Dreams, like hungry rats scurrying through a maze in search of food, chased each other through Deedee's sleep until they jarred her into consciousness.

She awoke feeling uneasy but unable to remember any of her dreams. She had the vague feeling that they had been about the little girl and the Shadow Monster, but she couldn't be sure.

It was just getting dark when she awoke. She lay in bed wondering if it was Monday night, or if she had repeated her sleep of the weekend, staying out until Tuesday or Wednesday evening.

No, she decided. It had to be Monday night. Julie would have called if she had missed another day.

Still weary, her joints and muscles stiff, Deedee got out of bed and went into the bathroom. She had to pee so bad, her sides hurt. She sat on the john for several minutes relieving herself. She thought about taking a hot shower or a bath, but she didn't have the energy to remain standing for a shower and was afraid that if she took a bath, she'd fall asleep again.

Not bothering to put on a robe, she stumbled naked to the living room and plopped herself onto the couch. Using the remote, she surfed idly through the channels, not paying much attention to anything, just trying to clear her mind and shake off the hazy lazy drowsiness that made her just want to crawl back into bed.

Her hand grew tired of channel surfing, and she dropped the remote onto the coffee table next to the couch, leaving the TV on channel 5, the local Fox

Network station. *America's Most Wanted* was on, and the host was describing a rapist at large in Florida. Deedee was dozing off when a picture was flashed on the screen that caught her eye. She came fully awake.

It was the little girl.

Sitting up, Deedee grabbed the remote and turned up the sound.

"This is Anna Wheaton," John Walsh said on the TV. "She has been in a coma in a small hospital in Massachusetts since Christmas Day."

The scene shifted and showed an aerial view of Towns End, Massachusetts. As John Walsh narrated the story of how Anna had gone sledding and had an accident, the screen showed pictures of Anna's house and Cemetery Hill. The scene shifted to a reenactment of a robbery at a hospital, identified as Middlesex Regional Hospital. Men from a van entered the back of the hospital and robbed the pharmacy. A guard interrupted them and was brutally stabbed.

The scene shifted to outside the rear of the hospital, at the entrance to the emergency room. John Walsh stood in the parking lot, pointing to the top of the hill. The scene shifted back to the reenactment, showing the robbers leaving the hospital just as Anna's father's car and a police car were coming over the top of the hill. Two of the bandits ran into the parking lot and opened fire.

The scene shifted back to the studio, where John Walsh addressed the camera. To his left, photographs of two men appeared. "These are the killers of Anna Wheaton's parents. Two of their gang have already turned up dead. One died at the hospital, when he was struck by police officer O'Dea's car; the other was found murdered, along with two innocent teenagers, in the woods just over the border in New Hampshire. The two men still at large are Rod Baylor and Gary Jergins, two longtime criminals. Both are considered armed and dangerous. If you have any information that might help lead to their capture, call our hotline or your local police. Do not, I repeat, do not approach either of these men in any way."

The program broke for a commercial, and Deedee turned it off. So that was what happened to the little girl, Anna. Deedee felt bad for her. She also felt scared for herself. This confirmed something she had feared about her out-of-body experiences: They brought her very close to death. The little girl, Anna, was in a coma while her spirit roamed the other side.

Deedee got up and began to pace from the living room into the kitchen and back again. She couldn't stop thinking about Anna Wheaton, her body in a coma, her soul in and out of that strange other world, constant prey to the Shadow Monster.

Deedee felt that she had to do something. A part of her rebelled against that thought, telling her she was crazy. The little girl, Anna, was nothing to her. Why should she risk her life for someone she didn't even know?

But she's just a child, the answer came. Deedee knew the fear that gripped *her* on the other side. How much worse was it for a child? And then there was the Shadow Monster. Sooner or later that evil thing would find a way to consume the girl, Deedee was certain of it. But for some reason, when she and the girl were together, they created a force that the Shadow Monster couldn't defeat, couldn't devour.

I have to help her, she decided. She couldn't leave the poor girl to the clutches of the Shadow Monster. No matter how frightened she was, she had to go to the other side and help the girl. She wouldn't be able to live with herself if she didn't.

Are you sure you're not doing this for the sex? Because you're really, deep down, just a slut, and this is an excuse to show your real colors? her conscience asked.

Maybe so, Deedee thought, but her mind was made up. Slut or not; right or wrong; whether she lived or died, she knew what she had to do.

She looked at the clock over the stove. It was three-thirty. The bars would be open for happy hour at four. Shedding her robe, she headed for the shower.

7

Rod Baylor was cold, hungry, and tired. The past week, they'd hidden out in the woods of southern Connecticut after getting out of Rhode Island as fast as they could. Now he had to decide what they were going to do.

But he couldn't think on an empty stomach.

There was a diner up ahead. The road they were on had been a major truck route until five years ago, when the state had remodeled I-95 South so that it was now quicker than the old route.

The diner was called Bob's Good Eats and was a run-down old place with a gravel parking lot. An old Ford pickup truck was parked near the entrance. Rod told Gary to pull in, and the big man eagerly did so.

"Oh, man, I'm starvin'," Gary exclaimed as he pulled the stolen van in next to the truck. Rod put his Uzi under the seat and took out his pistol, checked it, and put it in the inside pocket of his overcoat.

"Okay, let's go."

"Can I get pancakes, Rod?" Gary asked. He sounded like an excited kid talking to his dad.

"Whatever," Rod replied. He kept his eye on the road as they went into the diner, but it remained clear. Inside, a waitress was behind the counter across from a wiry old bearded farmer wearing a dirty gray sweatshirt, jeans, and a battered Red Sox baseball cap. They were watching a small black and white TV set at the end of the counter.

Rod led Gary to a booth at the far end of the front of the diner. From there, Rod could see the parking lot and the road. He pulled a menu from its stand on the table, looked at it, and fished his money out of his pockets. He counted what little they had, looked at the menu again, and frowned. All they had was enough for a couple of hot dogs with chips and a pickle. If the two of them weren't already so hot, he would have ordered whatever he liked, then robbed the place when it came time to pay. But after the murders in Rhode Island, they had to keep a low profile.

"We're getting a couple of hot dogs," Rod said. Gary was still looking at the menu.

"But I want pancakes," Gary whined.

"Tough titty," Rod remarked. "We only have enough money for dogs. The rest we gotta save for gas."

Gary looked despondent for a moment, then glanced cautiously at Rod. "What are we gonna do, Rod?"

"I'm not sure yet, but I got an idea. I know a couple of guys from the slammer that maybe can help us."

Gary started to speak, but Rod silenced him with a look as the waitress approached. She was in her fifties, hair, bleached blond; face, too heavy on the makeup; body, bloated from too many nights spent in front of the TV guzzling Narragansett beer.

"What can I get you boys?" she asked, pulling a pencil from behind her ear and an ordering pad from her apron pocket.

"Two hot dog plates," Rod answered.

"And what'll it be to drink?"

"Just water." Rod said. Gary looked like he was

going to say something, but Rod shot him a silencing look.

"Comin' right up," the waitress, whose name tag read "Lil," said.

She went behind the counter, stuck their order slip on a revolving wheel at the window kitchen, and called, "Two dog plates." A moment later she came back with two filmy glasses of water.

"Can't I at least have a Coke, Rod?" Gary asked as soon as she was gone again.

"No. Quit your bitchin'. We're gonna eat and get the hell outta here. I got a plan."

Lil came back with their hot dogs, which were wrinkled-looking pathetic things in soggy buns thrown on plates with a smattering of greasy chips and a limp-looking pickle each. While they ate, Rod, in a low voice, started to tell Gary about his plans.

"Hey, Lil! Come on. Our show's on!" the old farmer at the counter called to Lil, who was emptying the dishwasher near the kitchen door.

Interrupted, Rod looked up at the TV. *America's Most Wanted* was on. "Jeez! I hate that fucking show," he muttered, and went on telling Gary how they were going to unload the drugs.

They were just finishing eating and getting ready to go when Rod happened to look at the TV again. The farmer and Lil were scrunched up close to the thirteen-inch screen as if they couldn't get enough of John Walsh. There was a scene on the screen that looked familiar to Rod. Another look, and it dawned on him. That was the parking lot and emergency room entrance behind Middlesex Hospital. A feeling of apprehension swept over Rod. He could hear John Walsh talking about a family and a cop being murdered. Rod wondered if the cops had any leads. Another moment, and he knew. There on the screen were mug shots of him and Gary. It took less than three seconds for Lil and the farmer to turn, slowly, and look at Rod and Gary, recognition dawning on their faces.

The old farmer tried to make it to the door, but Rod had his pistol out before the man could get completely off his stool. He looked at Rod, his eyes wide, his mouth open, a pleading look on his face. Rod shot him, the bullet hitting him in the chest and knocking him spinning around his stool and to the floor. Lil screamed, and Rod shot her in the face. She fell into the TV, knocking it off the counter. It fell to the floor, and the screen exploded in a flash of light and smoke.

The kitchen doors burst open, and a large fat man—Bob, presumably—came charging out, a butcher knife raised in his right hand. Rod didn't even flinch. He calmly turned and shot the fat cook three times in the belly and chest, and once again in the back of the head when the man was down.

"Shit!" Rod swore, looking at the carnage. "We don't need this right now." He walked over to the TV and kicked it, sending it sliding a few feet into the farmer's body. "Goddamned TV! Don't these hicks know it rots your brain?" He laughed hysterically then. Gary, standing shocked and shivering next to the table they'd been eating at, looked fearfully at Rod.

"Rod, cut it out."

Rod stopped laughing and smiled at Gary. "Boy! When shit goes wrong, it really goes wrong, don't it?" He laughed again.

Gary didn't think he was funny. "What are we gonna do, Rod? You killed all these people."

"Yeah," Rod mused. He looked around, then out at the van and the farmer's truck in the parking lot. "Get out there and start the van."

Gary hesitated a moment, then did as he was

told. Rod went behind the counter, took a piece of apple pie from under a glass display bell, and wolfed it down. He punched the NO SALE button on the ancient register and took a measly thirty dollars from the till. He went into the kitchen and rifled the large stainless-steel refrigerator, eating some cheese and muttering at how little food the place had.

He went to the stove next to the grill and looked around it, behind it. There was a pipe running in from the back wall, connecting to the stove and grill. A propane gas line, he guessed. So far out in the sticks, the place would need to use propane. The tanks had to be out in the back. He turned the gas on for the burners and was glad to see they didn't light automatically. The pilot lights were probably clogged with grease. He turned on all the burners and went back out to the front of the diner. Gary was just coming in.

"I did like you said, Rod." In his hand he held a five-gallon gas can.

"Where'd you get that?" Rod asked.

"It was in the back of truck. I figured we could use it in the van."

Rod smiled. "No. Give it to me."

8

Deedee showered quickly, washing her face and underarms and between her legs. She figured her hair looked good enough—she didn't want to take the time to dry it. She got out of the shower and toweled off while going through her closet, trying to decide on an outfit. She chose her skintight black jeans and a low-cut black sweater to match.

By four forty-five, she was out of the apartment and in her car, heading south to a place she knew from her college days. At happy hour, the Red Deer was a big hangout for construction workers. It took her less than twenty minutes to get there, and she was glad to see the parking lot was full of pickup trucks.

Inside, the bar was smoky. A fire going in a huge stone fireplace gave a vague wood scent to the place, almost masking the stale beer and cigarettes. She went to the end of the small half-circle bar and sat. The bartender, a beer-gutted black man of fifty or so, came over, and she ordered a tequila with lemon on the side. While she waited for her drink, she surveyed the bar. There was an immediate prospect directly to her left, four seats down at the bar. He was big, six foot four at least, and he was dark, Indian looking. He had long, shiny shoulder-length black hair and a build that Arnold Schwarzenegger would be proud to own.

A quick appraisal of the rest of the bar, and it was obvious he was the best of the litter. He looked her way, and she smiled. He smiled back, but it was a funny smile. It gave Deedee the feeling it was the here-we-go-again smile of a man used to being approached by women. It was an egotistical smile, and Deedee didn't like it, didn't like him for a moment. But God! He was gorgeous!

The bartender brought her tequila, and she drank it straight down. She closed her eyes and felt the burn for a moment before sucking on the lemon.

"You do that good."

Startled, she opened her eyes. The good looker had moved down and was sitting next to her at the end of the bar. His face was broad and sharply defined. He had a long thin nose and large brown eyes. His lips were full and sensuous but had a sense of cruelty about them.

"What?" Deedee asked, trying not to dribble lemon juice down her chin.

"You do that good," he repeated, adding, "sucking, I mean."

Deedee blushed and felt a moment of fear. She had the sudden compulsion to get out of there. But that was crazy. This was exactly what she had been looking for, why she had come to this bar. She knew she'd get picked up fast here, no pussyfooting.

But there was something wrong. Still, she heard herself answering, even as she had to force herself to remain seated, "That's not all I do well."

He laughed, then smirked, and for Deedee the smirk said it all. This guy was so in love with himself, it wasn't funny. He knew he was good looking, and she had to give him that, he *was* good looking, but he also thought he was God's gift to women. There was something else about him, too, that Deedee couldn't put her finger on, but she just chalked it up to her dislike of his egotism. What the hell? She wasn't going to marry the guy. She only wanted him to come back to her apartment and fuck her into the next world.

"I'll just bet you can," Good Looking said.

"I'm Deedee."

"Hi, Deedee. I'm Dick."

She smiled at him and licked her lips slowly. "Well, Dick. Why don't we go back to my place, and you can find out if I lie or not."

He smirked again and looked around at some of his buddies. He must have made a face at them or mouthed something about Deedee, because they craned to see her, and several of them made crude noises. Deedee blushed hotly. This was really becoming a disaster. She decided it wasn't going to work. She left a five on the bar and slid off the stool, heading for the door. Dick caught her before she could leave.

"Hey, darlin', where you going? I thought you were going to show me some things."

Deedee almost told him to fuck off, but the thought of Anna alone on the other side kept her from it. As she'd thought before, so what if this guy was a jerk? All she needed him for was sex.

"Yeah, so I did," she replied. "You want to follow me?"

"Lead the way," Dick said.

All the way back to her apartment, Deedee waged a war with herself. One moment she was looking for a way to ditch the jerk in the pickup truck behind her; the next she was thinking of Anna and eager to use the jerk behind her to get to the other side. She still couldn't lose the sense of trepidation about what she was doing. This was more than the normal guilt and shame she'd felt with Paul and Barry; this was a real sense of something bad happening.

She shook it off. What could happen? He couldn't rape her, since she planned to have sex with him anyway. She ran it over in her mind. They'd get to her apartment, get naked, and screw, and when she left her body, he'd think she was dead. Being the jerk he obviously was, he'd split, and she'd be fine.

In what seemed like a lot less time than it had taken her to get to the bar, they were at her apartment. Dick parked behind her at the gas station and followed her up to her second-floor digs.

Deedee closed the door behind Dick and took off her coat, hanging it on the rack next to the door. She took Dick's coat and hung it next to hers.

"Would you like something to drink?" Deedee asked, suddenly nervous again, all her second thoughts crowding in upon her.

"Fuck that," Dick said, and grabbed her around the waist, pulling her to him. "I want to see what you can do." He grabbed her left breast with his free hand and squeezed it hard.

"Okay," Deedee said, wincing slightly at his roughness but also turned on by it. "Let's go in the bedroom."

She started to turn away, but Dick pulled her back, crushing her tiny body against his muscular frame. "No. Right here," he said. He brought his right index finger up to her face, rubbed her lips with it, then roughly forced it into her mouth up to the knuckle.

Deedee gagged and pulled away. Suddenly she was on the floor, her head was ringing, her thoughts ajumble, her face hot with pain throughout the left side. Her vision was crossed and took a second to right. For a moment there were two Dicks standing over her, arms raised, ready to strike her again.

The two Dicks became one as he started to undo his pants. "Don't you ever pull away from me again, if you know what's good for you, bitch." He pushed his jeans and underwear down to reveal a less-than-average-size penis. He reached down, grabbed Deedee by the hair, and yanked her to her knees. She cried out in pain and tried to claw his hand, but his other one came down fast and hard across her cheek again, and she blacked out for a moment.

When she came to, her face was mashed into his crotch, his small cock shoved into her mouth. He held her head with both hands, his fingers tightly entwined in her short hair, and moved his hips rhythmically. She couldn't breathe, and even though he was small, she started to gag. He pulled her face off his penis and pushed her lower, into his testicles.

"Suck those balls, you fucking slut," he commanded. Her nose and mouth were pressed hard into his sac. She felt like she was suffocating. She opened her mouth to breathe, and hairy soft flesh filled it. She did the only thing she could do. She bit down. Hard. Something crunched.

Dick screamed—low, hoarse, and panic-filled. He tried to pull away, but she wouldn't let go. Her teeth were embedded in his sac, and she could feel one of his testicles crushed between her side teeth. She tasted blood and spit him out.

Dick's scream ended, and an inhaling shriek began as he staggered backward. Blood ran down his legs and dripped from his testicles. They looked crimped, Deedee's teeth marks clearly showing, the flesh around them turning red and purple. They were beginning to swell.

Dick looked down at himself and sobbed. He looked up at Deedee with a questioning look that quickly turned to rage. He lunged for her but stumbled over his lowered pants. She scrambled back, away from him. He doubled over in pain with the effort, giving her enough time to crawl to the end table, next to the couch, and grab the pewter candleholder there.

Using the couch for leverage, she got to her feet and brandished the heavy candlestick in both hands. "Get the fuck out of here, you bastard, before I smash your skull in," she said breathlessly. Dick got up slowly, eyeing her carefully, gauging whether he could get her. But his balls hurt too much. He'd had enough for one day. He gingerly pulled up his pants, wincing as he did, and walked bowlegged to the coatrack.

He stopped with his hand on the door and looked back at Deedee with a glare that made her shiver. "This ain't over, bitch. Nobody does this to me and gets away with it."

"If you come back here, I'll kill you," Deedee said as fiercely as she could, shaking the candlestick at him. Dick smirked and left, slamming the door behind him. Deedee hurried to the door, did both locks, then hurried to the window to watch his truck leave. When he was gone, she went to the couch and collapsed on it in tears.

9

"What are you gonna do with that, Rod?" Gary asked. The van was running in the parking lot, ready to go. Rod was carrying the gas can from the truck.

"Cover our tracks a little, Dumbo," Rod replied. He began dousing the inside of the diner, and the bodies, with gasoline. "Get back in the van, and wait for me."

Gary went back outside and sat in the van, watching the road and the diner alternately. Rod came out carrying the old farmer over his shoulder. He put the old guy in the truck, then got in next to it. He backed it up and drove it straight through the front of the diner, smashing in the door and the walls on both sides and bringing down the overhang. The truck settled, half in and half out of the diner. Rod got out, lit a matchbook full of matches, and tossed it into the truck cab. He came running to the van, got in, and shouted, "Get the hell out of here!"

Less than a hundred yards down the road, they heard the diner blow as the flames reached the gas leaking from the stove. There were two sharp explosions, and what looked like a frying pan landed off the road to the left of them as they drove away.

10

The dream wouldn't go away. Deedee tried to ignore it, tried not to think about it, but that didn't work. Night after night it came back. It was funny really, considering the hellish experience she'd just undergone at the hands of Dick, that the dream would be about Anna.

She dreamed she had left her body. She was in Anna Wheaton's hospital room. The girl was in the bed, attached to tubes and wires, and hovering over her—all around her—was the Shadow Monster. Deedee was immobilized in the dream, helpless as she watched the thing devour the girl.

She awoke sweating from the dream, breathless and shaking, a soundless scream in her throat, staring terrified into the darkness of her room, imagining the Shadow Monster everywhere, ready to strike.

Deedee tried everything she could think of to stop the dream, or avoid it. She tried distracting herself before sleep with a magazine, but it insinuated itself into her thoughts. She tried staying up as late as possible, until she was so tired, she could barely keep her eyes open. It was a vain hope that she'd be too tired to dream when she finally fell asleep, but it didn't work. She tried setting her alarm to awaken her every hour, to interrupt her sleep and dreams, but she ended up shutting off the alarm and rolling over, back to sleep, without really waking up.

The worst of it was, she didn't have work to take her mind off the dream during the day. Her face was so bruised, she'd had to call in sick every day. She spent the time in the apartment, exercising, watching TV, reading, trying not to nap and trying not to think about the dream and how Anna was doing and not succeeding. By the end of the week, her physical appearance, in the aftermath of Dick's blows, was improving, but her mental state of health was deteriorating.

She just wished she could go back to work. At least then she could stop thinking about it for a while, but every time she looked at herself in the mirror, she knew she couldn't do that without making up a story to account for her bruised face. Though the swelling had gone down, her eyes were still black and blue, turning to mottled yellow and purple around the edges. It was still too bruised for even heavy makeup to cover it adequately.

On Thursday she called the office and told Julie that she did indeed have the flu (something she had hinted at when calling in the previous three days) and that she felt she should just take her two weeks' vacation. There was a girl who filled in regularly for Deedee as a temp. Julie said she'd call her and hoped that Deedee would feel better soon.

That night, drinking cup after cup of coffee, Deedee tried to stay awake all night. She was successful, but by dawn she felt like shit. Worse than shit—she felt like the proverbial cliché: death warmed over.

All Friday morning she sat on the couch like a zombie, staring at the TV, drinking coffee, getting up only to pee. Just past eleven, as she flipped through the channels with the remote, she suddenly sat bolt upright, knocking her coffee cup off the arm of the chair, spilling it all over the rug.

The Shadow Monster was on channel 13. Its hideous countenance boiled against the screen, pressing its flat dead eyes against the inside of the glass.

I have her, Deedee. I have her now inside me, and she tastes so good. So-o-o-o- g-o-o-o-d!

The thing opened its mouth in laughter, and there, peeking out from between its nasty teeth, she could see Anna's shocked face peering out at her, the lips forming in a soundless plea for help.

Deedee awoke with a shriek, nearly leaping from the couch in an effort to get away from the TV. But the Shadow Monster wasn't on the TV—it was Xuxa. Deedee stared at the blank-faced, blond kids'-show host and burst into tears. She collapsed on the couch, sobbing and muttering over and over a tearful, furtive prayer, "Please, God. Make it stop. Please, God. Make it stop."

11

Rod Baylor awoke feeling stiff, cramped, and cold. He was lying across the front seat of the van, legs jammed against the passenger side door, head at a right angle to the driver's. His neck hurt like hell. He sat up, stretching his legs beneath the dash and rolling his head on his shoulders until he felt his neck pop. He turned and looked into the back of the van, where Gary lay sleeping, curled into a ball amid the boxes of stolen drugs.

Rod rolled down his window and, placing a finger along the side of each nostril and blowing, cleared his nose. He took out a vial of the pharmaceutical coke he'd taken from one of the boxes and shook some powder onto the back of his left hand. He snorted it quickly and licked the residue from his hand. He took a little on his finger also and rubbed it over his teeth.

They were parked in the woods, on a fire access road in Blackstone State Park in Blackstone, Massachusetts. They'd driven all night from the diner in Connecticut, getting lost in a maze of country back roads until they found themselves passing through the small town of Blackstone, in the Blackstone River valley of southern Massachusetts. They'd been hiding in the park for the past three days.

Rod got out of the van, his breath blowing in clouds of steam in the cold air and his feet crunching in the frozen crusty snow underfoot. "This sucks," he muttered to himself. Massachusetts was not where he had planned to be by now. He wondered again, as he had nearly constantly since the hospital job, how things could keep getting fucked up so badly. He ignored the faint, self-accusing voice that told him it was his own fault for wasting the cop and that family in the Subaru. Back at the diner, when *America's Most Wanted* was on, he'd caught the bit of information that the cop hadn't been there to bust them—hadn't even known they were there. The girl'd had some kind of accident, the cop had been rushing her to the hospital. If he'd just taken off when he'd first heard the siren, the robbery wouldn't have been discovered for a day at least, just as he'd planned. Then Fred Wayne wouldn't have been killed and ID'd, through whom Rod was certain the cops had been able to make him and Gary. Now their faces were plastered on TV screens across the whole damned country.

But how could he have known? You're pulling a heist, and you see a cop car coming, you got to figure they're there to bust you. So you got two choices, run or fight. Rod had never been one to run from a fight. He knew if he had to do it all over again, he'd do the same thing, so it was stupid to kick himself in the ass over it.

Besides, the real reason things had gotten so fucked up was due to Carlo getting busted. If he really had to blame someone—and he did—it would have to be that no-good greaseball guinea Carlo. He drained his lizard and went to the side of the van, opening the sliding door.

"Hey! Gary! Wake up!"

Gary groaned and pushed the canvas tarp he'd taken from the farmer's truck off him. He shivered and rubbed his face with his hands and scratched his head.

"I'm cold, Rod. And I'm hungry too." He stood and got clumsily out of the van, his feet plunging to the ankles through the hard snow cover. "I don't wanna do this no more, Rod. This sucks," Gary whined. He pulled his feet from the snow and dug slush from around the edges of his sneakers. "I wanna get outta here. I wanna goes somewhere warm and have some good hot food." Gary got a wistful look. "I wished we'd ate more at that diner. It smelled good in there. Why'd you have to kill all those people, Rod, and burn that diner? I bet they had real good food, better'n those hot dogs we had."

Rod listened to Gary's whining and wondered, not for the first time (nor the last, he supposed), why he put up with the dumb fuck. Sure Gary was big, a lot of muscle to back Rod up, as he had on several occasions in and out of prison. But was that worth the aggravation? Deep down, the big guy was a pussy. As far as Rod knew, Gary had never killed anyone and refused to carry a piece. So why didn't he just dump him and keep the goods and the money for himself?

He didn't know, didn't have a clear-cut answer for the question. He just knew he couldn't. Gary was the closest thing Rod had ever had to a friend in his life; the closest thing to a brother, family. And despite the big guy's wimpiness, he was totally dependent on Rod. Rod owned him, and Rod liked that. Being small all his life and forever taking shit for it, he liked having the big goon at his beck and call. It was like constant revenge against all the big jerks who had ever fucked with him over the years. Still, Gary did get on his nerves sometimes. Like now.

"Oh, shut the fuck up, you fucking idiot!" Rod said in digust. "Just shut the fuck up." The disgust started to turn to anger. "I'm sick of listening to your whiny pussy voice. Don't you think I'm cold? Don't you think I'm hungry?" He kicked the snow and sent chunks of frozen cover skittering across the glassy surface of the rest of the snow. "It's not my fault that everything's gone wrong, so just shut the fuck up and let me think."

12

Part-time park ranger Dave Dewars was also cold, hungry, and thinking. He was thinking about heading over to the Mister Donut shop in Grafton and having a hot cup of decaf and a chocolate cruller, and maybe flirting a little with Mary, the waitress there.

He slowed his Jeep Cherokee on the park road. Just ahead was a fire access road that he could turn around in. He was supposed to make a complete round of the park, but what the hell? It was wintertime. There was no one in here besides him. He'd done enough patrolling this morning for the piddling sum the county paid him. They even made him use his own vehicle, for Christ's sake. And the road just past the fire access road was unplowed, making for a slippery, bumpy ride if he were to go on.

Fuck that, Dave thought. No way I'm putting my baby through that kind of punishment today. It's too cold. He figured he could finish his rounds on Thursday. Who would know? He only made rounds twice a week in the winter—it could wait.

He approached the fire access road and slowed the Jeep. He was about to turn in when he saw fresh tire tracks in the snow of the unplowed road. Dave stopped the Jeep and sat staring at the tracks. They hadn't been there on his last trip through the park last week. Whoever had made them didn't seem to care about covering their tracks. Probably a couple of kids had come out here parking over the weekend. Hell, he'd done it when he was in high school.

He started to put the Jeep in reverse, to turn around, but hesitated. He looked at the tracks again. There were only two tire tracks. Either the vehicle making them had backed out of the access road, which was a dead end, following exactly the tracks it had made going in, or the vehicle was still in there.

Dave Dewars shut off the engine and got out, crouching next to the Jeep to look at the tire tracks. This was something he liked to do on his rounds—stopping to study tracks in the snow. He looked at all kinds of tracks—animals, birds, vehicles. Sometimes he liked to fantasize that he was an Indian scout or a mountain man, but mostly he liked to make believe he was Sherlock Holmes. More often than not, though, no matter how hard Dave stared at a set of tracks, whether animal or vehicle, he couldn't tell anything from them. He told himself he could, though. He made up all sorts of things that he imagined he could see in the tracks. Looking at these tire tracks in the snow, he decided they were made by a 1995 Ford Explorer whose front end was slightly out of alignment and was driven by a man weighing three hundred pounds.

He had no basis for these conclusions, but he liked the way they sounded as he muttered them, staring seriously at the ground, feeling like a real goddamned detective and not just some flunky park ranger. Dave decided that the driver of the Ford had been smart enough, or lucky enough, to follow his own tracks out, when he heard a voice shouting, and not that far away.

"Shut the fuck up!" was all Dave caught, though

there was more. Dave quickly forgot all about his detective fantasy. There *really* was someone in there, in the park illegally!

He immediately thought of poachers. The county commissioner had warned him of them when he'd started the job a year and a half ago. Stories of winter poachers had been what had spurred the county to hire a part-time ranger to make winter patrols in the first place. Blackstone Park was home to a large population of red fox, about the only animal pelt that would bring any serious money if collected in sufficient quantity. There were also deer that could be targeted by illegal hunters. Whoever it was, Dave had to do something about it.

Dave went back to the Jeep and stood, his hand on the door, trying to decide what to do. He mentally kicked himself for not buying a gun, as he was going to do last summer. All he had for a weapon was a can of Mace in the glove compartment. He got in the Jeep and took out the Mace. Tucking it in his pocket, he got out and started following the tire tracks on foot.

They didn't go far, veering off the access road about twenty-five yards in, through an opening in the pine trees. Dave knew there was a nice little glen through there that was a favorite spot of picnickers in the summer.

He stopped next to the closest pine and crouched, listening. There were no more voices, no sound of an engine. He knew that whoever was in the park, their vehicle had to have four-wheel drive, or they'd never have attempted to go off the road in this snow the way they had. Which meant, if they got tipped to his presence, they could escape in any direction.

For a moment, Dave was going to go back to his Jeep and radio for help on his CB, but then he thought better of it. If it was poachers or illegal hunters in a four-wheel vehicle, they might just have a CB too and use it as a warning system. If he radioed for assistance now, they might get tipped off and get away without him ever getting a good look at them or a description of their vehicle.

Dave knew what he had to do. Picking his path carefully so as not to make any more noise than was necessary, he followed the tire tracks through the opening in the pine trees. Several yards off the road, the tracks went through a thin wall of laurel bushes. Dave stepped behind a thick pine tree and peered around it. The poachers were in the glen, all right. Dave didn't seem to notice that their vehicle was a van and not a Ford Explorer.

He could see one man in the clearing standing near the rear of the van. The guy was huge. Dave estimated him to be six foot nine, maybe more, and three hundred pounds at least, which made Dave smile that his guess had been right. He appeared to be alone, and Dave could see no weapons.

He was just about to circle around the glen to be able to read the license plate on the van, when he felt the cold muzzle of a gun against the back of his head. He had time to utter two words: "Oh, God!" before his brains were splattered all over the pine tree in front of him.

Gary jumped at the sound of the pistol shot. "Rod!" he cried in a weak, desperate voice. For a moment, he had a vision of Rod lying dead in the snow, shot in the back by some gun-happy local cop, leaving Gary all alone. He'd been alone for most of his life due to either his size or his lack of intelligence. He'd never been able to make friends easily. And when he did, it had been with a bad group who only wanted him around for his muscle and his willingness to take orders. It wasn't surprising that when the gang finally got busted for an armored car robbery, the two others, besides Gary, who got caught copped a plea and turned state's evidence against him, leaving him holding the bag and doing a full sentence of ten to twenty.

His ten years in prison had been more of the same—being a loner, most guys too afraid of his size to do anything but avoid him. Though he was ashamed of it and embarrassed about it, he had let prison gang members use him for sex. He knew he could have stopped them, he was strong enough, but he let them do it because it was a kind of acceptance and he was starved for even a morsel.

That had all changed when Rod entered the picture. Gary had been in the weight room with seven of the Soledad gang members. They had paid off a guard to give them some privacy and were taking turns sodomizing Gary, making jokes all the while about how he was big on the outside but nothing but a little faggot on the inside. That didn't bother Gary too much. Whatever little self-respect he had ever owned had long since been trampled and extinguished.

But what they were doing to Gary had bothered Rod Baylor. He had been passing by the weight room and had seen and heard the Soledads using and abusing Gary. A racist and a homophobe, the sight of a big white guy being gang-raped by a bunch of wiseass spics had been too much for him. He had quickly gotten together a dozen members of his own gang, the Iron Fist, bribed the guard again, and gone in the weight room, freeing Gary and nearly beating to death the gang of Puerto Ricans. From that day on, Gary had belonged to the Iron Fist, and he became Rod's shadow. He was as devoted to Rod as a dog is to its master. Though he didn't like the way Rod acted a lot of the time, and he didn't like it when Rod called him names, Gary knew he'd be lost without him. Rod was his friend. The only friend he'd ever had.

Gary ran in the direction of the gunshot and was relieved to see Rod emerge from a bramble of laurel bushes a short distance away.

"Rod! What happened? I heard a shot!"

Rod reached back into the bushes and pulled a man's body out by the collar of his jacket. Most of the man's head was gone, and his brains dripped into the snow at Rod's feet.

"Oh, shit!" Gary gasped. "Not another one! Why, Rod? Why'd you do it?"

"Because I had to, Dumbfuck!" Rod screamed at Gary. "He's a park pig. We've got to get out of here right now. He probably radioed the state cops and told them where we are."

Rod ran to the van, got in, and started it. He motioned frantically for Gary to get in. Gary hesitated, not wanting to just leave the body there in the snow, but he could see Rod was getting mad, so he got in too.

"But why'd you have to kill him, Rod? You been killing an awful lot of people. I don't know much, but I know that ain't good."

Rod laughed, checked to make sure the van was in four-wheel drive, and put it in gear. "Don't ever let anyone tell you you don't know nothing, Einstein. You don't have to know nothing—when you're as big as you are, who gives a shit. If you'd only realize that, you could've had it pretty smooth. As for killing, well, it was either him or us. I don't know about you, but I'll always choose us. Now let's get the fuck out of here." Rod tromped on the gas, and the van rumbled and slid through the snow and bushes, out of the glen. Gary looked back at the body and wished they had at least covered it up with something.

They came out of the woods onto the access road a short distance from Dave Dewar's Jeep Cherokee. Rod pulled the van alongside and got out. He opened the Cherokee's door, looking in, then got in. "Hey, Gary," he called a moment later. "I think we're in luck. His CB radio isn't even on. I don't think he radioed in about us after all."

Gary got out of the van and went over to the Cherokee, where Rod was just getting out of the driver's side. He had turned the Cherokee's CB on and put the volume up. Gary started to ask him what he was doing, but Rod hushed him. After several minutes of listening to static and sporadic transmissions on the CB, Rod turned to Gary.

"For a change, we're in luck. That dumbfuck didn't radio anyone about us. Probably thought we were a couple of kids. Come on. Let's ditch this Jeep in the woods and get the fuck out of here."

Gary didn't comment or ask questions, but he was thinking that Rod had killed the park ranger for nothing. It seemed to Gary that *all* the people Rod had killed since the robbery were people he really hadn't had to kill. Gary was starting to suspect that Rod just enjoyed killing people and didn't need much of a reason to do so. He'd always known his friend was violent, but he'd never really seen his killing side. Gary decided he didn't like it.

Rod drove the Cherokee off the access road and into the trees. Gary followed on foot. Rod drove to the edge of a steep embankment, stopped the Jeep, and got out. "Help me," he called to Gary. Together they pushed the Jeep over the edge of the embankment and watched as it crashed down through the snow and laurel bushes, ending up nosefirst, the front end buried in the snow, looking as if it had fallen out of the sky.

Next they got the body of the park ranger and put him near the Jeep, in the gully. Using branches, they brushed snow over the body and the Jeep, then covered them with the branches. When they were finished, someone would have had to be right next to the Jeep to see it.

"With any luck, he won't be found until we're out of New England," Rod said, surveying their work.

"Where we going, Rod?" Gary asked.

"First stop, New Jersey. I know a guy in Newark that I was in the pen with. If he's still on the outside, he can help us unload these goods so we can get some dough and head for Mexico. If he ain't there, we head for upstate New York, in the Catskills, where another ex-con I know can help us. It's time we stopped fucking around. We hang around this area much longer, we're going to be dead meat."

They reached the van and got in, Rod driving.

"Let's get the fuck out of here," Rod said. He started the vehicle and pulled onto the access road.

13

Deedee stood staring at the buttons on the telephone for a long time, receiver in hand, held to her ear. On the telephone table next to the phone, her address book lay open to the number she wanted, though she didn't really need to look it up. She had committed it to memory some time ago. With a trembling hand, she started to punch the numbers, then hesitated and depressed the disconnect button. She took a deep breath, closed her eyes, opened them, and dialed the number.

It rang only four times before being answered, but the wait seemed interminable to Deedee. A woman's voice came on.

"Hello?"

Deedee hung up, cursing softly. She dialed again. It was picked up on the second ring this time. Again the woman answered, again Deedee hung up.

She started to dial again, stopped, and put the receiver down. She forced herself to count to one hundred three times before dialing again. This time she held her breath and kept her fingers crossed, silently praying that the woman would not pick up the phone again. Her prayer was answered.

"Hello?"

His voice sounded angry, but Deedee didn't care. To her, he sounded like salvation.

"Jesse?" she managed to say, her voice thick and her throat tight with sudden emotion.

"Who is this?" His voice was still angry but was leavened with a tone of uncertainty.

"Oh, Jesse!" she stammered, and had to stop, take a deep breath, regain control. "It's me. It's Deedee."

"Deedee?" Now there was a note of relief, shadowed with doubt (or was it uncomfortableness?), in his voice.

"Did you just call here?"

"Yeah."

"Why'd you hang up?"

"I'm sorry. I don't know. I—I—just wanted to talk to you." Then the tears came, sobbing, hitching tears.

"Hey! What is it? What's wrong? Are you okay?" Concern filled his voice, and it comforted Deedee.

"I need you, Jesse. I need . . ." Her words were lost in a renewal of sobbing.

The uncomfortableness was suddenly back in his voice, full force. She could imagine him standing there, in his kitchen probably, his fiancée standing nearby, at the stove maybe. Deedee realized that he had every right to feel uncomfortable, the way she sounded. She was putting him in an uncomfortable position. And she was about to make it even more uncomfortable.

"Hey. Deedee. Come on. I thought we got through all this a long time ago. It's been two years. I—"

She cut him off. "It's not that, Jesse. It's not what you think." She took another deep breath, steadying herself.. "I need to talk to you. I need to see you. I need your help."

"Why? What's wrong?"

"I can't—I don't want to talk about it on the phone. Can I meet you somewhere? I can drive down to Helena."

Within half an hour, she was in her car and on

the turnpike, driving to Helena. Jesse had agreed to meet her at a Dunkin' Donuts not far from his apartment and had given her directions how to get there.

Deedee wondered what Jesse was telling his fiancée. Deedee had never met her, didn't even know her name. She'd heard through a mutual friend that Jesse was engaged. She'd gone on an eating binge for three days, making herself sick with Twinkies and Funny Bones by the dozen.

Deedee wondered if Jesse's financée was anything like her. She was probably the complete opposite. Deedee wasn't sure which would upset her more. If Jesse's fiancée were a lot like her, then that meant Jesse had continued to love her after they split and had looked for someone like her. If she was the opposite of Deedee, that meant, well—that was obvious.

This is stupid, she thought, slowing on the highway until an eighteen-wheeler coming up fast behind her startled her with a blast from its horn. She pulled to the right and let the truck pass, flipping the driver the finger as he went by. She thought about taking the next exit and turning around, going home, and then her eyes caught the sun glistening off the mountain peaks not far off. It reminded her of the day she and Jesse had gone hiking in the mountains surrounding Missoula. It had been at this exact time of day, with the sun low and peeking from behind the mountaintops, that Jessie had told her it was over between them.

Deedee knew at the time that she should have been expecting it. After all, it was par for the course, wasn't it? Every man she had ever dared to love had left her eventually. And they had all left for one reason—they couldn't deal with her near-death experiences every time they made love to her.

Jesse, she had thought before the breakup, was different. He had been more curious than frightened by her collapses, once he knew they were a common occurrence for her. He had questioned her extensively about her experiences and had suggested a dozen explanations.

For the first time in her sexual life, Deedee had begun to feel really comfortable with a man while making love. She began to trust Jesse. She knew that when she had an orgasm and stepped out of her body for a while, she wouldn't come back to find herself dumped in the bed—or worse, the floor—and her lover gone, running scared because he thought he had killed her.

But then all that had changed, been shattered that day in the mountains, when he told her it was over, and all she could think about was how beautiful he was, standing there in the late afternoon sun.

Same old same old.

"It's because of sex, isn't it?" she had asked in a dull monotone, when it had finally sunk in that he was leaving her.

Jesse had looked at her for a long time, with a look he had that made her feel as if he had X-ray vision and was looking right inside her brain and reading her innermost thoughts and feelings. "That would be the easy way out," he'd said at last. "I'm sure it's what you think, and probably what you've come to expect, but it's not the reason I'm leaving."

That had gotten Deedee's attention. "Then why? What's wrong? What did I do wrong?"

Jesse had become a little angry then. "Why do you think you did something? Why are you always so ready to blame yourself for everything? The truth is, Deedee, I just don't love you. I mean, I do in a way, as a person I care about, a friend, but not as someone I want to spend the rest of my life with. We've been together for three years. If I don't love you that way by now, it isn't going to happen."

Deedee was stunned, shocked. How could it be that he didn't love her? True, she had never heard him say the words *I love you*, no matter how many times she had said them to him, but she had just thought that he was the type of guy who didn't like to verbally express his emotions. His actions seemed to express his love for her so much better than words anyway. He was so good to her: kind, gentle, understanding, empathetic. No man had ever treated her that way, so when Jesse did, she thought it was because he was in love with her. It had never occurred to her, until that day in the mountains, that Jesse was just a really nice guy who treated everyone that way.

Deedee could have handled his leaving her because of the sex thing, but his leaving her because he didn't love her was crushing. The shock was so great that it took several days for it to sink in. When it did, she was devastated, crying constantly, suffering severe attacks of depression where she didn't get out of bed for days at a time.

After the depression, she had entered another phase. Instead of being mature and accepting what Jesse had told her, she vowed to win him back. During periods of adrenalized energy, she wrote him letters, called him at work and at home, bought him gifts, and stalked him in her car, following him everywhere.

Finally he had confronted her and told her it was over, finished, *done*. He told her that he wanted to remain her friend, but not if she was going to keep acting so crazy. He claimed he still cared very much for her and that if she ever needed his help, he would give it, but their love relationship was through.

She had accepted it then. After a few more weeks of tears and depression, she gave up and, with some difficulty, began to put Jesse behind her. Until today, she hadn't spoken to him in two years, though she'd thought of him often. She had never considered staying in touch "as a friend"—it would have been too painful. Besides, Deedee figured his offer of continued friendship had been the kind of standard crap people say to someone when they want to lessen the hurt of a breakup, but it never worked that way. All it really did was ease the conscience of the person doing the breaking up.

But now she needed someone like Jesse—she needed Jesse. As she drove to Helena, unmindful of the traffic around her, she hoped fervently that his agreeing to meet with her meant that he intended to stand by his last words to her: "Call if you ever need anything."

14

Deedee found the Dunkin' Donuts easily enough. It was right off the first exit for Helena. She drove through the parking lot looking for Jesse's motorcycle but didn't see it. Of course, she realized, he probably had a different vehicle by now. She sighed and checked her watch. He'd said to meet him there at 4:30, and it was 4:35 now.

He's probably inside, she thought, parking her car. Or maybe he had been there and left. If that was the case, then she'd just have to call him again at home. But deep down she knew she wouldn't do that. If he hadn't been able to wait more than a few minutes for her, then that meant he was really uncomfortable about meeting with her, and no matter how much she needed help, she couldn't put him through anything that would make him feel so weird.

"Might as well go in," she mumbled to herself as she got out of the car. She was so sure Jesse wouldn't be inside that she was quite shocked when she walked through the door and there he was, sitting in a corner booth, nursing a coffee and staring out the window at the traffic going by. He looked up, saw her, and smiled.

Up until that moment, Deedee had been unsure of what she was about to do. But when he smiled at her—and not a self-conscious, uncomfortable, wish-I-was-anywhere-but-here smile, but a true, sincere, glad-to-see-you-it's-been-too-long smile—she knew she had done the right thing. Jesse would help. She could count on him.

She sat across from him, and they stared at each other for several minutes. "Hi," he said at last. "Would you like a coffee?" She nodded, and he went to the counter to get her one. When he returned, he studied her face with concern. She knew he was looking at her bruises. They had begun to fade, and she had spent a long time on her makeup, trying to cover them. She had done a good enough job that a person passing on the street wouldn't notice, but indoors, in direct lighting, they were still visible.

"What happened to you, Dee?" he asked.

She started to answer, was overwhelmed with a sudden flood of emotions, and mentally kicked herself. She took a deep breath, calmed down, and started over.

"Some asshole tried to rape me."

Jesse was shocked and very concerned, which made Deedee feel good. It meant he still cared. He asked several questions, rapid fire, until she had to laugh, and he realized he wasn't giving her time to answer.

"Did you go to the police?" he asked.

"No," she answered, averting her eyes.

"Why not? Was it someone you know?"

"Look, Jesse, I didn't come here to talk about that. Well, I did, but that whole episode was just a part of a much bigger thing that I need your help with."

"What?" he asked quietly, and a touch uneasily.

She launched into the story of Anna Wheaton, hesitantly at first, but soon the words were pouring out of her at such a rate that she could barely find time to take a breath. Jesse listened quietly for the most part, nodding and saying yes as prods for her to continue when she paused. She ended with telling him about the near-rape by Dick, and the dream she kept having about Anna and the Shadow Monster.

Her coffee was untouched and cold by the time she finished. Jesse finished his and went up and got another one before saying anything. "I saw *America's Most Wanted*. Saw that little girl on there," he said quietly, stirring his coffee. He sipped, licked his lips, put the cup down, and looked at Deedee.

"So why come to me? What do you want?"

Deedee had to fight to contain the conflicting emotions of exultation and dread that suddenly surfaced within her. She could have kissed him right then and there for his immediate acceptance of what she had told him. He showed no doubt, no expression of you-must-be-crazy; just simple, sincere, acceptance. Jesse, as he always had, understood and believed. But the dread came from the way he asked "What do you want?" It was said defensively, not helpfully. The way he said it hit home the fact that their relationship was over and had been for a long time. Jesse was engaged to another woman. Suddenly she was certain that this was a huge mistake. How could she expect him to consent to do what she was about to ask of him?

He agreed to meet me, didn't he? she asked herself in answer. That had to say something for the way he still felt toward her, or maybe for the memories of her that he cherished. Maybe.

"This is kind of awkward," Deedee mumbled. Jesse said nothing, just sat, staring at her and sipping his coffee. Deedee had the feeling that he knew what she was going to ask him, but he was going to make her say it. She took a deep breath.

"Jesse, I've got to help that little girl somehow. If I don't, the Shadow Monster will get her, or she'll just end up lost in that Limbo forever. I don't know what I can do—maybe talk her back into her body, help her heal herself, I don't know. But I've got to do something. The thing is, I can't keep getting to the other side the way I have been. The incident with Dick proved to me how dangerous that is." She paused, giving Jesse a beseeching look, but he ignored it.

"Like I said, what do you want from me?"

She sighed. He wasn't going to cut her any slack at all. The hell with this, she thought. The worst he can do is say no, and that'll be the end of it.

"I was wondering, *hoping*, you might come and stay with me for a little while and help me get safely to the other side so that I can help Anna Wheaton," she said quickly. Jesse's expression didn't change, didn't show shock or surprise.

He leaned forward and spoke in a low voice. "You mean you want me to *fuck* you so you can get to the other side and help that girl," Jessie said, his tone of voice a trifle sarcastic.

"Crudely put, but yes," Deedee answered, smiling crookedly. Jesse looked at her, shook his head, and laughed.

At first, Deedee laughed along with him. But her laughter died out long before his. She sat there, smile frozen on her lips, and wondered how to interpret this reaction. He was laughing much too long. True, she had wanted to keep things light between them, especially considering the awkward subject, but his prolonged fit of hilarity was ridiculous.

Jesse continued to laugh, sitting back, arms outstretched along the top of the booth's back. Deedee became very uncomfortable. People were starting to stare.

"Cut it out, Jesse," she said quietly.

His laughter slowed to a chuckle. "You're incredible," he said, wiping a tear from the corner of his left eye, and then he was off to the mirth races again.

"Please stop," Deedee pleaded. She wasn't sure if he stopped because he caught the catch in her voice revealing her unstable state of emotions, or if it was because people were staring. But he did stop.

"I'm sorry," he said a moment later, a touch of a giggle still in his voice. "But you come to me and ask if I'll come stay with you and have sex with you so that you can have a near-death experience to save a little girl trapped in Limbo. I'm sorry, but I can't help but find that amusing. I know you're serious, and I believe you, but it just struck me that that is a story the *National Enquirer* would pay good money for."

Deedee tried to relax and understand his reaction, but her instinct was to flee. Jesse had changed. He was mocking her. This wasn't the Jesse she had known and loved and thought she could trust no matter what.

"You're right. I'm sorry. Forget it," Deedee said quickly. "I should have known better. I'm sorry to have bothered you," she managed to say before the tears came. She got up and hurried out of the coffee shop to her car.

Jesse didn't follow. By the time she reached her Hyundai, the tears wouldn't stop. She felt ridiculous, foolish, humiliated. She sat in her car, keys in the ignition, crying for several minutes. She hated herself. She had been such an idiot to think he would help her with such a wacky request. And she hated herself even more for the fact that she was sitting there hoping he would come out after her and tell her he was sorry, that he'd be glad to help.

He did come out, several minutes later, but not to

seek her out. He got into a brown Jeep and drove away, not looking her way once. She fought the impulse to follow him and tried to stifle her tears. She wouldn't break apart again. Not this time. She started the car, backed out of the parking space, and headed for the highway back to Missoula.

"You're on your own," she said to her reflection in the rearview mirror. "You're on your own."

Deedee was unaware of how fast she drove back to Missoula. Where it had seemed to take forever to get to Helena, the ride home felt as though it had taken mere minutes. It was bad enough what she was feeling—humiliation and degradation—but through it all, Anna Wheaton remained foremost in her mind. During the drive back to Missoula, when she could barely see the road through her tears and Jesse's rejection should have been dominating her thoughts, she couldn't stop thinking of Anna. At one point, she'd had the strangest feeling that the girl was very close, trying to communicate with her.

"I must be losing my mind," she said aloud as she turned the Hyundai onto Main Street and headed the two blocks for home. A part of her actually wished that were true. At least if she were crazy, she could get help. But there was no doctor who could help her with what ailed her.

15

Newark was a farce.

Newark was a joke. Worse, Newark was a near disaster. Rod and Gary were lucky to get out alive. Though Rod suspected that Gary didn't have a clue as to how close they had come to dying, Rod did. The funny thing was, it had left him with a strange exultation, an excitement, an energy that jittered through his nerves and made his muscles twitch in weird rhythmic patterns.

Rod marveled at how similar the high from killing someone was to the high from almost being killed and surviving. Of course, he preferred the former—that was a high he could control. But when circumstances forced the latter upon you, you had to go with the flow and dig it as much as possible, because the alternative was to never dig anything again, ever.

Still, he didn't like it when things went wrong, which had happened from moment one in Newark. He'd decided to try his connection first, a big black ex-con by the name of Rashid whom he'd met while doing time in Rahway prison in New Jersey. Rashid was the leader of the biggest gang in Newark, the Blades. Rod and Rashid had been anything but friends in prison. Both were racists; Rashid hated whites as much as, if not more than, Rod hated blacks, Hispanics, and Orientals. But they had always had a paranoid, hateful respect for each other's strengths.

The Blades had also been the biggest gang inside Rahway, thanks to Rashid's influence. Rod had been the leader of a relatively small gang of white supremacists called the Swaztikas, who were so completely gonzo that no one bothered them. Rod and Rashid's bond had formed when the Puerto Rican gang, the Comancheros, had tried to get uppity and take control of the black-market operations away from the Blades and Rod's gang. The Blades controlled the sale of narcotics and male prostitutes within the prison, while Rod's gang made moonshine whiskey, mostly for distribution to their own members, but they would also sell it at a high price to prisoners outside the gang. The Comancheros, who had been getting their drugs and booze at exhorbitant prices from the Blades and the Swaztikas, decided to go into business for themselves. Their threat had brought Rod and Rashid's gangs together in an effective, if uneasy, coalition against the common enemy.

Rod and Rashid were paroled at the same time, more than ten years ago, four years before Rod had been incarcerated at Walpole prison in Massachusetts, where he had met Gary and the Wayne brothers. Rod knew Rashid might well be in prison again by now, or dead, but he had to try. The Blades controlled a massive drug operation in Newark. Rod knew he could get top dollar there for the goods they'd stolen from Middlesex Hospital, as long as Rashid was still in charge. If he wasn't, Rod knew they ran a very real risk of having their throats slit and their being dumped in some landfill. But Rashid and Rod had promised each other, upon leaving prison at the same time, that if ever the other was on their turf, they could expect safe passage. Rod hoped Rashid would remember that and would like the drugs enough to help him out. If everything went well, it would only be a matter of days before he and Gary could be on their way to Mexico and the good life. The drive there hadn't taken too long, heading south on Interstate 95. Six hours of straight driving had gotten them there in the early evening, only to find that Rashid was dead of AIDS. The new leader of the Blades was an evil-looking punk named Leon, who must have had a very large hatred of Rashid. As soon as Rod had mentioned the deceased Blades leader, Leon had lost it, and Rod and Gary had almost bit the Big One. If Rod hadn't had the Uzi, or if it had jammed on him, they wouldn't have made it out of there alive. The Blades understood the power of such a weapon, and none of them were equally armed. While holding them off at gunpoint in the parking lot of an abandoned strip mall, Rod found out that Rashid had died—and more importantly, as far as Leon was concerned, he had given AIDS to Leon's sister before he died. Rod understood then the new Blades leader's hatred of Rashid.

Rod realized then that this deal wasn't going to work. Leon couldn't see beyond his own hatred of Rashid far enough to discuss any deals. Rod and Gary made it back to the van and took off, with the Blades giving chase in their beat-up cars and souped-up hot rods. The police got involved and actually saved Rod and Gary's butts, but Rod was sure the cops got a make on the van too.

Since leaving Newark city limits, Rod had stayed off the main roads and looked for another vehicle to steal. There were plenty of cars available but a sudden dearth of trucks or vans that could hold all the stolen drugs.

Eventually they came upon a vast parking lot

surrounding a large old paper mill. Rod killed the van's lights and cruised the parking lot's perimeter until he found a cherry red Ford pickup truck with a wide bed. He pulled behind it, and while Gary transferred the drugs from the van to the truck, Rod popped the ignition with a screwdriver he found in the glove compartment and hot-wired it. Rod parked the van behind a large snowbank at the far end of the lot, and he and Gary were back on the road, back in business.

Now the Catskills were their last chance of getting rid of their goods and getting enough money to get away. Rod told Gary to head for the highway while he broke out some coke and snorted several lines. He couldn't remember the last time he had really slept well, but that was okay. The coke was keeping him going.

They passed over a bridge, heading for the on ramp to Route 24 North to upstate New York. In between snorts, Rod happened to glance down at the highway passing beneath the bridge. Just beyond the on ramp, state cops had set up a roadblock.

"Shit," Rod swore, and slammed his fist on the dash, spilling a good quantity of coke onto the floor. "We gotta find someplace to lay low." He told Gary to forget the highway and keep going. The immediate danger of the roadblock was thus averted, but Rod had no idea where they were or where they were going.

16

Anna was aware of the doctor probing her, testing her reflexes, but she had neither the strength nor the will nor the desire to respond. Her life had become a weird existence between her hospital room—the real world—and the strange other world where dead souls passed through on their way into the light or into the darkness of the other thing. She and the pretty woman seemed to be caught between the two, never able to enter the light, stalked by the dark monster.

She thought a lot about the pretty woman when she was back in her body, in the hospital bed. And when she was on the other side, she searched for the woman as long as she could, until the monster showed up. She wondered why she could return to her body whenever she wanted but couldn't get to the other side as easily.

It was hard to think clearly when she was inside her body. The combination of medications and the injuries she had suffered made the time she spent in her body a nether world of fleeting images, dreams, and storming emotions that left her thoughts all confused. She had no idea of the passing of time. Not that the other side was any different, as far as the passage of time was concerned. Time seemed to be slower on the other side. She could leave her body, setting off the life-monitoring alarms attached to it, spend what seemed like hours on the other side, yet still be back in her body before the doctors and nurses rushed into her room to revive her.

She dipped into unconsciousness and came to the surface again. Aunt Kara was by the bed, crying and lightly holding Anna's hand in both of hers. Anna wished she could respond and make Aunt Kara understand that she was okay. She tried, but the opposite happened. She left her body, suddenly floating on the ceiling, looking down at her prone body in the bed, the alarms going off, and Aunt Kara screaming for a doctor. It all telescoped away until it became a bubble floating near her, and she was amid the crazy vegetation of the other side.

She didn't see the pretty woman anywhere. She began to concentrate on the woman's face, remembering what she looked like. She began to feel herself moving, gliding through the thick atmosphere under a power not her own, as if being drawn by something. A reality bubble appeared in the distance, and she was drawn to it until she was enveloped by it.

Then she was back in the real world, but not in her hospital room. She was hovering over a highway, watching cars zip along below her. A small red car passed under her, and she was pulled along with it, literally sucked into it, where she floated in the backseat, looking with astonishment at the driver—the pretty woman. Anna felt a flood of images and emotions, mostly bad, run through her when she reached out her hand and touched the pretty woman's shoulder. There was the image of a man drinking coffee, and an overwhelming feeling of sadness and despair. She pulled her hand back, as if from a flame, the emotions were so intense. The moment she did, she was transported back to the other world, expunged from the pretty woman's life sphere, which floated lazily away from her.

Anna felt bad. The emotional pain she'd felt in the pretty woman made her want to cry. But the worst thing she had sensed was the despair and fear. The fear stayed with her now and made her look constantly behind her, afraid the monster was sneaking up on her. Anna wanted, *needed* to talk to the pretty woman when they were both in the other world, but it didn't look like that was going to happen soon. Questions about the woman flooded her mind: Who was she? Where did she come from? How did she get out of her body? She didn't seem to be physically hurt in the real world, the way Anna was. It occurred to Anna that the woman could leave her body on purpose, and that brought up the bigger question of why she would want to do that.

These were questions that were not going to be readily answered. Her sense that the monster was about to show up any second became stronger, pushing her toward panic. She escaped into her bubble and returned to her body.

17

They were waiting for her.

Deedee had no hint, no suspicion. Everything seemed normal She unlocked the door and went in. As soon as she closed the door, they were upon her, coming out of the darkness of her apartment.

After the initial shock and scare, she wasn't really surprised that it was Dick. What did surprise and terrify her was that he had two burly friends with him. Deedee thought that a man like Dick would have preferred to batter and abuse his women in private, but he had obviously discovered a couple of kindred souls.

One of them grabbed her from behind, arms across her chest, a hand clamped over her mouth. The lights came on, and Dick got right in her face, grinning evilly.

"Told you I'd get you, bitch," he said menacingly to Deedee. To his friends he added, "It's bang gang time, boys." His friends laughed.

"Don't you mean *gang bang*?"

It was Dick's turn to laugh. "No, no, no," he said. "First she gets the bang gang, then she gets the gang bang."

He began to beat her.

It was the flashes of light that brought her back to consciousness. The laser beams of color beyond description brought her out of the depths of darkness, and she realized she was going over to the other side.

But how had she gotten here? She couldn't remember. Sex was usually how she got out of her body, but she couldn't remember having sex. Was it with Jesse? She remembered going to see him—but no, he had turned her down.

Then what had happened?

The ride through time and space ended as she emerged from her life sphere and watched it telescope away to a small bubble that floated nearby. She found herself floating an inch or two above the fungus floor of Limbo. She didn't sense the Shadow Monster anywhere nearby, but neither did she sense the presence of Anna Wheaton.

She began floating aimlessly, listening to the weird hum of the strange life around her. Her thoughts returned to how she had gotten over this time. She couldn't remember a thing after seeing Jesse.

A sudden chill made her shiver.

Why couldn't she remember?

Deedee began to grow frustrated. There was one way she could find out—she had to go back into her life sphere and return to her body. Strangely enough, that was the last thing she wanted to do. She felt a horrible sense of panic and fear just at the thought. What was going on?

She pushed the panic and fear away. This was what she'd wanted anyway, wasn't it? Hadn't she been trying to get over to the other side for over a week, so she could find and help Anna Wheaton? Well, here she was. She had to make the best of it.

Speaking of which, where was Anna? An overwhelming fear that the Shadow Monster had gotten her enveloped Deedee. Maybe her dream had come true, had been a premonition of reality. Maybe she was too late.

A bubble appeared very small in front of her and began to expand. Deedee backed away, then stopped. She could see the scene becoming clearer inside the growing bubble. It was a hospital room. In the bed was a child with tubes and wires running from her body to an array of electronic equipment, monitors, and IV poles.

It was Anna Wheaton.

18

Anna was drifting away again, sliding down that long slippery slide into oblivion. She was tired, a tired that left her feeling drained until she felt invisible. Sometimes it was nice to go down the slide and into the river of nothingness at the bottom. Like she was going to now, except—

There was someone in the room with her. She felt a presence pulling her back from the brink of unconsciousness. She didn't want to go back. She was too tired. And lately an intriguing idea had developed that if she went deep enough into the river at the bottom of the slide, she'd come out the other side, where the light would finally consume her, and she'd be with her mom and dad, and then she wouldn't have to worry about anything again, not revenge, not anything. If she could just be with her parents again, she'd be happy.

But now, here was someone disturbing that plan.

Against her will, she was drawn back to consciousness and beyond, rising straight through wakefulness and out of her body. It happened so quickly that she had the strange sensation that she had been squeezed through a very small hole, guts first.

Something was coming through from the other side, entering her life sphere. At first she was terrified that it was the monster come to eat her, but her heightened senses told her no. There was a popping sound and a rush of air, and suddenly the pretty woman was there, floating near the ceiling over her bed.

Anna stared in awe at her. She looked different. Her entire being had a golden glow to it that was beautiful to look at. Anna knew what that glow meant. It was the same glow she'd seen on every other person she'd seen on the other side, just before the light came for them and whisked them off to Heaven.

The pretty woman was dying.

Anna flew to her. *"You have to go back to your body!"* she shouted. *"You're dying. If you don't go back to your body now, the light will come for you . . . or—"* Anna couldn't finish the thought, couldn't mention the monster, couldn't put into words her fear that the evil thing, and not the light, would consume her new friend.

"What do you mean?" the pretty woman asked. *"I've been waiting so long to talk to you, I can't go back now."*

"You have to," Anna pleaded. *"You're beginning to glow. That means you're dying. Soon you'll go to Heaven, or . . ."*

"Yeah, or the other place. The Shadow Monster," the woman said. *"Yeah, I get your drift."*

"The Shadow Monster," Anna repeated softly. *"So that's its name. I just call it the monster."*

The pretty woman laughed. *"That's good enough for me."*

"No," Anna said. *"The Shadow Monster fits it better. But never mind that now. I'm telling you, you've got to get back to your body."*

"I don't know if that's such a good idea," the pretty woman replied. *"I . . . I'm afraid to."*

"You've got to try."

The pretty woman turned and reached out to her life sphere, but it remained small and out of reach.

"I can't."

Anna held out her hands. *"Concentrate on your body and your home. I'll help you picture them."*

"How do you know what my home looks like?" the pretty woman asked.

"I don't, but if I touch you while you're thinking about it, I'll be able to see it too. But we have to do it fast—your color is changing."

Deedee looked at herself and saw that her aura was a different shade of soft glowing yellow. The color of imminent death. What could be happening to her body? she wondered. How could she be so close to death? She wasn't sick, or at least she couldn't remember being sick. Was that why she'd been so afraid to go back? Had something horrible happened to her? Had she been in a car accident on her way back from seeing Jesse? All these thoughts and worse raced through her mind.

Anna took hold of her hands. *"Come on. You've got to get back."*

Deedee didn't want to, but the girl was insistent. They held hands, and Anna said, *"Think of your home. Think of your body waiting for you to return. I found that brings my bubble to me."*

Deedee listened, fear building in her, not wanting to go back, not wanting to see what bad thing was happening to her physical being. She knew it was going to involve pain, and she hated pain. But the bigger fear of losing her life overrode all the other fears, and she did as Anna bade her. She began visualizing her body in bed, though she had no idea if that was where she'd been when she left it. She closed her eyes and concentrated harder, Anna's hands clenched tightly in her own.

"Look!" Anna said breathlessly.

Deedee opened her eyes. Her bubble was coming closer, growing as it did. Out of the corner of her eye, in the distance, she saw the distinct blue aura of another soul moving toward them, but then her bubble blotted it out as it expanded. She got a very clear picture of her bedroom, with herself lying on the bed, fixed in her mind, and the bubble began to grow quickly, closer. Suddenly it was large enough for her to see figures within. She wasn't in her bedroom, and she wasn't alone.

The bubble reached her, pulling her in. She held on to Anna's hands, pulling the girl in with her. They emerged just under the ceiling of her living room. What they saw below them made Anna cry out in fear, and Deedee cringe as if in pain.

In the middle of her living room, a kitchen chair had been set, and Deedee's body was tied to it with cut electrical cords from kitchen appliances. She was sitting upright. She was naked, but so dressed in blood that at first glance, it was hard to tell.

Dick stood over her, bloody fists clenched, debating which part of her body he was going to maul next. His two goons were standing on either side on the chair, drinking beer and watching as Dick beat the shit out of some woman they didn't even know and had never seen before.

Deedee stared in shock at the scene. Who were the men with Dick, and why would they want to hurt her? In that moment, Deedee realized what a hopeless romantic she had been for ever thinking that all people were basically good. Here were two prime examples of the truth—men, fairly normal appearing and good looking, who found it visually and sexually exciting to watch another man beat a woman to death.

But they would only watch for so long.

"Hey, man! Enough of the bang. Let's get on with

the *gang* bang," one of the men said. He was heavyset, athletic looking, with thinning blond hair.

Dick looked at him, then back at Deedee. "There'll be plenty of time for that." He stepped back, cocked his right arm, and punched Deedee in the breasts.

Watching, dread and fear turned immediately to anger and fury in Deedee. Without realizing what she was doing, she rushed at the blond man closest to Dick. With a sound like a very large zipper being closed, her spirit entered his flesh and she was inside him. Before the man could recover from the shock of feeling an alien mind inside his own, she moved his arm, grabbing the heavy ceramic two-gallon Boston baked bean pot with the spider plant in it that was on a tall three-legged stool next to him, and brought it crashing down on Dick's skull.

Dick went down like a shot, a good deal of blood gushing from a considerable dent on the side of his head. Immediately she was expunged from the blond man's body and mind, and he staggered as if dizzy. The other man looked with horror and disbelief at what his friend had done.

The front door was suddenly kicked opened, and Jesse was there. He took one look at what was going on and charged in. The two goons were too stunned by what had just happened to react. Jesse glanced quickly at the bleeding, naked Deedee tied to the chair and went into action. He cold-cocked the nearest goon, the blond, who was still stunned and confused from Deedee's possession of his body. Jesse's fist flattened his nose, and he went down to his knees, both hands going to his face as blood spurted from between his fingers. His eyes rolled into his head, and he collapsed sideways onto the living room rug. The other guy, though much bigger than Jesse, started backing away, eyes searching for an avenue of escape. He backed against the bookshelf, grabbed a dictionary, and flung it as Jesse. When Jesse ducked, the guy bolted for the door.

Anna saw this, saw that he was going to escape. "No!" she cried, and felt a burst of energy flow from her mind toward the man. Just as he reached the door, it slammed on him, hitting him in the side of the head and knocking him to the floor. Jessie pounced on him, straddling his chest and pounding his face mercilessly until it was a mass of bloody flesh and the man was unconscious.

Jesse got off the man and went to Deedee's side. He untied her and pulled her into his arms. "Oh, God, Dee. What did they do to you?" He picked her up and carried her into the bedroom, putting her carefully on the bed. He became visibly choked with emotion as he looked at her battered, bloodied body. With his hand trembling, he dialed 911 and, in a cracking emotional voice, spouted out that he needed an ambulance and the police and gave the address of Deedee's apartment.

Deedee and Anna had followed him into the bedroom, passing through the wall, and now they floated over the bed, watching Jesse as he ran to the bathroom and got a wet washcloth. He returned to the bed and began gently washing the blood from her face.

Deedee looked at Anna, then down at Jesse ministering to her beaten body. She noticed that the glow of her aura had increased. She had to get back into her body. Anna nodded her agreement, though no words passed between them. Smiling at the girl, Deedee floated down to the bed and back into her physical being. She opened her eyes to see Jesse bending over her, wiping the blood from her face so gently and lovingly that it made her want to cry. Surprisingly, she felt no pain, only a numbness that was close to being paralyzed.

Jesse brightened when her eyes opened, becoming excited. "You're going to be okay, Dee. Just hang in there. The ambulance is on its way."

Outside, she could hear sirens approaching and stopping. "That's them," Jesse said, getting up. "You're going to be all right."

With an immense effort that brought such an intense pain that she nearly lost consciousness, Deedee reached up and grabbed his hand. "Don't go," she managed to say through her broken teeth and swollen lips. The effort cost her a great deal of pain, which was now spreading throughout her body, every nerve screaming out at the beating she had taken.

"I'm not going anywhere, Dee. I just got to let the cops and ambulance guys in," Jesse said, coming back to stroke her head and smile reassuringly.

"Promise me," Deedee barely whispered, feeling herself slipping into unconsciousness. "Help me. Promise."

Jesse looked solemnly at her poor beaten face and nodded to her. "I promise," he said softly.

Smiling, she let her mind drift away from the pain into cool unfeeling blackness.

three

Kevin and the Dead Guys

1

He would sit in the darkness for hours when thunderstorms rolled in from the ocean. He sat by the window, arms at his sides, head tilted slightly, as if listening for something beyond the rumble of thunder. Coming upon him in the darkness, one might have thought him asleep, until the lightning flashed and it became apparent that he was awake, eyes open, staring into the distance. He was immovable at these times, unreachable. It was the reason he lived alone.

The jump still came easy enough—it always had. And he had always looked forward to jumping, until recently. Now *he* was waiting for him. What bothered him most was knowing how long *he* had been waiting for him.

Twenty-six years.

Kevin Lucier sat in his wheelchair, in the darkness, struggling with the urge to jump and the fear of doing it. As they had so much lately, his thoughts turned back to the Nam. Pleiku City. The Tet Offensive.

His unit had just been ordered to hook up with A Company, First Battalion, 69th Armored Division on its way into the city. He and James, his best friend, had ended up walking behind a tank, entering Pleiku City at dawn.

Excitement had been the tone of the day.

Walking through the streets of a modern city torn by warfare, he had been able to imagine how his father must have felt in the Second World War. It was that sense of excitement that had brought on the foolish daydream that had left his guard down. And that had cost him his legs, and James's life.

He didn't have to try very hard to bring the memory vividly to mind: the tank, incredibly loud on the pavement; the stink of its blue smoke exhaust mingling with the clouds of dust it churned up from the filthy, rubble-strewn street; the smell of gasoline.

He saw a child in the window of a four-story apartment building, waving to him. Picturing himself in one of those old newsreels showing GIs liberating Paris, he waved back. That's when the attack came. From his side. And he wasn't ready. Didn't see it until it was too late.

Another kid ran out of the building. Couldn't have been more than twelve years old. He was carrying a portable one-shot, Soviet-made antitank rocket launcher. Before Kevin realized what the kid had, he was already down on one knee, firing the weapon at the tank.

A bright flash, a reverberating thud, and the entire undercarriage of the tank between the treads exploded. The tank reared up like a frightened stallion, came down hard, and began to do donuts in the street.

James never had a chance. The explosion sent hot oil into his face and eyes. He screamed and fell to his knees. The next moment, the tank whirled around, and he went under it, the sound of his body being crushed so horrible as to remain undescribable by Kevin to this day.

Kevin had barely had enough time to register

what had happened to James when the tank was spinning around again, coming at him. He tried to dive out of the way, but some shrapnel from the rocket had caught him in the left knee, knocking him to his side on the ground. He lunged to the side, rolling for the gutter, and knew, seconds before the tank rolled over his legs, that he wasn't going to make it. Those were the worst few seconds of his life—the dreadful anticipation of all that pain seared him. What was worse was seeing James's crumpled, bloody body being spit out from under the tank, just before the metal behemoth came on to take away his legs.

He shuddered at the memory and stared down at the remains of his legs, stumps ending just above both knees. He'd spent a long time, several years, wishing that tank had rolled over his head instead of his legs. He'd spent a long time in the VA hospital in San Francisco feeling sorry for himself, wishing he had died. And then he had discovered the thing he came to call jumping, and everything had changed.

The early days had been exhilarating. The more so because he'd discovered jumping quite by accident. He had gone to see a hypnotherapist at the suggestion of one of the other disabled vets at the VA hospital. The guy, a quadriplegic, had raved about it, saying that for a short time, while in a trance, he had got his legs and arms back.

Kevin hadn't believed him, hadn't believed that he'd ever know again the feeling of being whole, except maybe in his dreams. But the vet had gone on and on about how great it was, so that finally Kevin had decided to try it, if only to be able to shut the guy up. But the guy had been right, though Kevin's experience was vastly different. And an incredible experience it had been.

Kevin was like one of those people in a bad sitcom who swears they can never be hypnotized and then succumbs at the snap of a finger. The hypnotherapist was leading him through a wonderful hallucination of running along a beach, feeling his legs strong and pounding the sand beneath him, when something wonderful and fantastic happened. One minute he was running along the imaginary beach, exhilarated with the feeling of having his legs back, and the next he was on the ceiling, looking down at himself lying on the hypnotherapist's couch.

Over many more sessions, he had discovered that when he was out of his body, he could travel to any place he could imagine—all he had to do was picture it in his mind. He spent the following years traveling around the world and even into outer space. At first, he hadn't cared if it was a hallucination, or a dream, or whatever; he was just so happy to be having the experience. Eventually he began to realize that what he was experiencing was real.

It was from these experiences that he began to recover from his handicap. He started drawing again, a passion he'd had as a youth. Based on his out-of-body experience, he created the underground comic *Jumpers*, about three handicapped people who could leave their bodies and become, in effect, superheroes.

Jumping became like a drug to him. Neither cocaine nor heroin ever had a stronger hold on a man. Kevin knew he was addicted (as most addicts do), but he didn't care. Jumping *wasn't* a drug. He didn't think it was harmful, until he came back from a jump one day to find his body in a hospital, tubes and wires going in and out of him.

The doctors had been amazed at his quick recovery. He had shuddered when they told him how close he had come to dying. That had driven him to find a doctor who could help him, which led to Dr. Caroline Glendan, psychologist, hypnotherapist, and M.D.

Over the last two years, working with Caroline, Kevin had learned how to put himself into a "safe" trance, where his heart rate and blood pressure would remain constant, before he made a jump. In fact, he became so good at it that he could jump in and out of his body at will, anytime. And because he was in a wheelchair, he could do it anywhere without fear of his body falling and being hurt. All he had to do was feign sleep. Lately, though, he'd been spontaneously jumping, with no control over when or where it happened, or for how long.

The phone rang.

Kevin shook himself and sat up straight. The phone rang again as thunder boomed out over the bay. He touched a lever on the right arm of his motorized wheelchair and sent it into reverse. It hummed electronically and propelled him away from the window. He switched it to forward and glided across the dark room to the telephone stand. He snatched up the receiver.

"Hello?"

"Hello, Kevin?"

Dr. Glendan. Her voice, as it was in sessions, was soft, melodic, seductive.

"Hi, Caroline."

"Am I interrupting you?" she asked. She knew this was the time of day that he liked to jump.

"No, not really."

"Having trouble?"

"A little." He heard her waiting for him to go on. He didn't feel like it. Another change in his life.

"What's the problem?" she asked.

Ah! The probing question. God! he was tired. An exhaustion so sudden came over him that it was a few seconds before he realized he was going to jump. In the beat of a heart, he was outside his body, floating above it. This scared him, this spontaneous jumping he'd been doing lately. He didn't like not being in control.

He floated to the ceiling. Below him, his body had slumped in the wheelchair, the phone falling from his hand to the floor. He could hear Caroline calling him, urgency building in her voice.

This was the part of jumping he had first fallen in love with; being free of his crippled body, being able to soar and travel without that damned wheelchair. And to have his body whole again. He always thought it strange, but wonderfully so, that when he left his body, his spirit still had legs, as though they were always a part of him, despite having been amputated in Nam.

"Kevin! Kevin, if you can hear me, answer, or I'm calling an ambulance." Dr. Glendan's voice rose to him from the phone below. She sounded as close to panic as Kevin had ever heard her.

He pushed himself off the ceiling and swooped down to the phone. Concentrating hard, putting all his force into his spirit's finger, he pushed the zero button twice, causing the phone to beep in Caroline's ear.

"Kevin, is that you?"

Two beeps.

"Have you jumped? Are you all right?"

Two beeps.

"Was it spontaneous again?"

The last question went unanswered. Kevin didn't even hear it. A clap of thunder, not of this world, had enveloped him. Lightning, brighter than any he had ever seen in a stormy sky, burned through his eyeballs and left them stinging and blinded. When vision returned, the real world had become transparent and the Army of the Dead were marching through his living room.

As always, his first reaction was to scream. So many dead souls coming through the walls of his living room. And at their head was James. The sight of them, of *him*, was the most horrible thing he had ever endured, and he doubted he would ever grow used to it. This time was just as bad as the first time he'd seen the Army of the Dead.

He had been having pleasurable jumps for almost six years. Suddenly one evening less than six months ago, he'd been going into a jump when something strange happened. Caroline was there; she was still helping him while collecting data for a journal report about him that she was writing.

He'd been slipping into the trance that was the doorway to jumping when he heard the thunder and saw the lightning that was inside his head only and nowhere else. A moment later, the Army of the Dead were walking through his living room. Hundreds of them, thousands—millions! And among them was James, his best friend, whose death Kevin felt responsible for. He'd been carrying around guilt for James's death since he'd first awakened in the hospital in Saigon.

Seeing James that first time had been like getting hit in the chest with a sledgehammer. There he was, in Kevin's living room, the man he'd killed—his best friend. To say he was horrified would be an understatement. James had haunted his dreams for years, but they weren't always dreams of that day in Pleiku City, from which he invariably awoke screaming. Sometimes the dreams were good ones, fond memories of their youth together in Watts, going to school, playing basketball. Ironically, these dreams left him feeling worse than the ones of their last day together. Now to actually see James in front of him, his coal black skin dimmed to a horrible gray, shuffling along through eternity, was almost enough to drive Kevin mad.

He had approached James that first time, floating to him in his ethereal body. He'd hovered alongside his friend, trying to speak to him, following him and the multitude of other souls through the walls of his house and out into the night.

At first, James had paid no attention to him. Kevin pleaded with him to tell him why he was there and where was he going. James kept walking, saying nothing, not even looking in his direction. So intent on communicating with his dead friend was Kevin that he didn't notice that they were no longer in the real world. They had entered a strange flat dimension of geometric shapes scattered over a plain of gray—a scene that reminded him of a painting by Dali. The sky overhead was a bloodred, leaching into blackness at the horizons.

Frustrated, frightened, emotionally exhausted, he'd been near to tears, ready to give up, when James finally seemed to notice him. His friend looked at Kevin with a look that could only be called pity, and a moment later spoke.

"I'm waiting for you, bro."

The words had gone through Kevin like a blast of arctic air. After the initial shock, he'd pressed James to explain, but he got nothing more out of him.

Eventually he'd given up and found himself back in his body.

Since then, he'd been tormenting himself over what James had meant. Why was his friend's soul doomed to march through that bleak dimension forever? Was it Hell? It sure as shit wasn't Heaven. He didn't know what it was, only that it frightened him and so made him fearful of jumping.

He'd told Dr. Glendan about it, and she hadn't seemed surprised. She'd treated it as though she'd been expecting it.

"You've avoided dealing with what happened to you in the war for too long," she'd said. "I knew it would come up sooner or later."

He'd argued. She was treating this as if it were some kind of guilty hallucination conjured up by his mind.

"Well, honestly, Kevin," she'd rejoined, "isn't that what all this jumping business is? You induce a deep trance in yourself and live out your fantasies *in your mind*."

He wished he could believe it, but he knew it wasn't true. On too many of his normal jumps, he had witnessed events, sometimes thousands of miles away, that he would later read about in the newspapers or see on the nightly world news. These had convinced him that his jumping was indeed real.

Just as it was now, with the Army of the Dead walking through the walls of his living room, as if they weren't there at all. It was horribly pitiful the way they shuffled along. Old men and women, young men and women, but strangely no children. Their faces were somber, their eyes vacant. Their skin color reminded Kevin of the underbellies of dead trout. They existed in a dim world of gray tones that, as he stared, slowly seeped over and through the real world until the latter was just a faint reflection that faded completely.

He was in a surrealist painting. Dali could not have painted a scene stranger than the one in which he now found himself. He stood upon a plain of winter gray that stretched in all directions as far as the eye could see. Scattered here and there, like a child's discarded toys, were complex geometrical shapes and structures. The sky overhead was a deep red, the color of fresh blood, that became a fathomless black at the horizons. It all gave Kevin the sensation of being trapped inside a giant bell jar. Cutting the plain in half was a ribbon of black, upon which the Army of the Dead marched. The collective sound of their movements was like a continuous sigh to Kevin's ears.

Kevin didn't want to look, didn't want to be there. He knew what was coming—who was coming. He didn't want to see James again. It had been twenty-six years, for Christ's sake. Why did he have to come back now?

And there he was. James, walking at the edge of the column of dead souls. Suddenly, Kevin was beside him, his floating soul keeping pace with his dead friend. A feeling of despair and hopelessness overwhelmed him. He tried to shrink away from James, but his spirit body would not respond.

"Why, James?" he asked, but his voice was barely a whisper. *"Why are you here?"*

James ignored him. He reached out to touch his friend, and there was bright flash of light. A searing pain shot through him, and emotions of sorrow, and longing for life filled him. In the next instant, he was back in his body, slumped over in the wheelchair. The phone was still at his feet, the receiver lying with its cord tangled and coiled. He picked it up. The line was dead. He put the receiver back in the cradle. His head fell back against the chair, and he wept softly.

Dr. Glendan arrived within the hour. He knew she would. He let her in from his chair, pressing the appropriate button on the remote console of the wheelchair. He could control the entire house from the chair: lights, heat, air conditioning, opening and closing and locking doors. He could even start his van in the garage from the chair and run water into a tub for a bath. The entire house had been designed around his being handicapped. The money to do it had come from the *Jumpers* comic books, which had become a worldwide underground hit, netting him enough money to be able to build the house, on the bluff overlooking Butter's Bay, Washington, to his specifications and special needs.

"Are you all right?" Dr. Glendan asked, hurrying into the living room. She tossed her coat, gloves, and purse onto the narrow modern-design couch. All the furniture in the house, what little there was of it, was designed the same way—to take up as little space as possible, yet still provide comfort for guests. The furniture had been designed by a fellow vet who'd lost an arm in Nam and who now had a very successful business specializing in furniture for the handicapped.

"I'm fine," Kevin answered.

She crossed the room to the large bay windows where he sat, gazing out at the night sky over the bay. He was tempted to look at her as she came toward him, to watch her fluid, graceful movements, the smoothness of her legs, the suggested suppleness of her body within the confines of her clothing, but he resisted. He had dared to dream once that maybe he and Caroline could someday be more than therapist and patient, but now he was no longer foolish enough to wish for something like that. Since the jumps had taken on the aspect of a nightmare rather than the pleasurable experience he'd become addicted to, their relationship had suffered and now he realized the only thing they had in common was that they were both African-Americans.

For a while there, at the peak of his jumping, when travel and experiences had seemed unlimited, they had become very close, sharing and reveling in his incredible ability. Caroline had attended him personally on all his jumps then. To Kevin, she had seemed as excited as he each time, if not more so. She'd sat diligently by his side, keeping tabs on his vital signs while she anxiously awaited his return and all that he had to tell.

At least that was what he had thought. She'd seemed so sincere in her excitement and her belief that he was actually doing what he was doing and not hallucinating or dreaming. But now when he thought about it, he realized she had never said she actually *believed* that he was really having out-of-body experiences. In fact, the one time he'd asked her if she believed him—if she thought he was really leaving his body and traveling in spirit form, she had replied, "I believe *you* believe it's true, and that's all that matters."

At the time he had let it go, chalking it up to the fact that she was a psychiatrist trained to say things like that and never reveal anything about herself. But when he'd started losing control of the jumps, visiting the weird other dimension of the Army of the Dead, she had revealed her true thoughts: He was deluding himself; the visions and experiences were only the result of self-hypnosis and his desire to be normal again in any way possible.

When she'd first suggested this, he had grasped thankfully at it. The experiences with the Army of the Dead and James had scared the bejesus out of him, and he would have welcomed any explanation that made him believe it wasn't real. As time went on, though, he knew he was wrong. He began to realize the true import of what he had done, and when he'd tried to discuss it with her, she had played psychiatrist with him rather than really listening to him. That had pissed him off. He had gone to her as a friend, as someone he could trust to at least believe him, not as a doctor who would try to counsel him and explain away everything as if it were all in his head—that none of it was real.

As far as Kevin was concerned, that was bullshit. Though he had at first been willing to clutch at any straw that would explain his experiences as anything but real, something had happened on the jump before last that had proved to him that it *was* all real.

It had started just like all his other recent jumps. Reality had changed, becoming transparent. The Army of the Dead had marched through his living room. Suddenly all that too had disappeared, and he found himself soaring through an infinite nothingness, blacker than any darkness he'd ever seen. He felt dizzy to the point of nausea as his body tried to deal with the simultaneous sensations of falling and flying.

Just when those opposing sensations threatened to cause him to black out, he was distracted by intensely bright laser beams of colored light that, though they hurt his eyes, gave his body the feeling of having some bearing in relationship to his surroundings.

One particularly bright red beam of light had flashed before his eyes, blinding him. When his sight returned, he had seen that he was floating through a bizarre landscape of funguslike plants, through which floated great clusters of silver spheres that looked like bubbles of liquid mercury.

He had been marveling at this new plane of existence—especially the silver spheres, which seemed to be portals into the lives of other people—when he saw one of the dead marchers appear from out of nowhere. A second later, the dead soul, an elderly man, was absorbed by one of the spheres.

Kevin had rushed to the bubble, which was part of a large cluster of spheres, and been amazed to see a live scene going on inside the largest bubble, the one the dead soul had gone into. It was like being on a rooftop and looking through a small dome-shaped skylight on the activity below.

It was a street scene, with a lot of pedestrians bustling on the sidewalk and heavy traffic on the road. A small black boy, about age eight or nine, was being chased through an alleyway by another boy. They were playing tag or some such chase game, laughing and running headlong toward the busy thoroughfare.

Kevin saw the dead soul—a tall white man with gray hair, his shoulders hunched, his skin wrinkled—standing next to a telephone pole at the curb. The young boy ran on, shrieking hysterical laughter at the exhilaration of being chased. He reached the end of the alleyway at a moment when there were no pedestrians crossing the mouth of the alley. He looked back at his friend, or brother, who was chasing him, and turned, plunging headlong across the sidewalk, heading into the street. A large delivery van was coming along at a good clip, heading straight for a deadly rendezvous with the child.

Kevin had panicked watching the scene. He'd tried to shout a warning and reached out, his hands and arms plunging through the surface of the sphere up to his elbows. The sensation was strange—a cool tingling on his skin that sent electrical pulses throughout his body that were not unpleasant. The dead soul saw Kevin's arms break through. He looked up, straight into Kevin's eyes, and Kevin thought that he looked frightened.

The child was at the curb, head still turned back at his chaser, not watching where he was going. There were only a few feet of safety left between the boy and serious injury, even death. The boy was just about even with the dead soul, yet the man didn't seem to notice him. He kept staring up at Kevin. At the last second, the man's right foot shot out, caught the ankle of the boy, and sent him sprawling on his stomach at the edge of the street, a good foot from danger as the truck rumbled by.

The boy screamed and began to cry. His friend/brother rushed to help him to his feet. The smaller boy's chin and nose were scraped raw and bloody, as were the palms of his hands. The dead soul seemed unhappy with what he'd done. He looked at the crying boy, then beseechingly up at Kevin. A moment later, he disappeared, dissolving into thin air.

Kevin had backed away from the scene, trying to comprehend what had just happened. The strange landscape around him began to change, dissolving as the dead soul had done. Just before it disappeared completely and he was thrust back to the land of the Army of the Dead, he saw two people whose auras were not like those of the Army of the Dead. Their auras glowed with the same blue electrical light that his own aura and those of the living contained. He saw them only for an instant before that world completely disappeared, but in that instant, he knew and recognized them as living souls, like himself.

The idea that others could jump excited Kevin. He knew from his research into the phenomenon of near-death experiences that many people had had out-of-body experiences. But there were very few accounts in Western literature, outside of the ramblings of Shirley MacLaine, that described spontaneous out-of-body experiences such as he knew. And nowhere outside of Eastern religion and philosophy was there any mention of being able to control one's out-of-body experiences the way he had learned to.

The two live souls he'd seen (he wasn't able to determine their sexes, they were too far away) could not have been having near-death experiences. He'd witnessed one before while out of his body, and the illumination of the person's aura was vastly different from his own or that of these two souls he'd seen. The latter had most definitely been living souls temporarily displaced from their bodies.

He didn't tell Caroline about that episode. He didn't want to hear her analytical interpretation of what she believed was happening "only in his mind."

He looked at her, standing near the curtains, looking out at the cold moon rising over the bay. It was funny that she hadn't mentioned the incident with the phone, when he was out of his body. Maybe it was time to prove to Caroline once and for all that this was real.

"It's not in my mind," he said, breaking the stillness.

Caroline started, looked at him, and offered a patronizing smile that infuriated him.

"When I pressed the buttons on the phone earlier, I did so with my spirit. I was out of my body at the time," Kevin said evenly, trying to keep his growing anger in check.

"Kevin," Caroline said slowly, as if choosing her words carefully, "I think you've gone too far with this thing. It no longer serves a positive purpose toward your mental well-being."

"I'm not deluding myself!" Kevin shouted back at her. "I can prove it to you, Caroline. I never thought to do it before because I always assumed you believed I was telling you the truth."

"I do believe you are telling the truth."

"No. As you said before, you believe that *I* believe. That's not the same thing. Let me prove it to you."

"Kevin, you can't prove it to me. It doesn't matter what I believe. What matters is that you've taken this therapy as far as it can go. It's pointed up the real problem in your life—your guilt over what happened to your friend in the war. Now it's time to move on and deal with that guilt, to realize his death wasn't your fault. When you do, you'll finally be at peace with yourself and your handicap, and then you can get on with living life to its fullest, instead of escaping it through trances and hallucinations."

That did it. That was the last straw. "Get out," he said quietly, his voice quivering with suppressed anger. When she didn't respond, he lost it, shouting in a rage, "Get out! Just get the fuck out! We're through! I don't need you anymore. Get out!"

She tried to argue, but he screamed at her again to get out.

"If that's the way you want it, Kevin, fine. You know where to reach me if you need me." And she left, her heels clicking an angry rapid fire against the floor.

2

It was another week before he jumped again, and it was a spontaneous one at that. He spent most of the week in Los Angeles, in meetings with his agent and Tri-Star pictures. The movie company was interested in making a movie based on his comic book, *Jumpers*. There were two times during the week, both of them in the middle of meetings, when he thought he was going to jump spontaneously. With a great deal of effort, he had managed to keep himself under control and in his body.

Before he had lost his legs in Nam, Kevin had always wanted to travel, but now, with his handicap, he hated traveling. Despite a lot of good intentions and some laws for the handicapped, getting around out in the world in a wheelchair was a pain in the ass. He always made sure to book a hotel that had complete access and to arrange transportation with a limo company with a handicapped van, but that was generally as much control as he could manage. The rest of the time, he was at the mercy of buildings and structures created with no thought for the handicapped.

And the worst of it was, the trip had been a waste of time. Tri-Star decided the project wasn't right for them and backed out at the end of the week. Several independent producers were still interested, but his agent had really been pushing for a deal with Tri-Star.

Kevin had listened to his agent bitch and moan all the way to the airport, but the truth was, Kevin didn't care. *Jumpers* had been good to him, had afforded him a lifestyle he never could have known otherwise, but he had a feeling that it was about to take on a momentum and life of its own, becoming bigger than he could ever control. He had met the creators of *Teenage Mutant Ninja Turtles* at an awards banquet once and had talked with them at length. Now he was beginning to understand what they had meant when they said they felt like Dr. Frankenstein—their creation had turned into a monster that was no longer in their control.

But that was okay. Kevin didn't care if *Jumpers* took off into the stratosphere and became the latest fad. He'd already made more money than he would ever need. And in light of his recent jumps and the haunting message that James was waiting for him, a comic book seemed quite trivial.

Lately it seemed to Kevin that he couldn't stop thinking about jumping, his friend trapped in Limbo, and the two live souls he had seen on the other side. He would give anything to talk to them. He hoped too that they might be able to tell him more about the Limbo of marching souls where his war buddy waited for him.

He felt a sense of relief as the plane touched down in Olympia. His specially equipped van, complete with remote control for all functions, was waiting for him in the underground garage. With the help of a brawny male flight attendant and then a porter, he disembarked from the plane and made it to his van.

He felt better behind the wheel, finally in control of his environment. He often thought it was funny how whole, healthy people often give up control of their environment without even realizing it. They always think they're in control even when they're not. He had been the same once, disregarding his vulnerability to the environment. It had taken the wheelchair to open his eyes. Now he always knew when he wasn't in control of his environment, and he hated it.

The drive from Olympia to Butter's Bay, on the coast, took an hour longer than normal due to construction on the freeway. He ended up getting off the highway only eight miles outside of Olympia and had to travel the rest of the way on secondary roads.

It was dark by the time he got home. The overcast sky deepened the shadows around the house and turned the bay into a black void framed by the dimly seen rocks and the white sand of the beach around it.

His house was set on a bluff, overlooking the bay, a half mile from the water, giving him a stupendous view of the cliffs, the beach, and the Pacific Ocean beyond from his living room window. That was where he headed as soon as he entered the house. He didn't stop to unpack his valise or get something to eat and drink, despite being hungry and thirsty.

The thought of the two live souls he had seen had been dominating his thoughts since he'd gotten on the plane. He was certain that if he could communicate with them, they could help him understand what the hell was going on with his friend in Limbo and what he might do to help him.

He rolled the chair to the large window overlooking the black bay below. Then he started the process, as he always did, with controlled breathing. A deep nasal breath, exhale. Two deep nasal breaths, exhale. Three deep nasal breaths, exhale. And back to one again. He continued this for several minutes before he felt his soul loosening from its fleshy moor.

The familiar crack of thunder resounded in his head, and lightning seared his eyes. He felt the gut-wrenching tug at his solar plexus and the strange feeling of being pulled inside out. His body was slumped in the wheelchair below him and his ethereal spirit was bouncing off the ceiling, but the marching dead were nowhere to be seen.

This was just like the old days, when he had first started to jump. He was outside his body, free to roam. He wasn't being projected into any strange dimensions or meeting the souls of dead friends. Ironically, at any other time, he would have welcomed this return to normalcy. Now it was the last thing he wanted.

Damn! he thought. The one time I *want* to be in another dimension, and I can't. You can bet that if I just wanted to do some traveling, the dead would be all over me like white on rice.

He tried to think himself into the dimension of the reality spheres where he had last encountered the two live souls, but he had never entered that dimension before without first going through the dimensions of marching dead souls, where James waited.

Kevin floated through the window and into the cold night. The wind blew him out over the bay but did not chill him, though he knew it was very cold. The night sky was the blackest he had ever seen it. For a moment, he thought it was the void between dimensions, where the laser beams soared, but it was just the night.

The wind forced him back toward the cliff face, over the thin strand of beach at the bottom. Out at sea, lights from passing tankers blinked in the blackness. An updraft caught him suddenly, and he was flung upward into the night. Another strong wind off the ocean pushed him inland past his house, until he was over the small town of Islet. There seemed to be some sort of parade going on—the streets were filled with people marching. The wind dropped off, and he wafted down, closer.

The first chill of the night ran through him when he got close enough to see it wasn't a parade—it was the dead marching through the streets of Islet. He floated closer, and there, marching below him, was the old man he'd seen trip the kid.

"Hey!" Kevin cried, working his arms and legs to push himself closer. *"Hey, you! You! Old man!"* He was nearly level with the column, and the old man was just ahead of him. *"Wait! I need to speak with you!"*

Kevin pushed forward, reached out to touch the old man, and was blinded by an explosion of light that rocked him, sending a flash of intense pain through his entire being. When his eyes recovered from the blinding light, he saw that he had been thrown a good twenty feet by the explosion.

Kevin swam through the air, back to the line of dead souls, and saw the old man barely staggering along. He looked stunned. Kevin approached him again, and the old man shrank away from him.

"Don't touch me!" the old man screamed at Kevin. *"Get away from me! You've messed things up enough already!"*

Kevin tried to interrupt and talk to the man, but the old guy grew frantic, nearly hysterical, babbling about being left alone and trying to push deeper into the column of dead to get away from Kevin.

Kevin wanted to pursue him, but he was now afraid to get too close to any of the walking dead.

"Leave him alone," a voice behind him said. He

turned, and there was James, marching up behind him.

"Leave him alone, Kevin. He can't help you," James said. Kevin started to reply, excited at the prospect of finally communicating with his dead friend, but before he could say a word, the column of dead marching through the streets of Islet dissolved, and then the town itself faded away. He had the sensation of being caught in a drain, then being sucked through a small hole, and in the blink of an eye, he was back in his body.

As dawn streaked the sky, sending tendrils of light toward the dark western horizon, Kevin put his face in his hands and wondered what to do next.

3

The weekend passed slowly. He tried to work, but every time he went to his drawing board, he ended up just sitting there, doodling and staring at the title page of *Jumpers*, which ran on every issue of the comic book.

The drawing showed three heroes in dynamic, forceful poses rising out of their prone bodies beneath the title, which was written in fiery letters. He looked at the faces of his heroes. Each one had two—their regular face, and then the face of their ethereal being rising out of their mortal body. Their mortal faces were plain, even ugly and deformed, but their ethereal, out-of-body faces were beautiful, as were their bodies.

There were three heroes in the *Jumpers* comic: two crippled black men, and a deaf, dumb, and blind white girl. One of the black men had no legs, just like Kevin. But his spirit-body had powerful, muscular legs. The other black hero's body was twisted with deformity, but his spirit-body was perfect—muscular and beautiful. The girl was plain, even homely, until he drew her out of her body, when she became beautiful.

He studied his heroes' faces and felt a sense of recognition toward them that he'd had never felt before. The woman's face he had consciously modeled after Michelle Pfeiffer, but the men's faces he'd just made up, or so he thought. Now, looking at them, he recognized them as being variations on the features of his dead war buddy, James. It was so obvious, it was amazing that he had never seen it before.

That realization did nothing to help him work, though. It only distracted him more as he thought about his friend's soul and all the others wandering the surreal landscape of the afterlife. He wondered again why, for what reason, in accordance with what law they were compelled to do so.

He wanted to jump again, to try and find the two living souls he'd seen, but he was afraid he'd just end up back with the walking dead. After the last experience, he wasn't too keen to get close to any of them anytime soon.

By Sunday night, he was overtired and in a terrible mood. Even word from his agent that Tri-Star had called, had changed their mind, and wanted the rights to *Jumpers*, offering $25 million, didn't cheer him up. There had been a time in his life when he had thought he would always care about money and getting rich, but the sad fact was, now that he had done just that, he no longer cared.

His thoughts turned to Caroline, and he held his breath at the emotion that clenched his heart. If only things had been different in his life—but that was a self-pitying road that he had trod too often in the past.

Enough! he thought. He'd wasted enough time. Sitting around feeling sorry for himself, fantasizing about what might have been but never could be, was getting him nowhere and wasn't helping to resolve his problems.

It's time to jump and get on with it, he told himself. He rolled away from the drawing table and, with fingers deftly working the wheelchair's controls, steered to the living room bay window.

It was raining again, a fine misting rain that seemed to descend in clouds that shifted in the wind. He could not see any lights from ships at sea. The ocean was a black hole.

He began the controlled breathing and tried to focus his mind. He started to relax, started to go, but was suddenly snapped back. He didn't know what was wrong. Nothing had distracted him, as far as he could tell. The storm outside was a quiet one, no thunder or lightning, just the soft soothing patter of rain on the window.

He tried again. Controlled breathing—a focused mind. Relax. He felt reality shift, followed by the inside-out feeling and the flash and roar of light. He started to rise from his body, then fell back.

There was sound. A rhythmic shuffle. The dead marched through the far wall, oblivious to the fireplace or anything else. They came through the wall, walked through the furniture, and exited the opposite wall. If Kevin looked really hard, he could see through the wall to where the dead marched straight through all the walls of his house and out into the night again, where they became lost in the distance. The walls, the house, reality itself, became transparent around him. Mist filled the room, and rain blew through the walls of the house. Night invaded where the light had been, until there was nothing left of the everyday world except the wheelchair that he remained trapped in. The gray surrealistic plain stretched out to infinity in all directions. The sky overhead was bloodred, laced with the streaking fiery brilliance of the beams of light that coursed through it.

Kevin was afraid, more afraid than he'd been when he first came to this place and saw his dead friend marching across this weird plateau. He was more afraid than he'd ever been in his life.

Everything that was happening was the same as when he jumped, but this time he was still inside his real body, still trapped in his wheelchair. The experience scared the shit out of him. Did it mean he was trapped here and was going to have to suffer through all eternity in a wheelchair?

The dead marched by, one moment miles away, the next within inches. He cowered from them, the thought that he was going to spend eternity this way driving him to the edge of madness.

At one point, the dead drew so close that sparks flew between him and the nearest one. He lost it then, screaming. He wasn't able to stop. He hammered the arms of the wheelchair and rocked back and forth as he screamed. Tears ran down his face.

A voice brought him back from the edge of lunacy. *"Kevin. Bro. Shut the fuck up."*

The scream caught in his throat, was silenced. James was standing in front of him. A hundred yards behind, the dead filed by in their perpetual parade. Kevin looked at his dead friend and began to tremble violently.

"Take it easy, Kev, and listen. I don't have much time. Your marker has come due."

Kevin found his voice and spoke hoarsely, *"What are you talking about?"*

"I'm talking about borrowed time, bro."

"Borrowed time?"

"Yeah! The time you've been living on."

"What?" Kevin was confused. This was all too weird, a little too unreal.

"You took my time, bro. You took my life."

"No!" Kevin screamed. His head swam. This couldn't be happening. This couldn't be true. It was his worst nightmare, his worst fear. It had been the source of all his personal torment and guilt and had taken a lot of hours of therapy to deal with it—

the fear that he should have died too that day in Pleiku City.

"It's time to give it back, Kevin. It's time to pass the gift on, bro. It's the only way I can move on."

Kevin was crying. *"I don't know what you mean,"* he blubbered.

James reached out a hand to touch him. *"Yes, you do, bro."* The hand came closer. *"You know what I mean."* Sparks flew from his hand—

—and Kevin was falling. His head struck something hard—he realized it was the leg of the coffee table—on the way to the floor. He crumpled heavily in a fetal position in front of his wheelchair, sending it rolling away from him.

I'm back in my home, he thought. It was all there, his furnishings, his stuff. All solid, all real.

His head felt light; the back of his neck, sweaty. He had no strength in his arms. They trembled when he tried to push himself off the floor. After several futile tries, he gave up and lay with his useless body front down on the floor. With his face, hot with tears, lying against the cool wood floor, he fell asleep.

4

They needed a place to hide out, and they needed it fast. Rod knew that if they stayed on the road, it was only a matter of time before they were caught. The police roadblock on the interstate had convinced him of that. After getting away from the interstate and the roadblock, Rod and Gary had driven west on back roads, trying to avoid traffic and people.

Near nightfall, as they were driving along a winding narrow road through a heavily wooded area, Rod noticed the lights of a small town just coming on in the valley ahead. A sign told him they were entering Hanson, New York. Nestled into the hillside along the road a mile or two ahead, Rod noticed an abandoned building. At first he thought it was a factory or a mill or something like that. Then SOUZA ELEMENTARY SCHOOL, etched into the granite above the boarded front doors, revealed the building's true purpose.

He instructed Gary to drive the truck around the back of the school, looking for a place to hide it. Rod was glad to see there were no homes real close to the school. The nearest one he could see had to be a good 250 yards away, through a thick copse of trees that obstructed nearly everything except the light from one second-story window.

Rod was debating whether to pull the truck into

the woods and cover it with branches when Gary spoke up.

"There's a garage door, Rod. Too bad we can't park in there."

Rod looked to where Gary was pointing. At the rear of school was a garage door. Stenciled on the front, just below a row of dark windows, was the warning: CAUTION! SCHOOL BUS.

"Pull under those trees over there for a minute," Rod said. Gary obliged, and Rod got out, looked around, and crossed to the garage door. He could see nothing through the row of filthy windows until he came to the end and found a clear spot in the last window. There was a door next to it that appeared to be all metal. He tried it, found it locked, and peered through the small clear spot.

The garage was empty for the most part, except for a stack of bus tires in the far left corner and what looked like a tool bench running along the side wall. Rod grabbed the garage door handle, twisted it, and lifted. He wasn't surprised to find it locked. Luckily, garage door locks are fragile at best, and this one was rusted.

He grabbed the handle with his right hand and twisted it hard. A sharp pain went through his wrist, and his fingers went tingly numb.

"Shit! Son of a bitch! Whore!" he cursed, getting up and massaging his hand. He could hear Gary laughing in the truck and shot him a hard look that shut him up. "Get over here, numbnuts," Rod called to Gary. The big man got out of the truck and shuffled toward Rod, a sheepish expression on his face. When he reached Rod, he almost cowered before the smaller man, making Rod chuckle nastily.

"Let's see you do something with those muscles

for a change," Rod said, pointing to the door. "Open it."

Gary turned to the door and stood in front of the lock, legs spread a little, bracing himself. He grabbed the handle with both hands—the left palm up under the left side of the handle, the right held against the top of the right side. With one quick, hard movement, he pulled up on the left side while pushing down hard on the right. Inside the door, rusted metal shrieked and snapped, and the handle flipped into a vertical position. The door went up an inch and stopped. Gary put his weight into it, and lifted, and the door went up quickly and rustily, groaning and rattling. To Rod, it seemed like the loudest sound he had ever heard, but once the door was up and he looked around, watching and listening, it didn't appear anyone had heard.

He stood aside and told Gary to get back in the truck and pull it into the garage. He endured the racket of the door again as Gary closed it once the truck was in.

"This is cool, Rod," Gary said when the door was closed.

"It'll do," Rod muttered. "Let's go have a look around."

5

Kevin had decided—after much self-convincing—that it had all been a dream. He thought he might even have had a seizure of some kind.

He'd awakened after twelve hours of unconsciousness on the floor at the foot of his wheelchair. He was stiff and uncomfortable, but the strength had returned to his arms, and he was able to get back into his chair. Since then, yesterday, he'd been mulling over what had happened, trying to convince himself he had just dreamed it.

The phone rang, interrupting his thoughts. He pushed himself away from his drawing table, where he'd been sitting, doodling all morning, and motored the wheelchair to the phone on his desk.

"Kevin. Good news." It was his agent. Kevin listened halfheartedly as his agent outlined the preproduction schedule on the *Jumpers* movie. He agreed to fly down to L.A. again on Wednesday to sign contracts and meet the producers.

He hung the phone up and drove the chair into the hall and down the ramp to the living room. He parked in his favorite spot in front of the large window overlooking the bay. It looked like a nice day, sun shining, warm. Spring was coming early this year. Kevin looked out at the day and longed for the past, when he could leave his body and fly out over the bay, simply enjoying the freedom of movement, not having to worry about the dead, or about living on borrowed time, or anything.

He sighed and stared at the sails drifting across the blue of the bay. He wanted to be out there so badly. He ached to jump and soar through the spring sky, but at the same time, he dreaded it.

Without warning, he felt the familiar tug at his solar plexus. The sky darkened, and he knew he would have no choice in the matter. The thunder and lightning came, and he groaned with the feeling of being pulled inside out again. His head jerked once and dipped to his chest as his spirit left his body. The room had faded, growing more and more transparent. Suddenly it all disappeared, and he was standing in the middle of the dead's parade grounds once again.

He rejoiced at having his legs back, at having made the jump complete. It proved to him that what had happened last time had been a dream. He had been stupid to think otherwise. But he still felt a strong sense of apprehension as the long column of the dead approached.

Kevin let his spirit rise above the dead and searched the ranks for James, determined to approach and speak to him. He needed to prove once and for all that yesterday had been a dream.

Though he searched the rows carefully, Kevin couldn't find his friend. He floated closer, as close as he dared, and searched. The spirits of the dead shuffled past below him, and still he saw no sign of James.

At first, Kevin was upset that he couldn't find his friend. Then he began to get excited. It occurred to him that if James was no longer among the souls of Limbo, then he must have moved on. Perhaps the great light had come for him, the way Kevin had seen it come for others. But he had to be sure. The column of spirits stretched to the horizon and beyond. Kevin realized he could spend eternity looking for his friend and never lay eyes on the same soul twice.

But every other time he'd jumped here, James had been nearby, drawing him like a magnet. He had to consider that. Kevin decided to accept his friend's absence as proof that his friend's spirit was at rest at last.

He let his own spirit descend to the plain a hundred yards away from the dead. A new thought had struck him. He wondered why—if James's spirit had moved on—he had jumped to Limbo again. What was the point? Before, he had always presumed he was jumping here because of James. But here he was again, and no James.

"Kevin."

The voice startled him, and he whirled around. James stood behind him, a few feet away.

"It wasn't a dream, Kev," James said. *"A mistake was made. It happens. Now it's time to rectify it."*

"What do you mean? What mistake?"

"You're living on borrowed time, Kevin. You were supposed to die that day in Pleiku City, not me."

"Living on borrowed time? I lost my legs, man! What kind of life do you think I've had without my legs!" Kevin shouted angrily.

James looked long and hard at Kevin. *"You've had a pretty good life, despite your handicap, and you know it. You've maybe had a better life than if you'd come out of the Nam whole."*

That brought the guilt charging back upon Kevin with a weight equal to that of the tank that had taken his legs. His friend was voicing nothing new, nothing that Kevin hadn't already considered himself. He had often wondered how different his life would have been if he had come home from the war in one piece. Would he ever have developed his artistic talents? Probably not. The only reason he had was due to the boredom of being confined to the damned wheelchair. *Jumpers*? He never would have created it, because he never would have developed the ability to jump. And right about now, that didn't seem like such a bad thing.

Kevin looked sheepishly at his friend. Though he'd considered all this many times before, he had always avoided reaching the obvious conclusion: Losing his legs had been a godsend, the best thing that had ever happened to him.

"You've had a good run, bro, but now it's time to set things straight, to make things right," James said, his voice tinged with sadness.

"What are you saying? That I've got to die? Is that what you're saying?" Kevin questioned. But James was fading. The entire surreal plain around him was fading away too.

"Wait! Answer me! What do you mean? How do I make things right?"

James was nearly gone. He looked at Kevin, smiled, shook his head, and was gone. Kevin was plummeted into darkness so complete, he couldn't see his own fingers when he held them before his eyes. He felt that he was moving through the darkness, but he couldn't be positive which direction it was in. There was no wind, no air even to feel himself moving against. He'd never noticed a lack of air before during his jumps. He realized now that he didn't breathe when he was out of his body.

A frightening thought assailed him: *What if the reason I'm not breathing this time is because I'm dead?* Maybe that was what James had meant. But if that were true, then what was he doing here, and why was that red light suddenly appearing out of nowhere? It expanded until it engulfed him, and he went into it, through it, and emerged in the weird dimension of strange plant growth and floating herds of bubbles that were people's lives.

The light went out, and as he turned, his head passed through a cluster of bubbles. It wasn't a pleasant feeling being plunged into someone else's life. The onrush of thoughts, emotions, and details was overwhelming, but the physical sensation was the worst. Kevin likened it to how a sheet must feel as it is vigorously shaken out. The bubble passed, and he staggered, nearly falling.

Watchful for other bubbles, he floated slowly between the pillars of plant life. Up ahead, two solitary spheres of light floated into view, and Kevin recognized them immediately. Their light was like his own. It was the two souls he'd seen before—the two souls who were jumpers like him.

He started toward them, working his arms and legs like a swimmer. Halfway to them, he realized one of the souls was a little girl, the other a young woman. The little girl looked his way, and he was about to call out to her when two life bubbles appeared from above, rapidly fell on the two souls, consumed them, and sped off, all in a matter of seconds. Kevin tried to follow, but it was impossible.

They had returned to the land of the living.

6

Anna was lost and frightened. She was more than frightened, she was terrified. She was more terrified than she'd ever been, even in the presence of the Shadow Monster.

What she had seen those terrible men doing to Deedee had been horrible. Next to witnessing the deaths of her parents, it was the most horrible thing she'd ever seen. In some ways it had even been worse than seeing her mother shot in the head—all that had happened so quickly, and she'd barely been conscious.

The violence she had just witnessed in Deedee's apartment had been burned into her mind like a brand. It had been so brutal. But the worst of it was the looks on the faces of the men, especially the one called Dick by the others. He was *enjoying* beating Deedee to a pulp. They were all enjoying it. The men who killed my parents were like that, she thought. They enjoyed killing. They had to—how else could they just kill innocent people? They had to enjoy it very much.

Anna didn't understand how that could be. She knew there were bad people in the world, but before her accident and her parents' death, and now this, she had been lucky enough to have never been exposed to the presence of real human beings who were so evil that they could enjoy torturing or killing another human being. It was almost unbearably frightening.

The fear drove her up through the depths of her mind into the bottom of a shallow pool of semiconsciousness. She opened her eyes. She was back in the hospital room.

7

Deedee awoke from unconsciousness, striking out at the assailants that still beat her in her dreams. An arm went around her, and a hand clamped her leg. She screamed.

"Dee! It's okay! You're safe."

The voice cut through her panic. She immediately recognized it. Struggling, she tried to open her eyes. They didn't want to work. She managed to get the right one open enough to see a blurred figure leaning over her.

Jesse.

"You're in the hospital, Dee. You're going to be okay." His hand touched her shoulder affectionately. His other hand stroked her hair. He leaned over and lightly kissed her forehead.

"Don't leave me," she tried to say, but she wasn't sure if he heard or not. Her mouth wanted to work even less than her eyes. It didn't matter, though—the effort had cost her too much energy, and she slipped back into the forgetting embrace of unconsciousness.

She awoke not knowing—or caring—how long she'd been out. She woke up quietly this time, not struggling to escape her nightmares. Sleep had left her fear-free for a while. As she came awake, she heard the sounds of the hospital around her: a nurse, very close, admonishing a Mrs. Kerry to take her medicine; a PA announcement for a code blue in the ER. In spite of a sharp piercing pain that went from her cheekbone right through to the back of her head, Deedee opened her right eye and peered at the room. Her vision swam, her eyes watered, and she grew tired quickly.

She closed her eye and remembered that Jesse had been there. Or had that been a dream? she wondered. Another question raised itself. What was she doing in the hospital anyway? I must be hurt, she thought, or sick. But how had she hurt herself, and what was wrong with her?

Bits and pieces of what happened flitted through her memory, but their sequence was jumbled. She was too foggy to be able to understand and make sense of them.

She gave up and was slipping into sleep again when she heard Jesse's voice.

"Marcia! What are you doing here?" Deedee heard a new voice, a woman's voice, and she didn't sound happy.

"Never mind what I'm doing here? What are you doing here? What the hell is going on? You took off and said you'd be back in a couple of hours. That was yesterday. Where have you been?"

When Jesse answered, Deedee could hear the nervousness in his voice. He was on a spot. She surmised that Marcia was his fiancée.

"Take it easy, Marcia. Keep your voice down."

"Who is that?" Marcia asked. Her voice was closer and not any quieter.

"It's an old friend. She needs my help right now."

Deedee felt a thrill at Jesse's words. The sound of high heels approached the bed.

"Oh, my God! What happened to her?" Marcia's voice was softer now.

"She was attacked by three guys," Jesse answered.

Marcia whispered, "Jesus!" A little louder, she asked, "Was she raped?"

"No," Jesse said quietly. Deedee thought she heard something in his voice. It seemed Marcia had heard the same thing.

"What exactly is she to you, Jesse?" Deedee detected a note of fear in her voice.

There was an uncomfortable silence before Jesse answered, "I told you. She's an old friend."

"Old friend, or old girlfriend?"

Another uncomfortable silence.

"She was my girlfriend before I met you," Jesse said.

"So this is Deedee," Marcia said softly. "What's going on, Jesse? Are you still in love with her or what? Is that why you're here?"

Again Jesse hesitated before answering. Deedee realized she was holding her breath and let it out slowly, softly.

"My feelings for you haven't changed, babe. If that's what you want to know. But I still care about her, and she needs my help right now."

"How long is she going to need your help? And what exactly do you mean by help?"

"I just need to make sure she's all right," Jesse answered. He sounded like he was becoming irritated. Deedee knew that tone well. But whereas when she and Jesse were together, that tone would have would have upset her, now it elated her. The pain that seemed to come from everywhere receded to a small place, and she was filled with a wonderful sense of joy.

"Fine," Marcia answered icily. "But don't expect me to be waiting for you."

Deedee heard the swish of clothing and the angry tap-tap of heels on the floor, leaving the room.

"Marcia . . . ," Jesse said, but not too loudly,

Deedee thought. He didn't move. After a minute or so, Deedee heard him pull up a chair next to the bed. A moment later, she felt his hands caress her hair.

Everything will be all right now, she thought, and drifted blissfully into healing sleep.

8

Gary was scared. He did his best to hide it, but he didn't like the damp, dark old school building. The place brought back too many bad memories of his childhood, both at home and at Our Lady of the Lake school.

He was following Rod down a wide hallway, past wooden doors on either side that had large wire-mesh glass windows filling their top halves, just like at Our Lady of the Lake. The glass was thick and, with the wire mesh quilting it, was nearly impossible to see through.

They came to an open area, where a large oak staircase went up and around to the second floor. Over the stairs, three massive smoked-glass windows stretched up to the arched ceiling and let in a dim light. To the left, a short flight of stairs went down to the main doors—a row of four, with push-bar handles, wooden bottom halves, and glass tops that were poorly boarded over.

"This place is kind of spooky," Gary said, adding a little laugh so Rod wouldn't think he was scared. It didn't work. Rod let out a low evil laugh that sent a chill down Gary's neck.

"Hey . . . Cut it out, R-R-Rod," Gary said sheepishly.

"Whatsa matter? This place scare you? A big fuck like you?" Rod taunted.

"Cut it out," Gary said sullenly.

"I think this place is just fine! For a while, anyway. We'll hole up here and let the heat blow over. All we need is some food." Rod ran up the stairs to the first landing and peered through the window.

"Can't see shit through this," he said angrily. He turned and ran down to the row of main doors. Peering through a crack in the boards, he exclaimed, "Looks good."

He turned to Gary. "I'm going to sneak out and walk down the road into town. See if there's a store and get some supplies. You unload the truck. This might not be a bad place to stash the stuff if New York don't work out."

Before Gary could say anything, Rod had undone the second door's top and bottom bolts and was gone. Gary was left alone in the spooky school building. His breathing sounded weirdly amplified in the empty building. It gave him the creeps, so he held it. He shivered with fright as the sound of his breathing went on for a few seconds. For a second he had the thought that it was the school breathing; then he told himself it had to just be an echo. The empty front lobby and stairs, with the high ceiling and windows, created the perfect acoustics for an echo chamber.

Gary forced himself to laugh at his foolishness, but he could manage only a mental chuckle. "Hello-o," he called softly. The whispery echo of his voice gave him chills. It was too much what he imagined a ghost's voice would sound like. Looking around so nothing could sneak up on him, he returned to the garage.

It didn't take him long to unload the truck. He stacked the boxes in the corner of the garage and sat on them, hunched over, his hands clasped between his knees. He wished Rod would hurry back with the food. His stomach was gurgling regularly. And he was cold. He pulled the canvas tarp around his shoulders, but it wasn't helping much. He was tempted to go out to the main doors and look out to see if Rod was coming, but he didn't want to go through the empty school building again alone.

He shivered. He pondered starting the truck and running the heater, but he was afraid Rod might get mad. Someone might hear. The danger of carbon monoxide poisoning never crossed his mind.

There was a loud noise from somewhere in the building. Gary froze. He waited, listening for Rod's footsteps. He couldn't hear them.

"Rod?" he called, and went to the door. He put his ear to it and listened. Nothing. Jeez! This place gave him the creeps! He opened the door wide enough to stick his head out and looked up the stairs into the gloom. There was very little light, just a faint illumination from the windows. It was getting dark outside and darker inside. Gary didn't want to be there alone after dark.

He took a deep breath. There's nothing up there, he told himself. He pulled his head back and started to close the door when another noise—a door closing, he thought—came from somewhere within the building. It echoed a moment and faded. Silence returned. Gary's heart was beating fast, too fast. He was breathing fast too, getting dizzy, in danger of hyperventilation.

A muffled bang reached his ears. It was followed by another, and another—an entire series of them. It sounded like someone—someone *big*—was walking around in the building, then running.

The footsteps stopped.

"Where the hell are you, Rod?" Gary gasped. He

didn't like this, didn't like this at all. It was getting dark in the garage now too. Rod had been gone for a long time. Too long. What if something had happened to him? What if the cops got him, or worse, what if he decided to ditch Gary, like he was always threatening to do?

"No," Gary whispered. "He wouldn't do that. He wouldn't take off without the stuff." That brought some reassurance. But Rod might have been nabbed by the cops. Suddenly Gary was certain of it and was filled with dread. He was all alone. Worse—he was in this creepy old building all alone. In the dark. Getting darker.

I'd rather go back to prison than stay here, Gary thought. He began pacing, fretting over what he was going to do, stopping every few steps to listen, straining to hear some sign of Rod's return. Several times he went to the door and put his hand on the knob, but he was too afraid to open it. In addition to his fear that Rod wouldn't return, he'd become irrationally afraid that there was something waiting for him on the other side of the door. Something dark and hideous. Waiting for him to stick his head out again so that it could bite it off.

He shuddered.

Stop it, Gary, he told himself, imitating Rod's voice in his head, imagining Rod saying it. When Rod said something, it made a difference.

Gary paced some more and decided that if Rod didn't show soon, he would take the truck and leave the boxes of drugs here. He would ride around and look for Rod. If he didn't find him . . . Gary guessed he'd just have to turn himself in. It was the only thing he could think of; he couldn't face the non-prison world without Rod around to tell him what to do.

He waited some more, standing still, shallow breathing, counting to a hundred slowly in his mind five times. He'd just made up his mind to go and was about to get in the truck when he heard a muffled bang—like a door closing—and footsteps getting louder, coming down the three stairs to the door.

Gary was thrilled. Rod was back! The joy was immediately tempered, diminished greatly, by the thought that maybe it *wasn't* Rod outside the door coming for him. A dozen images of movie monsters flashed in his head, but none of them was just right for the fearful thing that he was afraid of.

He nearly bolted for the truck when the doorknob turned, but it was Rod after all, a bag of groceries in each arm.

"Hey, fuckface. Give me a hand. Didn't you hear me kicking on the door out there? What the fuck are you doing in here? It's about ten degrees colder in this fucking garage than it is in the school."

"Uh, sorry, Rod," Gary answered, and beamed. Not even Rod's anger could quell the happiness he felt now that Rod was back.

"What the fuck are you smiling about?" Rod asked as he put the grocery bags on top of the boxes of stolen pharmaceuticals.

"Nothing," Gary said quickly.

Rod frowned at him and turned to the stack of boxes. He pulled one off the side and ripped it open. He reached in and pulled out a small brown jar with a white cap and a typewritten label on the front.

"All right!" Rod said, and held the bottle up for Gary to see. "Pharmaceutical coke, my friend. It doesn't get any better than this." He put the jar in his pocket. "Well, don't stand there like a fucking lump—get the groceries, and let's go find a nice cozy classroom."

Gary smiled and nodded. He felt much better with Rod there. He still didn't like the idea of staying in the creepy school, but as long as Rod didn't leave him alone again, he'd be okay.

Hefting the groceries into his arms, he followed Rod out the door and up the stairs into the gloom.

9

Anna struggled through nightmares of bad men chasing her, beating her, shooting at her with guns. She dreamed about the events at Deedee's apartment, and she dreamed of her parents' deaths. The two became intertwined until the men who were beating Deedee became the men who had killed her parents.

When she rose to the semiconscious level, just below complete awareness, the image stayed with her. Of course, she knew they weren't the same men. In fact, she'd never seen the men who had killed her folks.

Who were they? What kind of people could they be to do such a horrible thing? What kind of people felt they had the right to go around beating people up and killing innocent people just because they felt like it? She couldn't fathom it. She knew about crime, had caught glimpses, when she was supposed to be in bed, of R-rated movies her parents were watching, had seen the nightly news when really bad things had happened, but the violence had all seemed so far removed from her quiet life in Towns End.

The reality of violence was a brutal shock to her that neither movies nor TV had really prepared her for. But the worst thing of all was the realization that the people who could do such evil things were very real and very close to home. Nowhere was safe.

They were evil. They were monsters. But that didn't give them the right to do the things they did.

Anger filled Anna again. Hot, restless, hateful anger grew in her, pushing her heart rate and blood pressure up and bringing her fully back to consciousness.

The hospital room was dark and quiet. All she could hear was the steady beat of the heart monitor.

My heartbeat, she thought. I'm going to live and never get the chance to find the men who killed my parents. She started sobbing. Why should she be alive when her parents were dead? Why couldn't she die too, and be with them? Why couldn't those evil men have killed her too?

She wished she knew who they were. She wished she had them in the room with her right now. She'd kill them, kill them with her bare hands, rip them to shreds, she was so angry.

She felt a thrill at the thought of being able to do that. She remembered how she'd stopped that guy with the power of her mind at Deedee's apartment. If she could do that, then she could do the same, or worse, to her parents' killers. If only she could find them before she made a full recovery.

Deedee knew who they were. She'd told Anna she'd seen them on TV on *America's Most Wanted*. She had to find Deedee. She had to find the men who'd killed her parents. If she couldn't die and be with her parents, she could make sure the men who'd killed them wouldn't live a moment longer than she could prevent. And just maybe the effort would kill her too, and she could join her folks.

10

Kevin was afraid that he was headed for a nervous breakdown. He couldn't sleep for the nightmares of being trapped in his wheelchair on the other side. He was nervous, jittery all the time, never knowing when he might jump out of his body. James's words haunted him.

Borrowed time.

Time is up.

He started drinking too much. It was the only thing that would allow him some peace of mind for any length of time. But after three days of steady drinking, even booze didn't bring relief anymore.

His work suffered. He stopped answering his phone and turned off his answering machine after listening to his agent's tenth tearful plea for him to answer or the deal with Tri-Star was going to go down the tubes.

He didn't care.

He didn't even care when Caroline called, leaving a short message asking after him.

Strangely, for three days, he didn't jump at all. Perhaps it was his fear of doing so that kept him from it. But he was equally wanting to jump. He was at war with himself—half of him scared to death to jump, the other half anxious to find out what James had meant and how it tied in with the other two jumpers he'd seen. He wasn't sure how or why, but he was certain those two souls were involved in this.

Borrowed time.

By the end of the week, his sleeplessness had combined with the alcohol to bring him to wit's end. He became very paranoid. It go so bad that he canceled his flight to L.A. for the Tri-Star gig (igniting a flurry of calls from his agent) and didn't answer the door when Caroline showed up on Saturday. He hid in his large wheelchair-accessible closet and sat there for two hours after she'd given up and left. He was afraid to come out, certain that Caroline had gotten in the house somehow, and he just couldn't bear to face her in the condition he was in.

It was dark in the house when he finally summoned enough courage to leave the closet. He went to the window and peered cautiously around the edge of the blinds. It was dark outside. No cars were in the circular driveway. He motored the chair through the dark house, heading for his studio overlooking the bay.

He felt feverish, near delirium. Suddenly, without warning, he jumped. It happened in a split second. The thunder/lightning shift in reality exploded on him, and he was outside his body, soaring over the plain of marching dead. He could see them like an army of ants below him.

There was a blinding flash of light, and he was hurtling through darkness. The big light burst upon him, and in an instant he was in the weird dimension of fungus pillars and bubble flocks of people's lives.

A mass of them was bearing down on him. He tried to avoid them by grabbing on to the nearest pillar and hiding behind it. The bubbles swarmed past, several brushing against him, leaving him with glimpses of rice paddies and Oriental children playing at the edge of a vast field, then it was gone.

He floated from behind the pillar and looked around. There, in the distance, was a solitary glowing sphere like his own. Excited, he moved as rapidly as he could toward it. He was frustrated by his clumsy propulsion efforts and swore profusely.

He got closer and could see the outline of the young girl within her aura. He pushed on. She turned when he was less than twenty feet away, and she saw him. A look of fear crossed her face, and she started away from him.

"Wait!" Kevin called. *"It's all right. I'm not going to hurt you."*

The girl stopped retreating, and Kevin moved forward slowly. *"It's all right,"* he kept repeating softly.

"Who are you?" The girl surprised him with the question.

"My name is Kevin," he said.

"What do you want?"

Kevin was suddenly unsure of how to answer. What exactly *did* he want? *"I—I'm . . . like you. Um, . . . you know, alive. I just want to talk to you."*

She came closer.

"What happened to you?" she asked.

Kevin didn't understand. He looked at himself and could see nothing wrong. *"What do you mean?"* he asked.

"Why are you here? What happened to you?"

Kevin was still puzzled. *"Nothing happened to me. I'm here because I've been looking for you and the woman I've seen you with."*

The girl's face darkened a moment. She asked, *"How do you get here?"*

Kevin laughed a little. *"I just meditate."* Now it was the girl's turn to look puzzled. *"I learned how to do it,"* Kevin explained, *"cuz I'm crippled. I learned how to do it so I could escape my wheelchair."* He surprised himself by blurting that out. He realized he'd never said that out loud before to anyone, not even to Caroline, to whom he thought he'd told everything. Now that it was said, he suddenly doubted if it was entirely true. After the episode with James, he wondered if he would have begun jumping even without learning how. If being here was his destiny, as James had implied, he would have ended up right here, right now, no matter what he did or didn't do.

It was a depressing thought.

"Oh," the girl said, matter-of-factly accepting his explanation as only a child could. *"Why are you looking for me and Deedee?"*

"Deedee? That's your friend's name?"

The girl nodded.

"What's your name?" Kevin asked.

"Anna. Anna Wheaton," the girl answered.

"Well, Anna Wheaton," Kevin said, *"I'm not really sure why I've been looking for you and your friend, Deedee. I've seen the two of you over here, and I realized that you were jumpers, like me."*

The girl looked confused. *"What's a jumper?"*

"You can leave your body, like I can, like Deedee can." The girl nodded, understanding. *"I guess I was hoping you two might be able to help me answer some questions."*

"What questions?" Anna asked.

Kevin told her of his experience in the dimension of the marching dead.

"I've never been there," the girl answered. *"I always come here,"* she added sadly.

"Do you have any idea why I'm here? Why we're here?" Kevin asked, feeling a little foolish asking desperate questions of a child.

"I don't know," Anna replied, *"and I don't care."*

Kevin looked at her. She was crying. He felt like a jerk. Here he was dumping all this crap on a kid. Selfish as usual.

"What's wrong?" he asked gently, moving closer.

The girl began to cry harder. *"Deedee . . . she . . . she's hurt. And my mom and dad . . ."* The girl couldn't finish for crying.

"It's okay," Kevin mumbled. He didn't know what to do. Normally, his instinct would be to hug a grieving child, but in this new plane of existence, he wasn't sure he could have physical contact. But he had to do something. He'd never been one who could ignore another person's pain, especially a child's.

He reached out to her. As he did, he entered her aura. He was immediately overwhelmed with her feelings. He felt her sorrow and fear, but most of all, he felt her raging anger—an anger more powerful then anything he himself had ever felt toward anything.

More than her feeling, Kevin knew her thoughts and memories all in a rush so swift, it left him dizzy. He knew about her family, could picture her sisters and her parents. The feeling of sorrow intensified with the latter. He could see completely in his mind's eye all the events that had led to her first out-of-body experience and everything that had happened since. He shuddered at the fear she generated when she thought of the thing she called the Shadow Monster. And he shuddered more at the deadly determination in her to hunt down and kill the killers of her parents.

Kevin was overwhelmed by all this. His head swam, and he felt nauseous at the force of her emotions and thoughts invading him. He tried to back off, but their auras were acting like magnets, pulling them together. He felt the urge to panic rising, and he pushed it down. He concentrated on remaining calm.

An amazing thing happened. As soon as Kevin began consciously calming himself, the barrage of intense emotions and thoughts from Anna subsided, and the color of her aura changed from red to blue.

"Will you help me?" she asked Kevin.

Kevin nodded. *"I don't think I have a choice in the matter."*

11

It was a week before Deedee was discharged from the hospital. During that time the police interviewed her numerous times, taking her version of what had happened. They were polite and all, but Deedee got the feeling that they weren't too sympathetic, especially after she told them about her first meeting with Dick. Some of the cops didn't even bother to hide that they thought she had been asking for it. They told her Dick and his buddies had been released on bail but had been ordered to stay away from her. A trial date had not yet been set.

Jesse stayed with her the whole time, leaving only at night to return to her apartment to get some sleep, or once to go back to Helena to get some clothes and pick up his paycheck from work. He had called in and taken some personal time he had accumulated. On her discharge day, he arrived with a dozen red roses and drove her home. Even though she could walk perfectly well, Deedee let Jesse carry her into the apartment. He carried her the way a groom carries a bride across the threshold, and the symbolism escaped neither of them. Jesse looked away, embarrassed. Deedee smiled.

"Where would you like to go? The couch or your bed?"

"The bedroom," she answered, resting her head on his shoulder.

He carried her across the living room and pushed the bedroom door open with his foot.

"You make me happy," Deedee said dreamily as he placed her on the bed. She felt him stiffen a little, and he pulled away. She took his hand with both of hers.

"Jesse, I know I have no right to keep you here. I overheard your conversation with Marcia at the hospital. If I'm messing up your life, you should go." She added in a soft voice, "You should go to her."

Jesse hesitated a moment before sitting beside her at the edge of the bed. "Deedee, I don't know, really, why I decided to come here when I did. I felt bad about blowing you off, I guess. But now I'm glad I came. I want to be here. I know you don't have anyone else. As for Marcia, maybe this was a good thing. I thought I wanted to marry her, but after seeing you . . . I mean, after this whole incident, I'm not so sure. I kind of feel relieved, and that says something in and of itself."

Deedee smiled and clasped Jesse's hands tighter. That was what she'd been hoping to hear. "Jesse," she said, "remember what I told you before at the coffee shop? I still need you to help me, Jesse. Now more than ever. That poor little girl is out there all alone in Limbo, and the Shadow Monster is sure to get her if it already hasn't." She began to cry. "I have to go look for her, and I need you to help send me there."

Jesse gave her a look of incredulity. "You're all beat-up and sore. You can't be serious. It's too dangerous. It'll hurt you."

"No. It's okay," she responded immediately. "I'm okay inside. I might be sore, but I can take it. I have to."

"No!" Jesse answered, his tone adamant.

"Please," Deedee pleaded. She searched for the right words to convey to him just how important this was to her, but her emotions got in the way. Her eyes filled with tears, transmitting her message much more effectively to Jesse than words could have done.

"Aw, Dee. I don't want to hurt you," he said softly.

Deedee could only weep in answer.

Jesse looked away, exasperated for a moment, then looked back, his eyes running over her body. "Maybe there's a way," he said, more to himself than to Deedee. "Lie still and relax," he told her.

He climbed on to the bed, straddling Deedee on his knees without putting any of his weight on her. He began unbuttoning her blouse. He went very slowly, cautiously, as he lifted her gently to slip the garment off her. He bit his lip, seeing the bruises and welts covering her chest and stomach. Her breasts were the worst. They were swollen, misshapen, purple and dark red with bruises. Jesse knew he couldn't touch them. They were too sore.

Carefully, he undid her slacks, a loose-fitting pair that one of the nurses had given her, since all of Deedee's pants were tight-fitting jeans that she never could have gotten into. She had insisted on pants to hide the bruises on her legs. He pulled the slacks off slowly, every bruise on her legs causing a pang of sorrow and anger inside him. Gently he removed her panties and spread her legs—not too far apart. He leaned over and blew gently on her exposed sex. She trembled. He blew again and followed it with the tenderest kiss to her clitoris that he could manage.

A soft moan escaped her lips. Ever so lightly, he let his tongue explore her, gliding over the delicious surface, tickling here, rubbing softly there, until she was moaning with every breath and gyrating her hips in rhythm to the ministrations of his tongue.

Jesse could tell by her breathing that she was building to a climax. He continued his gentle oral caresses with all the care he could muster. He felt her body begin to tremble. Her moans grew into cries of ecstasy. She shrieked. Her body convulsed once—and went limp.

Jesse raised his face from between her legs. Deedee's arms were flung out to either side of her body. Her face was turned to the left, her neck arched as if she were staring at an interesting spot on the wall just above the left bedpost. Except that her eyes were unseeing.

Jesse crawled over her prone body to the head of the bed. He knelt there and felt her neck for a pulse. It was there, but just barely. He lay next to her and pulled the heavy quilt over them. He wrapped her in his arms and held her close, waiting for her to return.

12

Deedee was scared. She had left her body easily—perhaps too easily—and was streaming through the darkness that was interrupted only by the colored beams of laser light. What if she couldn't get back to her body? What if it was too soon for her to be handling this? What if she died?

She shuddered at the thought that if she died, the Shadow Monster would devour her soul. After all, in her own opinion—and who knew her better than herself?—she hadn't been a very good person. She was certain that if she died now, she would be a meal for the Shadow Monster and spend eternity being digested in its murky bowels.

If it wasn't for Anna needing her, Deedee would have turned back. She couldn't do that, though. Anna was all alone out here, waiting for her.

Deedee felt the familiar falling sensation and knew she was about to pass over to Limbo. She kept her eyes open and her senses as alert as possible and hoped that the Shadow Monster wouldn't be waiting for her.

It wasn't. The landscape around her was empty even of the swarms of bubble clusters. That worried her. She knew from past experience that the bubble clusters tended to become scarce when the Shadow Monster was around. She was relieved when several large clusters floated by, followed by numerous smaller ones. She avoided them easily and examined her own aura, looking for any of the telltale yellow light she had seen before, when she had been close to death at the hands of Dick and his buddies. There was none. Her aura was filled with the life-affirming blue light.

Just like the two auras in the distance that were moving toward her.

"Anna!" she called. They rushed toward each other until they were hugging and their auras had become one, changing to a bright orange at their joy.

"I'm so glad you're all right!" Anna squealed, tears streaming down her face.

"Me too!" Deedee replied, beginning to cry a little herself. *"Me too."* She hugged Anna and looked over at the black man nearby, in an aura of brilliant blue.

"Who's your friend?" Deedee asked, stepping back from Anna.

"This is . . . Kevin," Anna said. She looked at the man questioningly. *"I don't know your last name."*

"I'm Kevin. Kevin Lucier," the man offered.

"I'm Deedee Blaine." She moved toward him, hand outstretched.

Kevin backed away. *"I'd rather not touch your aura,"* he said. *"I've got enough emotions of my own messing me up without feeling someone else's too."*

Deedee laughed, and Anna joined in.

"Kevin's going to help me," Anna said.

"Help you what?" Deedee asked.

"Help me find the men who killed my mom and dad. And kill them."

four

JUMPERS

1

Gary carried the bags of groceries, trying to see what kind of food was inside, and followed Rod out of the garage and down the hall to the lobby.

"Let's check out the basement first," Rod said. He led the way across the lobby to the archway on the right, which said "Boys" over it. "Come on," Rod said, and started down the stairs. Gary put the groceries down at the top of the stairs and followed. The stairway wound around once and ended at a low-ceilinged room, whose walls were cinder blocks painted a putrid shade of green. Arrows on the wall across from the stairs indicated that the boys' room was to the left, the gymnasium to the right.

"You check out the bathroom, I'll look at the gym," Rod said to Gary. Rod went through the double doors, which creaked ominously. Gary considered following him but knew how mad his friend would get. Reluctantly, he turned and headed for the boys' room.

He started around the corner to the narrow opening in the wall that served as the boys' room door—and stopped cold. He smelled something. Something sour, wet. Body odor. For a moment, Gary flashed on a time in prison when he'd been cleaning the men's showers, and that smell had washed over him. A moment later, two inmates had pounced on him and raped him.

Gary shivered involuntarily at the memory. The

smell scared him. It meant someone was in the boys' room. He held his breath and listened, and sure enough, he could hear wheezing from within.

Gary wondered what he should do. If he called Rod and no one was in the boys' room, Rod would make fun of him and get mad. But he was positive they weren't alone. There was someone in there all right.

Gary thought about what Rod might do to anyone he caught in the school. He knew his partner would do anything he had to to keep them out of the hands of the cops. Gary didn't want Rod to kill any more people, but he didn't want to go jail either.

The latter fear was stronger. He decided to go and get Rod. He was turning away when he felt a hand on his shoulder. He let out a shriek and jumped away. Cackling, raspy laughter followed him. He turned and faced a wizened, hunched old man, just as Rod came back.

"What the fuck?" Rod said. "Who the hell are you?"

The old man opened his mouth to speak but was seized by a coughing spasm. He hacked and wheezed until he he had hacked up enough phlegm to deposit a large wad on the basement floor. "I think I should be asking who the hell are you?" the old man said, and was seized by another coughing attack. He worked himself up to expectorating another juicy one and went on. "You ain't cops, that's for sure," the old man said. "This here's my place. Been my place for nigh on three weeks. You can stay a little while, but don't even think about taking over the place."

All the while the old homeless man was talking, Rod was slowly working his way behind him.

"We don't want to take anything over," Gary said

apologetically. "We just need a place to stay for a little while. Ain't that right, Rod?"

At that moment, Rod pounced. The old guy's back was to him. Rod pulled his hunting knife from his boot, grabbed the old man around the neck with his right arm, cutting off his air and any noise he might make, and drove the knife into the old man's lower back. He twisted the knife once, twice, making the old man jerk like a puppet on a string, and pulled it out. The old man slumped to the floor, with his last breath sounding like air leaving a deflating balloon.

"Rod! No!" Gary cried when he realized what his partner was doing, but as usual his reaction was far too slow. The old homeless man lay dead on the floor before Gary could take a step.

The old man lay there, blood running sluggishly from his mouth, his eyes open, staring at the small pool of blood that was forming around his face.

"W-Why?" Gary stammered, his eyes filling with tears, his voice cracking. "W-Why'd you have to kill him?"

Rod bent over and wiped the bloody blade off on the old man's filthy coat. He gave Gary a disgusted look for his show of emotion. "Why do you think I killed him? We can't let anyone know where we are. Don't you get it? We were on *America's Most Fucking Wanted*. Every cop, every couch potato in this country, will be looking for us. We are not taking any chances."

Rod reached down and grabbed the back of the collar of the old man's coat. Grunting, he dragged the body into the boys' room. "Hey, Gary! Come here and check this out." He sounded excited.

Reluctantly, Gary went into the boys' room.

Rod had stuffed the body into one of the stalls and closed the door, leaving the old man's feet sticking out. Rod was squatting in the corner of the room near the urinals, where a sleeping bag was laid out next to a round metal contraption that looked like a small Christmas tree stand.

"We got us a Sterno cooker," Rod said, smiling and holding up the round metal thing. "Now we can have some hot chow. Go get the groceries."

Gary did as he was told, fighting back tears and trying not to look at the feet of the dead man. He went up the stairs to the lobby as quickly as possible, grabbed the bags, and hurried back down to Rod, like a kid afraid of the dark.

"I thought we'd have to eat these cold," Rod said, grabbing the bag from Gary and rifling its contents until he pulled out a package of Oscar Mayer wieners and a can of B&M baked beans.

"I'm starved," he said, and tore open the franks with his teeth. He kept up a constant patter of small talk while he lit the Sterno cooker and skewered a couple of dogs on his knife. While he roasted them, he talked about going to Mexico after they unloaded the goods. How they would live high on the hog, have babes galore, and never have to worry about nothing ever again.

Gary listened in silence. For a long time, a feeling, a certainty had been growing in Gary that Rod was more than just a criminal, that he was bad—that he was *evil*. Gary had fought the feeling, pushing it away whenever Rod had acted crazy and done bad things, but since the robbery at the hospital, Gary found it harder and harder to do. Rod's actions at the hospital—killing that cop and that innocent family—and all the people he'd murdered since—most for no reason that Gary thought was good—had given birth to a distrust that was becoming deeper every day. Where before Gary had always thought Rod was his friend and would always look out for him, now he wasn't so sure. Through the slow-moving machinery that was his thought process, Gary was beginning to realize that Rod didn't care about anyone—didn't *take* care of anyone—other than himself.

Gary didn't want to believe that, but the thought wouldn't go away. The more he went over things, the more he came to believe Rod was just using him and would kill him in an instant—the way he had killed Tommy Wayne—as soon as he felt Gary was no longer useful.

Gary shook his head, trying to dispel the thought. Rod didn't notice. He went on chatting about what he was going to do with his money. Gary tried to listen, tried not to have bad thoughts about his friend, but it was hard to do, especially with the dead homeless guy's feet sticking out of the toilet stall less than a yard away.

Gary sighed and watched his friend gingerly pull a dog from his knife and, with lips pursed, wolf down the steaming piece of meat. Rod had saved his life in prison, and Gary knew it was a debt he could never repay, so he'd stick by him, at least for now.

But he was beginning to realize that he didn't like Rod very much.

2

Deedee didn't know what to say. Anna's aura had begun to glow a fierce red. She could feel the anger and hatred emanating from the girl as she declared that she was going to kill her parents' killers, and this guy, Kevin, was going to help her.

Deedee noticed something else too. The swarms of bubbles had become scarce. She hadn't seen one for a while. The liquid light belching from the holes in the ground had turned a bloodred that was deepening to black.

The Shadow Monster.

Anna was too worked up to notice the signs of the creature's approach, and the new guy didn't seem to notice that anything was wrong. Deedee started to warn them, but the Shadow Monster was there in the blink of an eye. Before Deedee could get out, "The Shadow Monster is coming," the Shadow Monster was there.

It unfurled around them, boiling up out of nowhere like a vicious black thunderhead, making the air crackle with evil. Static electricity ran like veins up through the shadows and into the dark clouds of bubbles that orbited the thing.

Panic shot through Deedee. In her weakened condition, the presence of the Shadow Monster felt a hundred times stronger—dangerously stronger. She could feel it pulling at her, drawing her as a magnet draws iron filings. Her ears were ringing, her stomach was in a tumult of nauseous spasms. Dark images flashed before her eyes—herself in bed with several men, them filling every orifice in her body with organs the size of baseball bats. The scene wavered, and the men became animals—a dog, a goat, a bull, and a large snake, each with grotesquely huge genitalia.

A whispering arose around her, inside her. A deliciously evil and seductive voice spoke to her of forbidden pleasures and undreamed-of, earth-shattering orgasms.

She couldn't take it. The Shadow Monster was too strong, and she was still too weak. She had to flee or succumb.

She chose to flee back to her body.

3

Kevin was frozen with fear. This thing in front of them, all around them, exuded such a force of evil that he was stunned. The thing was enormous. Its darker mass, in the center, bubbled like an oily stew, grotesque faces rising out of the blackness to within inches of his own face, screaming with foul air that nauseated him. He saw hundreds of tongues, like tentacles, slither from the presence and wrap around his aura, caressing it. Their touch was slick and oily and left Kevin feeling soiled.

A babble of voices that seemed to come from everywhere and nowhere at the same time spoke inside his head. Though he could make no sense of the jumble of words that were half spoken, half screamed, mixed with torrents of hysterical laughter, the voices brought vivid images to his mind.

He saw himself back in the Nam on that fateful day that he'd lost his legs and had caused James to lose his life. Only, in this vision, he grabbed James and, laughing, threw him under the treads of the tank. The vision dimmed, changed, and came back. He saw himself whole, his legs intact, walking into a hospital room. On the bed lay the young girl, Anna. Grinning evilly, he climbed on the bed and ripped the tubes and intravenous feeds from her arms. Ripping the hospital johnny from her body, he spread her legs.

"No!" he screamed in revulsion. The voices in his

head rose to a deafening pitch. He shouted again, louder, and felt the evil thing repelled with the force of his voice. All went black for a moment. He opened his eyes and was back in his body, slumped over in his wheelchair in front of the bay window, which rattled with the force of wind and rain from a raging storm.

4

Anna saw her two friends' life spheres approach, envelop them, and swiftly ferry their souls away from the Shadow Monster and back to their bodies. She was alone with the thing. But strangely enough, she was no longer afraid of it. The thing seemed to sense this, and it didn't pounce, didn't devour her. Slowly gathering around her, the Shadow Monster seemed in awe, almost *afraid* of *her*!

A feeling of inner strength and courage, like nothing she had ever known, filled her. Instinctively she knew where this strength and lack of fear came from: It came from not caring anymore whether she lived or died. All she cared about was revenge, making the men who had killed her parents pay for what they'd done. It had become an all-consuming lust inside her that left no room for anything else.

The thing read her mind and chuckled softly, evilly to itself. *Yes! Revenge!* it cooed lovingly. *Revenge is sweet meat, little Anna. Very sweet meat so good to eeaaat.* Laughter and screams bubbled up around her.

"Go away," she said flatly, turning from the Shadow Monster. *"I have more important things to do than listen to your bullcrap."* With the use of the expletive, a pang of sorrow pierced her. Her dad had always said *bullcrap*. Refusing to swear in front of his daughters, he had modified all the most common swears into acceptable phrases. *Bullshit*

became *bullcrap*. *Shit* was *shoot*. *Damn* was *dang*. The mother of all swears, the f-word, became *fudge*.

Oh, no, sweet Anna, the Shadow Monster whispered. *You don't want me to go away. No no no. No, you don't.*

Anna turned to the Shadow Monster abruptly. *"Yeah? Get real."*

Hideous laughter. *Real? Get real? I am real, little Anna, sweet little Anna. You know I'm real, so very real—real enough to eat you. But I don't want to eat you* (a whispered voice—high and thin and quickly gone—added *not yet*). *I want to help you.*

It was Anna's turn to laugh. *"You? Help me? What a joke!"*

The Shadow Monster laughed also. *I know! Sounds funny, huh? Sounds pretty damn queer, doesn't it? But it's true! Go figure, huh? I want to help!*

Anna sighed wearily. *"Look,"* she said, anger rising in her voice, *"if you want to eat me, then go ahead. I don't care. But I bet you'll choke on me. Why don't you just go away and leave me alone? I've got things to do."*

She floated away from the creature, but it followed, folding its billowing blackness around her.

And just how will you do these things? the Shadow Monster asked.

Anna hesitated.

You see? I know what you want, little Anna. I know! And I can help you. I can lead you to the men who killed your parents. I can help you get your revenge. And I only ask for a small thing in return. A very small thing.

Anna stood, thoughtfully regarding the beast. *"You can do that?"*

Oh! Yesssss! the Shadow Monster hissed.

"How do I know you're not lying?"

A hundred outraged, aghast faces boiled to the

surface of the Shadow Monster to look with reproach upon Anna. *Oh, sweetie,* the voices claimed in unison, *how can you say that? How can you even think it?* A multitude of laughing, giggling, screeching voices swept up around her. *But seriously,* the Shadow Monster said, cutting off the laughter as its face coalesced into the one hideous face, *you can trust me. As long as I get what I want.* The thing smiled, its tentacled tongue lolling from its mouth, the suckers each a tiny mouth with a tiny tentacled tongue protruding from it.

Anna regarded the monster warily. *"What do you want for helping me?"*

The Shadow Monster giggled, and a thousand incomprehensible whispers filled the air. *It's nothing. Nothing really. Just a small thing. Inconsequential really. Nothing,* the Shadow Monster said over the whispers.

"What?" Anna demanded.

The Shadow Monster giggled and shrugged all at once, and the answer came as all the whispers became one, sounding like an echo in reverse.

Your soul, sweet Anna. Your soul.

5

Deedee awoke in Jesse's arms. She pulled back and took a shrieking breath and stared wildly about her for a moment, unseeing of him or her bedroom.

"Deedee! Deedee! Are you okay?"

She looked at him, blinked, and focused. "The Shadow Monster," she mumbled.

"What?" Jesse asked, holding her by the shoulders.

"The . . . oh, my God! Anna! Anna's back there with the Shadow Monster." She shivered involuntarily as she spoke.

"It's okay," Jesse told her. "Calm down. She'll be okay."

"No! You don't understand! You don't know what the thing is like. I've got to get back. I've got to help her."

Jesse rubbed her arms, trying to soothe her. "Take it easy. Calm down."

"No!" Deedee shouted. "I've got to go back! Make love to me, now!"

Jesse laughed nervously. "Just like that? I don't think it's such a good idea, Dee. You just came out of it. You're still too weak."

"Fuck it!" Deedee swore, surprising both Jesse and herself. He drew back a little from her.

"Please, Jesse," she pleaded. "You have no idea what danger she's in. I have to go back *now*."

"Jesus, Deedee. This is crazy. I don't know."

"Please, Jesse. Anna needs me. I know you don't understand. You can't possibly comprehend what the Shadow Monster is like, but I tell you this, it's evil. Pure evil. It's the Devil Himself."

"I don't believe in the Devil," Jesse said matter-of-factly.

"I'm sorry, Jesse, but that don't count for shit, because He's real. I've seen Him."

"If what you say is true, then you're in as much danger as this girl Anna. And in your condition, you're probably in more danger. I won't be an accessory to your death."

"It'll be all right. I've got to try. Please, Jesse."

Jesse debated a moment, shook his head in exasperation, and gave in. He started to go down on her again, but she stopped him.

"No, not that way. It'll take too long. I need you inside me now, and I need you to fuck me hard."

6

Kevin sat up in his wheelchair as a strong gust of wind drove the rain against the bay window so hard, it sounded like machine-gun fire. In a flash of lighting—he wasn't sure if it was outside or in his head—he jumped out of his body again and found himself back in the Nam, Pleiku City, walking alongside the tank, right behind James.

His friend turned and smiled at him. *"You got to go back there, bro. That little girl needs you,"* James said. He looked sad, very sad. *"You can't leave her to deal with that evil all by herself."*

Kevin thought of the horrible, amorphous dark thing and felt fear course through him. *"I can't. I . . . can't,"* he stammered.

James shook his head and looked at Kevin with pity. *"Sorry, bro. You've got to. You've got no choice. Borrowed time, remember? You've got to pay the price."*

"But why that way?" Kevin asked. He looked around wildly. They were nearing the building where the sniper attack would come from. He could see the kid in the window waving. *"Why can't I just save you now and change everything?"*

"No can do, bro. This is a dream. This has already happened. You know it. I know it. Can't change what's done. There's only one way you can help me now."

The tank exploded. Kevin screamed, and in

another flash of light, he awoke back in his chair. It lasted only a second. The lightning and thunder exploded over him louder than the tank had ever been, and he quickly found himself back in that weird other place. A few yards away from him was the little girl, Anna, with the Shadow Monster swirling around her. They were moving away.

7

"Harder! Faster!" Deedee commanded Jesse. He was on top of her and inside her but being too cautious for her needs. "Fuck me harder, Jesse! Harder!"

Finally he obeyed, thrusting hard and fast into her. With it came pain, almost too much pain.

This isn't going to work, she thought with despair. Jesse was right—her body was too injured to take this.

But then, just as the pain was becoming unbearable and she was ready to tell him to stop, the pain changed. Suddenly it was like reaching the top of a hill and coasting down the other side. She felt detached from herself and began to feel pleasure. An orgasm built quickly inside. It was an orgasm unlike any she'd felt before. It came on her in a rush, exploding behind her eyes and sweeping down through her body instead of staying in her groin and spreading out.

She cried out, bit her lip, and went limp beneath Jesse.

The journey to the other side was completed in a fraction of a second. One moment she was feeling the orgasm burst upon her, the next she was watching her life sphere pulling away.

She looked around frantically for Anna, couldn't find her at first, then saw the miasma of darkness that was the Shadow Monster. It swirled in the distance, moving away.

"Stop!" she cried. With great effort, she propelled herself forward. From the corner of her eye, she saw Kevin's aura moving toward her.

"The Shadow Monster's got her," she shouted to him. *"We've got to help her!"*

They came abreast of each other and continued on toward the boiling darkness.

"Anna!" Deedee called. They were nearing the creature. She called again. The darkness of the thing billowed toward them. Its face, gigantic, formed from the shadows.

Go away! it said in a rumbling voice, not unlike the sound of belching. A foul wind blew over them, and the thing's tongue lashed out threateningly toward them.

Kevin stopped, a look of fear on his face, his aura turning from blue to a sickly green, but Deedee pressed on.

The Shadow Monster glared at her, its mouth opening wide as if to devour her. Suddenly its expression changed. Its eyes rolled back in its head, and its mouth closed. With a look of pain, the thing's face split apart, and Anna emerged from within the bubbling mass of shadows.

"Anna! Thank God! Are you all right?" Deedee asked, pressing forward. The Shadow Monster curled in upon itself and receded a few feet. Seeing this, Kevin came on.

"I'm fine," Anna said dully. Her eyes and expression were vacant, like someone just awakened from a deep sleep or trance.

"What's going on?" Deedee asked, drawing closer to Anna. The Shadow Monster took a menacing step forward at the same time, letting out a low

inhuman growl that set the almost-liquid atmosphere around them to vibrating.

"Back off!" Anna commanded over her shoulder to the thing. Amazingly, it whined and receded like a scolded dog. But underneath it all remained the constant hilarity of screaming, laughing, babbling voices.

Deedee watched with amazement. *"What the hell is going on?"* she asked emphatically.

"Nothing," Anna replied, none too convincingly.

Kevin, who had been hovering nearby, spoke up. *"What is that thing?"*

Deedee gave him a hard look. *"You have to ask? Can't you feel it?"*

Kevin glanced sideways at the thing and shuddered. The Shadow Monster howled with derision, and a babble of incomprehensible voices and animal sounds rose inside his head. Here and there, Kevin thought he recognized voices—those of his parents, old friends, James. He turned away from the creature and tried to shut the voices out.

"Anna, why were you with the Shadow Monster?" Deedee asked.

Anna answered but wouldn't look at Deedee. *"It's going to help me find the men who killed my parents,"* she said matter-of-factly.

"Oh, no! Anna, no!" Deedee said, aghast. *"Don't do it! You can't be serious."*

"Why not?" Anna asked.

"Because that thing is pure evil," Deedee said, glancing toward the Shadow Monster and adding in a low voice, *"it's the Devil!"*

The Shadow Monster burst into laughter. *Oh, puhlease!* It roared laughter. *How colloquial!*

"I told you to back off," Anna snapped, and the thing quieted except for bubbles of laughter that rose from it sporadically.

"I don't care what it is," Anna said. *"It's the only thing that can help me. The men who killed my parents were evil, so they have a connection to the Shadow Monster. It can help me get them for what they did."*

"Two wrongs don't make a right," Kevin put in.

Butt out, Sambo! the Shadow Monster bellowed.

Anna turned on it with a savage, angry expression, and the creature visibly cringed and seemed to diminish in size.

Hey! Just kidding! the Shadow Monster shrugged, but Anna only continued to glare until the thing moved back a few feet. *Jesus H. Fucking Christ! Can't you take a joke?* it said, and giggled nervously.

"Anna, please don't have anything to do with it," Deedee pleaded. *"You can't trust it. It has no reason to help you except to hurt you and devour you."*

For a moment, Anna considered revealing her deal with the Shadow Monster to Deedee, then thought better of it. *"I don't care,"* she said. *"It's the only chance I have of getting them."*

Seeing Anna's determination, Deedee tried to think of another tack. *"What about Kevin? He said he'd help you."*

"No offense, Kevin, but what can he do? The Shadow Monster knows who these men are. It's connected to them. And it will help me punish them. There's nothing you can do to stop me."

Deedee sighed, then shrugged, too. *"Well, you know what they say: If you can't beat 'em, join 'em."*

"I'm not asking you to go with me," Anna said.

"I know, but I'm going."

"Me too," Kevin added.

No way! No fucking way! the Shadow Monster shrieked. It came menacingly toward the three, growing in size and hideousness as it came. *Get the hell out of here, you two! She's mine, and we do this alone.*

Kevin cringed and backed away, but Deedee and Anna stood their ground and faced it.

"You don't make the rules now. I do," Anna said. *"Or our deal is off."*

The Shadow Monster considered for a moment, then let out a bright, high-pitched giggle. *What the heck? Right? The more the merrier, I always say*. Its form swirled and changed, becoming a huge dark man carrying a shadowy boom box to his ear. *So let's pa-a-arty!* the Shadow Monster sang as it danced around them. *Do a little dance. Make a little love. Get down tonight!*

8

Gary Jergins awoke shivering with the cold. He was huddled in a corner of the old school's main lobby, near the stairs that went down to the boys' room and the gymnasium. Rod was sleeping in the gym, next to the Sterno cooker, which provided little warmth. Gary had left the basement, unable to sleep so close to the corpse of the old man. He had pleaded with Rod to get rid of the body, to dump it outside somewhere, but Rod said no, explaining that the body was more likely to be found outside, which would lead the cops directly to them.

Ever since his childhood, and a particularly frightening experience at an aunt's wake, when he'd been forced to kiss her dead lips, Gary had been terrified of anything that was dead. Along with the fact that he felt bad for the old guy, who had appeared to be harmless, Gary just wanted to get as far away from him as possible.

All of which pissed Rod off immeasurably. For the first few days after killing the old guy, Rod had refused to give Gary anything to eat unless he went down to the gym, where Rod had set up camp. But even hunger couldn't force Gary into the basement now. After a week, the stench of the old man's decomposing body had become unbearable. Gary didn't know how Rod could stand it anymore.

His stomach growled loudly, reminding him of how hungry he was. He stood and leaned against the wall. It had been three days since he'd eaten, and he felt dizzy. He thought for a moment about leaving the school and going into town to look for food, but it was only a passing thought. The idea of him being alone, outside, was even more frightening than going into the basement.

He'd already searched the truck thoroughly for food and found only a half-empty bag of stale cashews. But that had been three days ago.

He sidled along the wall to the stairway and peered cautiously into the darkness below. "Rod?" he called softly. There was no answer. He took a deep breath and gagged. The stench rising from the basement was unbearable.

"How can he stand the stink?" Gary wondered aloud.

"I can't," came Rod's voice from behind him. Startled, Gary yelled, whirled around, almost losing his balance and falling down the stairs.

Rod burst into laughter. "You wuss!"

Gary smiled sheepishly and regained his composure. "How'd you sneak up on me?"

Rod cocked his head, indicating the other stairway, marked "Girls." "You know," Rod said, regarding Gary thoughtfully, "even though you wouldn't stay down there with me cuz you were scared, you were right all the same. That old fuck was really starting to stink up the place."

He laughed. "It never crossed my mind that he was gonna decompose and raise a stench. Maybe your stupidity is wearing off on me."

"I don't think so," Gary replied gravely.

Rod regarded the bigger man for a moment, then shrugged. "Whatever."

"Rod?" Gary asked. "Can I have something to eat?"

"Sure," Rod answered. "As soon as I get back from the store. We're fresh out of everything."

Gary looked disappointed. "But I'm starvin'."

Rod grinned evilly. "Hey! If you're too hungry to wait, there's plenty of meat in the basement."

It took several moments for Gary to comprehend what Rod meant. When he did, he gave his friend a look of disgust.

Rod was taken aback. It was the first time Gary had ever looked at him like that. He had killed guys for looking at him like that. "What bug's up your ass?"

Gary dropped his eyes and turned away.

"No! I wanna know. What the fuck is that look for?"

"Nothin'," Gary said sheepishly.

Rod looked at the big man's slumped shoulders and shook his head. "Yeah, right. Look, make yourself useful while I'm gone. Find us another room in this dump where we can use the Sterno stove without being seen from outside."

Gary watched in silence as Rod slipped out the front door, leaving him alone. Gary looked around frightfully and saw the Sterno cooker, the old man's bedroll, and the canvas tarp from the truck piled near the stairway to the girls' side of the basement.

He went to the pile and began to collect it, trying to keep his mind off what was just down the stairs in the basement. But the stench of rotting flesh wafting up from below made that difficult.

9

"I *want to know exactly how this thing is going to help you find the murderers of your parents,*" Deedee said loudly so that the cavorting Shadow Monster could clearly hear her. It stopped its gyrations, losing the form of a man with a boom box and returning to its normal amorphous state.

Oh, ye of little faith! it cried. *Don't you trust the Big D? After all we've meant to each other?* The Shadow Monster reshaped into an ebony clone of Dick, Deedee's attacker. A huge throbbing penis sprouted from him and kept growing, reaching out toward Deedee.

"Stop it!" Anna commanded.

Aw, shucks! I never get to have any fun, the Shadow Monster whined, but it did as it was told. Dick disappeared.

"She's right!" Anna said to the thing. *"How exactly are you going to help me? Tell me, or the deal's off."*

"What deal?" Deedee asked. *"That's the second time I've heard you mention a deal. What deal?"*

Before Anna could answer, the Shadow Monster swirled around the three of them in a rush of voices, punctuated by howls, grunts, and laughter.

I can and will help you in ways you won't believe! the thing crowed. In a thick southern accent and a sidelong glance at Kevin, it added, *Lordy! Lordy!* It went on speaking quietly, its voice seeming to insinuate itself into their very beings.

What evil lurks in the hearts of men? The Shadow Monster knows. It let out a phony scary laugh that turned into a bloodcurdling stage scream and went on. *That's right, chillun. I know all and see all evil! It puts a yummy in my tummy.* The thing belched, and bats with the bodies of spiders flew from its mouth and flapped around them for a few seconds before being sucked back into the creature when it took a huge breath.

I can take you to any man, woman, or child who has done evil. I have them all in tow, it said, indicating the life spheres hovering around it. *I can let you into their minds. I can help you.* The thing's voice was soothing, reassuring, convincing.

"I don't believe you," Deedee said, scared but defiant. *"I think you don't know anything about anything. You're just trying to trick us."* She turned to Anna. *"You can't trust this thing. Whatever deal you've made with it, forget it—it'll screw you."*

Whoa! the Shadow Monster said, acting surprised. *Is that any way to talk to a precious, innocent little girl?* In an aside, spoken from a tiny mouth next to its left eye, it said to Deedee, *But if anyone should know about screwing, it's you, slut.*

The Shadow Monster suddenly convulsed. Its face folded in upon itself, and the upper half of a man's body bulged out. The face solidified into distinctive features, the eyes opened.

Deedee gasped. It was the face of one of the men who had killed Anna's parents. They had shown his face on *America's Most Wanted*. He was the one who had died when the police car ran him over.

Reading her mind, the Shadow Monster answered from a mouth that opened in the man's belly, *That's right, ladies and gentlemen. I'd like you to meet Fred Wayne, one badass dude who has put a great big fat yummy in my tummy.* Eyeballs sprouted on the man's chest and rolled up, looking at the face above. *Say a few words, Fred. Tell these good people about yourself.*

The man looked frightened. He opened his mouth to speak and a worm slithered out, but he didn't seem to notice. *"I didn't do nuthin',"* the man stammered, trying to speak quickly. *"I never meant to hurt no one. I—I was abused as a kid. My mom beat me, and my dad raped me all the time!"*

Ah, put a sock in it, Fred! the mouth in the man's stomach said. A great black arm emerged from the dark blob of the main body of the Shadow Monster, holding an oily black sock. It stuffed the sock into Fred Wayne's mouth, until he gagged and his eyes bulged.

I hate it when these pussies whine about their abused childhoods! the Shadow Monster complained. With a great sucking sound, Fred Wayne was pulled back into the black mass of the creature. The horrid face of the Shadow Monster reemerged.

So, izzat proof 'nuff for ya?

"That doesn't prove anything!" Deedee said, stepping protectively in front of Anna. She looked to Kevin for support. He stepped forward hesitantly and spoke haltingly.

"Uh, yeah. That doesn't prove you can do any of the stuff you said you can do."

"Whoa! Sambo speaks! Can you dance too, boy?" the Shadow Monster asked maliciously.

Kevin's aura turned red with anger.

Oooh! You look good in red, brother! the Shadow Monster crowed.

His aura now a deep bloodred, Kevin moved angrily toward the thing.

Oh, yes! the Shadow Monster went on. *Red complements you. Goes so good with the black,* it said with an effeminate lisp. As it spoke, it swelled to large proportions, looming over Kevin.

Deedee sensed something was wrong. The Shadow Monster was not backing down from Kevin the way it had from herself and Anna. It was, instead, growing larger and more menacing. Its cavernous mouth was drooling, the spittle dripping from inch-long daggerlike teeth.

In fact, the Shadow Monster said, *you look good enough to eat!* The mouth opened and the tentacled tongue slithered out, snaking toward Kevin, who was so angry that he was oblivious to the danger he was in. Before Deedee could react, Anna had moved between the Shadow Monster and Kevin.

"Stop it!" she commanded. The thing let out a hundred differently pitched groans and closed its mouth.

"I want you to take me to the killers who are still alive, or else go away and leave us alone," Anna demanded.

The Shadow Monster cowed before her. *Your wish is my command, sweetcakes.* In an aside to Kevin, it muttered, *Later, boy.* It then swelled like a storm cloud ready to give up its rain. Slimy, shiny creatures belched to the surface all over its body, slithered this way and that, and were sucked back into the ooze that was the thing's flesh.

From the cloud of bubbles that hovered around the thing, two that were joined together in the middle began to descend toward them.

Ah! Here comes our bus now, the Shadow Monster said, smiling. The spheres descended faster, racing toward them. Anna and Deedee couldn't help but let out short screams, and even Kevin shouted with surprise as the life spheres fell on them and enveloped them in their reality.

10

Gary spread the bum's bedroll in a corner of a classroom at the end of the hall on the first floor. The room was empty, the wooden floor dotted with holes in circular patterns where the desks and chairs had been bolted. He'd chosen the room because it was the only one that had all its windows boarded up. Except for a small space, not more than an inch wide at the top of the far left window, all the glass was covered.

He set up the Sterno stove near the bedroll, folded the tarp into a cushion, and sat on it, his back against the wall, to wait for Rod's return. He was humming to himself, a tuneless, nameless song that was nothing more than soft groans in the back of his throat. He did this when he was very nervous or scared, which meant he did it quite a lot. The humming was having its normal calming effect on him and, combined with his hunger and lack of sleep, lulled him into a trancelike state.

The sound of thunder brought him awake with a start. He looked up at the small space of clear window and saw that the sky was blue. Besides, the thunder had sounded like it came not from outside but from *inside* the school.

Gary went to the door of the classroom and peered into the shadowy hallway. "Rod? Rod? Is that you?" No answer. He stepped into the hallway and stopped. There was a strange smell in the air that he hadn't noticed before. It was an electrical smell that reminded him of the electric bumper cars he used to ride as a kid at Canobie Lake Park.

He peered into the hallway, toward the lobby. The smell disappeared suddenly, but now he noticed something else. The shadows at the opposite end of the corridor, beyond the lobby where the garage was, seemed denser, blacker.

And they appeared to be moving.

Gary gasped. For a moment, he thought he had seen someone there, but the shadows shifted, and there was nothing but darkness—darkness that was swirling, as if eddied by a breeze that he could not feel.

He broke out in a cold, clammy sweat. "Something's not right," he whispered. The air suddenly felt heavy, oppressive, weighing upon him like a physical entity. He took a step backward and nearly stumbled, feeling the air push at him. He put out his hand to steady himself against the wall but pulled it back immediately. It felt hot and oily.

Gary shuddered at the touch, and his body continued shivering involuntarily. The shadows at the end of the hall were blacker and seemed to be multiplying, growing, surging toward him. The blackness swirled, came together. A shape appeared amid the shadows. At first it was just a silhouette of a figure, but it, too, took on form, substance, and color.

Gary shrieked and nearly fell down with terror. At the end of the hall stood a young girl, pointing her finger at him. But that wasn't what was scaring Gary. What scared him was that he could see right through her.

11

Anna was the first to see the big man in the hallway shadows. With a thrill of angry anticipation at her impending revenge, she pointed him out to Kevin and Deedee. But at the same moment that she thirsted for revenge—that she wanted to leap upon the man and rip him to shreds—she could sense nothing evil about him. His aura, though streaked with dark fear colors, was a bright, pleasant orange. Instinctively, she knew this man was not a killer. He looked like a child. Suddenly, he looked right at her, screamed like a kid, and ran, out of sight, into a room at the far end of the hallway.

What are you waiting for? the Shadow Monster, looming behind them, asked Anna. *Not quite as easy as you thought, huh, dumpling? This is where you really need my help. This is where I am in-val-u-a-bull!*

"That's one of them," Deedee said. *"I saw his picture on* America's Most Wanted.*"*

"There's something wrong here," Anna said, ignoring the Shadow Monster. *"Can't you feel it? That man's not bad. He's . . . he's just . . ."*

"Stupid," Kevin finished for her. He moved to Anna's side, away from the Shadow Monster, which had slid closer to the three and filled the hallway behind them.

"Yeah, I guess," Anna said, confused.

"A person doesn't have to be bad or smart to do evil things. To kill other people," Deedee said.

Right you are, my little nymphette, the Shadow Monster was quick to agree.

Anna turned on it. *"He didn't kill my parents, did he?"* she demanded.

The Shadow Monster shrugged. *He may not have pulled the trigger, but he's guilty just the same. There are many degrees of guilt, sweet thing. Whether you like it or not, revenge against yon gentle giant is part of your bargain with me. He belongs to me.*

Deedee and Kevin exchanged worried glances at the mention, again, of Anna's deal with the thing. Both had more than a strong inkling of what that deal might be, but neither had the courage to broach the subject.

Anna turned to Deedee. *"You said that was one of them. Where's the other one?"*

Her question was answered by the sound of a door opening and closing. It was followed by footsteps on stairs and the sound of paper bags rustling together.

"Oh, honey! I'm home," came a voice, followed by a nasty little chuckle! A small dirty-looking man came into view in the lobby ahead.

"That's him," Deedee said.

Behind them, the Shadow Monster giggled. *Oh, boy! We gwan have some fun now!*

12

Gary heard Rod enter the school, but was too afraid to move. He was afraid that maybe it wasn't *really* Rod. Then he heard his voice and laughter. He'd been hiding behind the door to the empty classroom since seeing the ghost in the hallway. It had taken all of his willpower to keep from crying.

When he was sure it was Rod, he crept from behind the doorway and peered around the corner into the hall. Rod was standing at the top of the front stairs. Gary's gaze went beyond him, to the other end of the hall, but there was nothing there now but normal shadows.

"Yoo-hoo," Rod called, placing the bags on the floor. "Where the hell are you, Dumbo?"

"Rod!" Gary called in a loud whisper, still peering around the corner of the doorway, only the top of his head and eyes showing. "Down here!"

Rods countenance quickly changed from smiling to concerned. He hurried to Gary. "What's wrong? Has someone come by here? Were you seen?"

"No, no, no," Gary whispered quickly. He grabbed Rod's arm, pulled him into the classroom, and closed the door.

"What is it then?" Rod asked, anger starting to tint his voice. His eyes gleamed with a drug sheen in the afternoon gloom.

"This place is haunted, Rod," Gary said breathlessly. "I saw a ghost in the hallway."

Rod let out a ridiculing snicker. "What? The old bum in the basement come looking for his Sterno?"

"No!" Gary whispered harshly. He paused a moment. In his terror at seeing the little girl, he'd forgotten all about the dead man in the basement. He was glad he hadn't seen *his* ghost! "It was a girl. A little girl. At the end of the hall. She was pointing at me," he told Rod. He nearly broke into tears as he finished.

Rod regarded him with contempt. "How can such a big guy like you be such an incredible pussy?"

"I'm not a pussy!" Gary said hotly. "I saw her! I did!"

"Yeah, right," Rod said, dismissing the subject. "Come on and help me carry the food in here." He opened the door and started into the hall, but he stopped when he saw Gary wasn't following him. "Come on," he said.

"I don't wanna," Gary said, eyes down.

"Listen, you stupid fuck. There's nothing out there. You must've dozed off and had a dream, that's all."

"It wasn't no dream, Rod. That little girl was there," Gary stated.

Rod shook his head and sighed. "So what if she was? I mean, a little girl, right? Are you afraid of a little girl? How can a little girl hurt a big guy like you?"

"She was a ghost!"

"Oh, for Christ's sake," Rod said, exasperated. "Okay. Fine. You stay here, and I'll get the stuff, okay, baby?" Rod stalked off to retrieve the grocery bags and returned to the room.

Gary quickly closed the door as soon as he was inside.

13

Anna watched the man put the grocery bags on the floor and go down the hall to speak with the other man, who was peering around the corner of a doorway.

"Okay, let's get him," Anna said, and turned to the Shadow Monster. The next moment, her life sphere appeared out of nowhere, swept her up, and disappeared again.

Anna didn't have to open her eyes to know where she was. She could hear the soft whisper of the respirator and the steady blip-blip of the heart monitor. Someone was holding her hand, caressing it. She heard a voice, far away at first but getting closer, speaking to her.

"Anna, honey. It's me. Auntie Kara. Wake up, honey. We all miss you so much. Haley and Jayne are here with me."

New voices. Her sisters, their voices mute and on the edge of emotion, "Hi, Anna." "Hi, Anna." "Please wake up." "Yeah, please?"

Anna had to smile at little Jayne's breathless plea. Aunt Kara's hand immediately tightened on her own.

"Oh, my God! Look! She's smiling. Haley! Jayne! She can hear us. Anna! You can hear us!"

Anna squeezed her aunt's hand back, in reply.

"Doctor! She just squeezed my hand," Aunt Kara cried.

Anna felt another presence over her. It had the strong smell of cologne, mixed with garlic breath.

"Yes. Yes," a male voice said. A finger lifted her right eyelid. Just before a light blinded her, Anna saw the doctor's face, clean shaven and very red, and Aunt Kara and her sisters in the background. Her eyelid was let go and closed. She wanted to keep it open but couldn't seem to do it. Floating doughnuts of light drifted behind the lid. The other lid was opened and the eye assaulted by the light also.

"The new treatment appears to have brought about an improvement," the doctor said. He was checking Anna's pulse, holding her left wrist. "This is very encouraging," he added.

"Can Anna come home now?" Jayne asked.

"Hopefully very soon," the doctor replied. "The new drug is working. If she continues to improve with it, she could be up and about, and even on her way home, in a few weeks. But right now she needs rest, lots of rest. You can come back and see her tomorrow."

Anna felt a light brush of lips against her forehead, followed by the touch of a hand on hers. "You're going to be all right, sweetie," Aunt Kara whispered.

" 'Bye, Anna," Haley said from somewhere near the foot of the bed.

"I love you, Anna," Jayne said quickly, and sobbed.

Tears and longing welled up in Anna. At that moment, she wanted nothing more than to sit up and tell them she was okay, to hug and kiss her sisters. To go home. . .

We have no home, she remembered. The anger that spawned the lust for revenge returned, stronger than ever. That man had done this to her family. He had to be made to pay.

She wanted to leave her body immediately. She *tried* to leave her body, *willed* her spirit to leave her body, *commanded* it, but to no avail. Nothing happened. She realized that something had changed in her. She had become stronger. The last thing that she wanted to happen right now, was happening. She was getting better. She was going to survive, where before it had been doubtful.

She remembered the doctor's words; *new treatment . . . new drug is working*. That must be it. The doctor was making her well, bringing her back from the edge of death.

No! No! No! Not now, Anna silently lamented. I can't get well now. Not now.

14

"*She's gone back to her body,*" Deedee said to Kevin.

He looked puzzled. "*But why? I thought she wanted this.*"

Deedee looked at the Shadow Monster. "*What happened?*" she demanded as strongly as she could. She tried not to be distracted or intimidated by the thing's grotesque shape-shiftings.

Modern medicine, the Shadow Monster replied with utter disgust. *That's what happened. The heroic efforts of medical technology.* It spat a wad of dark fluid that hit the floor and separated into a multitude of spiders, which crawled away at great speed in every direction. The Shadow Monster bellowed, frightening them. *Goddamned doctors can't leave well enough alone. Can't let a person croak in peace.* The creature's face writhed with worms that burrowed in and out of its jellied flesh.

"*You mean, . . .*" Deedee started, then stopped, suddenly afraid to ask the question. Afraid of the answer.

"*Is Anna dying?*" she finally raised the courage to ask.

The Shadow Monster chuckled smugly, and Deedee loathed the thing for it. *We-ell,* the thing said, its voice an exaggerated southern drawl, *she sure ain't livin' large!*

Deedee backed away from the creature. The

thing was growing larger, swelling its inky darkness around Kevin and herself.

She glanced at Kevin, saw the dark streaks of fear in his aura, and knew that he sensed it too. With Anna gone, something had changed. They were now in danger from the Shadow Monster. She could sense its predatory intentions the way people can sometimes sense when someone is staring at them.

She turned to warn Kevin, but before she could, he disappeared. Just vanished. Her astonishment was short-lived as, a moment later, her own life sphere came rushing out of the darkness and carried her back to her body.

15

The flash of light was so bright, Kevin was certain it had left him blind. But gradually he realized that wasn't true, he was just in a very dark place. At first he thought he was back in his body, in his house, and that it was night. But when he reached for the controls to his wheelchair and found empty air, he realized he wasn't sitting at all, but floating.

Dark movement far below caught his eye. He was floating at a great height. The multitude of dead were on the march on the plain below him. Inextricably he was drawn to them, floating slowly down, while the darkness around him gave way to the gloomy dull light that shaded everything in depressing tints of gray.

From twenty feet above the column, he spotted James. His friend was looking up at him as if expecting him. His face was somber, his eyes haunting.

"Go back, Kevin," James said, his voice hollow and distant. *"Go back and do what you've got to do. I'm depending on you."*

16

Deedee awoke and lay unmoving in the bed. Jesse was asleep in the armchair, pulled up next to the bed. She lay watching him for a few moments before he opened his eyes and saw her.

"Dee! You're back!" He leaned over and put his hand to her face. "I was worried. How do you feel?"

She tried to speak but coughed. "Dry," she managed to say. Her mouth and throat felt as if they had literally been coated with mud that had dried.

Jesse ran out of the room. A moment later, she could hear the refrigerator door open and the sound of bottles clinking together. He came back with a Coke.

She gulped the tonic noisily and hiccuped several times. "How long have I been gone?" she asked in a whisper, as he took the bottle from her and placed it on the nightstand.

"About two hours," he said, glancing at his watch.

"I've got to go back," Deedee said immediately. "Anna's in trouble. The Shadow Monster said she was going to die."

"No," Jesse said firmly. He sat on the edge of the bed and placed his hands on her shoulders. "You're going to rest."

She tried to protest, but he put his finger to her lips, silencing her. She didn't want to rest, but her body and mind weren't going to cooperate. She was exhausted. In a matter of seconds, she was drifting away into slumber.

17

Anna awoke in the middle of the night. She came fully awake for the first time since being brought to the hospital. Before, it had always been like rising to the surface of a pool, only to find it covered with a thin sheet of plastic that wouldn't let her through.

She felt better, stronger—and she despaired over it. She didn't want to feel well. She didn't want to *get* well. She only wanted to get the man who had killed her parents, and then she wanted to die.

She opened her eyes. The room was lit by the dim glow of lights from several monitors next to the bed. Running from them were tubes and wires connected to her arms, chest, and neck. She watched the blip of the heart monitor, willing it to stop, until sleep overtook her again.

18

Kevin went back.

As though watched through a rain-drenched window, his surroundings blurred, ran, and dissolved. Instantly, they reformed and crystallized, and he was back in the dark corridor in the building where the killers of Anna's parents were hiding.

He was alone. From down the hall, he could hear a murmured voice, but he couldn't make out what was being said. He whirled suddenly, looking behind him. He thought he had felt the presence of the evil thing the girls called the Shadow Monster behind him. There was nothing there, only normal shadows, normal darkness.

Maybe there *is* no such thing as normal darkness, he thought. Maybe shadows and darkness—any absence of light—*was* the Shadow Monster. He looked around again. He couldn't shake the feeling that the Shadow Monster was lurking about somewhere, watching.

A loud laugh from somewhere down the hall distracted him. He moved cautiously forward, gliding over the old boards of the floor. He stopped in the lobby, looking around at the stairs and the open area. It reminded him of some kind of municipal building that had been deserted. Maybe it was an old school or a vacated town hall.

A rancid odor, the color of pea soup, was wafting

up out of the stairwells marked "Boys" and "Girls." It curled in the air and floated toward him.

Kevin moved on, drawn by the voice from the other end of the hall past the lobby. He went to the door, raised his hand in the reflexive motion of pushing it open, and walked through it. He stumbled, his breath hitching in his lungs the way it would if he were to suddenly be doused with ice-cold water. No matter how many times he did that, it still came as a shock to him. He had to wait a few moments for his vision to clear. Whenever he walked through a solid object, his vision was blurred, haunted with the ghostly images of the inner structure of whatever he had just walked through. Right now, his eyes were clouded with trace patterns of wood fibers and grains of various primary colors that drifted across his vision. While he waited for his vision to clear, he listened to the voices in the room.

"I figure another couple of days, and we can get out of here," a nasal voice said.

"Why can't we go now?" a deep, slow, yet melodic voice answered.

"Because the heat is still on out there, thanks to that *America's Most Wanted* bullshit! When I was out for food earlier, there was a state trooper's car at the town hall. Maybe it don't mean nothin', maybe it does. I gotta listen to the radio later, see if there's any more news about us."

Kevin turned toward the speaker. Through a fading red-spiraled grain, he saw a short dirty man sitting slouched against a wall. The words that he'd just spoken had tainted the air around him a dark purple and swirled with a life of their own.

"I want out of here, Rod. I don't like this place." Kevin's vision cleared enough for him to see the other man better. He was sitting diagonally to the first, leaning against the back wall of the room. He was a good foot and a half taller than the other man and huge. The words coming out of his mouth were a deep green that wafted upward, dissipating slowly. They were pleasant to the eye, unlike the pulsing cloud of purple that came from the other's mouth.

The two men's auras were very different also. The smaller one had an aura of brownish red that was streaked with yellow, like lightning. The larger man's aura was bright clear orange, except at the bottom, where it darkened to a deep blue. A sad blue, Kevin thought, looking at it.

"If you don't quit your candyass whining, I'll make you go sleep in the basement with your buddy. I'll bet he's really *ripe* for some company," the smaller man said, laughing at his play on words.

Eruptions of red began to dot the surface of the large man's aura; the color of anger. "You can't do that, Rod. You can't make me. You might think you can, but you can't."

Silence fell between the two men. Kevin sensed something had happened. The small man, who was obviously the leader, was scrutinizing the larger man warily.

"Hey! Chill out, Dumbo. Everything will be okay. I was just fuckin' with your head," the small man said easily, but his words were black in the air and his aura turned a deep crimson red that flashed with streaks of yellow. He slid to the floor and pulled a sleeping bag over himself. "Get some sleep."

The larger man sat staring at his friend for a few moments before murmuring. "Good night." He lay down against a folded canvas tarp. A moment later he added, "And don't call me Dumbo no more. I don't like it."

The small man's aura seethed a dark red with more flashing streaks of yellow at this, but he said nothing.

Kevin backed away from the two and passed through the door again and into the hall. The effect wasn't so bad going backward. He'd have to remember that. His vision hardly retained a fading image of the intricate structure of the door's wood.

The one called Rod had mentioned someone in the basement. Kevin wondered if that was the foul odor coming up the stairs. A dead man in the basement. These men were criminals, that was for certain, but Kevin sensed a difference between them. It was as Anna had said—the big man wasn't a killer. The other one, Rod, was. Kevin believed he would kill someone for no reason at all, just for the thrill of it. But the larger man wasn't like that. It wasn't that he was stupid, as Kevin had thought earlier, (though he was certainly no bright bulb either); it was more an innocence about him, a trusting nature that only the innocent possess, which is why they are so often victims.

He's a dog, a rumbling voice said from behind him. Kevin felt a cold wind blow through his aura. He turned. The Shadow Monster billowed behind him, filling the hallway and the lobby beyond.

They're both dogs. Filthy dogs, the Shadow Monster said with a gravity of voice that Kevin had never heard from it. *But they're* my *filthy dogs* it added, and laughed.

Kevin backed away. *"Where's the girl, Anna, and Deedee?"* he asked nervously.

The Shadow Monster made a show of looking around. A huge pair of arms telescoped out of its body. Its hands gripped the darkness just below its face and pulled itself apart, exposing its insides. A writhing mass of tiny human bodies, bound hand

and foot with snakes, were being fed upon by a multitude of long-legged, slick-looking insects. The creature looked into itself, then back at Kevin.

They're not in here it said, and added, *not yet, anyway.*

Kevin shuddered but couldn't turn away from the sight.

I've saved a place in here for your friend James too. Right up front. VIP status. The thing laughed again. Inside its body, the snakes and insects opened their mouths and laughed also, in a weird mimicry of human laughter.

19

Anna awoke to silence in the hospital room. The quiet seemed strange to her. At first she couldn't understand why. What was it that she wasn't hearing? Then it came to her. She was missing the sound of the monitors and other equipment that were normally in the room. They were gone. She no longer had tubes stuck in her and wires running out of her. What did that mean?

It meant that she was really getting well. She'd be out of the hospital soon at this rate. And that meant she'd never be able to get out of her body and get her revenge. She had to be near death to be able to go to the other side.

Slowly she opened her eyes. She was in darkness. Carefully, she raised her right arm. It felt stiff and heavy, and her armpit throbbed with an aching pain. Summoning all her strength, she got her right arm up and flexed the fingers of her hand.

She took a deep breath and relaxed. That wasn't so bad. She tested and lifted her left arm next, then slowly brought her knees up and bent her legs.

Her eyes had adjusted to the darkness of the room, and she saw that there were metal guardrails on the sides of her bed. Grabbing the right rail with both hands and pushing with her feet against the mattress, she pulled and pushed herself into a sitting position against the metal headboard.

She felt dizzy to the point of nausea. She closed

her eyes and took deep breaths, holding the air in—and the sickness down—a few seconds before exhaling. She repeated it a few times and felt better, her head clearer, but her body felt incredibly weak. The effort of sitting up had wasted nearly all her energy.

She rested and thought about what she was doing, where she was going. She didn't know exactly—she hadn't gotten that far in her thinking. She just knew she had to get away from the doctors before they made her so well, she'd never be able to leave her body again.

"I have to get out of here," she breathed to the darkness. The guardrails presented a problem. She didn't have enough strength to climb over them, and she couldn't figure out how to get them down. She tried for several minutes but succeeded in only making a lot of noise, which in turn made her afraid a nurse or doctor would hear, come to investigate, and prevent her escape.

There was only one way out of the bed, and that was out the bottom. Moving slowly, being careful with every movement, she pulled her legs up under her. Using the guardrails for support, she turned herself around in the bed and crawled to the end. There she paused, resting and looking over the edge of the bed at the floor. It looked awfully far. She wondered if her legs could hold her weight and knew there was only one way to find out. Grunting, she put her hands on the low bedboard and got to her knees. She slid her right leg over and let it dangle as she straddled the bedboard. She started to lift her left leg to swing it over to the floor when the dizziness of exertion returned. The room blurred away, and she heard a distinct *thump!* followed by a groan. The dizziness passed. She was on the floor, lying in a fetal position. She guessed correctly that she had fallen out of bed, and the groan she'd heard had been her own.

Her right shoulder hurt, and her right knee, but other than that she was no worse for the fall. At floor level, she could see a dim crack of light under the door, a few feet away. She watched for what seemed like hours, but the bar of light under the door was not disturbed. She guessed it must be late at night or very early in the morning, with so little traffic in the hall.

Anna took a deep breath and pushed herself off the floor and up until she was on all fours. She didn't think she could stand—in fact, she was certain she'd collapse if she tried to. Concentrating on the movements of her arms and legs, she crawled to the door, wincing each time her sore right knee touched the hard floor.

At the door, she paused, resting her left shoulder and head against the jamb. After a while, she raised herself and reached for the handle. Sliding her body to the side, she pulled the door open a crack and peered out.

The hospital corridor outside her room was empty in the one direction she was facing. Pulling the door open more, she wedged her shoulders between it and the jamb so that she could lean her head out to check the corridor in the other direction.

It, too, was empty.

Hanging from the ceiling was a clock. The hands were at three. Considering the darkness of her room and the inactivity in the hallway, she guessed it was three o'clock in the morning.

She leaned farther out and gasped in pain as the door squeezed against her ribs. Far down the hall, she could see the nurses' station, but no nurses were in attendance there. With her right arm, she pushed the door open as far as she could. Moving as quickly as she was able, she crawled through the doorway but wasn't able to get into the corridor before the door banged on her left ankle, almost making her cry out in pain. Kicking the door open, she pulled her foot free.

She was exhausted from the effort, but she knew she couldn't rest there in the middle of the hospital corridor without being discovered. A few feet away was an alcove with a sign on the corridor wall, indicating the elevators were there. Groaning she got to all fours and crawled like an animal as fast as she could to them.

Half crawling, half falling, she pulled herself to the elevator but couldn't reach the call button. She knelt and reached as far as she could and clawed at the button. The elevator dinged, and the doors slid open. In the corridor behind her, Anna could hear the soft approach of rubber-soled shoes and hushed voices. She dragged herself into the elevator and swatted at the control panel, managing to hit the button for the basement.

The door didn't close. From the corridor, the voices were getting louder. Two women, presumably nurses, were talking. Anna swatted at the basement button again. The doors started to close but stopped and reopened with a loud *ding*! She realized her left foot was in the doorway, and the elevators sensors wouldn't let the door close while it was.

She tried to slide her leg in, but it had fallen asleep and she couldn't move it. Grabbing at her calf, just below the hem of her johnny, she pulled the deadened leg and foot into the elevator. Just as she heard the voices of the nurses and their footsteps come around the corner, the elevator doors closed. She fell back, lying splayed out on the elevator floor.

She opened her eyes and was completely disoriented for several moments. She had no idea where she was, where she'd been, or even where she was going. She sat staring at the open elevator door and realized she must have gone to another floor. The door started to close. She lunged at the door, throwing her body over the threshold. The door hit her hip and opened again.

She dragged herself into a sterile, white concrete-walled hallway. There were two signs on the wall opposite her. One indicated that the morgue was to the right, the other that the boiler room was to the left. She remembered then what she was doing. She had to find a place to hide so the doctors and nurses couldn't make her better. She had to get out of her body and back to the other side. She had to get back to where that evil man was hiding and make him pay.

She began to crawl in the direction of the boiler room.

20

Deedee awoke in darkness. She turned her head and saw Jesse's face illuminated by moonlight through the window. He was asleep, lying next to her. She snuggled up to him and kissed his nose, his cheek, his lips. His eyes fluttered open.

"Make love to me, Jesse," she said softly.

He groaned softly and buried his face in the pillow.

"Please, Jesse. I have to go back." She nibbled his ear, reached under him, and grabbed his penis.

"You know," he said, taking her into his arms, "if you don't kill yourself doing this, you'll probably kill me."

"Not a bad way to go," she answered as he mounted her.

21

The boiler room door was a large metal rectangle with a handle high up on it. Anna didn't think she could stand to reach it. She was feeling very weak. She didn't think she could go much farther. She leaned against the wall and felt it rattle behind her.

She turned and looked. There was a small metal door, just her size, set into the wall. It was slightly ajar. Gasping for breath, she summoned all the strength she had left and grabbed the edge of it. Grunting, she pried it open.

It was an access panel for pipes running from the boiler room. There was just enough space for her to squeeze in and lie down if she scrunched up. It took her twenty minutes to do so, and she had great difficulty pulling the door closed behind her, but finally she was successful.

She lay down in the warm darkness, the air humid from the pipes above her. Slowly, pleasantly, she felt her soul leave her body.

22

Company's coming, the Shadow Monster crowed. Kevin looked around. His ears popped, and the Shadow Monster disappeared for a moment, then reappeared with Deedee and Anna enveloped in its dark folds. Their auras began to glow fiercely, and the Shadow Monster backed off.

The gang's all here! the Shadow Monster exclaimed in a jolly voice. Its form swelled closer, and it swirled around them until it had encircled them with a wall of darkness.

"No more fooling around," Anna said determinedly. *"You're going to help me get that guy—I don't care about the other one—and you're going to do it, now!"*

Coitanly, the Shadow Monster answered, sounding like Curly of the Three Stooges.

Gather round and take my hands . . .

23

Gary awoke in darkness. He sat up, rubbed his eyes, and looked toward the crack in the boarding at the window above. He knew it should be dawn, or close to it. He always awoke at dawn, had since he was a youngster. He glanced down at Rod, who was curled up in the dead man's sleeping bag.

Quietly, Gary got up. He threw off the canvas tarp that he'd been using as a blanket and picked up his parka, which he'd folded for a pillow. Shivering with cold, he put it on.

He walked to other side of the room, to see out the narrow space in the boards better, and saw that it was indeed dawn. The sky was a smoky blue, tinged with pink. Gary stood, staring wistfully at the small patch of sky and jiggling his leg. He had to pee, bad, but there was no way he was going to go down to the bathroom with the dead guy down there. He remembered that the room across the hall from the one they were in had been marked, "Teachers' Room."

He went to the door, opened it carefully, and peered into the hall. It was dark, too dark to see anything. Moving quickly, Gary scooted across the hall and into the teachers' room, where there was a sink but the toilet had been ripped out. Whining with the need to go, he unzipped and relieved himself in the sink. As quietly as possible, he returned to the classroom, where Rod still slept.

Rod snorted and moved as Gary entered the room. Gary looked hard, trying to see his friend, but couldn't—the darkness in the room had become thicker instead of lighter with the dawn. Gary looked up at the window. Daylight was filling the sky, but none of it penetrated the room. Yesterday the clear space in the boards had provided plenty of light, but now it didn't.

Gary shivered. There was something wrong here. Something very wrong. He remembered the little girl in the lobby yesterday. He looked back toward the door, which should have been less than a foot behind him, but he couldn't see it.

Was she still out there? Who was she? A ghost? The thoughts hammered at him until a new, more frightening one took hold.

What if she was right . . . right in the room with him right now? She could be standing next to him in this darkness. . . . and he wouldn't be able to see her. She could be reaching for him, her ghastly hands about to grab him, about to close around his throat.

"Rod!" he screamed hoarsely. "Rod!" He stumbled into the room. He heard a grunt and a moment later nearly fell over his companion.

"What? What?" Rod said, jumping up. Gary could hear him pull out his pistol and cock it.

"I'm . . . I'm . . . I don't wanna stay here no more. I wanna go," Gary said, trying hard not to burst into tears.

Rod's hands grabbed him in the darkness and pushed him until his back hit the wall. A second later, he felt the barrel of Rod's pistol under his chin. "That's what you woke me up for, you dumb fuck? You big dumb baby fuck? I oughta blow your brains all over this wall, *right now*!"

Gary couldn't help it. He began to blubber. "I'm

sorry, Rod. I'm sorry. I just don't like it here. I'm scared. This place is spooky. That girl I saw yesterday. It's bad. We gotta get outta here. We gotta—"

Rod punched him in the jaw, and he stopped in midsentence, tears rolling down his face. "What the fuck am I gonna do with you?" He put his gun back in his jacket and zipped it. He began stomping his feet. "Shit! It's cold in here. Where the hell is that Sterno cooker? I can't see a fucking thing in here."

"See?" Gary said. "See?"

"What? See what? I just said I can't see a fucking thing, you idiot!"

"Nothing! That's it! You can't see nothing in here! It's *too* dark. It ain't right. There's something wrong with this place."

"No, there's something wrong with you. Shit! I should've wasted your ass and kept Tommy alive. At least he wouldn't have driven me crazy with this wimpy bullshit."

"Don't say that," Gary said, his voice frightened.

"What? You afraid Tommy's ghost is gonna come back next?" Rod laughed. "Actually, he might if he gets scent of your little girl ghost. He always did like 'em young. Or maybe the old guy in the basement will get up and come pay us a visit, huh?"

"Don't say that!" Gary said, more anger than fear showing in his tone.

Rod lit his lighter and glared at Gary. He turned and started for the door.

"Where you going?" Gary asked nervously.

"I'm going to the truck to see if there's anything about us on the radio," Rod muttered.

"I'll come with you."

"No!" Rod said, turning. The lighter flickered, throwing helter-skelter shadows over the walls. "You stay here. Get the Sterno going so we can have some coffee. It's in the bag." His voice was flat, calm.

Gary didn't like the sound of it. "But I don't wanna stay alone, Rod."

Rod's calm broke. "Well, I don't want you with me! You're driving me fucking nuts!" He turned, opened the door, and left Gary alone in the darkness, flinching at the sound of the door slamming.

24

The last thing in the world that Deedee wanted was to have the Shadow Monster touch her, but it did, and much more. Before she could make any attempt to escape or even protest, the thing was all over her. She felt one of its many slick-fingered tentacles wrap around her hand. With a scream of fear, she felt the thing enter her mind. Her thoughts clouded, darkened. Evil images boiled up and danced in her imagination, abominations too vile for words to describe.

From somewhere nearby in the billowing darkness, she heard Anna, her voice hoarse and frightened: *"No! You can't do this! You never said you'd do this!"*

Never said I wouldn't, either, the Shadow Monster answered slyly. *If you want your revenge, sweet-cakes, this is the only way. No matter how much you might daydream about ripping that man apart, you and I both know you could never do it. So we do it my way or the highway. Either way, our bargain still stands.*

Anna didn't answer. Deedee wanted to scream out an answer—demand that the creature get out of her mind and let her go—but her mouth suddenly filled with squirming things that made her gag.

Trust me, honey. You got no one else, the Shadow Monster said. *You got no choice.*

Deedee's vision cleared slightly, and she saw Kevin and Anna huddled within inches of her. Their auras had turned a smoke gray that crackled with thin purple veins of slow-moving light.

Now, the Shadow Monster spoke inside their heads, *it's show time!*

25

Gary whimpered like a frightened animal. He wanted to go after Rod—didn't want to be left alone—but he was more afraid of Rod's anger. He'd never seen his friend so mad without him killing someone.

He turned to the window, looking at the dim sky, wishing he could be outside, wishing he could leave this place. He sighed and took a book of matches out of his pocket. Striking one, he found the Sterno cooker and lit it. The darkness receded a little, leaving a safe little circle of light for him to sit in.

The Sterno sputtered, flickered, and went out. Gary lit another match and held it to the can, but it was empty. He glanced around the room. He knew there was no more Sterno, but he looked, hopefully, anyway. If they did have to stay in this spooky place, Gary certainly didn't want to do it without light.

He sat back against the wall, and the match went out. He felt the book of matches, counting two left. He debated whether to light them or save them. He frowned in concentration. Another thought invaded: Rod was going to be really pissed when he found out they were out of Sterno and there was no hot coffee waiting for him.

Gary thought of something else and smiled.

Without any fire for cooking or keeping warm, maybe Rod would want to get out of here.

Or maybe he'll send me into the basement to search for more Sterno.

He shuddered at the thought.

"I won't do it," he whispered to himself. "He can hit me. He can shoot me. I won't do it."

Approaching footsteps in the hall distracted him from his protestations. Rod was coming back. Gary stood and put his ear to the door. The footsteps stopped outside.

Gary was suddenly afraid to open the door, afraid of what was on the other side.

"Rod? Is that you?" Gary said through the door.

"No. It's the fucking boogy man, Dumbo. Who the fuck do you think it is?"

Gary laughed softly with relief.

"Come on," Rod said, and Gary heard his footsteps moving away.

"Wait, Rod, we're out of Sterno," Gary said, opening the door.

"Don't need it. We're getting out of here," Rod said.

Gary nearly jumped for joy. He stepped into the hallway, and even the impenetrable darkness couldn't daunt his happy relief.

But he couldn't see or hear Rod. "Rod? Where are you?" Gary asked into the dark, straining his eyes to see.

"Come on." Rod's voice came from ahead, moving off down the hall toward the front lobby of the school.

Gary strained his eyes and thought he could see a silhouette of a shape ahead. "Wait up, Rod. I can barely see a damned thing."

"Come on," Rod said again.

Gary moved forward. He didn't like this. Before, the lobby had been the best-lit place in the building, but now it was blacker than black. He wasn't even sure he was walking in the right direction.

"Rod? You there?"

"Come on," Rod answered. His voice sounded just ahead, but Gary couldn't see anything of him. "Rod? Why's it so dark?" Gary asked softly.

"Storm coming," came the answer. Rod sounded farther away now.

"Wait for me, Rod. I can't see a thing." Gary groped forward in the thick darkness, arms and hands stretched before him. They brushed against something, then Rod took his hand. Gary was touched by the gesture, almost to the point of tears. Rod had never done anything like that before.

"Where we going, Rod?"

"We're getting out. But first I want to show you something. A surprise."

Gary smiled. First Rod was holding his hand, now he was gonna surprise him. That wasn't like Rod. No, that wasn't like Rod at all. Gary began to get nervous. It *would* be just like Rod to act real nice, then do something really nasty.

Like lead him down to the basement and leave him in the dark with the dead guy.

Gary slowed his walk, but Rod's hand tightened on his, pulling him on.

"I don't like this, Rod. It's too dark."

"Don't be such a wuss," Rod said. Gary didn't like the tone of Rod's voice. It sounded very nasty all of a sudden. Rod was going to do it! Take him to the basement and leave him!

Gary was just about to pull his hand away from Rod's and grope his way out of the building on his own, when his foot hit something. He stumbled and had to step up.

"Watch it. Stairs. Step up," Rod said.

Gary stepped up awkwardly. One step, then another. They were going *upstairs*! Gary was infused with relief. Rod wasn't taking him down to the dead man after all.

Gary relaxed and let Rod lead him up the stairs.

26

Rod sat in the truck and breathed on his fingers. Steam blew in clouds from his mouth. It was a good twenty degrees colder in the garage than it was in the school. But it wasn't much lighter.

There must be a helluva storm brewing, Rod thought.

He put the key in the ignition, turned it to accessory, and turned on the radio. Static blasted from the speakers, making him jump. He quickly turned down the volume, then fiddled with the tuner, trying to find a station with news. He flipped through country, jazz, and classical stations that came in weak. A rock and roll station with a deejay announcing that he was on "the Big Mattress" came in clear, but he moved on after a few seconds. He turned the dial, finding nothing but static, until he hit the AM button and quickly found an all-news station.

Rod sat back, pulled a candy bar and a cigarette from his coat pocket, and listened to the news anchor run through a litany of stories about a three-alarm fire in Springfield, a robbery in Pittsfield, and various murders and a gang slaying in Boston, but nothing about him and Gary. That was encouraging.

A shadow passed over the dash. He turned quickly, looking out the back window. It was pitch dark behind the truck. He looked around. The entire garage was darker than it should be in the daytime, no matter how bad a storm was brewing outside. Thinking of outside, he could no longer see the row of windows in the garage door.

He shivered with a sudden chill. He hated to admit it, but Gary was right. There was something wrong here, something creepy about this old school. Rod had never been one to believe in ghosts or the supernatural, but if ever a place could be haunted, this would be it. He had to agree with Gary. It was time to get out of here.

He turned the ignition key to off, took it out, and put it in his pocket. Taking the Uzi off the seat with him, he got out of the truck quietly and closed the door softly. He looked over his shoulder several times. The feeling that he wasn't alone was strong. He tried to shake it off. There was no one else in the garage. He silently chided himself for letting the darkness, and Gary for that matter, get to him.

A shadow moved in the far corner of the garage.

"Gary? Is that you?" He strained his eyes to see. The darkness had become even thicker. Now he could barely see the truck, and he was less than a foot from it. Even though he couldn't really see, Rod had a sense of someone, or something, moving in the darkness.

Whatever it was, it was moving toward him.

"Gary?" He heard fear in his voice and hated it. He sounded just like Gary, all whiny and scared. "Jesus! I'm turning into a worse pussy than Dumbo," he muttered.

In the truck, the radio suddenly came on, blaring a classic rock song by the Rolling Stones. Mick Jagger was singing, "Please allow me to introduce myself, I'm a man of wealth and taste!"

Rod jumped at the sound of the music, a chilling sweat breaking out instantly all over his body. His bowels clenched in fear, and a cramp nearly made him double over. This was a new sensation for Rod. He couldn't remember a time in his life when he'd ever experienced fear like this. He didn't like it. It pissed him off.

"Gary! Gary! Dumbo! You worthless fuck! Is that you? Answer me!" He pulled the Uzi up. "You'd better answer me, fucker, or I'll waste you right now!"

No answer. On the radio, the Stones' song had given way to one of Rod's favorites: Blue Oyster Cult doing "Don't Fear the Reaper."

"What the fuck is going on?" he said under his breath.

"It's time to party, Rod," a familiar voice said directly behind him.

Rod whirled, gun ready to fire, but he couldn't pull the trigger. In the darkness a glowing pair of eyes stared at him. Slowly an illuminated face materialized around the eyes. The left eye winked at him.

"How's it hangin', Rod?" Tom Wayne asked.

27

It was so dark that Gary couldn't tell if his eyes were open or closed. He felt as though he were swimming in and out of a dream.

A particular dream.

The darkness was the same. He was walking upstairs too. There was that sense of something about to happen. Something scary.

He whined, deep in his throat. He remembered the dream all too well. He didn't like this dream.

"Rod, let's get out of here."

Rod's hand tightened on his, but no answer came. Gary was pulled onward and upward.

Gary's breathing came in panting gasps. He kept telling himself this wasn't happening; dreams don't happen when you're awake.

But there were the footsteps. He could hear them now too. Coming down the stairs toward him. Coming closer.

"Rod, please. Let's get out of here," Gary pleaded. He tried to stop and pull his friend back down the stairs, but he couldn't. In all the time he and Rod had been together, Gary had always known he was twice as strong as his friend. Strength wasn't power for Gary, it just was. Now, suddenly, Rod had become stronger?

The footsteps grew louder, closer.

"It's the Stick Man," Gary whispered. Rod's hand grew tighter.

With his free hand, Gary fumbled the matches from his pocket.

The footsteps were coming down the stairs, toward them. Awkwardly working the matches with one hand, Gary managed to bend one until he could flick the head of it against the striking pad. The flame burned for only a second—a flash—but what he saw in that flash of a second was enough to start him screaming.

It *was* the Stick Man. The Stick Man from his childhood nightmares. The dreams of being trapped in darkness. The footsteps getting closer, closer. The strobing light. The Stick Man, smaller, no more than a foot high, stalking him. Black line arms, legs, and body, a featureless black hole for a head, and a hat. A black fedora.

"Coming, Gary," the Stick Man would say.

"I'm coming."

The match in Gary's hand flamed to life by itself. Gary was startled from his scream of terror. The flame began strobing—flaring, going out, flaming again. Rod's grip on his other hand grew painful.

Gary looked up at his friend. Rod was gone. He wasn't there. But Gary's hand was being held.

By no one.

Gary shrieked. At the top of the stairs stood the Stick Man. He started down.

"Coming, Gary."

"I'm coming."

The light went out, flashed to life. The Stick Man was descending the school stairs, only it wasn't the school anymore. It was Gary's house on Payton Street. And it wasn't the Stick Man of his dreams coming down the stairs—it was his stepfather; his rail-thin stepfather, descending through the afternoon shadows of the gloomy house, coming to hurt him, coming to shame him, coming to make him wish he was dead.

"Coming, Gary."

"I'm coming."

"No, Ralph," Gary whimpered. The invisible hand holding him pulled him on to the Stick Man—Daddy.

"Coming, Gary."

"I'm coming."

The screams couldn't escape Gary fast enough. What came out was a high-pitched chortling garble of sounds. With every ounce of his strength, he tore his hand free. He felt the skin tear from his knuckles, as whatever held his hand clenched it even tighter, trying to keep him from getting away. He felt warm blood, his own, bathe the back of his hand. He didn't care. He tore his hand free, dropped the flaring match, and ran headlong, babbling loudly, down the stairs.

28

The first thing Rod noticed was that Tom Wayne was still dead. One glimpse of him was enough to tell. His color was bad. Like cooked chicken gone rotten. His eyes hung open, the orbs sagging over the rims of his lower lids.

His stomach and chest were torn up where the Uzi's bullets had exited his body. His insides hung from between his legs, where the bullets had entered.

Globs of his insides fell every few seconds to the floor of the garage. They made small wet slapping sounds on the concrete.

Even though Rod knew his ex-partner-in-crime was dead, he couldn't let the fact register on his brain. It defied everything that was his world, his reality. "Tommy," Rod said slowly, eyeing his former henchman with disgust, "can't say it's good to see you, ya *fuck*!" He pulled the trigger. The bullets ripped through Tommy's decomposing chest, sending flesh shrapnel spraying in all directions. Tommy staggered back a couple of steps, looked down at the further decimation of his body, and coughed. His lungs and rib cage fell out of his chest, intact, and thumped to the floor.

Rod gaped at the sight and felt his grip on sanity beginning to loosen. "I'm having an acid flashback," he mumbled, frantically trying to find an explanation to hold on to.

Tommy stood admiring his expelled body parts. He looked up at Rod's voice and grinned. He took a step forward. Rod could see Tommy's spine through his chest.

"Let's party, Rod," Tommy said, coming closer.

"Fuck you, deadmeat," Rod replied. He pulled the trigger again and ran.

29

Gary hugged the wall and stumbled down the stairs frantically. His howling babble had lowered to a spastic grunting. He descended blindly in the darkness, unknowing of what he was doing, where he was, or where he was going. The sound of footsteps clicking on the stairs not far behind him drove him on. Gunfire echoed through the old school, but Gary didn't hear it, couldn't hear it. For him, the gunfire was the sound of the Stick Man laughing, echoing through the darkness.

The stairs seemed endless, but eventually he reached the bottom, stumbled, and fell to his knees. The floor was hard and cold. It wasn't wood. It was stone. The lobby didn't have a stone floor, it had a wood floor. Part of Gary's brain registered this, but the terrible fear that had hold of him wouldn't let the information be used.

The footsteps were coming down after him.

And breathing. He could hear breathing. The Stick Man breathing.

"Coming, Gary."

"I'm coming."

Gary began to crawl across the floor. He could feel the cold stone beneath his hands but couldn't see it for the darkness. He was keening in a low, hoarse tone.

The footsteps, the breathing, were right behind him now. His neck muscles clenched in fearful anticipation of the long thin arms and clawing hands, each finger a spike, reaching for him.

He crawled faster. His right hand plunged into something mushy and slimy, something that smelled worse than anything he'd ever smelled before.

The darkness grew lighter around his hand. A figure began to appear as the light spread before him. It was a man. Glowing with a strange light.

It was the old wino.

Gary stared at his hand and couldn't breathe. His hand and arm were buried to the elbow in the old man's rotting stomach.

30

Anna felt as though she were swimming in thick oil. Everything was blurry, tinted with deep somber colors that pulsated slowly, liquidly. Images developed in the lights and oozed around her, and she found herself in the garage with the killer of her parents. She watched as the Shadow Monster disgorged the corpse of Tommy Wayne from deep inside, vomiting him into reality.

That was when Anna noticed the thickening atmosphere that encompassed her like a plastic skin. She realized she was very close to being consumed by the Shadow Monster. She was inside him already.

The funny thing was, she wasn't scared. She really didn't care what the Shadow Monster did to her, as long as it kept its end of the bargain.

She looked at the killer and wondered what kind of person could do such things. No sooner did she have the thought than she was inside the man's mind. It wasn't unpleasant. It was quite the opposite. She relished the fear the man was experiencing for the first time in his life. She wanted him to feel more of it. She wanted to torture him with fear, break him with fear. She wanted him to feel fear the way her parents must have when they saw him pointing his gun at them.

She searched his mind and was surprised when

she found the thing she was looking for. As soon as she found it, the thing began to materialize in the garage, in front of the killer. She watched it form and had to laugh. *This* was the big bad killer's deepest fear?

31

Rod banged into the truck in his haste to escape Tommy. He grabbed at it to keep from falling and glanced over his shoulder. Tommy's glowing body was gone. There was only darkness behind him, the same in front. He couldn't even see the truck that he was holding on to to keep from becoming completely disoriented.

There was a sound in the darkness behind him. He stopped. He had reached the front end of the truck. If he remembered correctly, the door was about five feet away, dead ahead. He cocked the Uzi and held it up and ready in his left hand. He reached out with his right to brace himself against the truck—and nearly fell over as his hand met empty air.

He stumbled and caught sight of something in the darkness. A flicker of light. A flash of red. A red orb, like a kid's rubber ball appeared, floating in the darkness. White began to show around it—a creamy white, spreading outward from around the red ball. Eyes formed over the red ball. A wide, upturned, grinning red mouth formed below it. The white bled out a couple of inches above the eyes and became a burst of orange hair tufting out around the red and white face. A billowing gold suit with a blue ruffled collar and blue pom-pom buttons down the front formed below the head. White gloved hands popped from the sleeves like a magician's trick. Feet clad in size forty-four, triple-E red shoes sprouted from the legs.

A clown.

Involuntarily, Rod whimpered deep in the back of his throat.

32

Kevin didn't like being within the Shadow Monster's aura. He didn't like the oppressive feel of the atmosphere against him. He liked what he saw even less.

The big guy, Gary, was a pathetic creature. Kevin knew the man was a criminal, but he couldn't believe that Gary had ever killed anyone, except perhaps in self-defense, and even then he doubted it. But even if he had killed, he didn't deserve what the Shadow Monster was doing to him.

Now Kevin watched as Gary knelt before the decomposing body of the old man his partner had killed. Kevin felt the big man's pain and heard his thoughts babbling incoherently. The man's fear was so powerful; it radiated out of him, permeating everything around. The Shadow Monster drank it in.

Suddenly, Kevin felt himself being drawn to the corpse. He felt as though he were being pulled by many arms toward the dead man. The Shadow Monster was doing it, he knew. It dawned on him what the Shadow Monster had in mind.

He tried to back away.

Out of the corner of his eye, he saw Deedee emerging from the dissipating shape of the Stick Man. He turned to her but could emit no plea for help. She looked on, helpless, as he was drawn into the corpse.

It's all part of the dance, bro, the Shadow Monster whispered inside his head as he was pulled into the dead man.

33

A hoarse scream tore from Gary's throat. It was choked off when he started gagging on the stench that rose from the body his hand was plunged into. He pulled back, his hand making a sucking, popping sound as it came free of the old man's stomach.

The corpse opened its eyes.

Gary fell back, scrabbling away from the dead man. Screams ripped through his mind, but no sound came from his mouth. The dead man rose awkwardly to one elbow, the other arm reaching for him.

"No," the corpse croaked.

"No," Gary echoed. "No, no, no, no, no, no."

"Wait," the corpse said.

Waiting was the last thing on Gary's mind. He scrabbled away from the corpse until he hit the wall. He turned and clawed at the stone. He looked back once.

The corpse was crawling toward him.

"Please, wait," the corpse said.

Gary screamed.

The corpse came closer. "Wait. I'm not going to hurt you," it said.

A shrill laugh erupted from Gary at that. It was not sane laughter. It went on and on and up and down in pitch. It echoed around him with the fury of a hundred church bells ringing in his ears.

The corpse reached him. Its arm came up, its hand came forward. Gary cringed, laughing madly, against the wall, nowhere to go. He closed his eyes. The corpse touched him, and his laughter stopped.

34

Rod turned and fled from the clown. Five steps later, he ran into the door. His face hit it first, flattening his nose and sending a wave of intense, sharp pain spreading over his face and entire head. Numbness followed the wave. Blood gushed from his nose, and he sank to one knee.

He looked back.

The clown was coming for him.

He struggled to his feet. He didn't have his gun. He dropped to one knee and felt around on the floor, never taking his eyes from the clown, who was less than ten feet away.

His knuckles scraped across the barrel of the Uzi, almost knocking it away. He grabbed it, fumbled it, righted it, and turned it on the clown.

He stood and pulled the trigger. The sound made his face throb. The flame from the barrel illuminated the smoke from the spitting Uzi. It also illuminated the clown and the bullets passing right through it.

The clown smiled as though the passing bullets had tickled.

"Oh, shit! This can't be happening," Rod muttered. He backed into the door, felt behind himself for the knob, and opened it.

"I'm outta here," he said, and fired one more burst at the clown for good measure and pulled the door closed behind him.

He was back in total darkness. He slung the Uzi strap over his shoulder and felt along the wall. He was expecting to hit the short set of stairs that led up to the corridor to the lobby, but they weren't there. He kept feeling along the wall, walking, walking, glancing behind every few seconds to see if the clown was coming.

"I'm in deep shit," Rod said to himself. "I'm in really deep shit." He came to a door, found the knob, and opened it. He'd hoped it would be a classroom, with windows, and brighter so he could see something. It wasn't. He could see nothing.

He stepped through, expecting open space, and hit a wall. He felt along it, walked away from it, and found another wall a few steps away. He was in another corridor. He tried to remember the layout of the school. He didn't remember any door off the main hallway that opened on another hallway.

There was a click behind him. He had let go of the door, and it closed. He walked back to it, but after far too many steps, he realized he'd gone the wrong way in the darkness. He turned around and went the other way. After counting ninety steps to himself, he stopped.

"What the fuck is going on?" Rod whispered into the darkness. He was shaking with rage and fear. He pushed on, feeling along one wall for a while, then switching to the other. After several minutes, he came to a door in the wall.

"Thank you!" Rod whispered. He opened the door. Complete blackness. He felt inside the door. It was another corridor. He stepped through, and the door seemed to pull itself from his hand and swing quickly shut behind him. He turned to grab it and bumped into the other wall. He tried to put his arms out at his sides and couldn't. The corridor was only a few inches wider than he was. Frantically, he reached for the door and found empty air. He *knew* he was facing the right way this time. He took several steps, arms up in front of him, but he found no door.

Though it was cold, Rod was sweating. If there was one thing he hated and feared almost as much as clowns, it was tight, closed-in places. He had to get out of there.

He walked along the corridor, arms at his sides, fingers extended out, brushing the walls. He walked for what seemed like hours, but was actually only minutes by his glowing digital watch. Eventually, his fingers met another doorjamb. He grabbed the knob, held his breath, and opened the door. Cold air washed over him. Though he could see nothing, the space before him felt big.

"At last," he breathed. "A fucking room."

He stepped inside, holding the door open. He was determined to check this out before he allowed the door to close. The darkness felt airy. He tentatively put out his arm. No wall. It had to be a classroom. The windows were just boarded up. It might even be the classroom he and Gary had been in!

"Gary? You there, man?" he called into the darkness. No answer. He turned to see if there was any way he could prop the door open, and in that instant everything changed. There was no door in his hand. There was no door behind him. The wide-open space he'd felt a moment ago was replaced with walls pressing against his body, front and back, nose to butt.

A moan of despair rose from him. He could barely breathe. Sweat poured from him, its odor polluting what air he could get. There was barely room to sidle along, but sidle along he did. Within a few feet, he came to another door, hitting the jamb with his shoulder. After much maneuvering, he squirmed over, and with his left arm bent along the direction of the corridor and his hand twisted around upside down, he grabbed the knob.

Sweating, shivering, he opened the door.

35

Gary's mind was abuzz with babbling voices and a noise like a swarm of bees until he felt the corpse of the homeless man touch him. Like a hush falling over a great crowd, the cacophony of madness in Gary's head stopped.

"I'm not going to hurt you," the corpse said in Gary's mind, speaking through its touch. Gary believed him. He opened his eyes. The corpse was no longer there. A black man knelt in front of him, his hand pressed to Gary's forehead. Gary realized he could still see the dead homeless man, but inside him was the black man. But Gary was no longer afraid. He was filled with a sense of calmness, of security, that flowed from the black man's touch.

"Who are you?" Gary asked, and smiled at the strange sensation of speaking without using his voice.

"My name is Kevin," the black man said. *"And there's someone I want you to meet."*

36

There was a light. Rod saw it dimly at first within the darkness behind the door. He couldn't tell where it was coming from, but it was enough to make him forget his apprehension and rush into the room.

The room was full of light that was coming from the stair windows. It was late afternoon. He looked back. There was no door behind him.

He was standing in the lobby of the school.

37

Kevin couldn't fight the pull of the Shadow Monster. He shuddered as he felt himself forced to enter the corpse of the old man. In his mind, he could hear the gleeful laughter of the Shadow Monster and understood what it intended.

Kevin was appalled. A sense of guilt overcame him at what he and Deedee had already done to the big man, scaring him half to death with the Stick Man apparition. What the Shadow Monster now had in store for the guy was too much.

Though the big man was a criminal, he was also an innocent. As soon as Kevin touched him, touching the man's mind at the same moment, he knew all there was to know of him. He knew all that the big man knew and had ever felt. He knew how the big man, through fear and trusting in the wrong people, had come to be arrested for robbery. He knew of the sexual terrors the big man had been subjected to as a child and again as an adult in prison. Kevin felt it all, as if the experiences were his own. Kevin felt the love and trust the big man once felt for the murderous bastard, Rod, but he also felt that that had changed to fear, dislike, and distrust.

Kevin grasped all this in a few seconds and knew he couldn't let the Shadow Monster terrorize and torture this poor guy any longer. There had to be another way. There had to be a way to use the big man without hurting him—a way to make him help Anna without torturing him.

A plan began to form in Kevin's mind, inspired by the growing dislike the man was feeling for his partner. He spoke to the big man, calmed him. As he did, he called Anna and Deedee to him with his mind, telling them his plan, hoping that together they would be strong enough to keep the Shadow Monster from interfering.

38

Anna tired quickly of the game the Shadow Monster had constructed for her to play with the murderer of her parents. At first, she had hoped she could scare him to death, make his heart stop beating out of sheer terror. When even his deepest fear, the clown, didn't succeed, she had hoped to drive him to the point of madness and despair, where he would take his own life.

But this man, this evil, evil man, was too strong-willed, too *bad* to succumb. She didn't know what else she could do until she heard Kevin's mind connect with hers, calling her to him. She listened to his plan.

Yes! That was it!

39

Gary watched in wonder as a cloud appeared behind the black man and came together into the form of the girl ghost he had seen in the hallway earlier. She was surrounded by blue light. She smiled at him. He smiled back. Behind her, another cloud formed and came together in the shape of a beautiful woman, also encased in a bubble of blue.

"Gary," the black man inside the corpse said, *"this is Anna."*

The girl came closer, put out her hand, and touched Gary's face. He shivered and stiffened as if feeling a mild electric shock. A river of images flowed through his mind in less than a second, showing him the girl's life, happy as it had been before that day in the hospital parking lot. Gary felt the love the girl had for her parents and the bottomless sorrow and hurt she had felt at their deaths.

The girl spoke to him. *"Gary, I need your help. That man, Rod, isn't your friend. He's bad. He's evil. And he must be stopped."*

As she spoke inside his head, the girl pulled memories from his subconscious, showing Gary all the terrible things Rod had done since Gary had met him. He saw the way Rod had treated him, lied to him, tricked him. Even more, he saw inside Rod's mind, through the girl, and understood what the man he'd considered to be his best friend really thought of him.

"I need your help, Gary. You can fix all the bad things you've ever done. You can help me make Rod pay for what he did to my parents, for what he's done to so many innocent people, including you."

Gary nodded. He understood. He felt the girl's anger and rage toward Rod fill him, and he knew what he had to do.

The black man, animating the old man's corpse, took his arm and helped him to his feet. Gary turned and started up the stairs to the lobby. He looked back once and saw that the black man/corpse, the girl, and the woman were following.

40

Rod started across the lobby, heading for the classroom where he had left Gary. He had to find the big dope and get the hell out of here. He didn't know if what he'd just experienced was real or some weird trick of his drug-addled mind, but he wanted no more of it and no more of this fucking place.

Halfway across the lobby, he heard footsteps coming up the stairs from the basement and froze.

No, he said to himself. No more.

Rod knew it couldn't be Gary coming up the stairs. Gary was too terrified of the dead guy in the basement to go down there. No. It couldn't be Gary.

Rod knew who it was, who it had to be. His throat went dry, and his legs felt suddenly weak.

"No more," he whispered. He couldn't take this. He couldn't take any more. He'd had enough of this place. He wanted out. Fuck the truck, fuck the stolen drugs, and fuck Gary too. He was leaving. *Now*.

He was just about to turn and bolt for the front doors when a huge, looming figure filled the boys' stairway door and stepped into the lobby.

"Gary!" Rod cried, his voice cracking. "Gary! Am I glad to see you!" He rushed to the big man and grabbed him by both arms.

"You were right, man. This place is bad. We gotta

get outta here. We gotta—" His words were cut off by Gary's right hand clamping on his throat.

"No, Rod," Gary said softly, slowly. "You're right where you need to be. We both are."

Gary's hand tightened on Rod's throat, cutting off his wind. Rod couldn't believe this was happening. He had noticed a change in Gary of late, a growing dissatisfaction and a certain new boldness toward him, but he never thought the big dumb fuck would actually turn on him.

Rod tried to bring the Uzi up, but Gary easily knocked it away with his free hand. It clattered to the floor a few feet away. Likewise, he pulled the pistol from Rod's waistband and tossed it aside. Gary then closed his other hand around Rod's throat and lifted him off the floor while he throttled him.

"I can't let you hurt any more people, Rod. They won't let me. You've done enough. Now you got to pay. We both got to pay."

Rod struggled in Gary's grip like a fish suddenly pulled from the water. His mouth gaped and his chest heaved, but he could suck no air past the vise-like grip on his throat. He began to see black dots at the edges of his vision.

Frantically, he began kicking his feet up and flailing with his hands, trying to reach his right boot.

His hand brushed his pant leg.

Gary squeezed harder.

Rod's hand touched his boot, slid off.

Gary lifted him higher until he was face to face with Rod.

"This is the end, Rod."

Rod kicked his foot and reached with his hand one more time. His fingers found the handle of his knife, jutting from the top of the boot, and closed around it, pulling it free.

You're right, Dumbo, he thought, staring into Gary's eyes. This *is* the fucking end!

With all the strength he had left in him, Rod thrust the knife up and into Gary. Again. Again. And again, until the big man began to stagger. Another stab, and the hands around his neck loosened. Another stab, and Gary let go, dropping Rod like a hot stone to the floor.

Gary staggered two steps backward, looked down at the blood seeping from his chest and belly, took one step toward Rod, and collapsed to the floor, groaning.

41

Animating the corpse of the old man was tiring work. Kevin had slowly followed Gary up the stairs, stopping just short of the top. He leaned against the wall and rested, listening. When he heard the choking, gagging sounds of Rod being strangled, he smiled. His plan was working. He turned and looked at Anna and Deedee, who were coming up the stairs behind him, and gave them the thumbs-up sign.

With Gary killing Rod, the Shadow Monster couldn't hold Anna accountable and couldn't hold her to their bargain. But something inside told him it wasn't going to be this easy, that the Shadow Monster wouldn't let them get away with it. When he heard the wet, slapping sounds like someone pounding raw meat and heard Gary fall and groan, he knew he was right.

With Anna and Deedee following, Kevin pushed the dead man's stiffened legs onward, forcing the corpse up the final two steps and into the lobby. With horror, he took in the sight of Gary lying on the floor, bleeding from at least half a dozen wounds.

What have I done? Kevin thought despairingly.

He looked at Rod, sitting a few feet from Gary, bloody knife in one hand, the other rubbing at his bruised throat, and lost it.

In a rage, he forced the clumsily moving corpse

forward, arms up, fingers clawing. Rod let out a shriek, dropped the knife, and scrambled sideways to pick up the Uzi. He fired. Kevin had the strange sensation of feeling the bullets tear into the dead man's flesh, but he felt no pain. It was like being pelted with tennis balls.

42

Rod backed away from the corpse until his back was against the wall, but it kept coming. He fired into the dead man again and again, ripping the rotting body to pieces, but the bullets didn't slow it. The charging cadaver kept coming, reached him, and its rotting hands clasped around his neck. Rod grabbed at the corpse's rotting arms with his free hand, but the dead man was too strong. The corpse's thumbs dug into his bruised throat, clamping his damaged windpipe closed again. Rod felt it being crushed and experienced more pain than he'd ever known in his life. He couldn't breathe. The strength began to leave his arms, and his struggles became more futile. His vision started to dim.

What happened next, Rod at first thought was a hallucination. There was a crackling sound, then thunder and a bright light. When he could see again, there was a transparent girl with a bright purplish red bubble of light around her, floating right behind the corpse that was strangling him. Next to her was a woman, also transparent, in a bubble of bright blue. And even stranger, Rod could see a black man inside the corpse, as if he were wearing it like a suit. It was *he* who was actually strangling him.

"Stop! He's supposed to be mine!" the girl said to the black man, and Rod heard it with his mind instead of his ears. *"Your plan didn't work. Now let*

me do what I have to do. Let me finish him!" the girl demanded.

"Get out of here!" the black man commanded, and tightened his grip, via the corpse's hands, on Rod's throat.

Rod felt himself dying. But instead of everything getting dark, everything was getting more colorful and alive to his senses. He was beginning to float up, out of his body, when the girl grabbed the black man and pulled him back, out of the corpse. The corpse immediately fell to the ground, releasing its death grip on Rod's throat. His body, too, slumped to the ground next to the corpse.

Rod didn't care. He liked this new existence, wanted it to go on. He fought the magnetlike draw of his body, which pulled at him until it became too strong. With a gasping, shrieking inhalation of air, Rod reentered his body.

43

"He's mine!" Anna said, weeping. *"He killed my parents, and I'm going to kill him!"*

"No, you're not," Kevin said softly. Deedee appeared from the shadows and drew close to Anna, comforting her. *"You can't, Anna. If you do, the Shadow Monster will own you. You're too young to die."*

A roaring scream of rage came out of the darkness around them. *Keep your fucking nose out of my business, nigger!* The darkness began to coagulate and form a shape, coming at them. *You tried to trick me, boy, but you don't know who you're fucking with!*

"Get out of here, now! Get back to your bodies!" Kevin yelled. He moved between them and the approaching form in the shadows. It was huge, and it had many legs.

The little bitch has got to kill that bastard! That's our deal. His life for her soul! the Shadow Monster screamed. Kevin could tell what it was becoming now. It had picked a nice fat fear out of his mind and was making a present of it to him.

44

Deedee rushed forward and merged her aura with Anna's, holding her back. She had thought Kevin's plan was a good one, had thought it would work, but now that it had failed, she saw that he had a backup—he would kill Rod himself. But if she didn't get Anna out of there, the girl would never let Kevin do it, and then she would be lost to the Shadow Monster forever. Deedee didn't know what Kevin's motives were for doing what he was doing, but he was an adult, capable of deciding his own destiny. Anna was merely a child, thrust into a situation no child should ever have to deal with. It wasn't fair, and Deedee wasn't going to let Anna pay through eternity for an act that was simple justice.

Summoning all her willpower, Deedee ignored the looming, threatening presence of the Shadow Monster and concentrated on calling Anna's life sphere to her. Two bright dots, far away and seemingly embedded in the wall of the lobby, appeared, slowly growing larger and larger. Though she hadn't been thinking of it, Deedee's life sphere was with Anna's, approaching with it side by side.

She heard the Shadow Monster bellowing with rage, felt it reach for them, just as she also heard Anna's hysterical crying and felt her struggle to get away. And then the spheres were upon them.

45

Kevin waited long enough for Anna and Deedee to be consumed by their life spheres before turning and going to Gary lying on the floor. The big man was still alive, though he was going fast. Kevin reached out to him and entered his body.

"All right now, big guy," he said inside Gary, *"let's take care of business.*

Gary nodded and slowly got to his feet.

46

Rod stood, keeping his eyes on the corpse on the floor, its body nearly in shreds from the pulverizing he'd given it with the Uzi.

He looked up. There was no see-through little girl, no woman, and no black man. He must have been hallucinating from lack of oxygen.

He let out a deep sigh of relief—and felt it cut off suddenly, as from behind him a pair of large hands closed over his throat again. He managed to turn his head just enough to see Gary behind him. Inside his friend's face, he could see the face of the black man, grinning fiercely at him.

Rod began to lose consciousness, his vision going black, but he still had enough sense to realize he hadn't dropped the Uzi. Gasping, grunting, he dragged it up until he could jam the barrel under Gary's jaw behind him.

Gary tightened his grip on Rod's neck and began to force his head back.

Rod curled his index finger around the trigger as he felt his neck bone beginning to give.

"This is for what you did to Anna and her parents," the black man and Gary said in unison. Gary jerked Rod's head back, snapping his neck. At the same moment, Rod pulled the trigger and the Uzi went off, taking Gary's head with it.

47

Gary's head exploding around his own jolted Kevin from the big man's body. He staggered back, blinded momentarily by the flash of the gun.

The Shadow Monster was howling with rage. As Kevin regained his sight, he saw the thing coming toward him. It was a giant cockroach, the one thing in the entire world that could make Kevin shudder in fear and disgust.

The Shadow Monster moved quickly, devouring Rod's spirit before it was halfway out of his body. It rushed forward and consumed Gary's soul as his headless corpse hit the floor. Rod screamed hideously as the Shadow Monster sucked him in, but Gary never made a sound. He looked once at Kevin, a deep sadness in his eyes, then smiled before he was gone.

The Shadow Monster faced Kevin, its cockroach antennae whirring in the air and its horrible insect mouth opening and closing, hungry to chew him up.

You're mine now, you black bastard, the Shadow Monster/cockroach bellowed at him. *And I am going to make you pay for eternity for cheating me of that sweet young soul.*

Kevin backed away as the Shadow Monster advanced on him, coming closer, its antennae reaching out like arms to puncture his aura and suck him in.

Suddenly, the room filled with light, a glorious light that appeared above his head and poured over him and the Shadow Monster. As the light touched it, the Shadow Monster screamed in pain. Smoke rose from it as the light seared it. The Shadow Monster frantically backed away, losing the shape of the cockroach and returning to its normal amorphous self as it cowered in the far corner and gathered all the room's shadows to itself, away from the light.

Kevin looked into the light. It was like looking into a long tunnel that radiated the most beautiful light he had ever seen. Every color of the rainbow, every color he had ever seen or could ever imagine, flickered in the tunnel of light.

From the center of the tunnel, a silhouette appeared, coming closer, growing larger. *"Kevin,"* a voice came from the figure, a voice Kevin recognized.

"James?"

James came out of the light, bathed in a glowing golden aura so beautiful, it hurt Kevin's eyes.

"You did good, bro. You made the payback. Now it's time to go," James said, smiling.

No! the Shadow Monster screamed from the corner. It had shrunk to a pitifully small size to escape the light. Its hideous face glared hatefully from the corner.

He's mine! the Shadow Monster raged. *He cheated me! He put himself in the girl's place. That makes him mine!*

James turned to face the Shadow Monster, and the thing cringed away from the beauty of his light. *"Tough,"* James said.

No fair! the Shadow Monster screamed, like a child cheated at a game.

James ignored it. He reached out, and Kevin took his hand. A feeling of incredible joy surged through

Kevin's entire being, and his aura changed from blue to a glorious gold matching James's.

No fair! the Shadow Monster screamed again, but Kevin barely heard it. Beautiful music, unlike any he'd ever heard, surrounded him.

"Come on, bro," James said. *"We're going home."*

Together James and Kevin floated up and into the tunnel of light, which closed after them and disappeared.

Slowly, the Shadow Monster expanded from the corner, filling the room. Faces rose and sank in its boiling flesh; faces in pain, faces in torment. Rod's was there; Gary's too.

The one face, the *true* face of the Shadow Monster appeared, and its horrible eyes surveyed the room and the corpses lying on the floor.

What a gyp, the Shadow Monster said, and disappeared.

48

Anna awoke in suffocating, hot darkness and started screaming. She thought she'd been devoured by the Shadow Monster. A janitor coming out of the hospital boiler room heard her, and within a short time she was being rushed back to the pediatric intensive care ward. She'd been missing for nearly twenty-four hours. The doctor would tell her later that she had come very close to dying during that time.

Her recovery, though, was quick. Within a week, she was moved to a regular room on the pediatric ward. Her roommate was a dark-haired, shy, thin girl by the name of Ashley. Ashley was having her tonsils out. Aunt Kara, Haley, and Jayne came to visit every day.

Anna's physical recovery was quick, but her emotional state remained poor. She cried a lot, cried herself to sleep every night, but the funny thing was, most of the time she was crying not for the loss of her parents but for the loss of Kevin, for the sacrifice he had made for her. And another funny thing was that her tears for Kevin were not always sad tears. What he had done for her filled her with a strange gladness. She didn't know why, but she couldn't shake the feeling that Kevin was all right, that he had escaped the Shadow Monster. She didn't know why, but she was sure he was in Heaven with her parents. It was this feeling that grew and eventually brought her out of her blue funk.

Over time, she began to brighten, having fewer bouts of tears. By the beginning of summer, she was out of the hospital, living with her sisters and Aunt Kara in the latter's house, feeling as normal as she could in light of her recent experience.

One hot July afternoon, just before the Fourth, Deedee showed up, driving into Aunt Kara's driveway in a rented car. Anna was overjoyed to see her, but she was quite a bit at a loss when it came to explaining to Aunt Kara who Deedee was and how Anna knew her. Deedee came to her rescue and told Aunt Kara that they were pen pals. Aunt Kara didn't look like she bought it, but she was an intuitive type of person, and she had already decided that she liked Deedee and that she was a good person.

Anna and Deedee sat on the porch, watching Haley and Jayne play on a tire swing hanging from a tall maple tree in the front yard. Aunt Kara brought them lemonade, then left them alone, going inside to watch the afternoon talk shows.

"I was worried about you. I called the hospital you were in as soon as I was able to. Did they tell you? I asked them to tell you I called," Deedee said.

"No," Anna replied. "But they might have. I was kind of out of it. A whole bunch of people called and wrote me letters and sent cards, and I didn't even know them."

"It's because you were on *America's Most Wanted*," Deedee said. "They did a special report on you and, you know, finding those two guys in the school. People like it when a story has a happy ending."

Anna changed the subject. "How have you been?"

Deedee sighed and shrugged. "A guy I was seeing . . . I was in love with. He helped me, you know?

Well, he left and went back to his old girlfriend. He said he couldn't handle . . . couldn't handle, you know, everything."

"I'm sorry," Anna said.

An embarrassing silence followed until Deedee asked, "Did you hear about Kevin?"

"No."

"It was on the news about two days after—well, you know. They found him in his house. They said it was a brain aneurysm."

Anna got up and went to the porch rail, her shoulders heaving. Deedee went to her and put an arm around her. Anna turned and they embraced, weeping for their losses.